CHEATING JUSTICE

JUSTICE TEAM SERIES

MISTY EVANS
ADRIENNE GIORDANO

ALG PUBLISHING

CHEATING JUSTICE

While investigating a government cover-up, former FBI agent Mitch Monroe is framed for murder. A wanted man, Mitch has no choice but to stay off the grid, and he needs Special Agent Caroline Foster—the FBI's top sniper and a woman who wants nothing to do with him—to clear his name.

After sharing a single night of simmering passion with Mitch a year ago, Caroline hasn't been able to get him out of her head. Or her heart. He's jeopardized her job once...helping him now could end her career. But a friend has been murdered, and no matter how Caroline feels about Mitch, he's not the killer. She needs answers, and she needs Mitch Monroe out of her life once and for all.

On the run and with no one to turn to, Mitch and Caroline can't fight the reigniting passion between them. She'll lose her career if she proves Mitch is innocent...he'll lose his life if she doesn't.

To the agents who work tirelessly behind the scenes to make our country safe.

1

unner's Paradise. That's what locals called Rock Creek Park.

As the sun sank lower on the orange horizon, Mitch Monroe was nothing but one of a dozen runners—just what he wanted—out on a cold, late-October afternoon, enjoying a piece of wilderness in the midst of Washington D.C.

His breath came in white puffs, fogging and disappearing in the crystal-clear air as he climbed another hill. The sun's weak light barely penetrated the heavy wall of trees on either side of the trail. No traffic sounds came from the nearby road—Beach Drive was closed on weekends so hikers, bikers, runners, and walkers could use the road for workouts and sightseeing.

*Thud, thud, thud...*his feet pounded a similar beat to his heart, light raindrops falling intermittently and making the trail wet. Running, running, running...his entire life had become running. Running from the FBI. Running from a mistake that he'd do all over again. Running from his past and a woman who haunted his every move.

What he wanted was to be home, but there was no "home" for him anymore. Running was all he had.

Behind him, another runner entered the trail and Mitch quieted his breathing to listen to the rhythm. Was the runner speeding up or slowing down? Following him or simply following the trail?

There was only one person who knew he was here, specifically on this trail at this time of day. He constantly varied his comings and goings, varied his runs and the places he went. Tonight was different. Tonight he was meeting a friend.

Mitch had few friends these days.

The footsteps grew louder, closer. One step, two...he eased to the side of the trail, ready to duck into the woods. As usual, he was unarmed. Fugitive or not, he'd never shoot a fellow agent or police officer. If they came after him, they were only doing their job and it would be his own damn fault if he got caught. Anyone else—say, a bounty hunter or random criminal looking for a sucker—was fair game.

Even though he'd once been a Bureau man with commendations in his personnel folder to spare, he wasn't a man of violence. He'd protect himself and those he cared about. Period. The level of violence depended on the threat.

The squeaking of sneakers drew closer, and a shorter, thinner man fell into step beside him. Kemp Rodgers. The only man who knew Mitch was here. A friend Mitch hadn't seen or spoken to in months.

The man who had requested this secret meeting.

Hearing Rodgers' heavy breathing, Mitch kept his pace slow and methodical. Jogging, not running. He pinned his gaze on the road ahead, putting one foot in front of the other and resisting the urge to grab his friend in a bear hug. *So wrong.* He wasn't a hugger. Months of little contact with friends and none with his family had made him crave human contact. "That cushy White House job is making you soft, man."

Rodgers snorted an out-of-breath chuckle. "Not like our days in the Bureau, huh?"

A wave of homesickness devoured him. Not for the Bureau specifically, but for what *had been*. His job, his friends, his life... all gone.

Rodgers' text earlier that day had been brief: *Rock Creek. 5:45 pm. TN.* The message had come from an unknown number, probably a burn phone. But Monroe understood. Rodgers had news about Tommy Nusco. About Tommy's death three weeks ago during a joint FBI-ATF assignment.

Mitch cut his eyes left, noting Rodgers was dressed in all black. Not a reflective stripe or bright color anywhere. *Definitely does not want to be seen.* "The cat burglar costume is really working for you."

"Hardy, har, har. Like you're some runway model."

"Not me. You've got the cheekbones for it."

"Too short. But I got brains. That's why I'm in the White House."

And I'm not. "I assume I'm freezing my ass off for more than idle chitchat about your doomed modeling career."

Rodgers snugged down his knit hat, his voice full of the classic sarcasm Mitch missed hearing these days. "You never minded freezing your ass off before. You love survivalist conditions. Probably why you're such a damn good fugitive."

It was rare Rodgers threw it in his face. *Nervous.* But whatever information he had, it was important enough to risk his job by meeting Mitch in the park. As an aide to the president, Rodgers couldn't be seen with a fugitive, even if he and Mitch had been friends since fifth grade. "Hey, meeting out here was your idea, not mine."

They jogged in silence for a few feet. Rodgers checked over his shoulder. "Any news from your end on Tommy?"

Like always, thoughts of their mutual friend's involvement in whatever this FBI-ATF assignment was brought on a flood of questions. Questions Mitch couldn't expose himself to ask and he knew no one would answer anyway. All he knew for sure was that Tommy had ended up dead in Roswell, New Mexico.

"Nada," Mitch said. "The few contacts still willing to talk to me claim ignorance. You?"

A tight sigh. "All I heard was something about Executive Privilege."

What the hell? It took Mitch a few seconds to process this unexpected tidbit, the damning implications. "The president's invoking Executive Privilege on the case? Why?"

"All my sources inside the House are closed lip. No one knows."

What the hell did you get yourself into, Nusco? Mitch slowed his pace, listening to the quiet *squeak-squeak-squeak* of Rodgers' sneakers on the wet ground. "Something definitely went wrong with Tommy's assignment."

"Or maybe he was dirty like the rumors claim."

Tommy had joined Mitch and Kemp during their sophomore year in high school. Long hair, ratty jeans, and enough anger inside him to fuel a freight train, the crazy teen had copped an attitude that pissed off Mitch from day one. But he'd seen a buried part of himself reflected in Tommy's cruel lips and flippant comebacks. Seen a reflection of his soul in Tommy's bring-it-on demeanor and me-against-the-world insolence.

Contrary to Kemp's advice, Mitch had immediately taken Tommy under his wing. Of course, Tommy being Tommy, he rejected all attempts at friendship, clinging to his outcast status with zeal. But Mitch was persistent. He watched and waited, and when the time came and Tommy finally dug himself into a hole he couldn't get out of, Mitch showed up in the nick of time to save Tommy's ass.

Along with Rodgers, they'd taken the FBI Academy by storm. Their instructors had dubbed them The Three Musketeers. Mitch figured it was better than The Three Stooges.

"The rumors are bullshit," he said. "Tommy had to be working an angle. Something went wrong and now the government is covering it up. That's the only reason for Executive Privilege."

"I don't know. You sure about that?"

It had been a long time since Mitch had been sure about anything, but this...*this* was different. *Cover up.* "The whole thing stinks, and it isn't because Tommy was dirty."

"If the president is threatening to invoke Executive Privilege, someone high up wants to keep the details secret. My guess? The parties involved are part of a bigger operation."

Tommy had always been a risk-taker, always reaching for the biggest fish in the pond. Had it gotten him killed? "Christ."

"Look, I know you were looking into what happened, but now you have to back off." Rodgers rubbed the end of his nose and sniffed. "You poke the wrong bear and the claws of the Justice Department will come down on you hard and swift. The FBI won't be the only entity hunting you."

Back off? *No way.* If anything, this Executive Privilege development fueled his desire to uncover the truth even more. But Kemp was a good guy—a good friend—and when the shit hit the fan, as it invariably would once Mitch started digging, he needed plausible deniability. Kemp had left the FBI to pursue politics, and in the process, landed a sweet seat in the White House because he didn't break the rules. Ever. Mitch, on the other hand, had more Tommy than Kemp in him.

Most rules were made to be broken. Executive Privilege or not, Tommy's killer wasn't getting away with murder, and the government wasn't getting away with pinning crimes on an innocent man. Tommy deserved justice.

"Mitch?" Rodgers' voice held a warning. "Promise me you'll leave this alone."

Mitch stopped, his ears ringing. The Three Musketeers

never called each other by their first names or made promises they couldn't keep. "Tell me you did not just go there."

Rodgers stopped as well, turned and came back to face him, his breath puffing out in white clouds around his face. "I did, and I expect that promise."

"Easier to open a vein."

"Tommy wouldn't want that."

"He also wouldn't want to be branded a traitor."

The two glared at each other in the shadowy light. Ahead, Mitch spotted a group of hikers crossing the road, dressed in expensive clothes and laughing about something. Their flashlight beams bounced off nearby trees and he automatically stepped closer to the woods.

His friend didn't follow. "I get it, man. You always had a soft spot for Tommy, and without you, he wouldn't have made it through high school, much less college and the Academy. But he was a wild one, and once you left the Bureau, there was no one keeping him in check. I don't know what happened in New Mexico, but what I do know is that Tommy might have crossed a line."

...once you left the Bureau, there was no one keeping him in check. Mitch's back teeth locked. *My fault.* He could hardly grind out the words. "Whatever happened, *he was* not *dirty.*"

Rodgers set his hands on his hips and looked off in the distance to where the hikers had disappeared. "I'll look into it *discreetly* from my end. You stay out of it. *Capisce?*"

Capisce, my ass. "Whatever gets you through the night, *Kemp.*"

"Mitch—"

He held up a hand, his nerves stretched thin with emotion. He didn't want his friend worrying about him and adding a new layer of guilt to his growing pile. "All right, all right. I'll stay out of it, but do me a favor."

"What?"

"*Don't* look into it, even discreetly. Whatever's going on could put you in hot water. You need to keep your nose clean, forget this conversation. I've got a buddy who can investigate what happened. He's discreet and he has an 'in' with the Bureau."

"Justice Greystone?"

"Better you don't know."

"Right." Rodgers blew out a breath, looked back the way he'd come. "Guess that's it, then. You need money or anything?"

Ouch. Mitch stepped forward, offered a handshake. "I'm living the high life. 'Go home. Find a wench, raise fat babies, live a good, long life.'"

Rodgers laughed at the movie quote, took Mitch's hand and dragged him into a manly embrace. "All for one?"

Mitch hugged him back. "And one for all."

As Rodgers jogged off, Mitch watched the deepening shadows gobble him up. What had happened to the three of them? Tommy was dead, Mitch on the run, and Kemp had sold his soul to God and country. Not the way Mitch had thought their story would go.

"All for one, and one for all," he whispered to himself as he took off in the opposite direction. "Don't worry, Tommy. I won't let you down."

At six o'clock the next morning, Mitch stood in a coffee shop sipping a cup of Joe strong enough to break his teeth. He stared at the overhead TV screen where President Perkins was giving a news brief about his new gun control legislation. He was flanked by his VP, the House Speaker, and the Attorney General and Deputy AG from the Department of Justice.

Two minutes later, the picture switched to the CNN newsroom and a newscaster started the next story. "Breaking News" flashed across the bottom of the screen and Mitch stared in disbelief.

Kemp Rodgers, White House aide, murdered in Rock Creek Park.

What the fuck?

And the picture of the suspected killer hanging over the somber newscaster's shoulder?

Fugitive Mitch Monroe, wanted by the FBI.

2

"*Y*ou're twenty-four clicks right."

Dammit.

Three days after taking a man's life, Caroline Foster lay on her belly in cold, moist dirt that seeped through her cargo pants and T-shirt. Not the worst conditions she'd ever faced. Besides, an unusually warm October sun drenched her back and spread its heat into her core while she practiced a shot that would give her bragging rights for six months.

In D.C., bragging rights meant something.

Whipping wind surrounded her and she eased back from her M-24 sniper rifle. Beside her stood Joe Harrelson, the retired marine sniper who owned this private range where her membership cost a good chunk of her salary but allowed her to avoid the Bureau facility when she needed distance from all things FBI. Particularly when she'd been forced to take a few days off. "*Twenty-four* clicks?"

How could that be? She stared across the windswept range to her target six hundred yards out. Behind the target, a small bush swayed in the wind and bent backward at a forty-five degree angle. She didn't want to question Joe's expertise. Not really. But, he was wrong. His twenty-four clicks would be solid if it was a fill-value wind. What they had was three-quarter value.

Either way, the shot had to be precise because her target was less than six inches in diameter and would be sliding along a cable at six miles-per-hour. Throw in the wind and this was a complicated shot. One only a handful of agents in the Bureau had made. And never in three-quarter value wind.

Didn't matter.

She'd happily be the first. And a woman to boot.

Still holding the remote that would put the target in motion, Joe eyeballed the wind flags, then checked mirage in his spotting scope. "Twenty-four clicks, darlin'. Or you can hold three feet into the wind. Your choice."

Behind her, two weekend shooters snickered. Joe glanced back at them. "You boys wanna try this shot? Last I checked neither of you could hit a bulls-eye at two-hundred."

Caroline sighed and repositioned herself behind the rifle. "No need to defend my honor, Joe. These boys are about to get schooled."

The assholes shut up.

Good boys. Here's a treat.

Laying her cheek against the stock, she checked the scope and adjusted the parallax. Her target once again came into focus and wavy lines of mirage danced across her scope. Caroline waited. Watched.

A shot like this was as much mental as physical and confidence played a bigger part than she liked to admit. Her confidence came from experience and hours upon hours of lying in wet, soggy dirt to simulate conditions that wouldn't be comfy-cozy.

After a few seconds, the mirage shifted from horizontal to vertical. Joe had nailed the wind speed, but his angle was off. A twenty-four click hold wouldn't work. Holding into the wind might.

Especially with a moving target.

"Watch and learn, boys," she said.

She nuzzled the stock, leaned into the bipod and loaded it forward.

I got this.

The small bulls eye came into view and she moved the crosshairs four Mildots to the right. Based on the bending bush, if she kept her right hold and pulled the trigger when the target got to the bush, she'd be dead on. Damned near impossible shot.

I got this.

She gritted her teeth, drew a deep breath, and exhaled slowly. Another breath followed, but she held half of it, let her body settle as she curled her finger around the trigger.

"Ready?" Joe asked.

"Send it."

He pressed the remote and the target lurched. *Here it comes. Wait, wait, wait.* Everything moved in slow motion, the target, the swaying bush, the wind, all of it. Calm silence brought her to a zone of concentration that gave her peace and a sense of order. She drew back a straight trigger.

Boom!

Joe looked into his spotting scope. "Eeee-doggies! Bulls-eye, baby. Damn girl, you might be the best I've seen."

She'd better be, considering the Federal Bureau of Investigation expected her, and the handful of other agents in the D.C. field office that were lucky enough to have been recommended for sniper school, to hit targets the average shooter wouldn't attempt. Sniper school had lured her to apply and—*eh-hem* —*make* the FBI SWAT team, a position taken in addition to her regular duties as a special agent.

Caroline glanced back at the jokers behind her. "You were saying?"

One guy stared at the ground as the two shuffled away. "Helluva shot."

"Bet your ass," she said.

Still grinning, Joe checked the spotting scope again. "I gotta try this shot sometime. I bet I can't do it. Damn, that sucks." His cell phone rang and he checked it. "I need to take this. You done here?"

"Yep. All wrapped up. Thanks."

Caroline leapt to her feet, dusted off what dirt she could and laughed. The boys at the office would love this story. Definitely helped alleviate the angst from her boss putting her on paid leave.

But rules were rules and blowing a target's skull apart tended to make a lot of people twitchy. Three days ago, Jeff Klausner, the ASAC—Assistant Special Agent in Charge—had summoned her to a hostage situation after negotiations failed. Negotiators liked to talk through issues. Caroline didn't mind. She had patience. If talking got someone out safely, that would be the best possible outcome. Unfortunately, that hadn't happened. As the best sharpshooter in the D.C. field office, she'd been dispatched to handle the creep who'd shot his wife.

Throughout their careers, most FBI snipers rarely fired their weapons. Caroline was the exception. In the three years she had been on SWAT, she'd eliminated a target three times. In each incident, she'd been given the standard time off until a full investigation had been documented. Her latest mission had gone as planned and maybe the time off irritated her, but she was a good little employee and didn't argue. Caroline, being Caroline, had taken the time to visit the practice range. To keep her skills sharp.

To keep from thinking about ending a life.

Because as much as she was bothered by that fact, as much

as she told herself it was part of the job and she was saving innocent lives by ending a not-so-innocent one, her finger was still the one on the trigger.

Criminal or not, her targets were loved by someone and those someones mourned their loss.

A lesson she'd learned on her second mission when everything the Bureau had done was questioned in a lawsuit filed by a grieving family. Every move she and the other agents had made was scrutinized and she relived the shooting day in and day out until the case had been dismissed. No wrongdoing had been discovered, and maybe for the Bureau it went away, but not for Caroline. She still thought about the nineteen year-old, bi-polar young man who'd lost his life at her hands and wondered if it could have been avoided. If the negotiators could have talked longer...if they'd known about his illness. *If...if...if.*

"I always said you had the best ass in the FBI."

Her body froze. Eleven months, five days and—she did the math—twelve hours had passed since she'd heard that voice. The one she'd thought about time and again after his last brief visit to her apartment, and she still managed to be equal parts pissed off, concerned and flat-out heartbroken. *That* voice could only belong to one person. Thus the remark about her ass and—*wow*—she always knew he had a set of stones, but this was too much even for Mitch Monroe. The man she'd spent all these months trying to forget. Months of burying herself in cases, months of begging her boss for every available opportunity to keep her mind occupied, months of a busy life that didn't allow for downtime.

Or thoughts of Mitch.

Without turning, she picked up her weapon. "Well, look what the cat dragged in. A girl puts her career on the line for you and you don't call, you don't write, nothing. To say the least, your technique needs work."

And then he laughed. She'd waited months to hit him with

that line and he *laughed*. Classic Mitch. She closed her eyes and —forget that he was a federal fugitive now wanted for murder —she'd kill him herself and be done with the whole affair.

Mitch, a murderer? She couldn't believe it. No matter what the White House was spinning about Kemp Rodgers' death, Mitch wouldn't kill his friend.

Then, again, she'd been Mitch's friend once...

Finally, she turned, bracing herself for whatever disguise might greet her, but found none. Brave.

As usual.

She took in his long brown hair pulled back in a low pony-tail, his dark eyes and ripped jeans, and shook her head. "You're insane for coming here."

He shrugged. "It's a private range. Not like I walked into Quantico."

It wasn't enough that he'd almost destroyed her career when he'd first started working The Lion case, now he wanted to have a second go at it. He was a fugitive wanted for murder and she was an FBI agent. She should arrest him.

Yet, she stood waiting for him to say something that would make a damned difference. I'm sorry? I didn't do it? Anything that would erase the idea that he could have murdered his friend.

She set her rifle on the table behind her, slid the bolt open. *Not loaded.* She knew it wasn't, but she checked anyway. Always.

Mitch shuffled behind her.

Too bad. He could wait like she'd waited for him all these months.

Her canvas carry case sat on the bench seat. Like many people, she preferred canvas over hard plastic because the softer material didn't make the rifle sweat. She dug through the case for her lens covers, popped them on, set the rifle into the case—bolt upward—and zipped it.

She'd clean the rifle later. For her, keeping a weapon in top working order meant cleaning it after every use. Even if only one shot had been fired, her weapons got cleaned. Every time.

She sensed Mitch moving closer, stirring the air around her, upsetting the energy, letting her know he was near. He had that way about him. Sometimes good, sometimes not.

"I need your help."

Of course he did. Should have known. Radio silence for eleven months and now he wanted her help. "I should shoot you and dump your body in the Reflecting Pool."

"Yeah, you should."

She spun and—*crack!*—smacked him, sending his head sideways and making her hand sting. She'd never physically attacked anyone before and she couldn't say it felt right or just, but unleashing it felt good. To let him know he'd hurt her. "We were friends. I helped you and you disregarded me."

"*Disregarded* you?" Mitch slid a hand over his cheek. "I've stayed away and I'm sorry. But what, Caroline? You want to do lunch or hit the shooting range with me? A guy wanted for assaulting your boss and now a federal fugitive?" Gently, he knocked on her head. "Think about it. I was protecting you."

She didn't need his protection. "I'm mad at you."

"Atta girl."

God, he was annoying. "You had a good reason to take a swing at Donaldson when he threatened you during The Lion case, but honest to God, Mitch, I think he should have swung back and ended it right there instead of trying to throw you in jail. But you should have manned up and never run from the charges, so whatever this is, I can't help you."

"Tommy Nusco."

"You murdered him, too?"

Surprisingly, he blanched. "I didn't kill anyone. I need to know what went down with Tommy."

Oh, please. He really had lost his mind if he thought she'd touch that subject. That involved ATF and the State of New

Mexico and she wasn't about to step into that snake pit. "You better worry about what went down with Kemp Rodgers and why the White House is after you. Turn yourself in, Mitch."

"Kemp told me the White House is buzzing about Executive Privilege being invoked on Tommy's case. A few hours later, he's dead. Put two and two together, Caroline. There's a cover-up in the works and what happened to Tommy is at the heart of it."

She faced him, still hating that he stood a good six inches taller and managed to make her feel small. She folded her arms and stepped forward, got right into his space. "No."

"Whatever they're concocting about Tommy is bullshit."

"I *don't* know that."

"Yeah, you do. When we all worked together, we hung out. You knew him."

"Not that well."

He rolled his eyes in that typical *I'm-Mitch-Monroe-and-I'm-bored* way of his. "He was *not* dirty. Whatever he was doing, the government is letting a dead agent take the heat. Why not? He's dead anyway. Doesn't matter that he was a decorated officer. The *government* obviously needs to clean up a mess and—" he inched closer, tilted his head and stared right into her eyes "—I know all about how the government cleans up a mess."

Back away. She should, but that would play into what he wanted. He wanted to control this conversation. His looming presence used to be enough that she'd give him that control.

Not this time.

She tilted her head the opposite direction, eased out a half-smile. "Mitch?"

"Yes?"

"Screw you."

She turned her back to him and scooped up her rifle case. Right now, she needed to walk away and not let him talk her into something that would wreck her career.

"You worked with him. You knew him. Are you going to let them do this? Are *you* going to do this?"

"I didn't work with him recently. I can't help you." She angled around him, bumping him as she walked by. "Goodbye, Mitch."

"Look into it, Caroline. That's all I'm asking. Just look into it."

3

*A*t 7:47 the following morning, Caroline dropped into her desk chair, stowed her briefcase under her desk and booted up her laptop. Happy to be back to the normal— and comfortable—tasks of her day, she watched the little hourglass on her screen spin and drummed her thumb on the side of the keyboard.

Mitch Monroe. Total poison. She'd finally—maybe—gotten him out of her system and now he'd returned. Needing something. *Not me.* Something else. Typical.

If she were smart, which her History degree from American University told her she was, she'd ignore him. And his looks. And that wicked sense of humor. All of it. She'd pretend he didn't exist.

As. If.

Her laptop dinged and she entered her password. A noise from two cubicles over sounded and she scooted her chair along the cheap industrial Berber carpeting to check it out. Beyond the cubicle walls she spotted Ron Mills, a fifteen year veteran she now supervised, getting settled.

"Hey, Ron," she called.

"You're back?"

Yes, thank God. "They cleared me last night."

Before scooting back to her laptop, she glanced right. The ASAC's office was dark. Perfect. It would give her a few minutes to snoop around about Tommy.

Even if she were ignoring Mitch, she'd been up most of the night obsessing over the possibility that the president, if the White House were subpoenaed, would invoke Executive Privilege on Tommy's case. God knew there were plenty of reasons politicians did certain things and hid others, but this one surprised her.

Someone knew something they didn't want the rest of the country to know.

And that was the thing keeping her from ignoring that pain-in-the-ass Monroe.

Back at her computer, she clicked a few times, found the drive she needed and started scrolling. As a relief supervisor, she had access to certain files. Whether she had access to whatever Tommy had been working on, she didn't know.

She scrolled directories for a few minutes, but found nothing remotely intriguing. Finally, she typed THOMAS NUSCO into the search field and a list—a really long list—of files popped onto her screen. This might take a while.

Twenty minutes later, she'd found a whole lot of nothing regarding Tommy's current cases. Nothing, as in, *oddly* nothing. Even when cases had been closed, the agents still had access to the files for future reference. In this instance, it was as if everything pertaining to his current assignment had been wiped away. Or hidden.

But there was one more place she could try. She clicked over to the drive and repeated her search.

Bingo. Four files. She clicked on the first one. *Access denied.* Interesting. Second file. *Access denied.*

"I see a trend here," she whispered.

The *bleep-bleep* of her desk phone gave her a start and she laughed at herself. Idiot. She scooped up the phone. "Caroline Foster."

"Yeah, Caroline. Good morning. It's Neil from IT. I got a ping on a file you were trying to open."

What now? "Hi, Neil. I'm looking for something and accidentally clicked on those files."

Twice. She winced. Terrible excuse.

"Okay, well, you don't have access to those files. They're classified. You need to speak to Special Agent Donaldson about that."

Ha. Now that was funny. Somehow, no matter how much she tried to avoid the man, Donaldson always wound up in her orbit. After that fiasco with Mitch, she was damned lucky to still manage getting bumped to a higher pay grade. Although, that was probably more the Assistant Director's doing than anything else. Despite her young age for FBI management standards, Jeff Klausner knew she was smart, could dig up leads like any twenty-year veteran, and more importantly, could blow open a case.

Donaldson? She didn't trust him. Although she knew there had been times he'd been backed into a corner with certain cases when he'd been forced to make unpopular decisions, she worried that all he cared about was his career track and his budget. As a relief supervisor, she could empathize. Everyone in management had to make cuts in the budget on a regular basis and reassign agents when necessary to other field offices. And as an agent at times putting her life on the line, she'd always felt he had her back. It was just in the office, surrounded by politics and cutthroat executives, she didn't trust him.

"Will do, Neil. Thanks for letting me know."

She dropped the phone into its cradle and laid her head on the desk sending her ponytail swinging. Damned Monroe. Twenty minutes into this covert operation and she'd almost blown it. The man was the worst kind of distraction. Trouble followed him like a horny teenaged girl...

"Foster!"

...or a pissed off FBI Special Agent in Charge.

She closed the window on her computer and shoved back from her desk, rolling into the aisle.

Bearing down on her was Donaldson in one of his ugly brown suits. The suit wasn't the worst of it. He had that pinched look on his face. The one where he scrunched his nose right before he tore into whomever stood in his way.

She popped out of her chair and shoved it back into her cubicle. "Sir?"

He stormed past her and she tugged on her suit jacket. His office assistant, Mary, hustled after him, files in her arms. Mary shot Caroline a *you screwed up* look. "My office. Now," he shouted.

As much as she didn't always trust him, Donaldson knew how to be scary and that awarded him a sort of twisted respect Caroline had given up trying to understand.

She trailed behind Mary, the little ducks following along, until they reached his office and Mary set the files on the edge of his desk. "I'll cancel those appointments for you, sir. Anything else?"

"Get me some coffee."

Nice guy.

Mary glanced at Caroline. "Would you like some too?"

Valium for me, thanks. "No, thank you."

Caroline waited for Mary to exit and faced Donaldson already seated and shuffling through notes. Had he even looked at her yet? She didn't think so. Why should he? She was simply a subordinate. And clearly, he wasn't happy with her. "Something wrong, sir?"

His eyes stayed on the papers. "What the hell are you up to this morning, Foster?"

"Sir?"

He slowly lowered the papers in his hands. Too slowly. His fingers tightened, creasing the memos. "Why are you trying to access classified documents on Tommy Nusco?"

Now what? *Crap.* "I was searching for another file on the Burnson case. I clicked on the Nusco files accidentally."

She had no choice but to go with that excuse after she'd used it on Neil in IT. One lie was bad enough—*thank you, Mitch* —two she'd never remember.

"The Burnson case. Hmm..." He set down the papers, leaned back in his chair. "Seen your pal Monroe lately, Agent Foster? The fugitive wanted for murder?"

Caroline stood stock-still. If she fidgeted, moved an inch, she'd be made. Making direct eye contact, she shook her head. "Mitch Monroe is off the grid. As you know. Why would I have contact with him?"

"He nearly ended your career once. Could still. We clear?"

Okey-dokey. What she had here was one of her bosses letting her know that the files she *accidentally* clicked on were important enough that IT had been directed to alert superiors when unauthorized access was attempted. Those files, what-ever they were, hid something. She'd have to write down those file names, see if Mitch could have his buddy Justice Greystone get into them.

"We're clear, sir. I apologize. Anything else?"

Donaldson shuffled through the stack Mary had left and grabbed a file. "I just came out of a meeting." He handed her the file. "Deal with this."

Eyeing him for a second, she took the folder and somehow knew whatever was in there was meant to be a very strong message. One thing about Donaldson, he was consistent. After the Monroe debacle, he'd done the same thing. Like she was a five-year old being put in the Bureau's version of Special Agent time-out.

She flipped open the file and perused the one-page report. A lead from another office.

But this one wasn't a meaty one that supervisors, or even relief supervisors like her, would normally be handed. This was a "nothing lead" from the Baltimore field office requesting the D.C. office comb through a dumpster behind a restaurant in Southeast D.C. in search of documentation on a fugitive.

Good. God. He expected her to spend her afternoon sorting through two-day old food and slimy raw meat. Donaldson didn't just want her busy, he wanted her out-of-the-office busy.

For a nice, long while.

"Yes, sir. I'll take care of it."

"Good. And do it alone. You shouldn't need help on this."

Alone. Sorting through a dumpster. It would take hours. Exactly what her boss wanted after she tried to access a classified file.

Damned Mitch Monroe. He'd sucked her in again.

4

"Saving the world, Justice?" Mitch sauntered over to where Justice "Grey" Greystone stood in front of a giant bulletin board. His voice echoed slightly in the abandoned army base, HQ for Grey's covert pursuit team shenanigans.

The stick-in-the-mud former FBI agent stood arrow straight, arms folded across his chest. Mitch could see from the stance that Grey was cataloging snippets of information pinned to the board. "Hard to save the world when my best investigator sleeps in and doesn't show up for work until..." he glanced at the clock on the wall—an ugly government leftover—"...three in the afternoon."

The covert pursuit team, nicknamed the Justice Team by Grey's girlfriend Sydney, was looking into election fraud by a senator.

Election fraud. *Kill me now.* "Just so happens, election fraud is not at the top of my to-be-investigated list at the moment. If you haven't heard, I'm wanted for murder."

"We heard." David Teeg, a computer hacker Grey had blackmailed into assisting the team, stared sullenly at a bank of computer screens in front of him. "I've got surveillance footage of you—and about a hundred other people—entering and leaving Rock Creek Park during the one-hour timeframe surrounding Rodgers' murder, but the murderer could have entered at a different location."

"You're investigating Rodgers' murder?"

The geekhead shrugged without looking at him. His T-shirt —one he'd stolen from Mitch—sported a "Come to the dark side, we have bacon!" saying on it. His jeans were worn worse than Mitch's, and a pair of headphones hung around the kid's neck as his hands moved over the keyboard with lightning speed. "Grey said it was important."

Outside, the October afternoon was moderately warm. Inside the old army base, it was freezing. No heat in the warehouse-like structure. Winter was going to be a bitch.

Better here than in prison.

The Justice Team setup was sketchy. No real oversight, no acknowledgement from the government they served. They investigated cases involving the untouchables—diplomats, elected officials high on the government food chain, judges, etc. Grey didn't trust many people, and so far, the team consisted of him, Mitch, and Teeg. And due to his fugitive status, Mitch was only a volunteer. No paycheck, no performance review, no paper trail.

Only the three of them—a renegade former Bureau agent, a fugitive from the law, and a black hat—all willing to bend, and even break the law as necessary, to find the proof needed to bring justice to those above the law. They already had dozens of cases to investigate.

Losing battle there.

And I might not be around to help if Caroline doesn't follow through.

Caroline. A beautiful, tough cookie to crack. He was asking a lot of her, like usual, and if she couldn't—or wouldn't—help him with the Tommy case, he was shit out of luck. No way could he drop the case on Grey when they were already balls-to-the-wall drowning in assignments.

"I probably shouldn't be here," he told Grey as he slouched against a battered desk the color of mud.

Grey was as Type A as you could get…a lot like Caroline… and drove Mitch crazy with his near obsessiveness on cases, but the guy always had Mitch's back. "Where else would you be?"

Few people, outside of Grey and Caroline, had ever covered for Mitch. Now with Tommy and Kemp dead…

An overhead light flickered, the fluorescent bulb long past needing to be replaced. "Best I bow out of this covert pursuit team. Too much heat on me. I won't endanger you guys."

Grey turned his gaze on Mitch for the first time. "You can't solve Kemp's murder on your own."

True enough. "I'm more concerned with Tommy's murder. Kemp told me if the White House is subpoenaed, the president will invoke Executive Privilege."

"Sounds reasonable."

Reasonable? "The government is covering something up."

"The government is always covering something up."

True. "This is different."

Grey rubbed his forehead. "I'll take you off the election fraud case and help you figure out who murdered Kemp, but I won't touch the FBI files on Tommy. Could get messy with conflict of interest and shit since I sort of work for them again."

"You don't have to do that, Grey."

"I can't save the world if I don't save your ass first."

One of Teeg's computers beeped. "Uh, Grey? Incoming call."

Grey and Mitch exchanged a look. Sydney called Grey on his cell. No one called the base. The whole operation was off the grid.

Grey marched to Teeg's desk. "We have a phone?"

"Technically, no, but it's coming through our computer system. I cloak everything we do, but someone must have hacked..." He hit several keys. "Wait a minute. I'll trace where it's coming from."

"Shit," Mitch and Grey said at the same time.

Mitch pushed off the desk, ready to run. Had someone followed him? Were they outside waiting for him?

Not possible. He'd been even more careful than usual. He always knew when someone was following him. His instincts were honed too sharply for someone to get the jump on him. "Could it be a wrong number or a telemarketer?"

"Got it!" Teeg looked up, his dark eyes round. "It's a cell phone with a number the FBI owns."

Grey leaned over the kid's shoulder, read the screen. "What the fuck have you done, Monroe?"

"Is that a rhetorical question? 'Cuz I've done a hell of lot of things."

Grey gave him a look that would have cowered most men. "Connect me," he said to Teeg.

"You sure?" the kid asked.

The intense gaze rained down on the hacker. "Do it."

Teeg's fingers shook as he tapped keys. He handed his boss a headset with microphone. "I'll put the caller on speaker, but whoever it is will only be able to hear you."

Hanging the headset around his neck, Grey propped the microphone to his lips. "This is Justice Greystone. Identify yourself."

"Well, well, Agent Greystone." A woman's voice—one Mitch knew all too well—came from Teeg's speakers. "Congrats on finally catching The Lion. Wish I could have been there for that take-down."

Grey didn't miss a beat. "Who is this?"

"This is Caroline Foster. *Special Agent* Caroline Foster. You might remember me. We worked together with Mitch before you two incinerated your careers."

Grey covered the microphone with his fingers and lifted an eyebrow in Mitch's direction. "You didn't."

Mitch hung his head, smiling to himself at Caroline's ability to hunt him down. She didn't have skills as a hacker like Teeg, but she was a good tracker, whether it was on the ground or the internet. Nothing less than impressive. Grey was probably shitting bricks. "I need her help."

"Bullshit. You *want* her help. Big difference."

Maybe. Maybe not.

Grey uncovered the microphone. "What can I do for you, Agent Foster?"

"I need to speak with Mitch."

"Mitch Monroe is a renegade wanted for attacking an FBI agent. As of yesterday, he is also wanted for the murder of a White House official. Sorry, I can't help you."

"Party line received and understood. Now put him on the phone. Please. Or I'll figure out a way to join your covert pursuit team—legitimately—and make your life all kinds of hell."

Grey shot daggers at Monroe then handed him the headset. Mitch had to laugh. The woman had it all, looks, brains, and a steel spine that scared the hell out of most males.

Even, at times, him.

He adjusted the headset, letting her stew a second longer because, yeah, that's when the fun really began. "You shouldn't be calling here on your Bureau phone."

"I need to see you."

Mitch smiled. "I love when women say that to me."

"I'm sure you do."

"Did you find something out about Tommy?"

"Tit for tat. Meet me and I'll tell you."

Grey shook his head, smelling a setup. Mitch's body buzzed with adrenaline. "How'd you get this number?"

"You know me better than that. I don't have much time. Our friend Donaldson is sending me to clean out a dumpster today."

"No shit? He gave a relief supervisor grunt work?"

"My punishment for trying to access classified files."

Got her. He hadn't made a mistake. Caroline, crazy as it was, wanted to help him. "There are worse things."

"Mitch, I don't have time for this. You wanted my help, now where do you want to meet?"

Her skills and training went beyond the gun range, and somehow she'd found a way to call the computer system, but that didn't mean she knew where the computer system—or he—was located. "Come here."

Grey—the poor guy—nearly self-combusted. "Oh, no. No, no, no..."

Mitch held up a hand to silence him. Caroline's end was dead air. Gotcha. Two could play the bluffing game. "Don't know where I am, do you, Foster?"

"The closed army base. I prefer we meet somewhere less..."

So she did know their location. "Less what?"

"Remote."

What was she scared of? "You've got thirty minutes. Then I'm gone."

"As if I'm the one on the run. If you want this information, you'll meet me."

Mitch smiled. So Caroline to insist on doing things her way. "Sorry, babe. Ain't gonna happen. I can smell a trap miles away. I'm out."

He tossed the headset on Teeg's keyboard, made a slashing motion across his neck. The kid cut the connection and the three of them looked at each other in silence.

Grey, of course, was the first to speak. "You've compromised our headquarters."

"Not if she doesn't show."

Walking to the board, Grey stared at all the case information. "How long?"

Ah. He knew as well as Mitch that Caroline would come. She'd gone to all that trouble to hunt him down. Something was eating at her, an itch she couldn't scratch. "Fifteen minutes. Maybe twenty."

"She can't see these files. They're all classified. You understand?"

Mitch nodded. If Grey wasn't throwing a shit-fit over his headquarters being compromised, that meant he wanted to hear what she had to say, which meant Grey believed she had important information. "Teeg? Keep your eyes on the screen and watch the perimeter in case she brings friends."

"You got it."

Grey turned to Mitch. "Call her back. She can't come through the main gate. Someone will see her. Tell her to take the access road. Teeg will open that gate."

Over the next twenty-plus minutes, Grey paced behind Teeg, all the while chastising Mitch. "I can't believe you're bringing her here. It's like you have a death wish."

"She's not going to kill me." *Strike that. She might.* "We're just talking."

"She's a weakness. Your weakness. Just like Tommy."

"Careful."

"She's here." Teeg pointed at one of the screens. The base still had all gates functioning and all were closed. The whole place looked exactly like it was...deserted. "Coming down the access road and kicking up all kinds of dirt. Lady is in a hurry."

"Anyone with her?" Grey asked.

"Not that I can see."

Grey turned to Mitch. "You're on."

.   .   .

Caroline drove through the gate at the desolate army base and decided she'd lost her damned mind.

If she were a serial killer, she'd lure her prey to a location like this one. Large, secure and abandoned. Even the access road she'd just driven down couldn't be seen from the main road.

Yep. If she were a serial killer, this is exactly how she'd do it.

Once through the gate, she drove along the crumbling pavement to the pukey-colored two-story building behind the barracks to her left.

Monroe stood on the sidewalk in front of the building. He wore jeans and a black windbreaker that looked as if he'd dug them out of the dumpster she was heading to. His hair was once again pulled into a ponytail—a look she wasn't sure she could get used to after seeing him day in and day out in a G-man haircut. Still, when she saw him her breathing did that little hitching thing that drove her completely insane.

How many things did it take to convince her she was an idiot? First, the lure of the serial killer and now she thought the serial killer was hot.

Just to be safe, she parked along the road and grabbed her Glock from the glove box.

She kicked open the car door, shoved her weapon into the holster with enough pizazz to make sure Mitch saw it and slammed the door.

"Mitch Monroe, I should kill you where you stand."

"What fun would that be?"

Damn him. Part of her couldn't resist the sickening charm. *Pain in the ass.* "Please. I'd apprehend a federal fugitive, satisfy my own need for retribution, *and* land a promotion while taking out your sorry ass. I'd be a hero."

"Harsh." He grinned. "I figured you'd tease out the

retribution—make it last beyond a single shot. But you always did like things tidy, didn't you?" He stubbed the toe of his sneaker into the ground. "I assume you want to do more than threaten my *sorry ass*. You said you had information."

Killer, that smile, but he knew that. He also knew that she knew that he knew. Whatever that meant. But this was the game with him. The push-pull of sexual tension that had existed long before he'd almost destroyed her career. "Yes, I want more than to threaten you. Donaldson was put on high alert when I tried to access those files. Something stinks here and it's not just the dumpster I'm heading to."

She stepped closer, got within a foot of him and glanced around. They were alone, but she didn't believe that Grey—Monroe's ever present partner in crime—wasn't watching from the pukey-colored building. "So, if you want me to dig around, you need to give me more because I'm locked out. Who do you know that'll talk to me about what Tommy was working on?"

Mitch focused on her, his eyes darting over her face, down to her chest. "Caroline, are you wearing a wire?"

A stab of anger...no, make that *hurt*...carved right into her. "No. Want me to flash you? Let you a cop a feel?"

"You already did, remember?"

She sucked in a breath—*shoot*—and stepped back. This man had ripped her heart out without even trying. Forget about the career implications; she'd considered him a friend. And after that night when they'd been at a hostage stand-off and she'd fired her rifle in the line of duty, they'd become more than friends.

Smart-mouthed, cocky Monroe had held her while she gutted through the realization she'd taken her first life. She'd looked down the scope of her rifle at the man holding an innocent woman hostage, and the moral and ethical repercussions had fallen away, only to come roaring back with a vengeance later. The guy had been a scum bag and deserved to die after killing and injuring over a dozen people in a church, but that didn't stop her from being sick over taking a life.

That awful, hellish night, Mitch was her anchor. He'd held her, talked her through the recriminations, and the two became friends in a carnal way that left them both howling until dawn when she rolled over and realized that, yes, they'd done the nasty—three, or was it four times?—and now had to face each other at the office. Every day.

And as much as she liked to deny it, that emotional part of her, the one who loved holding a man's hand or sharing a lazy breakfast, had imagined Mitch Monroe as a whole lot more than a one-night stand.

Fool.

She couldn't work with him *and* sleep with him. End of story.

Watching her working through her mental and emotional issues brought out a carnal smile on Mitch's lips. As usual, he'd known exactly where her thoughts went. His ability to read a situation was uncanny. When he got to know a person? That ability, much to her disadvantage, multiplied ten-fold.

But the thing about Mitch...he had weaknesses and she knew them.

Stepping forward again, Caroline tilted her head and inched closer, close enough that his warm, minty breath tickled her cheek. He watched her, his eyes slightly wide, waiting.

"Yes," she said. "I suppose I did."

With one giant step back, Mitch put distance between them. The man quite simply did not like people in his space. Even a woman he'd enjoyed a long night of intense, heart-stoppingly good sex with.

"There's a guy." No preamble, no further reference to their previous one-night stand. "An ATF agent Tommy talked about. He's now a blogger or something. I wanted to talk to him, but given my current circumstances..."

"What's his name? I'll find him."

"You don't have to find him. He's here in D.C. Name's Brice Brennan. He got fed up with the bureaucratic bullshit and left the ATF.

"Why do we care about this guy?"

"Tommy mentioned him a couple times. His blog is one of those government watch things. He doesn't do it under his real name and the government can't catch him. Tommy said he's uber-critical of ATF and regularly bashes them on his blog. Makes me wonder if he's had contact with anyone who knows what Tommy was working on. Maybe we can find him after you get done digging through that dumpster Donaldson assigned you to because he doesn't want you knowing what he's hiding."

On any given day, Mitch could be considered paranoid—a conspiracy theorist through and through. The problem was he was usually right.

Caroline puffed up her cheeks and blew air. "I hesitate to ask, but do you happen to know the name of this blog?"

"I do not, but if you're done being afraid I'll kill you and want to come inside, we'll put Grey's techy bitch on it."

She eyed him. "I thought you were worried I was wearing a wire?"

That Miracle Mitch grin slid across his face and he waved her off. "Nah. I was just fucking with you. I like getting you riled up, Caroline. It turns me on."

"Seriously, I *could* kill you."

Right this second. Just—boom! The man frustrated the hell out of her. He also made her laugh and that was the thing she couldn't resist. His caustic, inappropriate humor made a crazy, vicious world tolerable.

He swung sideways and held out his hand to the pukey-colored building. "Come on, Caroline. Take a walk with me."

5

What am I doing? Mitch opened the door and moved to the side to usher Caroline in. She always did that to him...caught him off guard. Just like mentioning the-night-that-never-happened. She was the one who'd insisted they never to speak of it. Yet, invariably she threw it in his face at random times.

She'd never gotten over that night. That intense, holy-fuck night. And what a holy fuck it was. He hadn't fully recovered from it either. At least, he hoped that was why she'd brought it up again.

A man could dream.

Caroline gave him the hairy eyeball before she carefully stepped across the threshold. As if she were stepping into a criminal's den. Or maybe hell. "I don't bite," he said, laying a charming grin on her once more.

She lifted her lip in a slight sneer. "As I recall, you do bite on occasion."

There it was again. A reference to the-night-that-never-happened. A reference that brought up a slew of memories. Her soft flesh between his teeth. The taste of her on his tongue.

His pants grew tight. From the memory and from the sarcastic look on her face. She pretended to be straight-laced but he knew better. The woman under the Bureau attire was as hot as they came. And she gave as good as she got.

Mitch adjusted his pants. He turned his attention to the main room and saw Grey frozen in his tracks, a look of utter fear on his face. "What the fuck...?"

"We need to find a blog," Mitch said, clearing his throat. Teeg had a similar look on his face. Disbelief. "A blogger actually."

"A *blog*? Are you out of your fucking mind?" Grey jerked his head to the board with all his classified information that was now, with Caroline's presence, officially declassified.

Yep, if Caroline didn't kill him, Grey would.

"Grey," Caroline said, "nice to see you. Apparently we're both suckers for Mitch."

He brushed fake dirt off his shoulder. "I do have a certain charm that's hard to resist."

Caroline laughed. "I never said otherwise. Which is my problem." She turned to Grey. "I won't look at what's on that board. Are you up to speed?"

"About Mitch's batshit idea concerning Tommy and a cover-up?"

"I'm afraid it may not be too crazy. I got my hand slapped this morning by your friend Donaldson for trying to read a protected file."

Good guy that he was, Grey pretended he hadn't overheard Mitch and Caroline's previous conversation. "No shit?"

"Yep. Now Mitch wants me to chase down some ex-ATF guy who runs a blog."

"Brice Brennan? Mitch already told me about him. Sounds like another dead lead to me, but Teeg here can find anyone."

Mitch huffed. "Hello? This is *my* case, everyone, remember?" He glanced at Caroline. "Caroline, meet David Teeg, the techy bitch I was telling you about."

"Hey," Teeg said. "I'm nobody's bitch."

Grey snickered. "You are, and you might as well face reality. Now help them out."

Grey headed for his board and Teeg made a nasty face at his back.

"I saw that," Grey said.

Teeg swore under his breath. "How does he do that?"

"Well," Caroline said. "I see nothing's changed with you boys. Still infants."

Mitch refrained from rolling his eyes. "How do we find Brennan, Teeg?"

Caroline walked over to the computer hub. "Mitch thinks he runs a government watch blog that Tommy told Mitch was highly critical of ATF. My guess is, it will have a lot of posts on gun control. Can we search blogs by subjects?"

Teeg hit a few keys and a second later said, "There are three thousand-plus government watch blogs."

"Holy shit," Mitch said.

Caroline's forehead wrinkled. "How do we narrow it down?"

Teeg hit a few more keys. "Nothing comes up associated with the guy's name, but we narrow it with keywords."

"Like what?" Mitch said.

"Gun control, ATF mismanagement or corruption, ATF watchdog," Caroline answered.

Teeg typed. A second later, a list of the most prominent watch blogs scrolled on the main screen. Caroline and Mitch both leaned forward, scanning their names. Nothing jumped out at Mitch. No "hey, I'm Brice Brennan's blog" which would have been nice, to be honest.

"This could take a while," Caroline murmured. "Can you do a search for Congressional cover-ups?"

"Sure." Teeg worked his keyboard magic again. "Okay, that leaves us with a thousand."

"Can you narrow them by the most recent posts on ATF specific cover-ups? Starting three weeks ago."

More keyboard tapping. "We're down to a few hundred."

"Hang on," Caroline said. "Try topics of ATF cover-ups and agents killed in the line. I bet Brennan's done at least a few posts on both subjects."

A new entry, a new list, this one much shorter.

A pang of homesickness struck Mitch out of the blue. Like it had with Kemp in Runner's Paradise. This was how it used to be, him and Caroline working cases together. It was fun to see her so fired up.

Teeg caught Mitch's eye. "I can get the IP addresses. That will at least tell you if the bloggers are located in the States. But if he doesn't want to be found, he could be bouncing the signal to other spots in the world."

"He's most likely not a supergeek like you." Mitch stared at the screen, thinking. "See if any of the top five have addresses here in the States."

"It'll take a minute."

Mitch drew Caroline aside. "Can I get you something to drink?"

She checked her phone. "No, thanks. I've got a date with a dumpster. Are you around tonight? Whatever Teeg finds, we can check out later."

She was willing to help him. Willing to go with him to locate Brice. His heart did a little weird *thump-thump*. "Yeah, I'll give you my number. We can meet up later."

"Try not to get arrested before then."

He snickered. "Try not to crawl too far up Donaldson's ass before then."

"Thanks to you, it's a little late for that."

He walked her to the door, her sensible shoes squeaking on the cement floor. "You'll survive."

She sneered at him again before exiting. He followed her out, watched her drive off. Yep, Caroline Foster would be the death of him. And she'd enjoy every minute of busting his balls.

Truth was, he might enjoy it too.

Caroline parked at the rear of the fast food restaurant's lot, nudging her car—no sense getting in trouble for using her Bureau car on an assignment she shouldn't be anywhere near —between a minivan and an ancient sedan. She checked the dashboard clock. 6:20. As usual, she was early and Mitch, bless his rebellious heart, would most likely be late.

Mitch, Mitch, Mitch. The man made her crazy in all the ways he shouldn't, but in a truly twisted way she loved.

After an afternoon spent dumpster diving, she'd gone home and showered for thirty minutes, scrubbing her skin raw, but somehow still carried the stench of rotting meat. Damned Donaldson. After handling all that bovine nastiness, she might just become a vegetarian. Tragedy that because she loved a good hunk of rib-eye.

A knock sounded on the passenger window and she jumped. Mitch's face appeared—well, how about that—five minutes early. She hit the lock button and he slid in.

Similar to that morning, his jeans rode low on his hips and were blown out at the knees. Under his leather jacket, a T-shirt read, *I can give a headache to an aspirin.*

How appropriate. And factual, but stupid. He was a fugitive who shouldn't draw attention to himself. Besides, he was already a bad ass who didn't need to advertise his attitude. Yet, in good old Mitch Monroe manner, that's exactly what he was doing. A rebel to the roots of his hair. "I see you've dressed for the occasion. And allow me to congratulate you on being five minutes early."

"Don't make fun of my clothes, Caroline. I dress for comfort these days. Unlike you in your pseudo-Bureau uniform."

Caroline glanced down at her slacks. After the marathon shower, she'd considered wearing jeans and the wicked leather boots she'd bought on a whim last month, but opted against it. Boots like that would entice Mr. Sexual Innuendo to make a comment, and they'd fall into old habits of one-upping each other. The last time they'd done that, they wound up in her bed working off major calories.

So, as clothing went, she'd done business casual: slacks, a turtleneck, and a blazer. No skin showing. At all. If Mitch didn't take the hint, he was blind. And dense.

Neither of which could ever be used to describe Mitch Monroe.

Not interested in verbal swordplay, she started the car. "No one followed you, right?"

He snorted. "I've been on the lam for a year. I know when I've got a tail. Afraid you'll get caught with a federal fugitive?"

"Bet your ass."

At some point they'd have to discuss the fact that she hadn't gotten over the last attempt he'd made to destroy her career. As unintentional as it had been, she'd allowed herself to be talked into things she shouldn't have been talked into regarding The Lion case. Going behind Donaldson's back, entering a report for Mitch she shouldn't have touched, getting herself involved in a hornet's nest.

Later. "This is your manhunt. Where are we going?"

"Teeg narrowed down the IP addresses to three possible street addresses. I had him run a DMV check of Brice's vehicle. Guy drives a Ford truck, red, D.C. plates. Teeg found the guy's

Facebook page—his personal one—and printed off a few shots of it. Brice is proud of his wheels. Got rebel shit all over it. Shouldn't be hard to spot."

Caroline entered the address he rattled off into her phone and waited for Andre—the name she'd given her GPS narrator —to spit out directions. Seconds later, she had a route mapped. "Twenty-five minutes."

Twenty-five minutes in a car with Mitch. Plenty of time to lay on his charm. Which, he most certainly would do. And her without ear plugs.

Pulling into rush hour traffic, she merged into the center lane and hit the gas. "When was the last time you talked to Tommy?"

Mitch fiddled with the car's radio, found a station playing old rock that made her want those ear plugs even more. "Labor Day. We had a standing boys-only trip—Tommy, me, and Kemp —every Labor Day to camp and fish. I picked a different location this year in case anyone knew about our usual spot, but Tommy couldn't make it anyway. Too deep undercover, he said. He was anxious...about what he wouldn't say."

A guitar riff nearly blew her hearing and she pressed a random button on the radio. Classical. She'd take it. Mitch gave her a WTF face.

"My car, my music."

"Since when do you like classical?"

"It relaxes me, and my ears were bleeding. Did Tommy tell you anything about the taskforce? They found his body in Roswell, in a parking lot near a residential neighborhood. Did you know he was down there?"

"He didn't share details. All he said was that he was hot and ready to be done with his latest assignment. Although, Tommy being Tommy, he had a lot to say about the women in town. Sounded like things were about to wrap up and he wanted to spend a few hours with a gal he was sweet on before he moved on to his next assignment. Next thing I know, Kemp tells me he's dead."

Mitch had his head turned, looking out the window, but the tight set of his jaw told her he was holding back emotions he didn't know how to deal with.

Caroline couldn't go there with him. As much as she wanted to, allowing him inside her head again would be torture. She wasn't sure she could survive another round of Mitch's brand of torture.

She merged onto the heavy, but moving expressway traffic. "Someone—besides this woman—had to be in contact with him down there. Someone had to know the details about the operation he was working on. We have to find that person. Maybe Brice Brennan might know who it was."

"Let's hope. Tommy liked working alone."

"That's what I'm worried about. The Bureau rumor is he was on the take. Selling assault weapons on the black market. I know he was your friend—"

"Yours too, Caroline."

Whatever. "I know he was *our* friend, but you know as well as I do, none of us were getting rich as FBI agents."

"He didn't need money."

"If he had a girlfriend, maybe he did."

"Seriously? You believe this crap? Nuh-uh. I know you better. If you believed it, you wouldn't be driving my ass on this goose chase. If you believed it, you wouldn't have gone looking for those files."

She glanced over at him, met his stare for a second, then went back to the road. "I'm not sure what I believe. Money makes people do crazy things. Maybe I'm here to satisfy myself. When we're through, I'll know for sure. *That's* all I know right now. Now shut up and let me think for the next fifteen minutes."

He punched the radio back to the rock station. Unbelievable. Most stubborn man ever. Well, guess what? She'd been known to be just as stubborn. Swirling her finger, she tapped the radio button to off. He sighed heavily.

Drama queen.

She waited for a response. Something. Anything. But Mitch only sat there, quietly staring out the window as Andre gave directions and they flew by clumps of trees on the side of the road.

Maybe she'd pushed him too far. Two of his best friends were gone and he was grieving and her only interest was self-protection.

After all they'd shared, how had they gotten to this place?

"I'm sorry," she said. "About Tommy and Kemp. About *us*. Whatever *us* is. We were friends and then we weren't."

Quite possibly for the first time ever, Mitch appeared speechless. He hemmed and hawed for a second. "We're more than friends, Caroline, whether you want to admit it or not. And I appreciate what you're doing here."

Sharp, ugly pain shot through her ribcage. That ache when thoughts of Mitch distracted her. Made her regret what never was. And here he was, working her over again. All that sincerity and the eyes—puppy dog eyes. He thought he could suck her in with those eyes.

Maybe he could.

She gripped the steering wheel tighter as she curved around the exit ramp. Just a few more minutes and they'd be back to business. "After this, we'll know what happened with Tommy. Let's just focus on that for now."

"If that's what you want, sure."

At the stop light, Caroline turned left and sent Andre into a fit. Clearly, she'd missed his command to turn right. Distracted. *Thanks, Mitch.*

After hooking a U-turn, she cruised down the four-lane

road leading to their first address. Three turns later, she drove past their target, a small white cottage with shrubs lining the house. On the porch hung a swing with bright red floral pillows.

In the driveway was a minivan. The ultimate Mom-mobile and about as opposite as one could get from a jacked up truck.

"Not looking too good," Mitch said.

Caroline laughed. "Excellent observation skills."

"According to Teeg, the other address is only ten minutes from here. Should we check that one out, and if it's a bust come back?"

Resting her forehead against the steering wheel, she mulled it over. If they went to the door and someone other than Brice answered—assuming this was his house—they'd lose all element of surprise. And considering she didn't see his truck, she wasn't feeling the love for this location.

Decision made, she sat up. "Yep. Let's see what the other place looks like. Then we'll know if we've wasted our time."

And, where Mitch was concerned, every last ounce of her emotional reserves.

Red truck. Lift kit. *Kiss my rebel ass* bumper sticker. Check, check, and check. "Bingo," Mitch said. "We found Brennan."

Caroline parked at the curb behind the truck and they scanned the house. Raised ranch. Dark curtains. Peeling paint. Overgrown bushes lined the steps to the front porch, and the sidewalk was cracked. *Real inviting.*

"I'll knock." Carline shut off her boring POS car. "You stay here."

"Hell with that. I'll knock and *you* stay here."

"A man wanted for murder showing up on your doorstep tends to freak people out, idiot. He'll never talk to you. Probably won't even open the door."

"He's ex-ATF. You think a Bureau agent won't scare him out the back door?"

"He doesn't know I'm FBI. You, on the other hand, have your mug on every news station and website in the tri-state area."

"You scream *FBI*, Caroline. The conservative clothes, the ponytail." He opened the car door and hauled out. "I'm going in."

Caroline, of course, jumped out on her side and slammed the door. "I'm going with you. You're not exactly dressed for it, but we'll pretend we're holy rollers. You could use a little of that in your life."

Just like the old days. She never could sit still. Had to be the one to drive. Had to be the one to call the shots. "Ever get tired of overcompensating?"

She tucked her classic navy blue jacket tighter to her body. A body he had memorized that single night he'd had her all to himself. A body he dreamed about having again. *Like that will ever happen.* "Overcompensating for what?"

"Being female. Being...I don't know. You don't have to control every fucking situation."

"When it comes to you, I do." They climbed the steps. "Just because you project carefree and laid back, doesn't mean you don't have control issues."

Mitch rolled his eyes and hit the doorbell. Stupid thing was broken. He banged on the door. "Do me a solid and at least try to act like you don't have a cob up your ass."

"A six-foot-two one?"

Deserved, for sure, but still he laughed. He'd missed this. Missed her.

The door cracked open an inch. A male said, "Yeah?"

"Hey, man." Mitch motioned with his thumb. He wasn't about to do the holy-roller act. "Nice ride. That your truck?"

A weighted pause. "What's it to you?"

"A buddy of mine told me about that truck. Said you'd done some sweet add-ons. Wondered if you'd share your garage contacts." Mitch pointed to the street and the god-awful car. "I need a new ride in the worst way."

The door eased open enough for the guy to look past Mitch. He spotted Caroline, lingered for half a second—*shit, we're blown*—then traveled to the ride in question. "Look, man, I don't know what you're selling, but..."

His attention came back to Mitch's face, then his eyes widened. "Wait, don't I know you?"

Play it cool. Mitch held out a hand. "Name's Mitch. I think you knew my friend, Tommy Nusco."

The door slammed shut.

Way to go.

"Nice work, ace." Caroline echoed his internal flogging. "Real nice. Anymore leads you want to blow for us today?"

Mitch knocked on the door again and raised his voice. "Brice, I'm not here to cause you trouble, man. I just need to know if what they're saying about Tommy is true. He's dead. All I want are a few answers."

Silence.

"Told you so," Caroline said.

"Real helpful, Caroline. Real helpful."

She pushed him out of the way. "Brice? My name's Caroline Foster. I was Tommy's co-worker, and also his friend. Mitch is telling the truth...we don't want to make trouble. We just need to understand what Tommy was doing when he died. We know you're a former ATF agent and hoped you might have some information or know someone who worked with Tommy in New Mexico."

Brice's voice came from the other side. "I don't know anything."

"Brice, I think you do. All we know is that Tommy is dead and he's being tagged a dirty agent. If that's the truth, we drop this whole thing. If it's not, we could use your investigative skills to expose the cover-up. Is it true?"

Silence. Caroline turned to Mitch and shrugged. He held up his hand. They'd wait. And wait a little longer if they had to.

"Brice?" Caroline said. "Can I at least leave my number in case you remember something?"

Mitch leaned forward, got right next to her ear where the strawberry scent of her shampoo teased his nose and triggered memories of her naked body. Last time he'd been that close they'd been tearing up her sheets, and the memory—although a damned good one—reminded him of the life and opportunities now gone. "Tommy and I went way back," he spoke toward the door, hoping Brice was still listening on the other side. "High school, in fact. No way I believe he was dirty. You?"

The door jerked open an inch. Brice spoke in low tones. "Get in your car. Drive around the block and park. Come through the yard and I'll let you in the back door."

"We weren't followed."

"You want answers, we do this my way."

The door slammed again.

Okay, then. "Guess we take a trip around the block."

They hustled down the stairs. Caroline had a grin on her face. As they climbed into the car, Mitch said, "What?"

She gave him an innocent look. "Good thing I went with you."

Good thing, my ass. "I was prepared to wait him out."

"Intimidation. Always effective."

She drove as instructed. They left the car, climbed through overgrown bushes and high grass in the back yard, and made it to the door. Brice was waiting for them. He didn't say a word, watching over their shoulders as he ushered them inside.

Paranoid much? Mitch had been on the run too long. He was paranoid, but this guy got a gold star in the department.

The inside of the house was a shocker. Clean, neat, total

opposite of the outside. *Hiding in plain view*, that's what Brice was doing. Mitch liked the guy on principle.

Brice didn't offer them seats or a drink. Nope, right to business. "Whatever we say is off the record."

"Fine with us." Caroline, always happy to get down to business, nodded. "We were never here, never spoke to you."

Brice seemed to relax a bit.

Two of a kind. Maybe it *was* a good idea she'd accompanied him on this adventure.

Mitch put space between Caroline and himself. That damn shampoo smell messed with his brain cells. And his libido. "Did you know Tommy?"

"Not personally. Some of my contacts did though."

"Any idea what he was working on?" Caroline asked.

Brice shook his head. "It was some taskforce, but nobody is talking. The agents, the good ones, are too scared. ATF isn't what it used to be. Management intimidation is the norm. You don't fall in line, you and your family get transferred to shit holes. Five different ones in two years. Any idea what that's like for a guy with kids in school? Worse than waterboarding."

Intimidation tactics at ATF had long been rumored but Caroline reserved judgment. If she was going to believe a government agency stooped to those levels she wanted proof.

Brice turned to her. "You're FBI?"

"I am."

"You sure you want to skip through this mine field?"

"If a good agent is about to be labeled a traitor, you're damn straight. I worked with this man and I'm not fool enough to believe people don't change, but I tried to get into a protected file about Tommy and was told—quite clearly—to stay out of it. That makes me twitchy. Makes me think good agents, ones like myself, could easily get screwed as well. So, if he *was* dirty, I want proof."

"Ho-kay," Mitch said. "Back on point. Brice, if you can hook us up, maybe we can figure out why ATF is covering up Tommy's death."

"Beyond that," Caroline said, "you run a blog. A popular one. If anything comes of this, you could be on the front lines."

"I use a false name and have some heavy security protocols in place."

"We found you. The government can too." Caroline touched his arm. "Help us figure out what Tommy was doing on this taskforce in New Mexico."

Brice shook his head. "I don't know any of those details."

Mitch tamed the anger rising in his chest. "A White House insider told me Tommy's body was found with a cache of weapons in the trunk of his car. Someone wanted him found with those weapons. Wanted to label him a dirty agent."

"Was he stepping on toes?" Caroline asked. "Could he have been threatening to leak info about whatever he was working on? Maybe even to you?"

Brice chewed on a thumbnail and looked guilty. Mitch's gut said Caroline had nailed it. Somehow, somewhere along the line, Tommy had contacted Brice. "I never spoke to him directly, but I do know the taskforce was super-secret and nobody knows what they were working on. Even some of the brass are in the dark, supposedly for security reasons."

Back to square one. "So we don't know why he was killed or why he was in that location when it went down."

Caroline cocked her head. "Or why he had those weapons."

He knew what she was thinking. Maybe Tommy *was* dirty. Hell, Mitch was having a fucking hard time believing his friend wasn't up to something bad at this point. "He wasn't on the take, Caroline."

"Then I guess we'll have to prove that, won't we?"

She didn't believe him. Didn't believe in Tommy's innocence. Like a kick to his gut, Mitch wondered if he'd gotten the wrong person involved. He should have done this on his own.

But he needed her. Plain and simple. "Yeah, that's exactly what we have to do."

And you're the best person to do it.

6

---

*C*aroline slid behind the wheel of her sedan and jammed the key into the ignition. What the hell had she done? For months she'd been going along just fine—well, maybe fine was a stretch—but she hadn't had Mitch in her life creating all kinds of chaos, because let's face it, the man lived for chaos.

But she'd been okay, living her life day-to-day working her cases, having an orgasm or two thanks to her trusty vibrator and then—bam!—Mitch Monroe walks in and disrupts her whole pathetic routine.

"Here's what we should do," Mitch said, slamming the passenger door.

"No, I'll tell *you* what we should do. We need to sit down and figure out what is going on with this case. We need to know who Tommy was working with and you have to be honest with me. Tell me everything you know. I respect that he was your friend, but I'm putting myself out there and I want total cooperation from you."

"Do you think he was dirty?"

"I don't know what I think, Mitch. But there's enough I don't know to make me wonder. So, we have to find a place where we can work this case like we would any other. We need a murder board, and a place to put it because I'm not taking you to my place."

"I have a place and a board already set up."

"Where?"

"Can't tell you. It'll compromise you."

Now he was worried about compromising her? He'd already compromised her in so many different ways, some of which she hadn't minded, she couldn't keep track of them all.

"Switch seats," he said. "I'll take you there."

"Ha! You're kidding, right? You want me—a person with not-so-minor control issues—to just hand over car keys?"

"That's exactly what I want. And, it gets better; I'm going to blindfold you."

"My ass, you are."

"I happen to like your ass."

He grinned that slick Mitch Monroe I'll-make-you-moan smile and something in her brain snapped. She should just stick with her damned vibrator. "Mitch—"

"Caroline, quit arguing. This is for your own good. I blindfold you, take you to where I'm squatting, and if Donaldson or anyone else comes at you, you'll be able to tell him that you have absolutely no idea where I'm hiding."

She tapped her fingers against the steering wheel, drumming, drumming, drumming, hoping for some flash of brilliance, because once again, Mitch's logic made sense. But that would mean handing over the keys, allowing him to take her to an unknown secondary location, *and* removing the battery from her phone so no one could trace it. The personal safety experts would consider her a failure.

But, if they were going to do this, they'd better do it right.

"Are you in or out, Caroline?"

Simple question with no simple answers. She could walk

away, without a doubt. He'd let her. She'd go back to her dumpster tomorrow and continue sorting garbage as her punishment for digging into a file Donaldson didn't want her digging into.

And that was the rub. The thing that would haunt. She shoved open the door to switch places with him. "Damn you, Mitch Monroe."

He went around the back of the car, passing her in a whoosh. "It's fine, Caroline. Trust me."

"Ha!"

He chuckled low and annoying, and regardless of how much she wanted to hate him, it made her smile. She'd missed this. The banter, the stupid arguments, the friendship. *I've lost all sense.*

She buckled her seat belt. "Are you seriously going to blindfold me?"

"I am. And I'm going to loop around, get you good and lost so you don't figure out where we're going."

"Two days ago if someone had asked me if I'd let you drive me anywhere blindfolded I would have shot them."

"I've always dreamed of blindfolding you. Just not for this purpose."

Something low in her throat hitched and Caroline swallowed. *Forget it.* "Oh, don't even."

"Right. Sorry. I forgot it's *the-night-that-never-happened.*"

She propped one arm on the center console and drummed her fingers again. The man had a comeback for everything and her snark wasn't as rapid-fire as his. She was good, but he was better. Another thing that irritated her.

What he didn't understand was that she'd made it *the-night-that-never-happened* because he, this man right here, the one ready to blindfold her and drive her who knew where, had reached inside her, grabbed onto her heart and ripped it right out of her body. After that crazy good night of sex, she simply didn't know what to do with him. For months before it had happened she'd been craving him and then—poof—they were back to being co-workers, because on an emotional level she was simply terrified.

Obviously, she'd been right, because he'd almost derailed her career by having her go behind Donaldson's back to file that stupid report about The Lion case.

Something to remember. Particularly when he removed his jacket and T-shirt—and my, oh, my—Mitch had been keeping in shape while on the run. Long, lean muscles, washboard abs, all of it shadowed against a darkening sky.

"What are you—?"

He tossed his T-shirt at her. "Blindfold. This will have to do."

She resisted holding the shirt to her face where she'd get his scent, that salty air smell that used to be part of her day every day. She missed it. Missed him.

Pathetic, Caroline. Was she a dog in heat now? Ignoring the Mitch-scent, she tied the shirt around her head. Not an easy task with so much material. This thing was more like a burka. Whatever.

The click of a seatbelt sounded. "Can you see?" he asked.

"No."

"You lying?"

She laughed. "No. I get it. Hey, grab my phone from my purse and pull the battery."

"Right. On it."

"How long until we get there?"

"A while. You okay?"

"I don't know, Mitch, am I?"

A second later, his hand wrapped around hers—*don't flinch*—and he squeezed. Being touched with a blindfold on was suddenly on her list of least favorite things. It left her questioning every decision, doubting herself and her actions. Worse, it made her vulnerable and she didn't do vulnerable.

"You may not believe it, Caroline, but I'll take care of you."

And dammit, this was why she'd fallen for him. Beneath that cocky, know-it-all exterior, lived a generous, funny, and uber-protective soul. "I hate you."

He patted her hand. "I know you do. I'm working on changing that."

The car moved, the engine revving as Mitch pulled out. He'd said he'd loop around and he did a fine job of confusing her because she lost all sense of direction after the fourth or fifth turn.

If nothing else, Mitch was skilled in the art of evasion.

For now, she'd have to sit back and wait. Again, not something she was particularly good at, and between the motion of the car and the blindfold, her breath backed up in her throat and her stomach rebelled, tumbling her undigested dinner. *Don't get sick.* She ran her hand along the cheap leather on the door—*handle, check*—and inched along until she found the window button and pressed it. When cold air hit her cheek, she let go of the button.

"You all right?"

Of course she wasn't all right. Not that she'd admit it. She closed her eyes, focused on...what?...anything that would let her not think about being totally defenseless. The range. She'd think about going to the range, the outdoor one where Joe would shout a greeting and maybe wander down to watch her shoot. She loved that. A man watching a woman shoot and it having nothing to do with her boobs or her ass or any other part of the female anatomy. She'd walk to the end of the row to her usual spot at her usual table, set down her case and remove her rifle, snapping the bipod legs into position. She'd load the magazine—five bullets—and send that baby home into the bottom of the rifle.

When Mitch's hand wrapped around hers again, she didn't fight it and held on. Let her mind wander to the-night-that-never-happened. Thought about those wicked hands on her. Tender sometimes, and definitely experienced. He'd handled her like a lover who knew her body inside and out. Just like she knew her favorite weapon and how to dismantle and rebuild it, that night, he'd known all the right places to touch.

For months afterward, every time she assembled her rifle, an image of Mitch's hands on her drifted into her mind, made her ache for that touch and the ease of it. The thrill of it. A thrill she didn't think she'd experience again.

Now she was here, vulnerable to him. Physically and emotionally blindfolded. Different circumstances, but her heart didn't seem to get it. It fluttered and banged around in her chest as if he were touching her for ulterior purposes.

And they'd been down this road before.

She slid her hand away. "I'm okay. Thanks."

Liar. He wouldn't know that, though, and for now, it was the best she could do because when Mitch touched her, every ounce of her common sense evaporated.

Finally, the car came to a stop. "We're here?"

"Yep. Keep the blindfold on until we get inside."

How the hell was she supposed to walk?

"And before you start yelling, I'll help you."

Smart ass. "If I break an ankle, I'm holding you responsible."

"I'll carry you."

"Not unless you want to get shot."

He laughed. "You carry a big gun, Caroline, and an even bigger attitude. But I like it. You keep threatening to kill me, though, and I'll develop a complex. I hope to change your mind so you'll keep me around for a while."

God, she didn't know what to do with this man. Every time she tried to hate him, he managed to diffuse it. "Mitch, please, just get me inside so I can take this blindfold off. I hate not knowing where I'm going."

. . .

Mitch took a quiet breath, turned the doorknob, and led Caroline into the east wing of Grey's deserted army base.

Seeing her blindfolded, holding her hand and guiding her, slayed him. Knowing what a control freak she was, this exercise had to be taking a piece out of her. Caroline wanted justice just like he did. It was eating her alive inside. She would never let herself be so vulnerable otherwise.

Especially to him.

He led her down a dark hallway, up a flight of stairs. The only light came from a few incandescents here and there along the concrete walls and the windows at each end. They passed what had once been sleeping quarters for the bigwigs and climbed another set of stairs. The first step was always the most challenging and she gripped Mitch's hand tighter until she found her balance, but once she did, her natural athleticism kicked in and she practically ran up the stairs.

Bad idea, his gut warned. *Bringing her here.* Exposing himself and the few facts he had to figure out this case and Kemp's murder. Worse, he was exposing himself to how he felt about her, and how desperately he needed her help.

Even if she *was* blindfolded, Caroline was smart. It wouldn't take long for her to figure out she was back at the base. If he could keep her focused on the case...if *he* could keep focused on the case and not her...it might all work out.

Jesus. He was doing it again. Just like last time. Justifying and lying to himself, and compromising her in the process.

Too late now. She was here, and he needed fresh eyes on Tommy's murder board. And now Kemp's. He'd divided the board in half, one for each of his friends.

Hell of a life you've got here, Mitch.

He guided her to the last room on the left. "We're here."

Caroline sighed with what sounded like relief. Pleasant relief. How many times had he heard that sigh? Heaven to his ears.

He'd installed a new lock on the room's door. Paranoia ran deep in his veins. He constantly ran just-in-case scenarios through his mind, and then went to work in reality making sure they never happened.

Yes, someone could still break in or pick the lock, but the average high school gang of kids looking for a party spot, or a vagrant looking for a place to squat, wouldn't go to the trouble.

He unlocked the door and helped Caroline across the threshold.

The room had been a classroom and came with a white board, a long table, and a bunch of metal chairs no one had bothered to take when the base closed. Not exactly homey, but workable as long as no one—including Grey—knew he'd set up camp here. He knew Teeg saw him coming and going on occasion, but the kid had never mentioned it. Teeg probably thought Mitch was doing something for Grey and one of Grey's rules was everyone kept their mouths shut about everything.

Moving behind Caroline, Mitch untied his shirt from her head. A piece of her hair caught in his fingers and he gently untangled it, enjoying the feel of the thick softness as it filtered through his fingers.

That hair. He liked it down. Remembered how it had tickled his face, his chest, his stomach. Lower...

Lust flared to life below his belt and he took a step back. A big step.

Which sent him into one of the metal chairs. The thing banged into the wall, causing the room to echo with the sharp noise.

Caroline didn't seem to notice. She smoothed hair away from her face, staring straight ahead at the whiteboard. Tommy's picture hung on the left. Kemp's on the right. Below each photo, Mitch had logged the date, time, and location of each of their deaths. A pitiful handful of other details.

Not enough.

He'd even slapped up some of his wild ass theories, trying anything to find a connection between them.

Drawn like a magnet to the board, Caroline walked by the table stacked with Mitch's files and newspaper clippings and went to stand right in front of it. "You've been busy."

He shrugged off his jacket and tossed it on a nearby recliner he'd found at the Goodwill store. How many nights had he fallen asleep in that thing staring at the board? "Busy twiddling my thumbs. As you can see, I've got jack squat for leads. Brice was my best hope to at least find out what Tommy was working on and why the government's trying to cover up his death by labeling him a traitor."

Caroline picked up a blue marker and started bulleting points under Brice's name. "Okay, let's make a list of everyone Tommy knew, ATF or FBI. Starting with me and Donaldson."

She turned to say something and stopped, her eyes zeroing in on his naked chest.

T-shirt. He should probably throw it back on.

Her mouth was still open. Her hand fell to her side.

He grinned. "Nothing you haven't seen before, Caroline." *And touched, and put those luscious lips on...*his gaze dropped to her mouth and those full lips that no doctor could recreate. Yeah, those lips just about did him in.

She closed her mouth, firmed her lips. All business.

Fine. He tugged on the shirt. "You were saying?"

She whirled back around, stared at the board. "Brice said most agents, and even some higher ups, were in the dark about this operation, but who had to be in on it?"

He plopped into a metal chair at the table. Her ass was directly in his sight line. *Just like the old days.* He laughed to himself.

She looked over her shoulder at him. "What?"

"Nothing," he said, but he couldn't keep the grin off his face. They might have been in a deserted army base, but everything else reminded him of the past. The *normal* past where he stared at Caroline's ass and never got caught.

Normal...he'd never wanted normal. That's why he'd joined the Bureau after college. He wanted action, adventure...to bring justice to the bad guys and have fun on the side with a woman here and there.

And here he was feeling normal when his life was anything but.

"Donaldson," he said, shuffling through his notes. "And Director Lockhart. Since ATF is involved, I'll take a wild guess and say the head of ATF in New Mexico, and the ATF supervisor in New Mexico are part of this. Whatever the op was, Justice would have had to sign off on it."

Carolyn scribbled each person's title under their agency headings. "If Justice is involved, the U.S. Attorney in New Mexico would be as well, right?"

She drew an arrow off to the side, wrote *U.S. Attorney NM* and added a question mark.

Mitch stared at the list of names on the board. "That's a lot of higher ups."

Caroline crossed her arms, inventorying the list too. "A lot of toes we'll step on once we start digging."

"You can back out any time."

She sighed, this time with annoyance. Pulling up a chair next to him, she dropped into it. "We have to be smart about this. Pick *which* toes to step on. These people won't talk to me. I'd have a better chance of meeting with God. And you certainly can't talk to any of them."

"That's why I started with Brice."

She tapped the marker on the table. A Caroline habit he knew well. "The field agents on the taskforce. They'll talk to me."

"If we can find any of them." Mitch contemplated the board.

"I'd like to see Tommy's autopsy report, the forensics and ballistics reports. All of it."

"Why?"

"No stone unturned and all that. You never know what we might find. I want to know who killed him, and what type of gun they used. No one was arrested, but did the locals or the taskforce have any persons of interest? Anyone they interviewed afterwards? There should have been a complete investigation and they have to have some idea about who killed him."

She drilled him with a look. "How do you propose we get those reports?"

"I have ways."

She faced him. "Can Teeg get them?"

"I'd rather not involve him or Grey with this until we have to. *If* we have to. You want to talk to the agents on the ground in New Mexico. Sounds like a field trip is in order."

She faced him. "You think I'm going to New Mexico with you?"

"You said—"

"I know what I said, but I can't just take off and fly to New Mexico. Not with you."

She was so self-righteous. And kinda cute. "I can't fly either, Caroline. Fugitive that I am. We'd have to drive."

Her eyes widened. "No."

"You could take a vacation day tomorrow and we'd have the whole weekend to get there and back."

"No."

He stared at her, saying nothing. A road trip sounded like fun to him. Especially with her. "I'll let you drive. I know how you like to be in control."

"You really do want me to shoot you, don't you?" She smacked his shoulder hard enough to make him laugh. "You make me crazy."

"I know."

She hit him again.

He raised a hand in mock surrender. "Forget it! I'll head out there myself. You stay here, be a good girl, and go back to your dumpster."

"Oh, screw off."

He started to rise. "I'll take you back now."

She grabbed his arm. "Sit your butt down. You're not going anywhere without me. Especially not New Mexico."

Gotcha. He resumed his seat. "It's okay, Caroline. I can handle the trip on my own. I'm a big boy."

"Oh, I'm well aware of that," she murmured.

"What?"

"Nothing."

Her chest rose and fell as if she'd been running. Was she pissed? Didn't sound like it. "Did you just affirm I'm a big boy?"

She met his gaze, her eyes flashing with emotion. Not anger. Lust. "Of course, the king of sexual innuendo would take it the wrong way."

Was he? Maybe. But Caroline was tricky that way. She may have been rolling her eyes and baiting him, but working cases always turned her on. In one way or another. He understood the rush. The challenge. The danger.

"I know that look," he said, putting his face smack in front of hers.

"The one that says don't come any closer?"

"Yes, but the one you're wearing isn't *that* look."

Hunger. That's what he saw when he looked in her pretty brown eyes. The same hunger lighting up his nerve endings.

"Mitch..."

The way she said his name was different this time, no snark, and it shot heat right to his groin. Goddammit. He shouldn't do this. Shouldn't let *her* do this.

But he remembered that soft, sexy tone from their one night together, and more memories tumbled into place. The dig of her fingers into his skin. The way she moaned into his mouth. "Whatever it takes, I'm going to make it up to you," he said. "It kills me that I hurt you."

Her breath hitched. There were dozens of reasons for her to leave. None for her to stay. "You did. But I knew exactly what I was doing, and I did it anyway. So whose fault is it?"

"It's mine."

She swallowed hard. "You were scared."

"Nah. *You* were scared. I was full of myself."

She scoffed. "You're still full of yourself."

"True."

"If we're going to make this work, you have to be honest with me...and yourself."

He hesitated for a second. "That's what terrifies me."

"You don't like to let people in. You don't want them to see the real you, so you pretend to be confident and snarky and you keep everyone at a distance. Hell, we worked together for three years and I...I slept with you...and I still don't know the real you. I bet even Grey doesn't know the real Mitch Monroe."

She had him there. And shit, didn't that sting. "Tommy and Kemp knew me. The real me. He's not a great guy, but they didn't care."

She put an arm across his shoulders and leaned in. "Who says he's not a great guy? Maybe he's a little screwy and has some baggage, but everyone has baggage. Lucky for you, I've seen the ugly side of Mitch Monroe. You don't have to hide him from me."

Yeah, he did. "Think we can start over? You and me?"

Her gaze didn't waver. "There's a lot at stake with this, professionally and personally, and as stupid as I was the first time, I'm not making that mistake again."

"You don't trust me."

"Not yet, I don't. So let's take it slow."

Slow. Right. He forced his eyes away from her lips. Not an

easy task when they were right there, ready for the taking. "Okay." He controlled his breathing, ignored the way his muscles twitched under the feel of her hand on his back. "First, I need to admit I actually can't go to New Mexico without you. I need you to interview those agents, whoever they are, if we can find any who will talk."

She smiled. Confident. "I know."

"Second...I really want to kiss you."

"Damn you." She grabbed his shirt, fisted it, and *bam*. Her lips crushed his.

The same lust he'd felt at the touch of her hair...all the old memories...flooded back in an instant. Caroline in his arms, her mouth on his, her legs wrapped around his hips.

That taste...the taste of her had haunted him.

She parted her lips and their tongues met. She moaned and the raw sound set his blood on fire. Making Caroline lose control had once been his biggest goal in life. Now...

Whatever it takes. Hadn't he just promised her he wouldn't hurt her again?

He pulled back, hating himself, but knowing it was the right thing to do. "You don't want this."

She blinked, her eyes half-lidded with lust. "Don't want...?"

"Me." He pushed away from the table, paced to the opposite side of the room, his pants too tight from his swollen cock. *Have to stay away from her.* "I'm a fugitive. I'm wanted for murder. You can't afford to get involved with me again, Caroline. We can't take it slow. We can't take this anywhere except friendship."

Her body stiffened. She licked her lips—God, what was wrong with him?—and smoothed her jacket. "You're right. That would be..."

"Stupid," he finished for her. "Unprofessional."

"Ha. Wouldn't be the first time we've been stupid or unprofessional. Maybe this time it'll be different and we'll find a killer." She stood and shoved in her chair. "I'll check in with

Brice tomorrow and see if he has any names for us of agents that might be willing to talk."

"Good idea." They were back on track. Back on the hunt. "I don't want to involve Grey if I don't have to, but it may come to that."

Caroline held out a hand, wiggled her fingers. "Ready?"

His cock jumped. "For what?"

"Aren't you going to blindfold me again?"

"Oh, right." He shucked his shirt, saw the way her gaze skimmed his chest. God, just don't let her lick...

Too late. Her tongue shot out and licked her lips. "You realize," she said, "with our history of joint stupidity, we're going to wind up screwing each other blind at some point."

He could only hope. He eased behind her and drew his shirt across her eyes. "Let's go to New Mexico, Caroline."

7

*C*aroline followed Mitch down the steps of the private plane her father had *loaned* them, tipped her head up to the bright blue sky and breathed in the warmth of a 92 degree October day in New Mexico. According to the weatherman, that temperature was still climbing due to a freak warm front plowing through the Southwest. She slid her blazer off, but left the sleeves of her blouse in place. She wouldn't have minded rolling them up, but no; keeping some sense of her professional armor would keep her focused on the case and not on...

What the hell am I doing in Roswell with Mitch Monroe?

Well, if she disappeared, everyone would say she'd been abducted by aliens. With these two, that might not have been far off. Brice, sensing a major corruption story about to break, had decided he wasn't happy sitting in the shadows of his blog. Not only had he come up with a source for them, he came on the trip, saying the guy wouldn't talk to them without Brice being there.

"Leave it to me," Mitch said, "to hook up with a girl who has connections."

Connections. Right. Considering her father ran a company that provided the U.S. government with technical advice on space missions, yes, they were darned lucky. Darned lucky the company owned a private jet, darned lucky her father trusted her enough not to ask questions, and darned lucky she knew how to lie. Because make no mistake, she'd given her father a line of baloney when she told him a friend from New Mexico needed to see a specialist in D.C. but due to her medical condition, couldn't fly above 32,000 feet. Only a private jet could guarantee that and Caroline wanted to help this friend.

Now she was lying to her parents like a fourteen-year-old wanting to sneak off with her boyfriend. And Mitch was the boyfriend.

Someone must have whacked me on the head.

Behind her, Brice whistled. "I tell ya, that was a helluva flight. First time flying private and it didn't disappoint."

Mitch reached the bottom of the stairs. "Yeah, Brice, too bad you were with us."

Oh, no. Pig that he was, she was sure there was some comment coming about joining the Mile-High Club. "Don't even go there, Mitch."

He unleashed one of his famous or maybe not-so-famous-but-famous-to-her grins and she rolled her eyes.

Throwing his arm over her shoulder, he gave her a squeeze. "Where to, boss?"

"Rental car. That's the only thing I couldn't manage, so I'll have to rent. No big deal. Donaldson probably thinks I called in sick so I could punish him for putting me on dumpster duty."

"Yeah, he thinks that highly of himself. Where's the car rental?"

"About two miles from here." She smiled. "At least one of us thinks ahead. The rental place said they'll send a shuttle. We just have to call."

He pointed to the small office plopped smack in the middle of four airplane hangars. "We going through there?"

"Not if I can help it. The fewer people who see us, the better."

"There's a gate," Brice said. "Next to the hangar."

Caroline pulled out her cell phone—her personal one—from her bag.

Mitch raised a brow. "Is that your Bureau phone?"

"No. This is one of my Dad's company phones I carry. Only my family has the number. When it rings, I know to answer it. I took the battery out of my Bureau phone again. That alone might get me fired, but I wasn't risking them being able to track my location. Even if Donaldson thinks I'm licking my wounds, he's a bastard and I wouldn't put it past him to try and catch me taking a mini-vacation when I'm supposed to be sick."

She called the rental car company—her father had an agreement in place with all the big rental companies for his employees, so she wouldn't have to use a credit card—and was directed to wait at the entrance to the airport office. Wait they would, but they'd stand at the end of the building, away from the office windows. Maybe she was paranoid, but an FBI agent traveling with a federal fugitive and a disgraced malcontent made for a great headline.

Where's my gun?

Caroline laughed at herself. Suicide might be the only way to get her stupid self to give up on Mitch. She glanced over at him, casually leaning against the light pole, his long, dark hair once again slicked back into a ponytail. His lean body clad in worn jeans and a short-sleeved graphic T-shirt that read, *I am not a minion of evil. I'm upper management.*

Stupid-self let out a little sigh. Something about this man drew her in. Every time. His looks alone could devastate a woman. Throw in the caustic humor and the balls-to-the-wall attitude and Caroline had been sunk from the first second she'd spotted Mitch Monroe.

Where. Is. My. Gun?

Sensing her attention, he lifted his face and met her gaze, smiling at her with that *caught-ya* smirk. Well, so what? They both knew the chemistry between them. They knew before the night they'd dropped into her bed and caused the angels to sing and they certainly knew it now.

Leaving Brice to his phone and answering posts on his all-important blog, she wandered over to Mitch. "Hey, sailor."

"Hey, Caroline. You were thinking naughty thoughts about me."

"In fact, I was. Only they involved my gun."

He threw his hand over his heart, but his quirking lips gave away a laugh. "Evil woman."

"I can't help myself."

"I know. That's what I love about you."

Love. There was a word she'd never uttered out loud about Mitch. Maybe she'd thought it a time or two—or twelve—because stupid-self liked to daydream about happily ever after. Well, stupid-self better wise-up. Happily ever after didn't include visiting Mitch in a federal prison.

"What you love about me," she said, "is I won't turn my back on you. I love that about me too. Most of the time. My loyalty has burned me in the past, though."

"Not this time. I've got your back." He reached up, ran his finger down the side of her cheek and as much as she knew it was coming, that instant *zzzppp*, the little buzz that happened whenever Mitch touched her, made her flinch. Like always, she craved getting closer to him so she leaned in and did just that, because—well—why not? Brice was obsessed with his phone and no one here knew them so she could pretend for just a few seconds that happily ever after really did exist.

She tilted her head, studied the strong angles of his face,

the dark eyes and softness around his lips. "You had my back last time, too. It still blew up."

Two years ago, when Mitch and Grey had first started hunting a serial killer, they'd zeroed in on a foreign diplomat, but couldn't get Donaldson to sign-off on pursuing their suspect. Mitch had come up with the genius plan of having another supervisor—namely Caroline who'd just been promoted and was a baby in the relief supervisor arena—enter a report outlining all the evidence into the FBI's system. Without entering it, the report wouldn't have been part of the case file and might as well have never been written.

But Mitch, having that giant conscience when it came to people he cared about, had gotten cold feet when the hellstorm came down on them and told Donaldson he'd stolen Caroline's password and entered the report himself.

None of it mattered. Donaldson, being Donaldson, did his magic and the report disappeared.

"Mitch, I don't blame you for involving me in The Lion's case. I'm a big girl and make my own decisions. These things you do are for the right reasons. I know that about you. But this time we could both lose everything."

"But if I'm right, you'll be a hero."

"And what about you?"

He shrugged. "I never cared about glory or power."

"You're a liar. There's something you want, and I'm not talking about this case. I'm talking about Mitch Monroe the man. Down deep, what do you want from life?"

Tilting his head back, he blew air through his lips. "I want peace. No more running. That's all."

"So when this is over and we clear your name and Tommy's, you'll be happy?"

"Not entirely."

Classic Mitch. Caroline huffed. "Well, big boy, if I'm putting my career on the line, I'd like to know what the hell we're fighting for here."

He turned to her, stared right into her eyes, not wavering for even a half-second. "I want you, Caroline. Then I'll be happy."

The look on Caroline's face said it all. Shock. Total and absolute. Her jaw dropped and she tried to form words, but nothing came out. In her eyes, Mitch saw a hint of fear. He'd scared the big, tough FBI sniper.

Way to go, idiot. "Don't worry. I know I'm too fucked up for you, but I wanted you to know. I'm not in it for a single night this round."

Her mouth slammed shut and she looked away. Glanced at Brice to make sure he was still absorbed with his phone. Then she simply stood, staring out at the runway, uncomfortable silence descending as the oppressive heat added to Mitch's discomfort. Damn, he was sweating in places he didn't know existed.

At least he'd said it. He'd never lied to her, but he'd dammed up his feelings for so long, danced around his attraction to her knowing she'd shut him down, he'd hoped his admission would bring him some relief. Her hair, her smile, the way she moved...it all screwed with his internal system. He wanted her and he wanted her bad. He knew she wanted him. But of course, he was a fugitive, not just from the FBI, but on the run for murder now as well.

Caroline didn't like messes, and he was one big fucking mess.

He slipped his sunglasses on. The shuttle arrived, saving him from any more embarrassing admissions and hopefully the heat. At least she hadn't slapped him. Or spit on him. He'd imagined both scenarios when he finally put that he wanted her into words.

At least, he'd finally said it. One thing he'd learned in the past year, you never knew when you'd meet the bullet with your name on it.

The three of them boarded the shuttle, riding in silence to the car rental building. Caroline went inside to rent the car, Brice and Mitch hung out by the fleet in the parking lot.

"Got a thing for her, huh?" Brice said, squinting in the late afternoon sun.

Mitch ignored him. "Think I'll have time to work on my tan while we're here?"

"If we don't end up like Tommy."

Any other day, he'd have knocked Brice cold for that flip comment. Today, the guy spoke the truth and Mitch respected him for that.

Mitch idly scanned the cars. He liked the flashy red Mitsubishi. Or the Cadillac SUV.

The silver Prius. That's the one Caroline will pick.

A minute later, she came out of the rental company and dangled keys in his face. "I'll drive."

Of course she would. And what do you know? She made a beeline for the silver Prius two rows back.

"Fuel efficient and extremely roomy," Caroline said.

"Extremely cramped," Mitch said, trying to fit his frame into the front seat.

Brice hopped into the back. "My contact said he'll meet us at the Le Feria farmer's market in thirty. He's pretty nervous, but he's bringing us information he says might help."

The car's GPS—certainly not her phone app with that squeaky voice—gave Caroline directions, and they wound their way through the city. Traffic was heavy this time of day with people heading home from work. They parked half a block from the farmer's market and walked the rest of the way.

All around them were rows of white tented booths displaying everything from sunglasses to baked goods to jewelry and wood carvings. If the heat was a factor in the attendance, it didn't show. People wandered the rows, bumping each other as they passed, and Mitch couldn't decide if being in the crush hid him safely in the throng or left him trapped. If he had to run, he'd be taking people out on his way.

"Big place," Mitch commented, eyeing a booth with green plastic aliens wearing miniature Roswell T-shirts. "Where exactly is your contact meeting us?"

"Don't worry." Brice acted interested in a booth with homemade salsa in every flavor imaginable. "He'll find us."

Caroline scanned the crowds of people milling by. "He knew Tommy, right?"

"Yeah."

They continued to meander and stop here and there. Halfway through the booths lining both sides of the road, a man in a Red Sox baseball cap and sunglasses nodded at Brice.

"Here we go," he said, taking them behind one of the larger booths and following the guy to a nearby picnic bench.

Brice and the man shook hands and exchanged a few comments. Brice introduced Mitch and Caroline. "This is Ethan Grimke. ATF."

Mitch shook Ethan's hand. "Thanks for meeting us."

Ethan nodded and tipped his cap a little lower, further shielding his face. "I shouldn't be here, but Tommy was a crack agent. If there was something I needed, he was there for me. It's my turn to do something for him."

Caroline, who'd stayed standing, smiled at Ethan. If anyone was watching, they'd think Ethan had just said something humorous. "Who do you think killed Tommy?"

Ethan shook his head. "I don't know. None of us do. I've been waiting for the ballistics report, the forensics report, anything. Nothing has showed, and there's no one left at this ATF office who even knows the name of the operation Tommy was involved in. It's like the whole operation disappeared...or never existed. I mentioned it to my boss and he said to keep my nose out of it, but a little bird in the system told me the case has been sealed."

Mitch's skin prickled. "Sealed? Why?"

Ethan shrugged. "You tell me. Everyone is on eggshells. Taskforce members working with Tommy have been fired or sent off to other offices in other states. The bigwigs are tight lipped, and the case is sealed."

"Shit," Brice said.

Shit was right. Mitch wondered if they'd come all this way for nothing, but the sealed case file only confirmed what Kemp had told him. There had to be a reason the White House would invoke Executive Privilege. "Tell me what you can about that night. The night Tommy was killed."

Ethan swallowed hard, fished his cell phone from his pocket. "I was the first one on the scene. I suspected something was going down with him because he called me that day. He sounded off. That night I gave him a call, just to check in. We made plans to meet for a few minutes. He said he had to make a couple of stops and would meet me at a bar on the corner of the street where he was killed. I parked in the bar's lot and cleared some emails while I waited for him. Then I heard shots and jumped out to see what the hell was happening. I found him on the edge of the lot near the sidewalk with a gun lying on his chest. An AR-15. Right on his chest, like a message from the killer. He was dead, but I tried to resuscitate him. Didn't work. Some woman tried to help and I told her he was gone already. I called it in, but while I was waiting for backup to arrive, I snapped photos of the scene and the gun."

He shook his head, his voice trailing off. "It still haunts me. I don't know what went wrong. Did someone find out Tommy was FBI or did they just get pissed at him for something and shoot him point blank? He never even drew his weapon."

The former agent in Mitch wanted to see the pictures. The

man in him didn't think he could handle photos of his dead friend. "What do *you* think?"

Ethan shrugged. "With the case sealed and no information coming out about it…" He let the words hang. "When Brice called me, I thought you might want to at least see the photos. I wasn't on the taskforce so I'm out of the loop on whatever they were doing, but there's chatter about Balboa, the gun runner we've been watching, being involved. He's got a huge cartel that goes back and forth across the border. Hell, it could have been one of his rivals. When I asked my ASAC about it, he made sure I got the message it wasn't my concern. Right now, I'm waiting like everyone else. Maybe if you see the photos, you might pick up on something I missed, or be able to rebuild the crime scene."

Without the reports, they were at a dead end. They needed to know what the ballistics report revealed about the bullets and type of gun used to kill Tommy. With that, they could trace the serial number on the gun, if it still had one, and find out who owned it.

Ethan tapped the touchscreen on his phone, his gaze skating over the people nearby.

Brice, too, was on high alert. He watched the crowd as he spoke to Ethan. "Anyone know you have those pictures besides us?"

"No one," Ethan said. Seemingly satisfied that no one was watching, he brought up the first photo.

Mitch's stomach turned to acid. There was the scene: Tommy, a bloody mess. A black assault rifle next to his body.

Ethan pointed at it. "That's the one he had lying on his chest. I had to move it to perform CPR."

Pressure filled Mitch's throat. His voice was trapped in a deep well. The danger came with the job, regardless of the letters that followed your name. ATF, FBI, DEA.

"Mitch?" Caroline had moved close and was leaning over

his shoulder to eye the photo. Her voice was soft next to his ear. "You okay?"

"Yeah," he bit out the word, his voice hollow. He took the phone from Ethan and entered his cell's number and Caroline's email address into Ethan's contacts. "Send us all the pictures, okay?"

Ethan nodded as Mitch handed the phone back. "I hope you can find out what's going on. Tommy was a damn good agent."

The pressure was back in Mitch's throat. Tommy and Kemp were the closest things he'd ever had to brothers. Now, they were both dead.

Good thing he still had Grey. One friend left in the world. *Helluva life.*

Mitch shook Ethan's hand. "Watch your back."

Ethan stood, gripped his hand hard, and cuffed him on the shoulder. "You, too."

Caroline rushed through the hotel room door with Mitch and Brice on her heels. The door smacked against the wall and she glanced at it not really caring, but the sound distracted her from her raging thoughts. *Forget the door.* She needed to get her laptop fired up and look at the photos Ethan had emailed.

"Caroline—"

"Shut up, Mitch."

The crappy faux wood desk was shoved into the corner of the room next to the windows and she hustled to it while fumbling with her briefcase. She hit the button to boot up the laptop and plugged it in while it whirred. No sense in wasting her battery.

Mitch's big feet landed next to her, his body close—too close—and she caught a whiff of his soap. That clean, salty air smell.

"Caroline, slow down."

"What's up?" Brice asked.

Mitch turned back to him. "Give us a sec."

"No. He's fine," she said. Being alone in a hotel room with Mitch would be a mistake. Whatever his problem was with her looking at these photos, he'd turn into the master she knew him to be and talk her into something. How pathetic was she? She knew—*knew*—how persuasive he could be and fell for it every time. And she didn't even know what it was he was about to talk her into.

Her difficulty with this situation came with standing in front of him, this man who had brought her equal amounts of pleasure and pain, and knowing her intelligence—her common sense specifically—was seeping from her body. No. Not seeping.

Gushing.

"Caroline, I need to *talk* to you."

She looked up at him, met his gaze, so focused and unyielding, and the gushing continued.

Caroline glanced at Brice. "Go get settled in your room. I'll call you when I've got the pictures."

Mitch followed Brice to the door and flipped the safety latch.

The laptop dinged and she typed in her password, her fingers flying over the keys. Mitch grabbed her elbow and tugged. "Stop. Please. What do you think you're going to do with these photos?"

"Well, gee, Mitch. I'm not quite sure."

"You going to call someone at Quantico and offer to send them over?"

"You're kidding, right?"

"No. I'm not. We need a plan for these photos. You're moving too fast."

She breathed in, closed her eyes for a second. *He's right.* Of course he was. This was Mitch, and as crazy as he made her, as risk-oriented as he was, he typically had amazing instincts.

"I think the plan is, we study the photos and see what's in there. I'd like to get a look at that rifle. We're assuming it's the murder weapon, but how do we know? It could have been a plant."

"We need the ballistics report," he said.

"Please! First of all, the case is sealed. Second, this happened three weeks ago and it involved a federal agent. Even if they unseal it, which who knows why they would, they're not going to release reports until they have this thing all nice and tidy. It could take months. Right now, we need to figure out if the gun in this photo was the murder weapon and where it came from."

Mitch narrowed his eyes. "Serial number. If Ethan got close enough, we can get the serial number."

Now he was thinking. "We still need the ballistics report. They could be back already, but without me making a few calls, I don't know how we get that."

"I can call Grey. He'll put Teeg on it."

"You want your friends to hack into the FBI? You said you didn't want to involve them unless necessary."

Mitch shrugged. *Shrugged.* God help them. The man acted like infiltrating a government database ranked right up there with deciding whether dinner should be chicken or beef. "I know what I said, but after seeing those pictures..." He shook his head. "Besides, Teeg's hacked the Bureau database before. Remember a couple years or so ago when the black hats took down the FBI and DOD websites?"

"That was *Teeg*?"

"He was one of them."

She burst out laughing. "Mitch Monroe, you will be my ultimate downfall. I know it. I stand here looking at you and I immediately turn dense."

He smiled at her, all Mitch, conqueror of evil, and heat spread low in her belly. Mitch inched closer. She should move back, out of his gravitational pull, but there were a lot of things regarding Mitch Monroe she should do. Instead, she hooked her fingers into the waistband of his jeans and those focused eyes—well, they shot wide. Who was in control now?

She tugged him forward and kissed him. Whammo. He drew her closer, gripping her hips hard and...and—*yes, yes, yes* —this was what she wanted. Lips and tongues and fire that somehow only happened with Mitch.

Every date she'd been on since the-night-that-never-happened had been a sorry letdown. Each time she went into it hopeful that she'd find the one person who could eject Mitch out of her mind and heart and, in a lot of ways, her body, because her body craved him like an addict. But with each date and each man, she quickly gave up trying. Whether the world should be thankful or not, there was only one Mitch Monroe.

The chime of her email sounded and Caroline gripped Mitch's waistband, bunching the fabric in her grasp, pulling it tight and holding him in place because the damned emails could wait a second. Even if she'd been in a hurry before, her mind had suddenly derailed.

"Ow," Mitch cracked, but kept kissing her. "Don't damage me. I may need what's down there later."

Oh, and the thought of that. Between the two of them they were about fifteen feet tall, all long legs and lean, athletic bodies that could go all night.

Intelligence gush complete.

"I hate you."

He backed away, shoved his hands into her hair and hit her with a wicked, vagina melting grin. "My dick doesn't care. Not sure the rest of me does either."

The evidence of that was obvious from the bulge against her tummy. Caroline jumped back, her breaths coming fast and hard and—yowzer—it was like being let out of sexual prison. Freed from a lifetime of boring men who couldn't figure out how to crack the Caroline-needs-an-orgasm code.

"Stop!" she yelled. "It's too much." She paddled her hands. "It's like...like...I don't know. But it's too much. You've been gone too long and this isn't what we should be doing now. Right? I mean, we're professionals. You're a *fugitive*. You could go to prison and then what? Conjugal visits once a month?"

Mitch's lips quirked. "Only if you marry me. I don't put out for free."

"Marry you? I want to dismember you!"

Dammit. She sounded insane right now, but this is what happened with him. His fault. *He* made her this way. Every time. "Laugh at me, and I will get my gun and shoot you. Then we'll see who needs conjugal visits."

Finally, he laughed and yep—*where's my gun?*—hearing that sound, that deep belly laugh she'd missed so damned much, made her laugh too. Hopeless. That's what she was. Stupid *and* hopeless.

But maybe, for a little while, stupid and hopeless was tolerable.

8

etach. Disassociate. Disengage. Mitch hovered over Caroline's shoulder as she sat at the desk and opened each photo one by one.

You've viewed hundreds of crime scenes. This one's no different.

Except it was.

But he needed to do this for Tommy. For Kemp. For himself. He had to think and act like a Bureau agent again. Cut out the damn emotions and stick to the facts staring him in the face.

Caroline didn't speak, but occasionally snuck a glance at him as she scrolled through the pictures. The photos devoid of Tommy's body were easiest to take. Those were area shots. The bystanders, the location, the street sign. Buena Street. No one should die on a street named Buena.

After they'd looked through all the photos, Caroline went back to the one with Tommy and the gun. "Let me enlarge this one."

She did, blowing up the pixels until they could make out the serial number on the AR-15's magazine well. At least a partial number. At this magnification, the numbers were fuzzy and the last one was half hidden by one of Tommy's fingers.

"Can you clean it up any?" Mitch asked.

"I don't have a program on this computer for that kind of thing."

"We need Teeg. He can find out if the ballistics report is in and he can clean up this photo so we can trace that number."

Caroline harrumphed. "This is a bad idea."

"Cold feet?"

"Smart feet. How far are we willing to take this investigation?"

"That's a question *you* have to answer. I have nothing to lose."

She stewed. Knowing Caroline and her Type-A personality, she was making a list of positive and negative outcomes and ticking off her mental boxes. "Call Grey."

"You sure?"

"I've come this far. I have to know why this case is being buried. Why Ethan was told to stay out of it and why, quite possibly, someone framed you for murder."

Mitch didn't need further encouragement. He withdrew his phone and emailed Grey with the basic details of what he needed Teeg to do. If Grey or Teeg had qualms and didn't want to join this circus, he'd respect that and try a different route, but he doubted they'd even blink.

He sat back and scanned the photos. "If it was one of Balboa's minions, why leave the gun on Tommy's body and the rest in the trunk?"

"Maybe, like Ethan theorized, someone tipped him off that Tommy was a UC agent. He might have thought the guns were tagged."

True. "So he kills Tommy and leaves the gun he used as a statement."

Caroline waggled her head. A habit he'd learned long ago meant she didn't like whatever it was running through her brain.

"What?"

"Maybe Tommy had the gun himself. It could have been one from the stash in his trunk."

"If he did, there was a reason. He was *not* selling them. I know it."

Caroline wrapped her hand around his wrist and squeezed. "I'm spit-balling here. That's all. I feel like we're all over the place."

She hit the computer keyboard a couple of times and opened a new document. "We need to record everything we know. All leads. Then we'll go from there."

Forty minutes later, they had hashed over everything they knew, a couple of possible killers—disgruntled criminals Tommy had busted while in New Mexico, gunrunners, gang-bangers—and Caroline had worn the carpet bare in spots from pacing. She needed her murder board, but even if they'd had one here, no way Mitch would have let her set it up. Better not to freak out the housekeepers. And if they needed to head out of town quickly, no need to leave anything like that behind.

His phone beeped with an incoming email. "BatHat" was the sender's ID. Had to be Teeg. The kid was a Batman fanatic as well as a criminally good hacker.

There was no message, just an email attachment. Mitch forwarded it to Caroline's email. It showed up a few seconds later on her laptop.

The marvels of modern technology. He clicked the attachment button and a screenshot of a ballistics report popped open. As expected, neither Grey nor Teeg had an aversion to hacking into the Bureau's system. "Teeg found the ballistics report."

FBI Laboratory, it read across the top. There were multiple pages. The case number, the lab's identification number, the department number, and the date were clearly spelled out.

The first page was a summary of items examined. The rest

of the pages detailed the results of the examination. Fingerprints were taken from Tommy's car, the gun found on his body, and the ones in the trunk. The only positive conclusion was that Tommy had handled the weapons. No other fingerprints, not even partials, were found on any of the weapons.

Damn. Not what Mitch wanted to hear after Caroline spitballed her theory about Tommy possibly selling the guns.

Next on the report was a list of the bullets that had been removed from Tommy's body. Each had been given a simple letter-number designation. All the times Mitch had read ballistics reports, it had never seemed quite so...sterile.

Turning a discharged bullet that had killed someone into nothing but a simple ID reinforced why he needed to remember his Bureau training. *Stay detached.* He'd always struggled with detachment, unlike Grey who could shut down his emotions with ease.

But then Mitch had never before had to solve a crime involving someone he cared about.

Focus. Mitch scanned each entry until he hit the one he was looking for.

Caroline saw it at the same time. "Look."

Exhibits 1.1, 1.2, and 1.3 were found upon microscopic comparison to have been discharged from the barrel of Exhibit 1.

Bingo. His eyes combed the list of weapons again. Exhibit 1...the AR-15. Mitch clicked on the photo screen showing the magazine well of the gun with the serial number and put the two screens side by side. Caroline read off the serial number on the photo as he followed along on the report.

A total match, except for the last digit on the photo they couldn't read.

Caroline did a fist pump. "Ethan was right."

It wasn't much, but it was all they had. And the way his heart was triple-timing it told him they'd only scratched the surface. Or possibly it was the way Caroline stood over him, her breasts pressing into his shoulders, giving him A-fib.

"Now we can run that serial number for chain of custody," she said.

Caroline stared at the ballistics report, not really seeing it, but nonetheless trying to absorb it. They had a sealed report they'd just broken any number of federal laws to acquire and it only told part of the story. The information she needed—the critical information of who purchased the gun and where—could be found by using her login for the FBI database. A few simple finger strokes and they'd have what they needed.

Simple.

Sure.

Simple if she wanted to flush her career. Maybe get arrested to boot.

Mitch pushed away from the desk. "Forget it, Caroline. You can't."

Actually, she could. Whether or not she should was the question. And when it came to Mitch, that question could apply in so many ways.

"ATF is overwhelmed with gun tracing requests and has been beta testing what will soon be a shared firearms tracking system," she told him. "It'll give law enforcement agencies limited access to information so they can quickly identify if a weapon has been used in other crimes. All local law enforcement will eventually have the new system, but right now, it's just the agencies under Justice. We're the guinea pigs and only supervisors have admin rights. I have access to it so if I have a case involving a firearm, I run the gun through the system and report any bugs."

"No, Caroline. Logging into that system is the equivalent of standing on good old Donaldson's desk screaming 'Look at me! Look at me!'"

Having already experienced Donaldson's wrath—dumpster diving anyone?—if she ran the gun when she was supposed to be out on a sick day, she'd definitely ping Donaldson's radar.

Mitch gripped her upper arm. "We'll figure out another way. I can send the make, model, and serial to Teeg. Maybe he can track it without tipping our hand."

"Maybe. But we'd lose time. He got this report fast, but who knows how long it would take him to crack into the ATF tracing system."

He shook that off. "ATF and the FBI have the serial number of the gun that killed an FBI agent. They've already run the number and traced it to its owner, but there haven't been any arrests. Instead, the taskforce has been disbanded and the case sealed. What does that tell you?"

It told her she only had one sick day and time was short. It told her that whatever the FBI and ATF were up to, it wasn't good. It *told* her that a good agent—an honorable and very dead agent—was about to be the government's sacrificial lamb. If the roles were reversed and she was the agent about to be posthumously crucified, she'd want someone to step in and make it right. She jerked free of Mitch's hold. "Get up."

The stubborn mule didn't move. Fine. She leaned over him, unplugged the laptop and picked it up. She'd sit on the bed and do this.

"Caroline, you're harboring a fugitive whom you transported across no less than seven state lines. If Donaldson gets wind that you're logging in remotely, he'll trace the IP address, figure out you're in New Mexico and your career is toast. He'll not only end your career, that dickhead will send you to prison."

She locked eyes with him and grinned. "Only if he catches me."

He finally moved, leaving the chair and crossing his arms as he stood at the end of the bed. "Don't throw your life away for me."

Oh, she had him this time. "That's the thing, Mitch. It's *not* for you. It's for Tommy. The thing you've wanted all along. Now shut up and let me do this." She returned to the desk. "No offense, but you distract me, and if I'm about to jeopardize my career, I don't want distractions."

"You don't have to do this."

"Yeah, I do."

She double clicked the icon and the system's welcome screen popped up. *This is it.*

"Caroline—"

"Zip it."

She'd made her decision and he, of all people, should know when she made decisions, that was it, no going back. No matter if she spent a minute or a year deciding, when she reached a conclusion, she went to the wall with it.

She typed in her username and password and sat back in the crummy chair in the crummy motel and one last time considered the crummy situation.

Tommy doesn't deserve this.

Boom. She smacked the enter key.

"Ah, Christ, Caroline. You're in it now."

"Mitch, I was in it the second you stepped onto that range."

While the hourglass chugged, she tiled the screens alongside each other and prayed no one would flag her.

Quickly, with tingling fingers, she entered the serial number and double checked it. Missed a digit. Dammit. She fixed it, hit enter and jumped from her chair—*oh, God, oh, God, oh, God*—waiting the few seconds for the result to pop up. She rubbed her hands over her head and down her ponytail. What had she done?

Mitch extended one arm, reaching for her. No way. Not now.

Not when she had to concentrate. His hands on her muddled her normally surgical thinking.

She smacked him away and a second later another screen popped up. She and Mitch leaned in.

"Notes," he said, grabbing the notepad on the desk while Caroline skimmed the contents of the screen.

She rattled off the manufacturer, the model number, and serial number. And how fascinating that the gun shop where the gun was purchased and the purchaser information had been left blank.

Bastards.

Beside her, Mitch scribbled. On his best day, his handwriting was atrocious. What he had in front of him, he'd better be able to interpret.

She clicked on the download arrow. "I'm downloading it. Don't have a coronary."

"What's that code number?" he asked, pointing to a five digit alpha numeric code next to the where the purchaser's name should have been.

Government agencies were chock-full of codes and acronyms, but she'd never seen anything like this on a trace report. "I have no idea."

"I've got it. Shut it down."

Mitch dropped his pen and jumped back like the chef in one of those television cooking shows that had reached his time limit.

Now, now, now. Dragging the arrow to the logout button, she clicked. There. *Done.*

Career in flames.

Worrying about it wouldn't help her. She spun away from the desk, found Mitch tapping the screen on his phone. "What now?"

"We call Brice. If you don't know what that code is maybe he will. It could be an ATF thing."

Within three minutes, Mitch opened the motel room door for Brice.

"What's up?"

Caroline shoved Mitch's notes at him. "We were able to get a copy of the ballistics report."

"Get the fuck outta here."

Mitch smacked him on the back as he strode past him. "Welcome to the dark side."

"How?"

"I don't kiss and tell," Mitch said.

Caroline sighed. "Meaning, in this instance, you don't want to know. All you need to know is the gun Ethan found on Tommy's body is indeed the weapon used to kill him, and even though it probably just ended my career, I ran a trace on that serial number."

"Lady, you've got some solid steel balls."

Working around loads of testosterone-filled men each day gave her a warped sense of achievement because a man telling her she had steel balls, in her world, was the absolute king of compliments. She waved the paper again. "The trace came back with a GBL code. I don't recognize it."

He skimmed the paper, flicked his eyes back to her, then to the note again. "This was in the trace report?"

"Yes."

Mitch leaned against the windowsill, crossing his arms. "You recognize it?"

"Yeah," he said. "I do."

Caroline paddled her hands. "And?"

"When I was in ATF, we used the GBL codes on a couple of taskforces to track guns bought by identified straw buyers. That code lets an agent know to go to a separate database for more information on the gun, the straw buyer who purchased it, if known, and where the weapon turns up—say if it's used in crime."

Guns being legally purchased by people—straw buyers—was nothing new. People with criminal records had to acquire their guns somehow and since they couldn't purchase said guns themselves, they paid others to do it for them. The guns would be purchased by the straw buyer and then simply turned over to the third party. If the gun were traced back to a crime, the straw buyer would say the gun had been stolen.

Gun shop owners routinely reported suspected straw buyers to ATF, but it was a matter of catching the buyer off-loading the weapons.

"Jesus, with all the databases," Mitch said. "How the hell do we get into those files?"

Caroline cocked her head. *Hold the phone.* "Wait. This gun has an ATF tag? As in the taskforce agents knew it was purchased by a straw buyer but it was still on the streets?"

"If that code was in the report, yes."

If the ATF, and the taskforce Tommy had been working for, had flagged a guy as a straw buyer but hadn't picked him up or confiscated the weapon...

"Oh, shit," Mitch said.

9

$\mathcal{T}$he rattling air conditioner kicked off, leaving the room in silence.

Mitch uncrossed his arms and grabbed onto the windowsill to steady himself. *Couldn't be.*

His breath jammed in his chest. He forced air into his lungs, his brain running at warp speed. "Tommy was killed by a gun the ATF let walk. A gun that should have been confiscated by Tommy's taskforce before it could be used illegally. How the fuck did that happen?"

"Hold on," Caroline said. "Tommy was found with a bunch of weapons. Maybe he *had* confiscated them and was going to arrest the straw buyer."

"Or," Brice added, "he was using his undercover status to work with the straw buyer to follow the guns to the big fish, the gun runner Ethan told us about. Balboa. There was another taskforce a few years ago that tried a similar thing. Unfortunately, it didn't work."

Caroline frowned. "Or..." She hesitated and glanced at Mitch. "Tommy really was dirty and using the straw buyer to cover his tracks while he sold the guns to Balboa or one of his rivals."

Silence fell again. Mitch drilled her with a look that conveyed all the pent up anger raging in his body. How many times did he have to insist Tommy wasn't a dirty agent? "That's what they want it to look like, Caroline. It's the perfect setup."

She took his hand and squeezed it. "Agreed." Releasing him, she moved to sit in front of the laptop. "We need a list of higher-ups who would have seen this report and want it kept under wraps."

Of course she wanted to make a list. "What good will that do?"

"We're taking this information to the New Mexico Attorney General. At least we'll start with him. He needs to investigate this operation, and maybe the Justice Department does too."

"Whoa, whoa, whoa." Brice started backing up. "If someone's covering this up, there's got to be a legitimate reason."

"Legitimate?" Mitch hollered. "You of all people, Brice, recognize a conspiracy when you see it. Tommy was killed with a gun ATF knew was purchased by a straw buyer and they let that gun walk. Wake up and smell the conspiracy! They don't want an official investigation that would make all parties involved look like idiots."

"Don't forget the press and bloggers like our Brice here," Caroline said. "They'd have a field day with this." Her fingers typed furiously. "Okay, since this was a joint taskforce between ATF and the FBI, the New Mexico ATF director and the head of the New Mexico Bureau office had to okay letting guns walk. They had to know. Who else?"

Brice shook his head, but gave up arguing. "DEA. They might be involved because of the drug cartels and the guns they ship across the border. Balboa probably moves drugs as well as weapons. And the top prosecutors in the border states had to sign off."

"There's no way that many entities knew about this operation and no one raised a red flag about letting guns walk," Mitch said, finally understanding Caroline's need for the list. "But this might prove someone set up Tommy, and if they did, all these state level people are shitting bricks. There's a cover-up here, and it starts with them. Kemp Rodgers told me the prez will invoke Executive Privilege if the White House is subpoenaed. This cover-up goes all the way to the top."

Mitch glanced out the window, checking the parking lot. He felt antsy, unnerved. Too many months on the run and now this. Who exactly was involved with Tommy's death? Who had pulled the trigger, and why were they making it look like Tommy was a traitor? Was it the same person responsible for Kemp's murder? "Why kill Kemp? He didn't know any more than I did."

Caroline stopped typing. "Maybe he did, or someone believed he did. Either way, they know you were with him that night at the park. You could be next on their hit list."

Mitch moved away from the window and went to Caroline. Her ponytail brushed his arm and all that dormant heat and the trouble he'd already brought to her made him crazy. He should put her on a plane home. Get her as far away from this as possible. Too late now. *Gotta do it.* "There's one way to smoke out the bad guys."

Caroline shifted sideways and eyed him. "How?"

"Brice leaks the ballistics report and the trace information on his blog."

Gasping, Caroline gawked at him. "Are you *crazy*?"

Brice was already across the room, grabbing his messenger bag and laptop off the floor. "Send me those files."

Caroline sprang up. "Wait. Not so fast. Let's think about this a minute—"

"What's to think about?" He started typing, his fingers flying over the keys as if he couldn't get the information out to the free world fast enough. "We've got government corruption and a dead agent."

A loud ring came from Caroline's briefcase. She shrugged out of Mitch's grip and dug around in it, bringing out her cell phone.

"Who is it?"

"Donaldson."

"Shit." He'd told her this would happen. "Cocksucker is fast."

"Only my family has this number. Oh, my God. My career is over." She stared at the phone as if she might actually answer it. Mitch grabbed it from her hand, and dropping it on the floor, he stomped on the phone, killing the thing in mid-ring.

"Hey!"

Mitch started gathering their things. "He's probably already traced that phone. We need to move, Brice. Now."

"A couple more seconds," Brice said, still typing furiously.

"What have we gotten into?" Caroline said.

Mitch fought the urge to grab her and run. "Whatever it is, it's big. And we're about to blow the lid off it."

Caroline shoved her laptop into the hatch of the Prius. Next to her, Mitch and Brice scrambled to stow their gear, all of them moving fast in the oppressive heat. Each intake of air so harsh, it burned all the way down her throat.

They needed to get away from this motel. Donaldson obviously knew she'd downloaded the report and most likely had traced the IP address. For all she knew, federal agents would soon be swarming the place.

Mitch closed the hatch and the three of them piled in, buckling up as Caroline started the car and got them moving. *What am I doing, what am I doing, what am I doing?*

In contrast to the unseasonal heat wave, goose bumps rose

on her skin. Icy, slick panic hurdled up the back of her neck, pounding at her, making her realize that, yes, once again, her attachment to Mitch, the stupid lust mixed with all the emotional what-if scenarios, had led her somewhere she had no business being.

All because she loved him.

"Damn you, Mitch Monroe," she muttered.

"Hey, I said I'd put you on a plane."

"I know. It's not your fault. It's mine."

"Then don't be pissed at me."

"I'm not. I'm pissed at myself."

"Holy shit," Brice said from the backseat.

Mitch angled back. "What?"

"I'm watching my blog on my phone. That fucker just exploded."

Caroline checked her rearview. "Exploded how?"

"Comments are about to crash me is how."

"Already?" Caroline asked. "It's only been a few minutes."

"Yeah, but I have social media links. Hang on."

Taking her eyes off the road ahead, Caroline glanced at Mitch.

"It's Twitter," Brice said. "We've gone viral, kids."

"Fucking A," Mitch said.

"Oh, my God," Caroline added. *Twitter.* A gurgle of nervous laughter itched in her throat and she made a strangled sound. "Twitter. Unbelievable."

"Not really. I have seventy-five thousand followers."

Now that was interesting. "You're kidding."

"The world is full of anti-government conspiracy theorists. They love governmental watch dogs."

Caroline stopped at a traffic light and checked the GPS. "Fellas, where are we going?"

Mitch held up a finger, thinking. "We need to hide in plain sight."

The light turned green and Caroline drove through the intersection while Mitch hit buttons on the car's GPS. *GPS.*

"Dammit!" she hollered.

"What?"

"We need to ditch this car. Donaldson is probably already tracking where my phone pinged last. He's a pain in the ass, but he's not stupid. In ten minutes, he'll have figured out that we needed wheels and that I rented a car. Hello, GPS."

She slid a sideways glance at Mitch, hoping he'd have something inspiring to say.

"Shit."

So much for inspiring. "Quick, find me a rental location where we can drop off the car."

"Brice," Mitch said, "you know anyone here who can help us with wheels?"

"Let me make some calls."

An hour later, after returning the rental car and cabbing it to a rundown restaurant on Roswell's west side, Caroline slid into a booth beside Mitch.

Her leg bumped his and a second later he patted her thigh. Did he have to put his hands on her? Maybe that pat was casual, a meaningless gesture so innocent he hadn't even looked at her, but he wrapped his long fingers, the ones she'd spent so much time thinking about, around her leg and gave it a little squeeze. That casual but supportive squeeze did things to her. Things she shouldn't be focusing on right now.

She shifted sideways.

Not that she minded, but she minded. *You're a mess, Caroline.*

Through the window, she watched Brice wander the parking lot in easy, random circles—no hurry—while he talked on his phone. Beyond the lot, intermittent cars cruised along the two lane road. All in all, not a bad place to squat for an hour. Not too busy, not too slow. In a place like this, they wouldn't stand out due its proximity to Highway 285 and all the tourists that traveled it.

"If he can't get us a car," she said, "we're screwed."

"No, we're not," Mitch said. "I'll find us a car. I'll owe someone a monster fucking favor, but I'll get us a car."

"See, this is what I love about you. You never abandon the fight. You always have a plan. It might be half-assed, but you make it work."

He grinned. "Is that a compliment?"

"As crazy as you make me, there are times I wish I could be more like you. Not so Type A. Not worrying. Not hung up."

"You're cautious. If everyone in the world were like me, it would be chaos." He cracked up. "Jesus, that would be a hot-ass mess."

Caroline snorted.

"Anyway, Type-A personalities like you and Grey give people like me balance." He tucked a few strands of her hair behind her ear. "You give me balance, Caroline."

A whooshing noise sounded and Caroline flinched as Brice slid into the booth across from them, her gaze on him. He smacked the menu open and looked down at it. Could the man be so hungry that he hadn't realized he'd interrupted what might have been a big moment in the Caroline-is-a-fool saga?

After a second, the weird silence finally drew his attention. Slowly, he raised his head, glanced at Mitch then Caroline. "Did I miss something?"

Mitch bumped Caroline's leg with his, but kept his focus on Brice. "No. Wheels?"

"Yeah. It's not pretty, though. Five calls later, I've got us a pickup. It has a bench seat so we'll all fit."

"Hey, we'll take it."

Caroline nodded. "Thank you, Brice."

"My guy is bringing it here. He's also got a trailer we can

squat in. It's at an RV camp site near Bottomless Lakes State Park."

"I was at that park once," Caroline said. "My family took a vacation there when I was a kid. There's a bunch of lakes. Ten maybe?"

"Nine," Brice said. "But yeah, that's it. He said the RV is in a remote area so we should be good to go."

"Who is this guy? You sure you can trust him?"

Brice nodded. "He's solid. Helped me out before."

A remote RV, a truck, it all sounded too convenient. "I don't like it," Caroline said. "How do we know he won't give away our location?"

"Well, Caroline," Brice said. "I guess we don't. I'm open to your brilliant suggestions, though, so fire away."

"Don't get pissy," Mitch said.

As if she needed him to defend her. "I wasn't questioning you, Brice."

"Yeah, you were."

She sat back, held up her hands. "Never mind. We're all on edge. And hungry. Let's eat, chill out for a few minutes, and regroup."

As if a beacon had flashed over their heads, a waitress stepped up to the table. Caroline needed food. And to sleep for a month. Sleep wouldn't happen any time soon, so she'd settle for food. Food always helped her focus.

After taking their order, the waitress swished off, her rubber soles squeaking against the tiled floor. Brice had set his phone on the table and was busy scrolling so Caroline reached across and gave him a gentle poke. "Hey, I'm sorry. You've gone above and beyond. I didn't mean to sound ungrateful."

"No sweat, Caroline. You think too much. Whoa."

Mitch leaned in. "Whoa, what?"

"What the fuck?"

He tapped the front of his phone and using two fingers, expanded the screen.

"What is it?" Caroline asked.

But Brice continued reading, ignoring them and that same panicky itch in Caroline's throat returned.

"What. The. *Fuck*?" Brice repeated. "You guys are not gonna believe this one."

10

———

"**W**hat?" Mitch asked.

Phone in hand, Brice slid from the booth. "We gotta go. Now."

"We have food coming," Caroline protested.

"Forget it. Let's move. Got a gun shop to visit."

Mitch dropped money on the table to cover the food they wouldn't eat, grabbed his and Caroline's duffels, and followed Brice out of the restaurant, Caroline on their heels.

"What gun shop?" she huffed. "This better be worth me leaving behind that quarter pounder and fries."

"It is." Brice stopped in the parking lot, waved at a truck pulling in. "There's our ride."

Mitch was surprised the damned thing actually ran. The color might have been blue. There was so much rust and mud on it, it was hard to tell. The rusted-out body made it look nearly skeletal. The front fender was missing and the windshield looked like a baseball had hit it in the lower passenger side, spider web cracks inching out from a central circle.

One of the side view mirrors hung suspended from a

broken piece of plastic and a few wires, swinging erratically as the truck bounced into the parking lot.

"*That's* our ride?" Caroline's voice had a tight, high sound to it. "You can't be serious."

"No GPS. No actual record of the thing. Buddy runs a junk yard. The plates on it are from another vehicle chopped up for parts a few months ago." He grinned and slapped Caroline lightly on the back. "You wanted off the grid. This is it."

He jogged off to say a few words to the guy who climbed out of the truck and handed Brice a set of keys.

Mitch was grinning but hid it from Caroline. If she saw his face, she'd slug him. "What was that you said about wishing you were less Type A and more easy going?"

He dodged just as she swung a balled fist at his arm. "Shut up."

Brice's friend took off on foot without glancing at them. Brice motioned for them to join him. Mitch started walking, realized Caroline wasn't following, and pulled up short. "It won't kill you, Caroline."

Her face was pale, lips tight. "It might. I'm not sure my tetanus shot is up to date."

This wasn't about the condition of the truck and Mitch knew it. "You don't have to come."

"Oh, I'm coming. Just give me a sec."

Mitch held up a finger to Brice who waved frantically from the driver's seat. "I know you want to drive, but I don't think in this case you have a choice."

"It's not that." She fingered the strap of her briefcase. "What's this gun shop we're visiting? He's not telling us what's happening."

Her voice now held a thread of paranoia. "Brice is on our side, Caroline."

"We barely know him."

Yep, paranoia had entered her bloodstream. All thanks to him.

Mitch walked back to her, put his face in front of her and smiled, turning on the charm. "I'll protect you."

Her eyes narrowed, zeroing in on him like she had him in her sniper scope. "I don't need you—"

He put his hands on both of her elbows. "I know. I'm just kidding. If Brice turns out to be a douchebag, you'll take him out before I have time to blink, right?"

"Right. And down deep, where it counts, I know he's on our side. I just don't know how far reaching this thing is and I'm worried."

"Comes with the territory."

"What territory?"

"Being a renegade."

She shivered under his hands. "I'm not a renegade. I'm just an agent looking for answers."

He put an arm around her shoulders and steered her toward the truck. Brice had it running and revved the motor as he watched them approach. The engine choked and sputtered. "You *are* a renegade. You always have been. You've just been living in denial."

She hit him in the gut with her elbow. Exactly what he was hoping for. He'd forced the old Caroline to rise to the surface again.

Her voice lost some of its tightness. She chuckled under her breath. "You are so full of shit."

"Go with it, Caroline. The dark side can be a lot of fun."

He helped her into the cab, smacking her on the ass for good measure. The truck smelled like marijuana and fast food fries.

Caroline shoved an assortment of coffee cups, 8-track tapes, and dirty tissues to the floor. "This is the most disgusting thing I've ever seen."

That was saying a lot when you were an FBI agent who'd recently gone dumpster diving. "Told you the dark side was fun."

She made the *I'm about to shoot you* face and scooted over the bench seat. The upholstery was stained and torn in places. "I'm afraid I'll contract a disease in here."

Mitch climbed in beside her and before he even shut the door, Brice shifted the truck and they took off.

"Where are we going, Brice? And don't say a gun shop. We know that."

He hung a right onto the main road and hit the gas. "I just got an email from a firearms dealer in town. He saw my blog post. He's only about ten minutes out."

"And we're going there why?"

Brice stopped at a red light and dug into his pocket for his phone. He tapped the screen and handed Caroline the phone. "Read this."

Mitch leaned close, enjoying the excuse to put his head next hers and breathe her strawberry scent, although it was getting a little ripe after all the sweating they'd been doing.

On the screen was an email. It appeared to be from the gun shop's owner.

I have information about that dead FBI agent. We need to talk. In person. How soon can you get here?

It wasn't long before Mitch saw a huge red and black sign, the name of the gun shop spelled out in gaudy gold letters. MH Firearm and Supply. His pulse sped up.

Brice took a left and there they were, in front of the dilapidated old building. He eased the pickup into the small lot, shut off the engine. "We're here."

Heat rose in shimmers off the blacktop. Mitch grabbed the

door handle. The door squeaked as he shoved it open, a paper coffee cup falling out onto the ground.

The three of them trailed inside, a bell over the door ringing and an alarm beeping as they entered. Security system. Not unusual considering the long narrow space contained three glass display cases that formed a U-shape in the middle of the store. Each case was stuffed with handguns of every caliber imaginable. Behind the cases, the walls were lined from one side to the other with rifles ranging from shotguns to semi-automatics.

Mitch let out a low whistle.

"No kidding," Caroline said.

Brice tapped one of the cases with his fingernails. "Lotta money."

He breathed in and the stale, gun-oil laced air burned his throat. "Yep."

In the back corner of the store, a guy in his thirties sat at a desk talking on the phone. He held up a finger. Sure, they'd wait. Considering this might be the guy who emailed them.

A short, balding man in blue denim emerged from the back, wiping his hands on a towel. "Can I help you?"

Brice stopped at the counter. "I'm looking for Marty. Name's Brice Brennan."

The guy scanned Brice, then Mitch and Caroline. "I'm Marty."

Brice held out his phone, the email still visible.

Marty glanced behind Mitch to look out the window at the empty parking lot. "Anyone see you come in?"

"No one," Mitch said. "Now tell us why we're here."

"Who the hell are you?"

Caroline stepped forward, digging for her ID. "We're feder—"

Mitch stopped her. "We're friends of the agent who was

gunned down. The one Brice wrote about. All we're trying to do is find out what happened."

Marty fiddled with the towel, glancing at the guy still on the phone. He motioned them to come behind the counter. "Back here. I don't want anyone to hear us."

Caroline and Brice both looked at Mitch. He nodded and signaled for everyone to follow Marty. They circumvented the glass counter and shelves of ammunition, entering a back room.

A tabletop was covered with parts of a gun Marty must have stripped and was cleaning. He tossed the towel on the table and led them to an office. Once inside, he sat at a beat-up metal desk and waited for Mitch to shut the door.

"I know about that gun you're claiming killed Agent Nusco." Marty flipped a paper clip end over end and glanced up at Brice. "The one you posted on your blog. I sold it."

Mitch kept his body still, not a twitch, not a shift, not even a damned deep breath—but holy hell—his system went into overload. "We need information on the guy who bought it."

Marty nodded. "Young guy. A local. He comes in on a regular basis and buys a lot of weapons with cash. If I ask about any of them, he puts me off. A few months ago, I followed him after he bought a rifle and saw him give it to a guy parked down the street in an expensive Humvee-like vehicle. I called ATF to let them know. I mean, if he's running guns, I don't want my license pulled because of it. All my sales are legal. What happens when the gun leaves the shop, I can't control."

"What did ATF do?" Brice asked.

"Pfft. Nothing. Told me they had him under control and to go about my business. I kept my mouth shut, but I followed him again a few weeks later and he did the same thing."

He tapped his head with an oil-stained finger. "I got to thinking about it, talked to a few of my friends in the area who run gun shops. We'd all had the same couple of guys that didn't seem the type purchasing guns. Me and my friend, Shonny Bridge—he runs a shop about forty miles from here—we got nervous. He knows a guy who knows a guy who works for ATF. Shonny talks to him, tells him we're seeing these guys hand off their purchases to someone in a Humvee. Could be perfectly legal, but Shonny and I've run into trouble before with gangs. Legitimate buyers being forced to buy for gangbangers, druggies, you name it 'cuz the criminals got some blackmail hanging over them, or they need the money. Shonny and me, we don't want to see those weapons end up down in Mexico being used for some drug shootout between cartels or with the police."

Brice shifted to lean against a file cabinet. "What did ATF tell Shonny?"

"Said they'd keep an eye on these buyers. Again, told us not to worry about it." Marty ran a hand over his face. "Thing was, it kept happening. I called the ATF to make a formal complaint. Got the runaround again. Next thing I know, some asshole shows up here one night after closing, telling me to open up. I don't let him in, tell him to come back the next day. I thought he was part of the cartel and I got nervous. Pulled out Patty, my H&K I keep under the front counter. I pointed Patty at him and told him to haul ass before I shot him. Then he pulled a badge. He was from the goddamned ATF."

Mitch kept his eyes on Marty. Still no sign of deception. *Holy shit.* "You let him in?"

"After I saw that badge, hell yeah."

"What did he say?"

Marty picked up a paper clip and flicked it between his fingers. "He said, 'You want to keep your license, keep your mouth shut. The ATF is running an operation and you need to cooperate with us and continue selling to those men you've been asking about.'"

Brice fisted a hand and smacked it on the file cabinet. "Damn."

Damn was right.

Marty nodded. "I told him to go to hell."

Mitch grinned. Marty reminded him of the truck they'd ridden there in. A little rusty around the edges, but still running. "Bet he didn't like that."

"Sure as hell didn't." He fiddled with the paper clip again. "Told me I'd lose my license if I refused to keep my mouth shut. The next day, Shonny said he had a visit from the same asshole."

"Did you get a name or number from his badge?" Caroline stood in between Mitch and Brice, looking uncomfortable but even more determined. "Did you confirm with ATF that he was an actual agent?"

"He was legit. I checked him out good and proper. Name's Will Atkinson. He's the Assistant Special Agent in Charge of the local ATF office and brother to George Atkinson, the U.S. Attorney here in New Mexico."

Caroline pulled a small notebook and pen from her briefcase and wrote down the name.

Marty watched. "I wrote letters starting the next day. This is America, and I'm a tax-payin' citizen. No one's going to threaten me." He tapped his index finger on the desk. "I wrote to my local district attorney, the state congressmen and to the goddamn governor. Told 'em a thing or two about small business and the kind of voting clout me, my friends, and my customers have in this state. I laid everything out and suggested they look into the situation. All I got was the standard political bullshit letters back. *Thank you for contacting us. Your letter is important. Please vote for me. Blah, blah, blah.* Not one of them mentioned ATF, the U.S. Attorney, or the possibility of gun running."

Mitch liked this guy. "Any more threats?"

"Nope, but those two guys who were constantly buying the guns stopped coming in. They stopped visiting Shonny too. Not long after, I was having a beer with some shop owners south of here at a gun show. Same deal. They were sure a few of their repeat customers were selling guns to a drug cartel. I told 'em my story, and told them to contact the feds or the governor or somebody. They didn't want to make waves."

He put his head in his hands and rubbed his bald head. "Then that kid got killed not far from here. It was all over the papers about him being FBI. I've been wondering ever since if he was killed with one of my guns. I've been following that blog of yours. Now I find out it's true." His eyes were haunted when he looked up at Mitch and Brice. "I did everything I could to make sure them bastards weren't giving my guns to the gangs, but what else could I do?"

Caroline leaned forward and laid a hand on the man's forearm. "Do you have copies of the letters you sent?"

"Every last one of them."

"Could I see them?"

Caroline, Miss Type A, was crossing her T's and dotting her I's. She wanted to confirm Marty was telling them the truth and not just trying to cover his ass. For once, Mitch appreciated her anal retentiveness. No matter how believable Marty was, you couldn't be too careful.

Marty opened a desk drawer and removed a file folder stuffed with letters. "Got 'em all right here."

Caroline shuffled through the contents, making a note here and there on her notepad. Names, dates, who replied and who didn't.

"What are you going to do about this mess?" Marty asked.

Brice released a deep sigh. "We're going to bring those guilty of killing Agent Nusco to justice and expose everyone involved in this cover-up."

"Good." Marty nodded his head. "But there's one more

thing," he said, his eyes bouncing between Mitch and Brice.

Mitch had that feeling again...the one that told him they'd stumbled onto something big. "What?"

"He's back. That first buyer I followed to the Humvee? Came in yesterday and bought another gun."

Before Mitch could jump out of his skin, Caroline gripped his wrist, hoping to hell he would keep his mouth shut and let her handle Marty. If she knew him at all, which she most certainly did, he was about to ask Marty for the address of that straw buyer. An idea Caroline could get behind, but also one that would break any number of privacy laws and get Marty in trouble.

What they needed here was careful, thought-out, and concise strategizing. Something Mitch, in all his blazing glory that turned Caroline on in every possible way, simply didn't know how to do. He was more the race in, kick some ass, and get the info kind of guy. Sometimes that came in handy. Not now though.

She'd have to do it for them.

"Marty," Caroline said, "I want us to be very careful about this conversation so we don't break any privacy laws. That being said, I'd like to find a way for us to get the address you have for the gentleman who purchased the weapon yesterday. Is there a way we can do that?"

From the corner of her eye, she spotted Mitch shaking his head. The eye roll would be next so she didn't bother to face him. She'd seen that eye roll hundreds—thousands—of times and had learned infinite patience because of it.

Marty leaned closer, craning his neck as if that extra few inches would allow him to hear better. "You want his address?"

"Yes. But gun sales are not public record in New Mexico."

"Fuck the privacy laws."

Fuck the privacy laws? This from a gun shop owner? Leave it to her to find Mitch's long lost brother.

"Hot damn," Mitch said.

Marty glanced at him, then went back to Caroline. "I'll give you whatever you need. Let them take away my license. For six months I've rattled every goddamned cage I can and now an FBI agent is dead from a gun I sold. Living with that'll give me a heart attack. I need to make this right."

Part of her wanted to argue, to stress to this man that they had options. Like a warrant. But warrants took time and if this was truly a cover-up involving a U.S Attorney and New Mexico ATF, a warrant would be impossible to obtain. Those involved would make sure of it and she could finally light the fuse attached to her career and blow it to pieces.

Hell with it. Caroline finally looked at Mitch. *Damn you, Mitch Monroe.*

"We have to do this," he said.

They didn't *have* to. They could take ten minutes and talk privately. Try to find another option that wouldn't risk Marty's license.

"Forget the options, Caroline. You know there aren't any good ones. Not in our timeframe."

A clock on the desk chimed the top of the hour. They'd left the hotel over an hour ago. Plenty of time for Donaldson to confirm she wasn't where she was supposed to be.

Go time. She turned back to Marty. "Get us the address and we'll do what we can to keep you out of it. Sound fair?"

"Fuck fair."

"I love this guy," Mitch said.

Marty shifted in his seat and put on bifocals to look at his computer. He tapped a few keys, glancing between the keyboard and the screen while Caroline's nerves suffered a seizure. Each pulse point throbbed and she ran her hands along the underside of her wrists, gently squeezing.

It's the right thing. She sure hoped so. It had to be. Getting this address might be the first step in finding the answers they needed. Professional suicide? She'd already committed that anyway. Personal triumph? Righting a wrong? Definitely. Either way, they'd have answers.

The printer beside the computer hummed. Marty snatched the paper it spit out and spun back to them. "Here you go."

Caroline and Mitch both reached for it, but he smacked her hand away. "I've got it. If the shit hits the fan, we say I had it first and I gave it to you."

Please. No one would believe that. Not after their history. She snorted. "You think that'd fly?"

"If your prints aren't on this sheet of paper, it can only help keep you in the clear."

Point there. She dropped her hand. "Thank you, Marty. We'll check this out and let you know."

She dug into her purse, grabbed one of her cards, and wrote down her cell number. *Wait.* Mitch destroyed her phone. Terrific. No phone. She'd have to pick up a burn phone. She passed the card and pen to Brice. "Write your cell number down so Marty can reach us if our straw buyer comes back."

As Brice wrote the number down, Mitch bounced on the balls of his feet, his endless energy crackling and reaching out to her, surrounding her. This was such a mistake. Intellectually, she knew it. Emotionally, she denied it. Because when Mitch got on a roll, when he saw his target and homed in on it, she wanted to meet the woman who could resist the pull of him.

Magic. That's what he was like when working a case. Excitement and lust and power all rolled into one package. And, despite agreeing with his mission, but not necessarily his approach, Caroline gave in to the magic.

He shoved the paper into his front pocket and shook Marty's hand. Then he clapped his hands together. "Let's roll, kids."

11

*T*he house that matched the address was a two-story shack that looked as if it started out as a one-story shack. "Do a drive-by," Mitch told Brice.

"We need a plan," Caroline said.

She sat nestled between Mitch and Brice on the bench seat, and in her typical 'Caroline way' kept inching closer to Mitch to avoid body contact with Brice. All so Ms. Uptight didn't let her Type-A-self invade the space of a guy she barely knew. Mitch couldn't say he minded all the closeness, but his thoughts kept wandering. And God knew his body went right along with them.

"The plan is," Mitch said, "to knock on the door and see who answers. *If* anyone answers. No cars in the driveway."

At the corner, Brice braked at the stop sign and checked the cross traffic. He hooked a left and Mitch stared out the side window, already thinking ahead to knocking on the front door of that beat-up two-story.

Still avoiding a squirming Caroline, Mitch caught sight of a neon "Bar" sign damn near begging for his attention. He could use a shot of bourbon right now. One that would fry his throat and make him forget about his dead friends. Sunlight flashed off of something and Mitch shifted his gaze to the green street sign with reflective white letters. *Buena.*

The shock ripped into him. Adrenalin, an enormous hit of it, plowed into his limbs. He jerked sideways, bumping Caroline.

"Hey!"

But he couldn't take his eyes off that street sign. "Son of a bitch. Stop this truck."

Brice pulled to the side of the road. "What now?"

"Buena. That's the street. Brice, pull up those pictures Ethan sent us. Quick."

"Mitch," Caroline huffed, "what is your problem? You damn near broke my hip."

Annoyed with Brice's slow pace, Mitch grabbed the phone and starting swiping through photos. No. No. Not it. Nope.

There.

Son of a bitch.

"That's it. Holy fuck." He hopped out of the truck while scrolling back to the photos of Tommy's body. Had to be. Had to.

Caroline followed him, stalking behind, trying to keep pace. *Right here.*

He stopped. Studied the picture for a second, looking for...*there.* A street sign visible from the parking lot. He looked around and squinted against the sun, judging the distance between the bar in the backdrop and Tommy's body.

Son of a *bitch.* "This is it. He died right here."

Caroline ripped the phone from his hands. "What are you saying?"

"Buena. I saw the street sign in the photos earlier." He pointed to the green and white sign at the end of the block.

Her mouth dropped open. "Ethan said Tommy went to his girlfriend's house and then had a couple of things to do. And then he's gunned down a block from a straw buyer's house? That cannot be a coincidence."

"Well, shit," Brice said from behind Caroline. "We need to knock on that door and see if our guy lives there."

According to Marty's report, the straw buyer's name was Jesse Lando. Brice had googled the guy and found nothing. Not even a Facebook page.

"And if no one's home?" Mitch asked.

Caroline narrowed her eyes at him. "We are not breaking and entering."

Fuck that. "Of course not. You can sit in the truck and wait for someone to come home."

"And what will you do?"

"Best you don't know. Let's go back."

They did, parking on the side of the street and killing the engine. Mitch looked at Caroline. "Are we going with your lame bible salesman act or do you have another idea?"

"Bible salesman?" Brice said.

"Don't listen to him, Brice." Her cheeks were flushed, her eyes bright with the chase. "He's trying to annoy me by yanking my chain. As he so often does."

And what a nice chain it was. Mitch chucked her under the chin. "Stay here. I'll go to the door and see what happens."

Mitch got out, hearing Caroline protest under her breath. He ignored her. Never mind her and the adrenalin rush, he had to focus. Had to calm down, get his thoughts in order and concentrate.

No telling who he might be dealing with on the other side of that door. Could be the man who'd gunned down his best friend. At the very least, it was a straw buyer who might've sold the gun to a major black market gun runner. Either way, Mitch's fist was going to find the guy's face.

Behind him, he heard a door slam. He turned to tell Caroline to get back in the truck, but found Brice walking up to him.

Brice held up his hands in an act of surrender. "She's worried you're going to kill this guy. Told me to back you up."

Smart woman. Mitch surveyed the house. No activity inside from what he could see and hear. The neighborhood was rundown, nobody out in the heat of the day. Maybe the owner of the house was at work.

Or maybe he was inside watching Mitch and Brice approach his house and wondering who the fuck they were.

A front window was open and a lace curtain blew in the light breeze. A planter by the front door held succulents and a glass ball. Homey touches for a straw buyer.

It would have been helpful if Caroline hadn't burnt her bridge to the FBI's databases. He could have had her look up the owner. Mitch was running totally blind here.

What's new? He signaled Brice to stay back as he walked straight up to the door. If the bastard was going to shoot him, so be it. He was done dicking around.

The wooden door had a knocker of all things. He raised it, let it fall. Waited.

Seconds ticked by. He glanced back at Caroline in the truck. She was watching, eyes wide. He'd bet anything she had her handgun drawn.

He knocked again. From inside the house, he heard someone call, "Coming!"

It wasn't a man's voice. No, sir. That was a female voice if he'd ever heard one. And he'd heard plenty.

Sure enough, the door opened and he found himself looking at a petite, dark-haired woman. "Yes?" she said. "May I help you?"

Not exactly the image of a hardened criminal. She looked to be early twenties, if that. Her large brown eyes sported glittery eye shadow and false eyelashes, and she was dressed in a simple tank top and cut-off shorts. Her feet were bare, toenails painted bright red. JLO had nothing on her.

Except this girl was the total picture of innocence.

Looks could be deceiving. She could have a weapon hidden behind her back. Mitch gave her a charming smile. "I'm looking for Jesse. He around?"

The woman's face shut down. "What do you want with him?"

"A friend of mine said he knows a lot about guns. Got a few questions for him."

Her dark eyes shifted to Brice, then back to Mitch. "He's not here."

"Know where I can find him?"

"He moved out a few weeks ago. I don't know where he's living now."

Damn. Still, if this chick was recently deep-sixed by Jesse, she might be willing to drop a dime on him. "You kick him out?"

"What's it to you?"

Mitch shrugged. "He cheating on you?"

She gave him an incredulous look. "He's my brother, idiot."

Aha. Leverage. A bitter ex-girlfriend might have an ax to grind, but a sister would want to protect her brother. How could he use that to his advantage?

Mitch heard footsteps behind him on the cracked sidewalk. Caroline sidled up next to him. "Jesse's your brother?"

The woman scanned each of their faces, stepping back a few inches. Retreating. "Who are you people?"

Caroline flashed her badge. The woman flinched. "Your brother has landed himself into a federal mess. We need to speak to him."

Look at her—strong-arming the only lead we have. First, she was all—*we need a plan.* Now, she was charging in like a bull. Mitch rocked back on his heels, waiting to see if the Bad Cop act worked.

Jesse's sister stared at them, her lips firmed, but she didn't slam the door in their faces. "I don't know where he is. I can't help you."

"Can you get a message to him?" Caroline said. "Surely you have his cell number?"

If she could get a message to her brother, Mitch was sure it would be, *get the hell out of town.*

The woman shook her head. Her long hair fell in waves over her shoulders. "You're not the only people looking for him. He stopped returning my calls two days ago."

Interesting. "Who else is looking for him?"

"A couple of men came by here the other night. I told them the same thing. My brother's skipped town and I don't know where he is."

Caroline was all FBI agent. She handed the woman a card with Brice's number handwritten in the corner. "Your brother purchased a weapon used to kill a federal agent just down the block from here. He can't stay on the lam forever. He needs to contact us or he'll spend the rest of his life in prison."

The woman froze, reworking her facial features into a detached look. "I don't know what you're talking about."

Right. And he was an angel in disguise. "The gun used was traced back to him," Mitch said. "He's in deep. But we can help."

She started to say something, stopped. "Why should I trust you? Even if I did, I can't help you."

Caroline was still holding the business card. She lowered it, turned to Mitch. "Give me a second here."

He didn't want to. Didn't want to give her control and walk away. He did it anyway. Gritting his teeth, he spun on his heel and motioned for Brice to walk back to the truck with him.

Before he was out of earshot, he heard Caroline switch from Bad Cop to Good Cop. "Ms. Lando—"

"It's Maria."

"Maria. I understand. I do. I have a brother and I know what it's like to want to protect him. Like you, I'd do anything for him. But Jesse is up to his eyeballs and the only way out is to talk to us."

Leaning against the rusted front bumper of the truck, Mitch watched Caroline once more offer the card. Miracle of miracles, the sister took it.

Then she quietly closed the door and Caroline returned to the truck.

As they all climbed in, Brice driving and Caroline sliding into the middle, Mitch said to her, "Since when do you have a brother?"

"I don't. But I know what's it's like to love a man who can't help himself and I definitely know how to manipulate a potential witness."

Hot damn. This woman was all he'd ever wanted. All her gumption and determination, and the way she was laying it all on the line to help him. Maybe it wasn't such a bad thing, letting Caroline take control of this case. "What's next, Bad Cop?"

She cut her eyes to him, then back to the road. "I'm the good cop. You're the bad cop."

He continued grinning. "Not from what I've seen today."

She sniffed, but was smiling. Ah, yes, she was enjoying this walk on the dark side whether she'd admit it or not. "Brice, I want to talk to Ethan again. Can you arrange a meeting?"

He grabbed his phone from the dashboard. "I'm on it."

Mitch slouched down and let out a long, slow breath. We're going to get this figured out, he mentally promised Tommy. I will clear your name. Even if it's the last thing I ever do.

Brice parked at the end of a row at the Town Square shopping mall, one of those mammoth buildings with five huge anchor stores and an endless amount of smaller shops rounding out the assortment. Caroline, being a destination shopper, in and out in ten minutes or less, never understood the lure of malls. Unless, of course, the patrons were shopping junkies. Then this would be a crack house and they'd never want to leave.

"Ethan said he'd meet us in the food court. It's dinnertime so it'll be packed. Orange baseball cap this time."

Mitch yanked the handle, threw his weight against the door and shoved it open, the usual squeal grating Caroline's nerves. What she wouldn't do for that little Prius.

She slid to the end of the bench and hopped out, adjusting her blouse that by now must have stunk like a sewer. Along with that Prius, she could use a shower. Hopefully, the RV they'd be squatting in had one, because using their credit or ATM cards for a hotel would be a major no-no. Donaldson, if she knew him at all, probably already had her transactions being monitored. And she'd only brought two hundred in cash with her. They'd have to make it last.

Inside the mall, the frigid air-conditioning blasted her, bringing her mind into sharper focus. If her energy had been lagging, the cold air instantly took care of it.

Mitch checked the mall map. "Food court is dead center. Can't miss it."

"We're eating while we're here. I could eat a cow right now."

Mitch grinned. As usual, his mind had probably gone straight to the gutter. Caroline sighed. "Is everything an innuendo with you?"

He shrugged. "I'm a guy."

"It's true," Brice said. "I can't go ten minutes without thinking about sex."

Caroline threw her hands up. "Too much information! Did I really need to know that? You know what? Forget it. Let's just do this."

The three of them marched through the gigantic mall, a

modern day Mod Squad on a mission. This was one for the Caroline Foster books for sure.

They passed store after store toting short skirts and sexy, cleavage exposing tops. Caroline glanced down at her rumpled clothing and decided she needed to update her wardrobe. Maybe add some sass to it.

Maybe.

Not with Mitch around though. He'd be a pain in the ass about it.

They reached the food court and, just as Ethan had said, the place was packed. The only open tables were on the far side near an indoor playground. All around her, the aroma of cooking meat and frying French fries alerted her ravished system. *I'm definitely eating a cow before I leave here.*

"Do you see him?" Caroline asked.

"Not yet. He's here though." Brice's phone whistled. "This is him. He sees us. He's at a table straight ahead."

Caroline scanned the tables, her gaze landing on a man lifting an orange cap to scratch his head. "Got him."

"Yep," Mitch said.

He took a step, stopped and reached back to let Caroline lead the way, his hand landing on her lower back and guiding her forward.

How things had changed. In their Bureau days, no matter how innocent the gesture, he'd never have put his hands on her. Here they were, once again in that complicated world that fell between co-workers and one-time lovers. They simply had to navigate the landscape.

Not an easy task when spending so much time squeezed into a pick-up and its not-so-roomy bench seat. The closeness threw her, made her want more of it and that was something she needed to reconcile. Because, unless they figured out what Tommy had been up to, Mitch might be going to prison.

They approached the table and she met Ethan's gaze. He

remained seated, which Caroline understood to be his effort to not draw attention. Brice took the seat next to him and Mitch and Caroline sat across from them.

"What's up?" Ethan asked.

With the noise level, whispering would be impossible, but she'd speak only loud enough for Ethan to hear, eliminating any nosey-bodies around them. "We have the name of the guy who bought the weapon."

Ethan's head dipped an inch. "The one that killed Tommy? You're shitting me."

"I shit you not."

"I thought the ballistics report was sealed."

"It is indeed."

Mitch propped his elbows on the table and scooted forward. "You don't want to know."

Ethan nodded, accepting Mitch's advice. "Who's the buyer?"

"Jesse Lando," Caroline said. "We visited the gun shop where the weapon originated. MH Firearm and Supply. It's owned by Marty Highland. Have you heard of him?"

"I know the shop but I've never dealt with the owner. He moves a lot of guns though."

"Yeah," Brice said. "According to Marty, he's been bitching to ATF about the number of weapons bought by this guy Lando. ATF told him to keep quiet. He's written to every official in New Mexico and no one is investigating."

"What does that say to you?" Caroline asked.

Ethan eyed her. "You think Lando is undercover?"

"Could be, right?"

"I know all the undercovers in my office. If he's undercover, he's not ours."

Mitch drummed his fingers on the table. "Can you ask around? We talked to his sister—she lives at the address Marty has on file—and he's in the wind since Tommy died. The kicker is, she and her brother live just down the block from where Tommy was killed."

"No shit? So maybe Tommy was meeting with him that night. He killed a federal agent and is laying low."

"According to his sister, he's never been in trouble. We know he doesn't have a record or he wouldn't have been able to buy a gun. Add that to what his sister said and this guy is suddenly murdering a federal agent? Makes no sense."

"Look, Ethan," Mitch said. "Can you run this guy's name by some people? See if it rings a bell? You said you were out of the loop on whatever Tommy was doing. Maybe one of the task-force agents knows something about this guy."

Ethan sat back, nudged his cap and scratched his head. *Stressed.*

Leaning forward again, Caroline touched Ethan's arm with just the tips of her fingers. "I'm sorry. I know what we're asking. I'm right there with you on that limb. My SAC already caught me poking into this case. He'll catch up with us soon so we need to move fast. If you can ask around about Lando, it'll save us time. But don't do it if you don't feel right about it. When this is over, *you* will have to deal with the backlash. For us, it doesn't matter anymore. We're knee deep. You can still walk away."

A woman pushing a stroller squeezed behind Caroline's chair, bumping her. "Oh, so sorry!" the woman said. "We're like sardines in here tonight."

"No problem," Mitch said. He unleashed one of his magic smiles, drawing the woman's attention from Ethan and Brice's side of the table. Flirting complete, he hunched forward. "We should get some food before people start noticing."

Yes. Food. Good idea.

"You go ahead," Ethan said. "My wife is waiting on me. I promised her I'd be home tonight."

Brice and Mitch stood, but Caroline stayed seated. "Mitch, get me the biggest burger and fries you can find."

"Will do."

The two men walked off and Caroline rested her chin in her hand. "I meant what I said. These two cowboys have nothing to lose. They don't work for the government anymore. You and I, we have careers. You have a family."

Ethan dragged a pen and a notepad out of the back pocket of his jeans. "Jesse Lando?"

This was it. He'd do it. Caroline relaxed her shoulders and the tension stuck there broke apart. This was a good man. "Yes. L-A-N-D-O."

"I'll see what I can do."

12

$\mathcal{T}$he RV was nothing but a popup camper alongside a small lake. A few trees gave some cover, but otherwise, it was all lake. Mitch sighed as he, Brice, and Caroline stared at it. They were going to be squished together again, which would have been awesome if it was just Caroline and him.

She looked as thrilled as he was about the tight quarters. "Please tell me this camper has a shower."

Brice shook his head. "We'll be lucky if it has running water."

Mitch sauntered to the door and opened it, the stale smell of mothballs hitting his nose. Popping his head inside, he saw nothing that suggested there was a sink or toilet. He'd squatted in worse places, but at least those all had running water and a toilet. "Bright side? At least there's a lake."

Caroline groaned. He knew the feeling. What he wouldn't give to be home at his old apartment, kicking back with a beer and watching a game. Funny how people took the little things —like a shower—for granted.

The three of them trudged into the tiny camper and the

sauna-like air nearly suffocated him. The damned heat wouldn't give. There was a table with a bench seat, a counter, a dorm fridge, and two single beds, one at each end.

No air conditioning.

No bathroom.

"Perfect!" Caroline's too-cheerful voice held an edge to it. "Mitch, you're sleeping outside. Good thing New Mexico is having a heat wave or you'd freeze your ass off."

Even though she'd consumed enough food at the food court to fill three of him, she was tired. Plus, he knew she was still stewing about Donaldson and the mess she'd made of her career. A snarky comeback was on his lips, but he squelched it. What he really should do—wanted to do—was take her in his arms and erase the tight lines around her mouth.

Caroline wasn't the only one who could use some extra-curricular exercise to take her mind off things.

Now wasn't the time. He went to an overhead bin and found what he was looking for: a rolled up blanket and a pillow. "No problem." He grabbed both and brushed past her to head outside. "I don't mind sleeping under the stars."

"I can sleep on the floor," Brice offered.

Mitch shook his head and kept going. Better he wasn't near Caroline in the middle of the night, remembering how much he loved kissing the skin at the base of her neck, or the way her hands and lips did evil things to him. Brice might end up scarred for life if he witnessed what Mitch wanted to do to her.

Outside, he took a breath of fresh air. God, he hated the smell of mothballs. At least out here, he'd be forced to keep his hands and mouth off Caroline and he wouldn't smell like some old lady's underwear drawer.

For a long while he sat near the edge of the lake, half-hoping Caroline would come out and talk to him. He heard an occasional noise from inside the camper, but soon all was quiet. The only thing keeping him company was an owl in the distance. He unfolded his blanket and stretched out, knowing he wouldn't be able to sleep. As he lay there, listening to the waves gently lap the shore, he decided a dip in the lake might be what he needed. He smelled ripe and a swim might relax his nerves.

He stripped down and dove in, the water warm and inviting. Probably snakes lived in these waters. After everything he'd survived recently, it would be his shit luck to die from a snakebite.

He swam out to the center of the lake and started back. The bottom wasn't too deep in most spots and before he was halfway to shore, he stopped and put his feet down. They sank into mud. Yep, shallow waters indeed.

Everything they'd learned that day nagged him. Straw buyers, ATF agents leaning on gun shop owners, the New Mexico AG's brother threatening people. Tommy's murder occurring a block away from a straw buyer's house.

Jesse Lando going AWOL.

Had the government gotten to him or the gun runner?

Mitch started swimming again, hoping the rhythmic exercise would clear his mind. *Stroke, stroke, stroke.* One thing was for sure. He had more to fear from the snakes in Washington than the ones in this lake.

When he came to a stop a few minutes later, movement on shore caught his eye. As he blinked water from his eyes and swam in place, he realized it was a mirage. Had to be. Not in this lifetime could he get that lucky.

He rubbed at his eyes. The heat, or possibly the mothballs, had fried his brain.

Nope.

The mirage remained.

Caroline stood on the shore, the moon glowing down on her long hair and naked shoulders. Naked *everything*, in fact. High, taut breasts, flat stomach, and never-ending legs.

She was beyond beautiful. His heart—and his dick—did a little *come to papa* dance. Because, really, what man in his right mind wouldn't be attracted to Caroline?

Once she knew she had his attention, she walked slowly, tantalizing, into the water. Had to be a mirage. After all the bad things he'd done in the world, there was no way God was rewarding him with this.

"Hey, Caroline."

"Hi, Mitch."

The moonlight illuminated something small and white in her hand. "What have you got there?"

She made a humming noise. "Why, it's soap."

That explained it. She'd wanted a shower and was forced to bathe in the lake instead. He recognized her evil plan...to taunt and torture him by making him watch.

She half-walked, half-floated to the spot right in front of him, swimming in place and staying just out of reach. Her eyes were dark pools. Her slender arms created waves that lapped against his chest. She didn't say anything, just circled around behind him.

"What are you doing, Caroline?"

"Turns out, Brice snores like a maniac. I'm taking a bath." She ran her hand across the top of his shoulders, her voice low and husky. One of her long legs brushed against his. "Maybe you'd like to join me?"

Mirage or not, God was doing him a solid here. *Don't say anything. Not. One. Fucking. Word.* Sure as shit, if he opened his mouth, he'd screw up this fantasy.

She worked over his shoulders, then trailed her fingers with the bar of soap down his spine. His dick was hard and straining and he clenched his jaw together as her breasts bumped against his back, her hands going lower.

"Shit, Caroline." He couldn't hold back. "I think you know how I feel about you. I can't play this game."

"What game?" her voice was low and seductive in his ear as she dragged the soap up his back.

"I want you so damn bad." Why couldn't he keep his mouth shut and just take what she was offering? "But if this is going to be a repeat of the-night-that-never-happened, I'm not going there."

"I sort of liked—make that *loved*—that night. That may have been the only unguarded interaction we've had." Soap still in hand, she wrapped her arms around his waist, bringing her front into complete contact with his back. Her lips nibbled at his ear lobe.

"The night itself was awesome. I'm talking about the day after when you couldn't look me in the eye."

"I know." She sighed. "Neither of us are in a good place for a relationship. Never have been, and quite possibly, we never will be. But I know what I'm doing right now. With the mess we're in, this might be all we get."

He had to work his arms harder to keep them both afloat. "You sure about that? You think you've detonated your career, and oh, hey, there's Mitch. Let me go work out my anxiety on him."

"Fair enough. You could be right." She laid her cheek on his shoulder. "But you said you'd do whatever it took to get back into my good graces. I'm calling in the chit."

"Sex will get me into your good graces? Well, hell, Caroline, why didn't you tell me this sooner?"

She goosed his ass and he laughed. "What I meant was, I don't know what will happen when we go back to D.C. We may both wind up on the losing end of this deal. Me out of job, maybe facing criminal charges, and you in prison. I'm taking advantage of the time we have. Plus, you're vulnerable right now. I could have hid your clothes."

His cock throbbed, scrambling his thoughts. He didn't like her behind him...he wanted to look her in the eye, make sure she wasn't taunting him so she could have a good laugh and swim off, leaving him in misery. "Caroline?"

She kissed his shoulder. "Yes?"

"Are you trying to even the score?"

"What score?"

"From the-night-that-never-happened. I didn't mean to take advantage. Then again, you haven't been vulnerable a day in your life."

"Not true about the vulnerable part, but I'm glad you see me that way." She released him, and damn, he knew it...she swam a few feet away and stared up at the sky. "It's really beautiful out here."

She floated on her back, closing her eyes. Her nipples broke the surface of the water and he nearly moaned. If only he weren't a fugitive. If only he'd told Caroline how much he wanted her—not just sexually—during the-night-that-never-happened.

If onlys. He hated them. "Tease," he said, trying to get a rise out of her.

She stopped floating, looked at him. "Back in D.C., I told you we'd end up screwing each other blind. You really think I'm out here just to tease you?"

"Seems that way, regardless of what you've said."

Bingo. She let go of the soap and swam back to him, getting in his face. Her legs wrapped around him, putting her exactly where he wanted her. "The-night-that-never-happened," she said. "Round Two. And believe me, you won't forget what I'm about to do to you."

His cock wedged in the soft spot between her legs, and he had to hold himself back from plunging home. "The-night-that-*did*-fucking-happen, and believe *me* when I say, I've been fantasizing about round two for a long, long time. You won't ever be able to pretend this didn't happen."

She laughed and he kissed her. A soft moan escaped her,

but there was no surrender in it, only the anticipation of pleasure. Her fingers scraped into his hair as she molded her body to his. The points of her nipples pressed into his chest, and he let his hands roam over her shoulders, her back, her ass. There he cupped her cheeks and prepared to guide himself home.

The owl *whoo-whoo*ed in the distance and in the back of Mitch's mind he heard another sound. Something...*a door opening?* Caroline stiffened, her arms and legs a solid mass around him. She broke the kiss.

Yep, it wasn't a figment of his imagination. She'd heard it too. Her eyes were round as she stared straight at him. "Brice?" she whispered.

Mitch glanced over her shoulder, and sure enough, Brice stood on the camper's front steps.

He held up a hand and the moonlight glinted off what looked to be his cell. "Sorry to interrupt," he called. "But I figured you'd want to know about this ASAP."

Caught.

In the lake. With Mitch. Naked.

Humiliation backed up in her throat and Caroline gasped. Even in the cool water, heat stormed her cheeks. Mitch moved in front of her, blocking any view Brice might have even in the darkness. Hadn't this been her worst nightmare from the night-that-never-happened? That a co-worker would know about her and Mitch and think of her as nothing but an easy lay? A woman sleeping her way to the top?

Brice wasn't a coworker, but once again, Mitch was in the middle of it. All because Caroline continued to allow it to happen. Continued to allow him to break through all that anger and hurt she'd stored up since he'd gone off the grid and ignored her every attempt to contact him. Superman had Kryptonite, Caroline Foster had Mitch Monroe. Mitch made Kryptonite look weak.

She'd have to consider the consequences of that later because at this moment, she was naked and Brice clearly enjoyed the show.

"I can't get out of this water," she whispered.

"I'll get rid of him." Mitch lifted his head to where Brice stood on the shore. "What is it?"

"Ethan has an update on Lando."

Caroline flinched. "Oh, my God."

"Brice," Mitch called, "do me a favor and turn around."

Following instructions, even if he did snicker loud enough for them to hear, Brice turned his back to the lake.

"Unbelievable," Caroline said.

"Stay behind me until we get to shore and I can get your clothes. Did you bring a towel?"

"Yes. Two. I found them in the cabinet earlier."

Slowly, they waded out of the water. Caroline stayed behind Mitch, that amazing body with his long, lean muscles gleaming in the moonlight and offering shelter should Brice morph into an ass and sneak a peek.

After a quick dry-off, Caroline shoved her legs into the yoga pants and T-shirt she'd left on shore and tied her wet hair into a knot. The humiliation of getting caught would not derail her. Not now. They had a case to solve and limited time to do it. Any juvenile jokes Brice might throw at her—men were dumb that way—would have to wait.

Plus, she was way beyond putting up with crap from anyone.

Not waiting for Mitch, she marched to the camper. "What's up?"

Brice swung around, eyeballed her wet hair and winked. "Too bad about the missing shower, huh?"

"Brice," she said, "one more snide comment and I will lay

you out right here."

Mitch stepped next to her. "I'd take her word for it."

"You two think I'm blind? The second you came to my door I knew you were either banging each other or would be soon."

Caroline closed her eyes, fought the humiliation of failing to hide her feelings for Mitch. "Uh, *Ethan*?"

Brice held open the camper door. "We need to call him back. I wanted us all on the call."

Inside the camper, the three of them squeezed into the seating area where Brice parked at the small, two-person table while Mitch dropped into one of the two bench seats. Caroline took the opposite seat while Brice dialed Ethan and put the phone on speaker.

"Hey," Ethan said.

"Hey," Brice said. "Sorry about that. We're all here now."

"My fucking mind is blown right now."

The gravelly tone in Ethan's voice, like glass scraping his throat raw, ripped through the phone line. Caroline gave Mitch her *what's this now* look.

Mitch sat forward. "What happened?"

"I made a few calls. Tommy was part of Operation Bullet-proof, and it was indeed, a secret taskforce, very hush, hush. One of the agents in my office is still in contact with one of the taskforce members. He was sent to one of the New York field offices after Tommy died. They wanted that son of a bitch as far from this as possible."

"Sure seems that way," Caroline said. "You spoke to him?"

"Yeah, half hour ago. I asked him about Lando. Hold on to your panties, kids, because Lando was Tommy's *informant*."

Caroline snapped her gaze to Brice, not really looking at him, but having him directly across from her put him in her sight line. What the hell was going on with this case? Tommy was killed by a gun bought buy a straw buyer who was his *informant*?

Movement from the corner of her eye drew her attention to Mitch. He wrapped his hand around his forehead and squeezed with such force his nail beds filled with color. "Informant for what exactly?"

Good question. Caroline had a few more. First off, if Lando was a known straw buyer and, according to Marty, had been buying excessive quantities of guns, did the taskforce knowingly let those guns walk? All of them?

Couldn't be.

"That's what I'm trying to find out." Ethan let out a long sigh. "With the case sealed and the taskforce members scattered, it's going to take some time."

Caroline was still trying to wrap her brain around it, but it made sense. "Tommy knew this guy was buying all these guns legitimately and turning them over to some gun runner, so he didn't arrest him and turned him into a snitch instead?"

"Yeah," Ethan said. "According to my guy, Tommy and some of the taskforce agents started moaning about the number of guns Lando and a few others were buying. They were told to stand down."

"Why?"

"No idea. My guy said hundreds, if not thousands of guns walked. Without busting the straw buyers, the taskforce had no way of tracking all of those weapons. It's a clusterfuck."

Caroline sat back and stared up at the top of the camper where a streak of dirt ran at least three feet. She needed to back up and start at the beginning. See if she could follow the timeline and understand where it all started. "What was the point of this taskforce?"

"Ha," Ethan said. "Get this. New Mexico is trying to crack down on gunrunning. What the agent told me is that the taskforce was supposed to follow the guns until they reached whoever the big dog was. Someone higher than Balboa even.

The fucking genius who developed this plan didn't count on losing track of the guns before they reached the big dog."

Mitch let out a derisive grunt. "That fucking genius happen to belong to the Justice Department? As the parent of ATF, in their infinite wisdom—because hey, we all know government agencies *never* screw up—they approved a plan to allow legally bought weapons to be transferred into the hands of criminals. And agents were forced to let it happen?"

"Pretty much."

Mitch slouched back, shaking his head and Caroline, she... she didn't know what to do. Or say. Thousands of illegal weapons had been unleashed on the general public. Who knew how many people were dead because of it? At least one person.

Tommy.

Kemp might be two.

Buzzing anger slashed at her, making her skin burn. Stay calm. She glanced down at her foot, tapped it one, two, three, four times. All she needed to do was get through this call and then she could spew.

"Okay," she said. "We need to find out who authorized this plan. Did it come from New Mexico ATF or Justice?"

"Why do we care?" Mitch asked. "Both organizations are responsible, aren't they? And we still don't know who actually shot Tommy."

Caroline met his eyes. "We'll find him and see justice done, I promise you. It starts with investigating who initiated this operation. I think Tommy is dead because of whatever he was doing on this taskforce. He may have been killed by whomever Lando turned that gun over to, but ATF allowed that gun to walk. We have to make sure ATF—and Justice—are held accountable, because in the end, it's not just about nailing the bastard who shot Tommy."

Mitch nodded. "We have to clear his name."

"And make sure this never happens again."

13

*C*aroline threw the camper door open and stepped out into the still oppressively hot night air. Needing to walk off some energy, that buzzing anger flick-flick-flicking at her from inside, she marched the length of the camper and turned back.

On her second lap, Mitch appeared in the doorway. "What's up?"

"I can't believe it. An agent is dead because ATF let a straw buyer turn over an assault weapon. Isn't this the thing we're fighting against? I mean, for God's sake! How the hell does ATF stand back and let thousands of weapons be turned over to criminals? Thugs? *Murderers*?" She waved her hands. "It's so stupid. And Donaldson let Tommy walk right into this snake pit."

"Because he's a dickweed, Caroline."

Oh, and here he went on the 'Donaldson' bender. Just what she needed. To get him started too. "Mitch! We all know he's a dickweed. The problem is, he's always been a dickweed that made sure not to put his agents in obvious danger. He's a lot of things, but he's FBI to his bones. I don't see him sacrificing the lives of his people."

Mitch shrugged. He was so pigheaded when it came to Donaldson that he refused to acknowledge her point. Fine. He didn't need to. What did it matter when Tommy was dead? A good agent and his superiors put the weapon that killed him into a murderer's hands.

Dear God.

She started pacing again. "We need to find out for sure who approved this operation. With all the secrecy, New Mexico ATF could be going rogue here."

"Don't tell me, we're making a list."

"Damned straight. Think about this. Who's the federal law enforcement officer in each state?"

Mitch shrugged. "The U.S. Attorney."

Caroline stopped walking and stared up at Mitch. "Who, in this case, is...?"

For three, maybe four seconds, Mitch stood staring out at the night, and Caroline waited. She knew him. Not just in a carnal way, but in all the ways that count when two people worked a dangerous job together. She'd learned his thought process, the way his mind ticked off ideas and filtered them. *Come on, Mitch, you've got this.*

In the darkness, with only the interior camper light illuminating him, she saw it, the recognition. That slight widening of his eyes before he snapped his fingers. *There we go.*

"Atkinson. Brother to..." he jiggled his fingers.

"Will Atkinson. The ATF agent who visited Marty. His brother is George, the U.S. Attorney for New Mexico."

"The question is, does brother number one, the brother responsible for prosecuting federal cases, the one who can intercept weapons illegally transferred via a straw buyer or are part of a gun trafficking scheme, know that brother number two was strong-arming gun shop owners to let the guns walk?"

Brice appeared behind Mitch and Mitch stepped off the landing. "So, what? Now we have to dig up dirt on a U.S. Attorney?"

Caroline moved around Mitch to Brice. "Is it possible the U.S. Attorney in New Mexico didn't know about this taskforce? ATF may be under Justice, but they don't report to the New Mexico U.S. Attorney. He could be in the dark about what his brother, the ATF agent, was doing."

"Seriously? You don't think one brother knew what the other was doing?"

Mitch shrugged. "Could happen."

Brice held up his phone. "Let's ask Ethan. He's so fired up, he'll get right on it."

Behind her, Mitch scraped his sneaker over the ground. "Before we get too deep into that, and discover this guy's in on it and then we're blown—let's check him out. Ethan'll know if he's a stand-up guy. If he is, maybe Brice and I can talk to him."

Caroline spun on him. "You're insane! The second you step into his office, he'll arrest you."

"I can talk to him though," Brice said. "Maybe I call him. Tell him I'm doing a follow-up post for my blog. See if he'll comment. On or off the record."

Caroline waved him off. "He won't comment. I can guarantee that."

"Yeah, but we may get a feel for what he knows. Or doesn't know."

"And," Mitch said, "we can put some heat on his brother."

The next morning, Mitch felt like he'd been run over. Twice. By a dump truck. He'd ended up sleeping on the camper floor instead of outside, but he might as well have slept on a bed of rocks. He'd tossed and turned, driven crazy by the ideas spinning in his head, and by the soft, sexy sounds Caroline made in her sleep. If only Brice hadn't interrupted their late-night swim.

At least there was coffee. Mitch washed his face in the lake and stared out at the water. The previous night's memories of Caroline naked on the shore made his cock twitch.

She was all business this morning, brushing her hair into a ponytail and making coffee while Brice went into town for food supplies. *Too damn perky.* Even with the perfect opportunity opening up for them, his guess would be she had no interest in picking up where they left off last night.

Nope. First thing on her list today was listening in when Brice called George Atkinson, the New Mexico U.S. Attorney. Mitch didn't know whether to hope the guy did or didn't know what his brother had been doing with ATF and the taskforce, but either way, he smelled a rat. A couple of them, in fact.

Tommy was killed with a gun the ATF let walk. No wonder there was a goddamn cover-up. And there was no freakin' way he was letting them label Tommy a traitor just so they could save their own asses.

He tamped down the pain and anger, locking them away. His stomach growled. First thing on *his* list? Breakfast. A full stomach would help him focus when Brice made his call. He wished he could be there to study the attorney's body language, but beggars—or in his case, fugitives—couldn't be choosers.

After that, Mitch wanted to go back and visit Maria. Even empty, his gut was never wrong, and since yesterday, it had been nagging at him about her. She knew more than she had let on. Good Cop and Bad Cop needed another go at her, especially now that they knew Jesse had been Tommy's informant. Had Jesse pulled the trigger? He'd bought the gun that killed Tommy, and then disappeared after Tommy's murder. Odds were, he was either responsible or dead. If he wasn't the one who set up Tommy, then someone, possibly whoever Jesse was buying for, had discovered Tommy was FBI and that Jesse was feeding him info. In that case, Jesse was either running for his life or had already met his Maker.

Both options sucked.

The sound of the truck returning made Mitch turn. Sure enough, Brice hopped out, arms filled with grocery sacks. He looked as tired and strung out as Mitch felt.

Neither man spoke as they headed into the camper and began unloading the groceries. Caroline moved with her normal energized efficiency, bumping into Mitch more than she avoided him, breaking out donuts and milk.

"No fruit?" she quizzed Brice. "What about yogurt?"

He gave her a tired look. "Really? That's what you're worried about this morning?"

She narrowed her eyes, and Mitch thought, *oh shit*, but she held her tongue, and made work of handing Mitch a napkin. She'd definitely requested fruit and yogurt when she'd handed over cash to help with the cost of the food. *She'll nail him later, just watch.*

But maybe she wouldn't. If Mitch had said that to her, she would have laid him out. Brice didn't have a history with her, and Caroline, for all her attitude was deep down a team player.

They ate in silence, then Caroline sat back and eyed Brice. "Eight o'clock. Ready to make that call?"

Brice googled the number, dialed and punched the speaker button. A receptionist answered and transferred Brice, not once but twice. He was put on hold. Finally, after explaining who he was and that he was trying to reach George Atkinson, he landed the man's voice mail.

Caroline sat next to Mitch on the bench seat, her left leg bouncing and whipping her nervous energy around like a downed power line. Unable to stand it, Mitch put a hand on her leg to stop its movement as Brice left a short message. Nothing too detailed, but Brice mentioned Will, which should snag the man's attention.

Then they waited.

And waited.

Caroline spent her time pacing outside, keeping the camper door open so she could hear the phone ring. Brice played a zombie game on his phone. Mitch kicked back, closed his eyes, and napped.

Bbrrring. The sound startled him out of a nightmare about Tommy and guns and dead bodies lining a sidewalk.

"It's him," Brice announced. Mitch and Caroline filed inside to their places at the table and Brice hit the call button. "Hello?"

A man's deep voice came from the speaker. "This is U.S. Attorney Atkinson. To whom am I speaking?"

"You can call me Hawkeye. Like I said in my message, I run the First Amendment Patriot blog where I recently exposed a government cover-up of the death of FBI Agent Thomas Nusco. Have you read it?"

The guy chuckled. "Yes, Mr. Hawkeye. I've read your accusations. Quite entertaining. I'm sure your conspiracy fans enjoy the propaganda."

A muscle in Brice's jaw jumped. Mitch was right there with him in the annoyed department. "Yeah, well, I'm doing a follow-up post," Brice said. "I've uncovered evidence that members of an interagency taskforce were told to look the other way, and gun shop owners were bullied into keeping their mouths shut regarding hundreds, if not thousands of weapons allowed to walk into the hands of criminals. One of my sources claims your brother was involved. Care to comment?"

There was a slight pause, not long enough for Mitch to tell whether the guy was forming a lie or not. "My brother is an ATF undercover operative, Mr. Hawkeye, and I'm the New Mexico U.S. Attorney. Yes, I have knowledge of the various operations that ATF, DEA, ICE, and Homeland have in motion in my state, but I don't hold my brother's hand while he's working. I can, however, assure you that I know nothing about these accusations or this so-called evidence you have. I strongly suggest you use care when posting such allegations on your blog."

"It's a free country," Brice said.

"It is that, but there are far more *real* patriots than false ones. You might step on toes with this type of nonsense."

Was he insinuating First Amendment Patriot was a joke? Seemed that way to Mitch. Must have to Caroline as well because that leg started its rapid motion again, *up-down-up-down-up-down.*

Brice, however, grinned, rolling his eyes like he'd heard it all before. "Do you know anything about the straw buying, Mr. Atkinson? Anything about the claims your brother, Will, was blackmailing gun shop owners to keep quiet about the straw purchases or lose their licenses?"

"No, sir, I do not, and if you'll excuse me, I have more important matters to attend to."

The line went dead.

Brice leaned forward and yelled at the phone. "It's Hawkeye. Just Hawkeye, you douchebag." He glanced up at Mitch and Caroline. "The guy has probably never read a Marvel Comic in his life."

Hawkeye was a comic book superhero that had recently had a resurgence in popularity thanks to the Avenger movies. " Apparently, not," Mitch snorted.

Caroline looked like she wasn't listening. She was off in Caroline's World, making her lists and analyzing every word good ol' George had uttered.

"Well?" Mitch said to her. "Is he lying? Trying to cover up for Will?"

Caroline shook her head. "Can't be sure. He didn't sound defensive so much as irritated. Like he's not worried, because the blog, in his mind, isn't credible. If the source isn't credible, neither is the information."

Brice pulled out his laptop. "I'm writing that follow-up post anyway. When we go back to town, I'll upload it to my blog and once again list my email. My conspiracy fans may love the 'propaganda'"—he made air quotes around the word—"but they're incredibly connected. Someone knows something here in New Mexico, mark my words."

Mitch touched Caroline's hand, drawing her attention. "We should go back to Maria's."

"I think so too. She could be in danger."

"She could be." He slid out from the table and offered her a hand up. "She could also be holding out on us about her brother."

"Oh, I'm sure of that." Caroline took his hand and stood. "Let me get my briefcase."

"Are you going to be Good Cop or Bad Cop this time?" he teased as they left the RV. Her ponytail swung from her confident walk to the truck.

She gave him a grin over her shoulder. "Maybe a little of both."

14

*I*n the blazing midday heat, Caroline plucked at the front of her blouse, pulling it from her sticky skin. Giving in to the heat, she'd ditched her suit jacket. Maintaining her FBI persona was crucial, but she'd rather not take a heat stroke during this freak October heat wave.

She climbed the brick steps to Maria's house, noted the broken edge she'd spotted on their prior trip and sidestepped it. Better not to sprain an ankle or blow out her knee while fumbling in a case she had no business fumbling in.

At the top of the steps, she waited for Mitch and Brice to reach the landing, then nodded. "Mitch, don't get crazy. Please. Let me handle this."

He offered up one of those maddening grins of his and Caroline knew without a doubt reining this man in would be impossible. But really, didn't the good girl in her, the obsessively controlled one who thrived on order and strategy, sort of love the uninhibited chaos Mitch created?

Unfortunately, yes.

She sighed and banged the cheap metal doorknocker. No answer. Caroline cocked her head and listened. Feet shuffling.

Just inside the door. "Maria, this is Special Agent Foster. We have information about Jesse. Please open the door."

Mitch waggled his eyebrows. *Chaos.*

A second later the door swung open and the petite brunette stood there, one hand on her hip. She wore hospital scrubs adorned with pink pigs and a scowl mean enough to frighten a hardened gangbanger.

"Hello, Maria."

"You people need to stop coming here."

Not likely. At least not until they located Jesse. "Maria, we have information about Jesse. Information you'll want to hear."

Maria huffed as if Caroline had saddled two hundred pounds on her. "Fine. I'll give you ten minutes. Come inside, though. I don't want any trouble, and in this neighborhood, someone will recognize you as law enforcement."

Caroline followed Maria into the house toward an over-stuffed blue sofa that looked relatively new in comparison to the scarred floors. Behind her, Mitch and Brice entered, then closed and locked the door.

Maria didn't invite them to sit. Caroline couldn't blame her. Whatever Jesse was into, straw buying might have been the least of it, and his sister obviously didn't want to suffer for his sins.

"What about Jesse?" Maria asked.

"Were you aware Jesse had a relationship with FBI Special Agent Tommy Nusco?"

Instantly, something in Maria's cheek twitched. Whether the reaction was due to Tommy's name or the fact that her brother had a relationship with law enforcement, Caroline couldn't know.

Not yet.

A cat meowed from somewhere near the back of the house and Caroline was grateful for the distraction in the otherwise silent room. "Maria?"

"I don't know what my brother does in his spare time."

Interesting. And also not the question asked.

"Maria," Mitch said, "we're not screwing around. You need to be straight with us and you need to do it quick."

The woman flinched and stepped back, literally, moving away from them. Terrific job alienating a potential witness. When Caroline got Mitch alone, she'd...she'd...she didn't know what she'd do, but it would be damned ugly.

For now, she skinned him with a hard stare that would hopefully remind him he'd agreed to let her handle this. In typical Mitch and his balls-to-the-wall fashion, he stared right back.

Fine.

She'd play.

"Mitch," she said, "why don't you two head out to the truck and follow-up on that lead from this morning? Leave us girls alone. Hmm?"

Mitch rolled his eyes.

She offered up a syrupy sweet smile. "Please."

He shifted his gaze to Maria, who retreated another step. Pretty soon she'd go right out the back door.

Finally, Sensible Mitch, the alter ego that showed up only in desperate situations, appeared and headed for the door. "Sure. Whatever you say."

The two men left and Maria locked the door behind them. "Thank you. His name is Mitch? He makes me nervous."

"He's harmless."

Unless you screw his brains out. Then, like the diehard shoppers at the mall, he's a crack house you never want to leave.

Caroline cleared her throat. "Maria, it's just us now. The guys are gone. I'm an FBI agent trying to figure out what happened to our friend, Tommy Nusco. He was a good man and he's dead. Not only from a gun your brother purchased, but now we find out your brother was Tommy's informant."

Maria stayed silent, not an ounce of surprise on her face. The cat meowed again. "I don't know anything about that."

Her gaze wandered to the stairs. *Upstairs.*

Prickles of unease poked at the back of her neck and Caroline angled sideways toward the stairs, looked up. Nothing. What was that about?

"No one is here," Maria said.

Maybe. Maybe not. Caroline rested her hand on the butt of her gun just in case. "I think you know something about Jesse being an informant and you're afraid to tell me. Why are you afraid?"

The woman dipped her head and closed her eyes. "Please," she said. "You have to leave. I just finished a fourteen hour shift and I'm tired. I need sleep. Desperately."

"Why are you afraid?"

"You need to go."

"Tell me why you're afraid."

Finally, Maria looked up. "Because someone was in my house while I was at work last night. You people showed up yesterday and someone came in my house last night. Okay?"

An intruder? Now they were getting somewhere. "Do you know who it was?"

"No."

"Did they break in?"

"The window in my bedroom has a screen missing. They came through there." She pointed at a floor plant by the base of the stairs. Some kind of cactus big enough to trip over. "Plus, there was dirt on the floor. Like someone knocked over the plant and tried to clean it up, but missed some dirt."

That would explain her distraction with the second floor. "Did you call 911?"

"In this neighborhood? Good luck. I called my neighbor and he helped me search the house. Whoever it was left, thank God. Nothing is missing."

"Are you sure your cat wasn't digging in the pot?"

"I've had that cat five years. She doesn't dig in my plants, and she's smart enough not to get near that cactus."

"Maybe it was Jesse?"

"He has a key, and if he'd been here, he'd have told me. He knows I'm nervous about living alone. He'd have left a note or something. Even if I'd be mad he came here, he wouldn't want me scared."

That sounded reasonable enough. "What were they after? Jewelry? Money? Drugs?"

Maria glared at her like she'd just bombed the block. "I don't do drugs." Then her gaze shot upstairs again.

"Sorry. I wasn't insinuating you did. Prescription drugs are all the rage right now and easy to steal."

"And because I work at the hospital, I have a lot of those lying around, right?" She walked to the door and held it open.

Dammit. Hoping to stall, Caroline stayed put. *So close to cracking her.* "We can help you."

"No," Maria said. "You really can't."

Caroline wandered to the door, but didn't step out. "If you're right and someone was in the house last night, I don't want to leave you alone. They could be dangerous. Is there somewhere you can go?"

"Sure. But if I go there, whatever trouble my brother is in will follow me and then the rest of my family is in danger."

That was probably a safe assumption. And one Caroline refused to ignore. If Maria's suspicion was correct and someone had searched her house, something worth finding might be here.

Time to kill two birds with one stone.

Mitch would wet his pants when she, supposedly the straight-laced one, suggested he search Maria's house while Caroline found her a safe place to rest.

"Maria, obviously you're exhausted. Let me take you somewhere safe so you can sleep."

"Are you crazy? I'm not going anywhere with you. Why should I trust you?"

"You have no reason to, other than I know what it feels like to be alone and scared and tired. Your fatigue might be influencing your decision so I'm offering to see you safely to a hotel where you can rest. You can drive your own car and I'll stay outside your room. Once you get some sleep, hopefully you'll reconsider and help us. If not, we'll leave you alone. End of it. All I'm asking is that you think about it."

"I can't afford a hotel."

They'd have to cover it for her, and Caroline couldn't use her credit cards. She also didn't want to burn through her cash in case they needed it. She'd be into Brice for a truckload when this was done. "We'll take care of that. What have you got to lose?"

"I can't leave my cat."

Some hotels accepted pets, right? "We'll figure out a place where you can bring him."

"*Her*." She motioned at the open door. "Tonight will be my first night off in fourteen days. First, I'm going to take a shower and clear my head. I'll think about your offer, but not until I've cleaned up and eaten."

Better than nothing. Caroline nodded. "I'll wait outside."

Mitch stood beside the truck cab while Brice sat in the driver's seat playing a game on his phone. The heat wave showed no signs of backing off and perspiration dotted Mitch's forehead. The more he wiped, the faster the sweat came back so he simply gave up.

Maria had opened the door a minute ago but Caroline

hadn't emerged yet. He craned his neck, trying to hear what Maria was saying without looking like he was eavesdropping.

Out of the corner of his eye, he saw the unmistakable black and white markings of a police car as the vehicle trolled the neighborhood. A glance in that direction and he saw the gold State badge emblem on the door.

Fuck.

The rack lights weren't on and the car appeared to be doing a simple drive-by. He ducked around to the passenger side and slid in. "Heat on our six," he said to Brice. "Keep your head down."

"Shit," Brice did as he was told and continued to stare down at his phone. "What do you want to do?"

More sweat ran down the back of Mitch's neck. Was this really a drive-by or had someone in the neighborhood tipped off the police? He slouched in the seat, wishing he had a baseball cap to hide his features. "Sit tight."

Taking off like a bat out of hell would only bring the cops running, and there was no way he would leave Caroline. If she noticed the car, she'd be smart to stay inside, even if the lights came on and cops brought the wrath of God down on him.

Just as the cruiser drew even with the truck, Caroline popped out of the house.

Ditto on the *fuck.*

She saw the car, hesitated a second, then looked over her shoulder at Maria, turning slightly so her sidearm was out of view from the street. She raised her hand and waved at the woman. "No rush. See you soon!"

Like they were best friends. Maria cocked her head, shook it like Caroline was a psych ward escapee, and shut the door.

Caroline pretended to be interested in the landscaping—if you could call sand with a few sprouts of grass landscaping—and kept heading for the truck.

The cruiser slowed but then continued down the street, braking at the stop sign.

"Time to go," Mitch said, sliding over so Caroline could get in.

She sat next to him. "We can't go."

"Did you not just see the state police drive by?"

"Maria's scared. Someone broke into her house last night. She claims she doesn't know who or why, and she *claims* nothing was missing, but I know she's lying about something. I just don't know what. I offered to take her to a motel so she can sleep. I'll keep watch on her from the parking lot just in case. Meanwhile, Mitch, you will love this—you and Brice can search her house."

She motioned at Brice's cell phone. "Give me that. I need to find a pet-friendly hotel."

Mitch was still in adrenaline overload. "Are you fucking kidding me? First of all, look at you, encouraging illegal activity when the police might be on my ass. And, hello...you're looking up pet-friendly hotels?"

"If the police were 'on your ass,'" she said, punching the screen, "they'd already have you in handcuffs. They were in the neighborhood, that's all. They probably drive through here on a regular schedule."

"Yeah, and not at night," Brice added.

"Here!" Caroline held up the phone. "Two miles away there's a motel with outside doors. Direct access to the room and they allow one small dog or a cat. Perfect."

Mitch controlled his pounding pulse by breathing slowly. In. Out. In. Out. "So where is she?"

Caroline made note of the motel's address on her note pad. "She's taking a shower and eating. She'll be out soon, I hope."

Caroline never said those words. She was always clear cut about everything. "You *hope*?"

A shrug and she studied the landscaping again. "She's thinking about it while she showers."

Perfect. He was stuck in a disgusting old truck during a heat wave while police circled the block and he was forced to sit tight while this gal took a cool, relaxing shower. Even getting laid turned into a bust. "It's like Christmas in hell," he mumbled.

Caroline shot him a look, her forehead creasing. "What?"

"Nothing." He used his shirt sleeve to wipe off the sweat trailing down his cheek. How could she look so unfazed by the heat and law enforcement being within a few feet of them? "Are you feeling all right?"

"Yes, why?"

"You're acting completely out of character."

A faint grin skipped across her lips. "I know. It's kind of... exciting. I feel like we're Bonnie and Clyde without the bank robbing."

His heart surged. He couldn't help it. Grabbing her by the back of the neck, he brought her face to his. "You're the sexiest woman I've ever met."

Brice made coughing noises. Caroline's grin turned into a real smile. "I know."

He kissed her then, hard and fast. There would never be another woman for him. Never.

He just prayed his Clyde to her Bonnie didn't take her down in a hail of bullets.

Maria made the right choice. At least Caroline thought so as they followed the woman's not-quite-ancient Toyota to the Desert Sand—how innovative—motel. Hopefully, Maria would get some sleep, clear the stress from her mind, and decide, yes, she would indeed cooperate before her brother wound up spending his life in a federal prison.

Or dead.

Brice swung into the motel's parking lot and parked in front of the office. Caroline sat forward so she could see Brice beyond Mitch who was still sitting in the middle. "I forgot to mention, you need to pay for the room."

He craned his head. "Say what? I just paid for our rooms."

"I know. I'm sorry. I can't use my credit or ATM cards. Donaldson could be monitoring them. And Mitch..." she glanced at him. "Well, no need to talk about that. You're the only option. I'll repay you. I promise."

Brice jerked the door handle. "Don't worry about it."

Dressed as he was in cargo shorts and a T-shirt, he looked like no one in particular. Just a guy needing a room. Exactly what they needed him to look like.

"So," Mitch said. "Wanna make out?"

Caroline snorted, but moved closer to the door lest he decided to hit her with one of those vagina-melting kisses again. And speaking of which. "What's with the lip-lock in front of Brice?"

"Uh, he caught us getting busy in a lake last night. Unless he's blind—and possibly deaf—he's aware of our personal relationship. If that's what the hell we're calling it. What *are* we calling it?"

O.M.G. Mitch Monroe talking relationships. "Let me borrow your phone. I need to check CNN."

"Why?"

"Because the world must be coming to an end if you're talking about a relationship."

"Hardy, har, Caroline. I'm being serious."

Seriously! Serious? She didn't want to even think about that, never mind discuss it. What they needed to discuss was how to figure this mess out and get home. Then they'd talk about a relationship. Or whatever it was. Not that she'd have minded having a conversation about their complicated history and potential future, but sitting in a truck, rushing it, was not happening. When they talked, they'd really talk. It might take hours, and if she had to tie him to a chair until they hashed out whatever this was they were doing, she'd be fine with that.

Hell, he'd probably be fine with it if it included tying him up. Instantly, her boobs started to tingle. Mitch, ropes, relationship. Oh, the things they'd do together.

Beside her, Mitch nudged her with his elbow. "You're thinking naughty thoughts again."

And silly him, thought he'd rattle her. *Try again, mister.* A minute passed with Mitch focused on her and Caroline focused on the back of Maria's car.

"Caroline, you can't ignore me."

Sure, I can.

"Oh, look. Here's Brice."

Thank you.

She turned and locked eyes with him just as Brice reached the front bumper of the truck. "Incredibly naughty. It involves ropes. Just so you know."

She gave him a full-teeth smile as Brice hopped into the truck.

"It's all good," he said.

Sure is.

"That's just mean, Caroline."

Caroline laughed. A pouting Mitch. Classic.

She took the key Brice handed her. Room 115. Perfect. First floor, probably at the end of the row since the room to her right was 101. "Thanks. Okay, here's the plan. I'll keep watch over Maria while you two head back to her place and see what's what. She's an eagle eye so don't mess anything up."

"Caroline," Mitch said, "you're crazy if you think I'm leaving you here alone."

"I'm crazy then because you have to. It's the middle of the day. You need to be in and out of Maria's place fast or risk getting seen by a nosey neighbor. If there are two of you, it'll take less time. One of you does the first floor, one does the second."

"No."

His chivalry was sweet, but incredibly annoying. "All I'm going to do is sit in Maria's car while she sleeps. She's just worked fourteen hours. She'll be out for a while. My gun and I will be fine. Besides, look how busy that main road is. Nobody would be dumb enough to try anything with all those witnesses."

Brice started the truck and eased out of the parking space to move down to room 115. "I hate to say it, Mitch, but she's right. We're losing time and the three of us sitting in this parking lot won't help."

Mitch grunted.

After parking, Caroline handed Brice the key back. "Would you mind hopping out a second and showing Maria the room? By the time you get back, we'll have a decision made."

Brice took the key. "You have five minutes. Then I don't give a shit, I'm going back to Maria's."

The second Brice hopped out, Mitch swung to face her. "I'm not leaving you."

Yes, he was. She flattened her hand against his chest and he glanced down. Then she crumpled his T-shirt in her fist. "Listen to me, Mitch Monroe. I get it. I love this alpha-caveman thing on you, but we have an opportunity here. I strongly believe Maria is hiding something in her house. Specifically, on the second floor, but I'm not sure why I think that. Something about the way she looked at the stairs when I was talking to her. Anyway, go find what she's hiding and maybe we'll get a lead on what happened to Tommy."

"I don't like it."

Sigh. Time to go to guns. "I have a question."

"Sure."

"Would you rather A) spend the rest of your life in prison, or B) come home to me every night and have me screw your brains out?"

He narrowed his eyes sensing her trick. "You know the answer to that, but it's not in the cards. Even if we figure out what happened to Kemp and Tommy, Donaldson still has that assault charge waiting for me. So humor me. I have to make sure nothing happens to you, and that when this investigation *does* end, you'll be okay, with or without me."

This guy, this one right here, who every once in a while stifled the smart-ass comments and turned serious and thoughtful and well, *loving,* was why she fell for Mitch Monroe.

She reached up, ran her hand down this warm cheek, the stubble of his beard lightly scraping the inside of her hand. She cupped it under his jaw and squeezed. "I'll be okay. Without you, I might not be happy, but I'll be okay. I'll be the Caroline I've been all these months while you were gone. I can survive that. I already have. Maybe I don't want to just survive, but I will."

"What do you want?"

"I want you to get back to living your life so we can see where we go. Finally. That's what I want. And I need you to go to Maria's and search for the evidence that can make that happen. Can you do that for me?"

Mitch grabbed her hand and smacked a kiss against her palm, letting his lips rest there for a second. For once, there was nothing sexual about it. No tongue darting over her hand or prolonged licking. Just a simple kiss filled with affection and Caroline's chest cracked. *Bam.* All the pent-up heartache and anger skipped away, leaving her with nothing but a fresh batch of watery, happy tears.

Mitch was back.

The truck door wrenched open and Brice hopped in. Caroline snapped her head to the window and wiped her drippy eyes. Silly girl.

Brice fired the engine. "Maria is locked in. Said she'd call me when she wakes up. Now, I'm going back to her place. Who's coming with me?"

15

*M*itch left Brice to search the first floor and he took the second. Caroline's instincts had always been spot on. If she had an inkling that Maria was hiding something on the second floor, he bet odds she was correct.

If only he knew what he was looking for.

Maria might not admit it, but she knew her brother was into some bad shit. Most likely she wasn't hiding anything per se, only covering her brother's ass.

The second floor had two bedrooms and a bath. Maria's room matched the flashy JLo look she'd worn the previous day. The bedspread was black and purple zebra stripes with sparkly beads. The nightstand held a lamp with a fur-trimmed shade.

He visually scanned the contents of the chest of drawers and nightstand, checked under the bed and between the mattresses. Nothing caught his eye or seemed out of place. She had a black desk with a laptop, but he left that alone initially to search the second bedroom.

That room was sparse and done in neutral desert shades... brown, drab green, and more ugly ass brown. Definitely gave off a masculine feel but if Jesse had been sleeping here, the guy had left little behind. A few shirts hung in the closet and two pairs of shoes sat on the floor. There was no dresser and nothing under the bed. The only items in the nightstand were a TV remote and a pack of condoms.

He was in the bathroom checking the medicine cabinet when he heard Brice's footsteps coming up the stairs at a fast pace. "Dude, we gotta roll."

Mitch met him in the hall. "What's up?"

"Ethan texted me. Something happened. He's freaked out but refuses to talk over the phone."

"Let me guess, another meeting."

Brice's eyes were lit with anticipation. "He said there's a skatepark near the mall. Two miles south. Said to meet him by the mural."

Mitch and Brice left the house empty-handed. Whatever Maria might be hiding was still safe. And Caroline wouldn't be happy.

The skate park was busy for a weekday and music blared from a large boom box one of the dozen teenagers had set up on a picnic table.

"Shouldn't these kids be in school?" Mitch asked as he and Brice searched for the mural, winding their way around the half pipes and other outcroppings and staying out of the way of the skateboarders. There were murals all over town done by local artists, but this one seemed to be hiding.

Brice pointed. "Maybe they're not in school anymore. There. The mural's on the other side of that concrete wall."

Mitch took his word for it, following him past a bench. Sure enough, they rounded the corner and there was the mural of a mermaid. A seriously hot mermaid with blonde hair and...*don't go there*. Going there only brought memories of Caroline naked on the lake shore.

Brice elbowed Mitch. "There's Ethan."

Yes. Ethan. Standing under a pinyon tree next to the mural of the hot mermaid. He wore a Diamondbacks ball cap and skipped pleasantries. "What the hell did you guys do?"

"Do?" Brice asked.

Ethan paced a few steps away, turned and came back. His eyes darted around, scanning the area. "The New Mexico U.S. Attorney ring any bells?"

Mitch exchanged a look with Brice. "What about him?"

"He called the ATF Special Agent in Charge this morning—my boss's boss—wanting to know who this 'blogger guy'"—he made air quotes—"was and how the hell did he get a report on a sealed case. Everyone from the taskforce, including the U.S. Attorney's brother still here in the New Mexico ATF office, got a tongue lashing. Oh, and a little bird inside the office told me the ATF SAC and my boss went behind closed doors for a while. Supposedly they were on the phone with an FBI Special Agent in Charge in Washington, asking him what he knew. That had to be Tommy's boss at the FBI."

"Shit," Mitch said. "Donaldson."

Ethan put his hands on his hips. "It gets better."

"What?" Brice was smiling like the shit about to rain down on them was the best thing that could happen. Mitch knew the feeling. They were kindred spirits in not caring how they shook things up, just that they did.

Ethan gave Brice an aggravated look. "This Donaldson? He jumped on a plane today to meet with my boss and the ATF SAC. All the higher-ups who put the taskforce together. Shit is going to hit the fan big time."

Both Ethan and Brice looked at Mitch. "He was probably planning to come here anyway. He knows Caroline is messing with this and that she accessed one of the databases from the hotel."

"What do we do?" Brice asked.

"The same thing we've been doing. Lay low, keep digging. We knew we'd ruffle some big feathers when we started this."

Ethan raised his hands in the air. "I'm out. I'd like to help you guys, but my ass is on the line here. I'm one of the only ATF guys left in this office who had any involvement, and mine was only finding Tommy's body. They have to know I'm the one feeding you information. I can't risk my career. I have a family."

Mitch reached out and shook his hand. "You've done enough. We appreciate it."

Brice and Ethan exchanged a handshake and a man-hug complete with slaps on the back before Mitch and Brice headed back to the truck.

"Where to now?" Brice asked, his tone sounding slightly defeated.

It was one thing to bring chaos down on your own head, another when the chaos started thinning the ranks.

Mitch watched a kid landing an Ollie. "We need another set of burn phones."

"I just bought the ones we have this morning."

"I know. Just in case. We'll switch 'em out. And I want to go back to Maria's and have a look at her laptop."

6:56.

Caroline checked her text for typos, then read it again. WHERE THE HELL ARE YOU BOYS?

No typos. Perfect. She punched the screen and sent the message off to Brice. They'd been gone almost five hours. Not that they hadn't checked in. They had. Once. Three-and-a-half hours ago to tell her Ethan wanted another meeting. Since then, radio silence.

So Caroline sat in Maria's sedan, continuously checking her surroundings while Maria's motel room door stayed perfectly, quietly...shut. Not a peep out of there. Caroline supposed, after a fourteen hour shift, the woman could still be sleeping. Five hours—in sleep time—wasn't that much.

Five hours sitting in a car doing nothing? That was a lot.

Still, as the sky darkened, and her bladder filled, Caroline wondered about the brilliance of talking Mitch into leaving her alone. Food she could live without for a few hours. A bathroom? Not so much.

Her phone whistled and she hit the little message envelope. ON OUR WAY. HAD TO MAKE A DETOUR FOR MORE PHONES. MITCH IS PARANOID AND WANTS TO SWITCH AGAIN. YOU OKAY?

Phones. Excellent. Paranoid or not, switching couldn't hurt. Considering Mitch had crushed the phone her father had given her.

I'M FINE. ALL QUIET. SEE YOU IN A FEW.

She set the phone down, shifted in her seat, and glanced out the driver's side window to the main road. Rush hour traffic had trickled to a car every ten seconds, but headlights were steady and the road well lit.

The parking lot on the other hand, was in desperate need of ten or fifty more street lamps. Hadn't the owners ever heard of parking lot safety?

She lifted one hip, slid her sidearm from her holster, and set it on the console for easier access.

Just.

In.

Case.

Pressure in her lower belly made her wince. "Watch that door, Caroline," she muttered. "Forget your bladder."

And hunger. Forget the hunger.

She shot Brice a second text—BRING FOOD—and tossed the phone on the passenger seat.

It would delay them a few minutes, but her body was most definitely crashing. The second they got here, she'd bolt into the office and use the restroom. Then she'd eat. Mitch had better remember to super-size her order.

He wouldn't forget. Not after all the time he'd spent harassing her about her ability to pack away food and still stay at a healthy weight. What could she say? Tapeworm?

Headlights flashed in the rearview. Couldn't be them. Not that fast. She set her hand over the gun, ready to arm herself if necessary. She kept her eyes glued to the mirror, waiting. The car swung left out of the parking space in the row behind and exited the lot. Caroline let out a small breath. So, maybe she was a little edgy.

Her phone whistled and she leaned over to reach for it.

Smash.

Broken glass rained down on her, tiny flying knives slicing across her bare forearms where she'd rolled up her sleeves then dropping into her lap. Caroline gasped, the horror and shock paralyzing her for a few seconds until a hand—a man's hand—reached in from the driver's side window.

Fight.

Trapped in the seat by the console, Caroline jerked sideways and smacked, connecting with bare skin. *Gun.* Console. She reached for her weapon, but the man's hand came at her again and she lurched sideways, knocking the gun with her elbow to the floor.

Son of a bitch.

Plan B. *Door.* If she could shove the door open, she'd buy time and maybe get a look at her attacker. She grasped the door handle and yanked. Nothing. Locked.

That relentless hand came at her again and she smacked at it, shoving her attacker away. Next time she'd bite. Or scratch. Whatever it took. She craned sideways hoping for a look at her assailant over the door frame. No chance. Too tall.

"Relax, bitch," the man said.

"Screw you."

A second man laughed.

No, no, no. A wicked hissing filled her head—*focus*—and she sucked in air because no, absolutely not. She would not die in a crappy motel parking lot for a crappy reason she didn't fully understand. *I'm in trouble.* With her training, she might be able to fight off one man. Two? Gotta try. She hit the lock button, yanked the handle, and threw her weight into the door.

Barely any movement. Not with two men blocking the other side.

Get a look at them. She leaned left, looked up, but the only thing she saw against a starry night sky was the giant fist coming at her.

Boom!

Caroline's world went fuzzy. No pain. Just...fuzz. Her vision floated, every colorless edge suddenly vibrant and flexing and she moaned a little.

The door opened and she sagged left. *No.* It couldn't end this way. *Get up.* As much as her mind willed it, her body gave in and dipped left again. One of the men caught her and the second man laughed again as her head looped and looped and looped and noise from outside, cars and birds and voices, mingled into a pot-luck of sounds all coming together and forming nothing but *rowwwr, rowwwr, rowwwr* over and over again. She gave her head a small shake.

The pot-luck cleared for a second.

"Hey!" another male voice shouted. "Police are on the way."

Police.

"Shit," one of her attackers said.

"Leave her. No time."

Something flashed. A light? Or did she make that up? *Don't know.*

Didn't matter. Again she lifted her head, but it lolled forward, hanging there. Dead weight. She closed her eyes. A nap. That's what she needed.

No sleeping.

Yelling startled her and she opened her eyes, followed the sound, her vision blurry. The clerk from the office ran toward the car, his longish blond hair flying behind him. He'd saved her.

From what?

No telling, but later, she'd thank him. That's what she'd do.

Caroline sighed. Just a little nap.

And then, finally, darkness came.

16

"*M*aria? Can you hear me? Come on, Maria. Talk to me."

Something poked Caroline's cheek. *What the hell is that?* She moved her head sideways and pain ripped through her jaw, lashing at the bones in her face. Dear God, that hurt.

"Maria? Wake up, Maria."

Female voice. *Where am I?*

"Maria?"

"Not. Maria," Caroline said.

Something touched her eyelid and—yow—sudden brightness blinded her.

"Cut that out," she mumbled, smacking at the offending light.

"Welcome back. My name is Hillary. I'm going to check you out. Okay? Do you remember what happened?"

"Oh, hey," a man said. "She's not Maria. She's Caroline Foster and she's FBI. Just found her badge in her briefcase."

In a rush, the fog in Caroline's head cleared and she came fully awake, her eyes darting left and right. Where was she? *Maria.*

Directly above her a blonde woman stared down. "Hi," she said. "I'm Hillary. We're going to get you fixed up."

Fuck hi. Caroline lurched up, swung her head left and right and, *holy crap,* agonizing stabs shot through the side of her face and she let out a gasp.

Motel parking lot.

It was fully dark now, and for the first time Caroline and her aching head were thankful for the bad lighting.

"No way," Hillary said. "You need to stay down. We're about to load you into a bus and run you to the hospital. Do you remember what happened?"

She shifted her eyes right and beside the gurney stood a uniformed cop holding her briefcase. Cops.

"Caroline? Tell me what happened."

God, the left side of her face was screaming. Like an ax hacking at bone one swing at a time. Over and over and over. Her vision blurred again. "Assholes. Two of them. One punched me. No hospital."

She rolled sideways and the cop whooshed in, helping Hillary shove Caroline down.

"Caroline!"

Mitch's voice. *No. Stay away. Cops.*

"Whoa, buddy," the cop said. "Who're you?"

Don't tell him.

"She's with me. What happened?"

Run, Mitch.

But there he was, looming over her, out of breath as if he'd run hard for miles and she lifted her hand, grasping for him. He latched on and squeezed.

"Sir," Hillary said, "you need to back away."

The gurney moved and then, clunk, it dropped, her stomach going with it. "Hillary, I'm sure you're a nice person, but do that again and I'll arrest you for assaulting a federal agent."

Hillary smiled. "Well, at least you still have a sense of humor. Sorry, Agent Foster."

"I'm riding with her," Mitch said.

"You can meet her there," the cop said. "Meantime, I need some information from you."

Listen to him, Mitch. Her eyes locked with Mitch's. *Please.* "It's okay. I'm okay."

Mitch focused on her for a solid minute—*please*—then turned back to the cop. "Absolutely. Whatever I can do to help."

Charming Mitch. The guy nodded and headed for the motel clerk who was giving the play-by-play to onlookers. Brice made some kind of hand motion at Mitch and he started backing up, watching the cop and then scanning the area as if memorizing the faces of everyone standing around.

"What hospital?" Mitch asked as Hillary locked the gurney in place.

"St. Luke's."

"Caroline, I'll follow right behind the ambulance."

Stupid man. She waved one hand. "Stay here. I'm fine."

The bus doors banged shut and Caroline winced at the movement and abrasive sound. Had Mitch heard her? He must have. They needed to stay with Maria. She was the important one. They knew that. They knew they needed to protect their witness.

She had no doubt.

Stay here? Was she delusional? Fuck staying here. Mitch swung away from the cop who had taken a brief statement and seemed satisfied Mitch hadn't seen a thing. Mitch had lied about his name and worked at keeping his face in shadows while he'd schmoozed the nice police officer. "Brice?"

"Yo." Brice had hung back and eyed the cop now a few feet

away. He hustled to Mitch and handed him the truck keys. "Go. I'll take care of Maria and move her. We'll meet up later."

Mitch hung his head for a second, for just a goddamned second, and inhaled. The sight of Caroline on that stretcher, her cheek red and swelling, made his chest lock up.

"My man," Brice said, not using Mitch's name, which was smart with all the people filing around. "Keep it together, okay?"

He was trying. Dammit, he was trying. He wanted to punch something. Someone. Really tear that fucker up. Who had done this and why? Once again, guilt ate a hole in his stomach. This was his fault. He hadn't wanted to leave Caroline alone. Hadn't wanted to get her involved in this goatfuck in the first place.

Liar. You always wanted her in your life, one way or another.

He had to get his shit together and pronto. Stuff all the feelings and worthless emotions into a deep, dark hole. Raising his head, he gripped the truck keys, feeling them bite into his palm. "Go to ground, Brice. We don't know who or what was behind this. Could have been a random attack, but we've pushed buttons in the past two days, and I don't believe in coincidences. We've stirred the hornet's nest and now we're going to see who comes out. Keep your eyes open and watch your six."

"Gotcha." Brice cocked his chin at the truck. "You do the same. Take care of your gal and watch your back."

Mitch was tired of watching his back. Tired of running. His first rule of survival was to stay away from the police and look what he'd done the moment he saw Caroline...ran right into the fray. *Stupid, careless...*

Caroline. He'd do anything for her.

He jumped in the truck and wheeled out of the parking lot, cursing himself. Some fugitive he was.

But then, you've always been a sucker for a pretty woman, just like Tommy. Not any woman, though. Only Caroline.

Pretty woman. An image of JLo Junior flashed through his mind. No. No way. Maria couldn't possibly be...

Now who's delusional?

It had been one long, fucking day. His mind was a mess. His heart too. No wonder he was having errant thoughts.

Get to Caroline.

"Okay, Agent Foster," the ER doc said, "we're sending you up for an x-ray."

An x-ray? Based on the noise level in the hallway, the place sounded packed. She'd be here all night and she didn't have all night to waste. Now that she'd gotten a dose of that handy-dandy pain medication, she was good to go. Ready to roll out of this bed, away from this stuffy, antiseptic, dead germs smelling place, find Brice and Mitch, and check on Maria. Hopefully, they stayed with her.

Both men were smart enough to know that.

The ugly striped curtain separating her bay from the hallway flew open and in stepped Mitch. One of the two men who should have been smart enough to stay with their witness.

Caroline swung her hand in the air. "Oh, my God. Please tell me Brice stayed behind."

"Relax," Mitch shot. "It's fine."

The doctor extended his hand. "Doctor Winston. You are?"

"A friend. We're traveling together. How is she?"

"She took a significant blow to her left cheek. I'm sending her for an x-ray."

Yada, yada. Whatever. The doctor made notes on her chart, told them he'd return when he got results and whooshed out. Mitch waited until the doc cleared and whipped the curtain closed again.

And suddenly—maybe it was the painkillers—her body

collapsed. Every tense muscle, like a fist uncurling, released as she watched Mitch move toward the bed. Toward her.

She lifted her hand, reaching for him like some weak-kneed high-schooler begging for his attention. For once, she didn't care. Not when he reached for her. Not when he closed his fingers around hers. And definitely not when he kissed their conjoined hands.

The moment drifted between them, only the noise from the hallway filling the space and Caroline blinked a couple of times.

He spotted it and knowing she'd hate that he'd seen the weakness in her, he released her hand, set it back on the bed and patted it. No pity. *Thank you.* And, dammit, she loved him.

He bent to examine her cheek. "Holy shit, Caroline. That fucker popped you good. Did you get a look at him?"

"No. There were two of them though. Both men. The one guy had huge hands. Enormous hands, Mitch. Like a pile driver. It happened so quick I couldn't get a look out the window."

"You think they were after you or Maria?"

"I'm not sure. They didn't say anything. Other than 'leave her' when the clerk came running out. But forget that. What did you find at Maria's?"

"Nothing."

Really? That was his response? They'd been gone five hours and had nothing? "Well damn."

Mitch shrugged. "There's more bad news."

Well, this would be good...considering the mess they were already in. "Lay it on me."

"Ethan's SAC went ape-shit after the U.S. Attorney called him complaining about Brice poking around."

"Oh no."

"Yeah. Ethan's one of the only guys left in that office that even knew Tommy and he's scared."

She knew where this was going. Ethan had a family to protect. He wouldn't want to be caught up in this fiasco. She couldn't blame him. *She* didn't want to be caught up in it.

"There's an upside." He tilted his hand back and forth. "Eh, an upside and another downside."

If Mitch was trying to make her feel better he was doing a crappy job. "Mitch?"

"Yeah?"

"You're driving me crazy."

"Ethan also said the big shots involved with the taskforce called a meeting. He suspects the shit's about to hit the fan."

A meeting. Considering the taskforce was housed in New Mexico, she made the assumption the meeting would be held here. But Tommy was still an FBI agent, basically on loan to Operation Bulletproof.

And Donaldson was his SAC. Which meant...

She closed her eyes and breathed in. The slight movement sent hot pain ricocheting through the left side of her face. *Please don't let it be fractured.* Maybe she needed a fresh cocktail of drugs.

The pain eased to a dull throb and she opened her eyes. "Is Donaldson coming?"

"He's already here. At least I'm guessing. Ethan said he jumped on a plane this afternoon. If he's not here, he will be soon." Mitch stepped closer, ran a hand down the good side of her face. "He won't find us. You haven't used your credit cards and Brice moved Maria. We'll meet up with them once you're done here, and hopefully, she'll talk to us."

Caroline threw back the sheet and sat up. "Forget the x-ray."

Mitch held her in place. "Nuh-uh. Medical complications won't help us. Get the x-ray and we disappear again."

"Mitch—"

"No, Caroline. You're getting the x-ray." Before she could

argue, he spun toward the curtain separating the room from the outer hallway. "I'll see what the wait time is."

It better not be long. She'd give them twenty minutes. That's right. If someone didn't wheel her up for the test in twenty minutes, Mitch or no Mitch, she was gone.

The curtain parted again and she looked up, ready to let Mitch know exactly what her plan was and—*oh crap*. If she had any spit left in her dry mouth it just evaporated. *Cocktail, please!*

An extremely pissed off looking Donaldson, his face redder than she'd ever seen, stood in the doorway.

"Foster," he said, "what the hell do you think you're doing?"

17

Two things shot through Caroline's mind. Well, two things after the *shit-shit-shit* stream that lasted a full thirty seconds. The first involved Mitch and whether or not Donaldson had spotted him. Probably not. Otherwise, Donaldson would have grabbed him or at least started hollering. And knowing Mitch, he'd have hollered back and security would have come running and then the police. All resulting in Mitch in handcuffs.

Caroline rolled her bottom lip out. Clearly, Donaldson hadn't spotted him.

The second, more obvious question was how the heck did Donaldson know she was here?

She stared up at her boss, every word stuck in her throat like a giant piece of steak she couldn't force down. She swallowed once, twice, three times and croaked a "Sir?"

He grabbed the cheap metal chair next to the bed, dragged it over, hitched his ugly brown suit pants and sat. For added effect, he shot his cuffs. "You did a decent job of laying low. Except I received a courtesy call from the PD telling me one of my agents got the stuffing beat out of her. Now, you tell me exactly what you've been up to on this Tommy Nusco thing and then I'll decide if I fire your ass."

"Sir, please."

"Start talking, Foster. I've got a meeting first thing tomorrow morning to discuss how a sealed document pertaining to the death of one of my agents got leaked to a blog. And then I get here and find you."

"Sir—"

Donaldson raised his hand, his eyes hard and mean, a snake about to strike. "Fuck the *Sir* crap. The only thing I want to hear from you is you didn't leak classified documents. Tell me that, and maybe I can help you."

She couldn't tell him that. Not even close. Sure, she could lie. But she wouldn't. If she got fired, so be it, at least she'd go down knowing she tried to clear Tommy's name.

And Mitch's.

"Sir, something is screwy here."

Donaldson jumped out of his chair, heaving his weight like it took every ounce of strength. Uh. Oh.

"I asked you for one goddamned thing!"

Caroline flinched and he paced to the wall, turned back to her, his face an odd shade of reddish purple she'd seen one other time. Of course, that time involved Mitch as well.

He pressed his palm into his forehead, took a deep breath, then dropped it. "Why do I think Mitch Monroe is behind this?"

Motherfucker.

Mitch pulled up short on the other side of the curtain, listening to the voice of the man he hated. He didn't just hate Donaldson, he despised him with a fury that would devour a continent.

Rage filled him, sparking every nerve and making his fingers twitch. *Stay cool.*

Donaldson.

The man who'd let a serial killer murder innocent women in order to keep his political friends in Washington from getting their reputations tarnished. The man who'd ruined his and Grey's careers.

You did that all on your own.

No matter what Caroline believed about Donaldson being a standup guy when it came to his agents, Mitch knew the FBI SAC would screw his own mother if it meant rising up the ranks of the Bureau. He was never focused on seeing justice done, only on furthering his career.

And now he was here, threatening Caroline. Every one of Mitch's protective instincts—already on overload—went Code Red. It would be stupid to go in there. Stupid to confront the one man who wanted his head on a platter. The man who'd put a target on his back in the first place because he hated the fact Mitch had been right all along.

You knew he was coming. Deep down, you've been prepping for this confrontation all along.

Like he had in the parking lot after the ambulance pulled out, Mitch hung his head for a moment, closed his eyes and breathed.

Stay cool. For Caroline.

Because in the end, this wasn't about him. It was about Tommy and Kemp.

And Caroline.

What was the right move here? Turn on his heel and save his ass so he could clear his name and Tommy's? Or go toe-to-toe with his ex-boss and end up in prison where he could help no one, least of all Caroline?

"Well?" Donaldson was saying to Caroline. Mitch could feel

the anger vibrating off him through the curtain. *"Is Monroe behind all of this?"*

Time to face the music.

Mitch gripped the curtain, reaching deep for a calm he didn't feel. He couldn't—wouldn't—let Donaldson or Caroline see anything in his body language but pure confidence and resolve, no matter how bad his gut cramped.

He shoved back the flimsy curtain, and against his better judgment, stepped into the room. "Leave her alone."

Donaldson stood at the end of the bed, his face mottled and the knuckles of his hands white from the tight grip he held on the footboard. His head whipped around and his watery eyes glared at Mitch. "I knew it." He let go of the footboard and puffed out his chest. "You piece of shit."

Donaldson had made him lose his temper once. Mitch swore to himself he'd never let the cocksucker do it again. Shoving his hands in his pockets so he wouldn't reach out and strangle the SAC, he rocked back on his heels and nodded at Caroline to let her know it was all right. "Agent Foster has been through a traumatic event. How about you and I step outside for this discussion?"

Caroline's face was white as the sheet covering her body. Her voice was low, full of warning. "Mitch...?"

"It's all right." He kept his own voice light and easy. Caroline usually thought the worst of him and his knee-jerk reactions. This time, he wanted her to see that he could keep a handle on his temper. "Agent Donaldson and I have a lot to talk about, don't we, Harold?"

Donaldson's glare turned sharper. He took a step in Mitch's direction, putting his chest in Mitch's personal space. "I ought to arrest you, right here, right now."

Intimidation? Really? *Stupid SOB.* "Yes, you should. Agent Foster had nothing to do with the information about Tommy's taskforce, his murder, or the cover up being leaked. It was all me. I hacked into the case file, forced Agent Foster to use her password to run a trace on a gun, and leaked the information to the blogger. I take full responsibility."

Donaldson took another step closer, putting his face in front of Mitch's. His stomach brushed against Mitch's belt. "That's bullshit."

Caroline echoed the sentiment. "I wasn't coerced. I volunteered."

Damn woman. Couldn't she let him be the hero just once? He held up his hands, showing Donaldson his wrists. "Cuff me. Lead me out of here. I'm all yours."

"Damn it, Mitch!" Caroline pushed into a sitting position. "I will not let you take the fall for this."

He pinned her with a look over Donaldson's shoulder. *Just let me get him out of the building...*

And then Donaldson pulled the trigger he knew would set Mitch off. "You're a selfish, self-centered jackass who's never cared for anyone but yourself."

Donaldson chest bumped him as he spoke to Caroline while keeping his eyes glued to Mitch's. "He burned you again, Foster. You're busy trying to get his attention and didn't see he was using you. You're worthless to the Bureau, and once I'm done lighting Mitch up, I'm going to burn you. You'll be lucky to find a job as a checkout girl at Wal-Mart."

Burn her? Mitch's resolve to stay calm disintegrated. Donaldson wasn't only threatening to end Caroline's career with the FBI, he was planning on hanging her out to dry so she never got a job with another government agency. "Do whatever you want to me, but leave her out of this."

Donaldson chest bumped him again. In his younger days, the SAC had been a tank. "Try to stop me."

Mitch absorbed the chest bump. Took a breath. *Do not hit him. That's what he wants.*

Oh, no. He wasn't going to lay-out the arrogant SOB. Not

again. But backing down wasn't in his DNA, and he needed to prove to Caroline he could handle this, not blow his stack.

Using two fingers, Mitch shoved them into Donaldson's chest and pushed his ex-boss back a step. "I've been on the run because of you for nearly a year." Another step. "You really want to throw down that kind of challenge? Because I'm sure you know what happens when you corner a wild animal."

Another push and he had the man backing up another step. Donaldson's legs hit the edge of Caroline's bed. Through the cold rage pounding in his head, Mitch heard her talking to him, telling him to stop it and calm down.

He *was* calm. Calmer than he'd been in a long time. He poked his fingers into Donaldson's chest again. "You can have me, but you leave her out of this. Tommy wouldn't want her to take the fall. There's a cover-up surrounding his murder, and regardless of what she says, I *did* coerce her. I couldn't do the digging, get the information I needed, because every law enforcement agency in the land is after me. I needed her and I knew if I kept asking questions, she'd have to find the answers."

"I was not coerced!" Caroline yelled.

Mitch turned on her. I can't let you take the fall for me. I can't lose you again. "Shut up, Caroline."

"There is no cover-up," Donaldson said. "Tommy went rogue."

"My ass," Mitch said. "He was one of the best damned agents in the field, and you know it. You're trying to cover your ass, like the rest of the higher-ups who let those guns walk. You helped put the gun that killed Tommy into a murderer's hands and now you're going down. I don't give a shit how long it takes. Every one of you dickweeds will be dealt with."

"Mitch!" Caroline hissed. "Knock it off."

"No, Caroline. A good man is dead over politics. And that, I can't stand."

That must have stung, because Donaldson stood silently,

absorbing the words. That alone was more fucking bizarre than a tap dancing elephant. Typically, the SAC volleyed back, yelling just as loud if not louder because—yeah—in his mind he was right. All day long.

Not this time, asshole.

Caroline extended her hand and wiggled her fingers. Mitch stepped away from Donaldson, taking a second to regain his composure. He grabbed hold of Caroline's hand and she pulled him in. "I want you to go outside."

"No."

"Then stand in the damned corner while I talk to my boss."

He stared down at her, huffing a little. She was putting him into adult time-out. What a kick in the teeth that was.

She squeezed his hand. "Please. For me?"

Ha. For her. She knew how to play him. But what the hell, he'd give her this. She always was better at reading people.

But if Donaldson makes one more threat...

His resolve returned. He wandered to the window and stared out over the parking lot where street lamps lit the place like a runway. From the corner of his eye, he saw Donaldson drop into the chair next to the bed, his shoulders drooping forward. *What the hell?*

"I didn't know," Donaldson said.

"Bullshit!" Mitch turned, ready to go at him again.

Caroline pointed a damning finger at him. "Don't make me throw you out of here."

That shut his mouth. Who the hell's side was she on? "I'm not leaving until Donaldson agrees to leave you out of this."

"Look, Monroe," the SAC said, "we may despise each other, but I don't deliberately put my agents in harm's way. My decisions aren't always popular, but I don't sacrifice my people."

Mitch huffed again and turned back to the window. *Cocksucker.*

"Sir," Caroline said, "I don't know what all we're into here, but it's not good. Thousands of guns have walked and ATF supervisors knew it was happening. They told Tommy and the other taskforce agents to stand down."

"Caroline," Mitch warned, but she held up her hand to silence him.

"How'd you get that file?" Donaldson asked. "I don't even have access to it."

Mitch glanced back.

Caroline's face went innocent. "What file, sir?"

Good girl.

"Fine," Donaldson said. "Don't admit it. Probably better that way. The less I know for tomorrow's meeting, the better." He stood. "A little advice, Foster. Come back to D.C., and fast. Whatever can of worms you've ripped open has snakes in it. You think these boys hauled my ass out here for nothing? There's a reason they wanted to meet in person. Hell, I wouldn't be surprised if they checked me for a goddamned wire. I never did trust that son of a bitch Atkinson. He and his *U.S. Attorney* brother are both assholes."

Donaldson eyeballed Mitch for a second. "You think *I* play politics? That bastard would prostitute his own mother."

He went back to Caroline. "I'm going to that meeting tomorrow. If I don't like what I hear, I'll look into these allegations of yours. But if they show me proof Tommy was rogue, you're gonna have problems." He turned to Mitch. "And I'll take you to prison myself. I'll hunt you down like the dog you are and put you in jail."

Mitch laughed and held out his wrists again. "Right here, pal."

Donaldson snorted. "That's the problem with you, Monroe. You don't think long-term. I could arrest you right now if I wanted. My problem is, as with your friend Justice Greystone on The Lion case, I might need you. You being in jail doesn't help me. For now, I'm keeping my options open until after this meeting tomorrow."

Caroline rested her aching head back on the pillow and blew out a breath. Once again, Mitch's spontaneous actions had almost cost her. That alone should have been enough to send him on his way. Tell him she never wanted to see him again. Get her life back on track. Even if being on track meant being lonely, she'd live with it. Lonely versus chaos, when it came to her career, was the safer bet.

And she'd always been the safer bet girl.

Except when it came to Mitch.

"Caroline—"

She held up her hand. "Listen to me. You have to stop this."

"What?"

"You're like a Molotov cocktail. Someone lights you up and you go boom. I can't take it, Mitch. I love your determination, your single-minded can-do attitude when it comes to people you care about, but you get reckless when your emotions are involved. When you get emotional, you swing first, think later. I can't do it. You're my partner in this and I need to trust you. When you pull this caveman routine, I can't trust you."

"Hey, I thought I was doing pretty damned good controlling myself. He was threatening you. You think I'm gonna stand in the hall while that happens? You know better. "

Oh, she knew. "I'd hoped you would have thought ahead. Donaldson could have arrested you and then where would I have been?"

Mitch huffed. "He wouldn't have done that. He said it himself. He might need me. I knew that from what happened with Grey. I had it under control."

"But I didn't know that, did I? You never discussed it with me."

She wanted to add *just like last time*, but based on Mitch's narrowed eyes and pinched mouth, she guessed she'd hit her mark. Still, a little piece of her broke away. Taming Mitch Monroe shouldn't have to bring him pain. Knowledge, yes. Pain? No. She didn't want that.

Fix this. "Before we have a blow-out here, all I'm trying to do is make you understand. You've been alone and on the run for a long time. You're used to working solo. Right now, we're partners. What happens to you, happens to me. And to Brice. Please, work *with* me. Control your emotions and work with me. I'll never hurt you or betray you. You have to know that."

"I do know that. I just..." He circled one hand, then dropped it, letting it flop to his side. "I don't want to be responsible for you losing your career. I don't care what happens to me. You're a different story."

"I'm a big girl. I willingly joined you on this. My career is not your responsibility. That's on me. But if we're going to help each other, we need to communicate. You can't just decide how it's going to be and jump in."

An orderly cruised in with a wheelchair. "Hey, folks." He grabbed her chart, then checked her wristband. "Okay, Caroline Foster, your ride is here. Sir, I'll have her back as soon as they're done. Might be thirty minutes or so."

"I'll be here." He reached his hand to Caroline to help her out of the bed. "I'll be waiting for you. From now on, I'll always wait for you. Whatever it is."

Like a magic password to her heart, the words released a rush of...something. Relief? Hope? Fear? Maybe all of it. Before that moment, she hadn't realized how long she'd waited to hear that. Years probably. She just hadn't known it. For every man who'd ever taken her on a date or even managed a second or a third, none of them did this to her.

None had given her the password.

She squeezed his hand, blinked a few times to chase some ridiculous moisture away. "I know," she said. "And I love you for it."

18

---

*A*fter the ER doc declared her face sufficiently banged up but unbroken and wrote her a prescription for pain meds, Caroline considered this hospital detour complete.

Back to work.

Mitch opened the passenger door of the beat-up truck and offered a hand to help her out. True to his word, he'd waited for her to return from x-ray and discussed his plan with her. Haza. Baby steps were sometimes monumental. The plan included driving all over town to ditch any possible tails and then meet up with Brice—and Maria—at yet another crummy motel.

As with the last motel parking lot, The Raceway offered poor lighting, outside entries to all the rooms, and allowed pets.

While Brice unlocked the motel room door, Caroline rubbed her eyes. Almost midnight. This day felt like a month. She needed sleep. And a shower. As in now. The painkillers overrunning her system only added to her fatigue.

But sleep and the shower would wait. Apparently, Caroline getting accosted nudged Maria to admit she had information regarding their case. As soon as they got that information, Caroline would sleep. Long and hard.

Slumber would clear her mind, bring her sluggish thinking back to its normal snapping pace just in time for Donaldson to meet with the ATF supervisors.

Caroline stepped into the motel room where pukish Berber carpet gave the whole place a depressed feel. Add to that the floral bedspread featuring every color known to man and— wow—the place needed an overhaul.

"What year is it?" Mitch asked.

"It's ugly," Caroline shot, "but it's not a time warp."

"Thank you. I expected my grandmother to walk out of the bathroom wearing cold cream."

Brice snorted. "Hey, you want the Ritz, you pay for it."

"It's fine," Maria said. "I shared a double bed with four sisters until I was sixteen. This is luxury."

Mitch pointed to one of the two vinyl chairs at the small veneer table. "Sit, Caroline."

Gladly.

Maria took the other chair and Mitch parked on the low dresser. Brice glanced around, but opted to stand rather than sit on the bed.

"What's up, Maria?"

Mitch, Mr. Compassionate. Caroline sighed, but couldn't summon the energy to shoot Mitch one of her *don't-be-an-inconsiderate-dumbass* looks.

Apparently, her sigh conveyed the same message. He held up his arms. "Oh, excuse me. Let me rephrase. Maria, how can we be of service?"

That made Caroline laugh. What a smartass. If she didn't shoot him first, she'd love him forever. Mitch grinned at her and waggled his eyebrows.

"Swear to God," she said, "you're begging to get shot."

Maria hunched her shoulders. "You people are cray-cray."

"I'm sorry," Caroline said. "Long day."

And I need a damned shower and clean clothes and a soft place to rest. To go home to her normal life. Whatever that was before finding out the government wanted to sacrifice a good agent. And if they'd do it to Tommy, they'd do it to her. At some point, she'd have to reconcile that. If she even could. Prior to this, she'd been a Bureau Woman through and through. Sure there were some bad seeds, but she had the vision, the dream, the silly ideals that came with wanting to make a difference.

Maria clutched at her purse, working her fingers over the worn leather strap. Her gaze moved from Brice to Caroline to Mitch, where she lingered a few seconds, studying him as if some recognition sparked. Odd.

But Mitch had that way about him, the rough, tough bad boy always drawing a woman's attention. Even women who couldn't decipher if he was a lunatic or not.

Maria kept her eyes glued to Mitch. Caroline gritted her teeth and forced herself to stay quiet. To not rush the process. *I'm so tired.*

"I knew him," Maria said.

Mitch flipped his hands palm side up. "Who?"

"Tommy."

Relaxed Mitch evaporated. Even from across the room, Caroline noticed the transformation, the stiffness. "Knew him how?"

"He was...um...kind and gentle."

Her voice hitched, just a little, but enough to send Caroline's feeble brain to full speed. She reached across the table, laid her hand flat, but Maria didn't move. Just kept working the strap on her purse. *Something is in there.* "Maria? We'll help you. Whatever it is."

"I was with Jesse one day. My car was in the shop and it was my day off. He took me to the grocery store and to the bank. Stupid errands. He got a call and told me we had to make a stop. Business that couldn't wait. I wasn't sure what that meant, but what could I do?"

"Where'd he go?" Brice asked.

"We drove to a strip mall. He parked and told me to stay in the car while he went into the coffee shop. I didn't like the sound of it. He'd always been a decent kid and tried to stay out of trouble, but in a lot of ways—his friends, his attitude, his obsession with money—he was straddling the line. I followed him into the shop."

Mitch shifted his weight causing the dresser to creak and they all glanced at him. "You saw him with Tommy."

"Yes."

She half smiled and that small hitch of her lips, that little bit of movement, forced Caroline to hold her breath. How was it that one gesture could be so miniscule yet stuffed with regret? "What is it, Maria?"

"His hair was long, his clothes a mess. He looked like someone my brother shouldn't be hanging around with."

"Did you know he was an undercover agent?"

She shook her head. "Jesse jumped up and we left. Just like that. I knew he was up to something, and I kept asking him, but he wouldn't tell me. I was scared he was doing something illegal and I kept hounding him about it. I guess he couldn't take it anymore and told me he was helping the government. That the man he met with caught him buying a gun for someone else and told him if he agreed to give him some information, the man wouldn't arrest him. I didn't believe it. I thought that was craziness. A few days later, Tommy showed up at the hospital. He found me in the cafeteria on my lunch break."

This time it was Caroline's turn to be shocked. "He broke cover?"

Maria thought about that. "I guess he did. He told me who he was and to leave Jesse alone. That he was a good kid doing the right thing. He gave me his card. Told me to call him if I ever needed anything. Jesse too."

"Did you ever call him?"

"No." She slapped both hands over her eyes and burst into tears.

"Maria?" Caroline urged. "It's okay. What happened?"

She looked up. "He started showing up after my shifts. The first time, it scared me. He was in his car, parked two down from mine. I almost had a heart attack when he got out and said he wanted to make sure I got home okay. After that, he showed up most nights, and each time...well..."

Her lips broke into a shy smile, and Caroline's gut bottomed out. She knew that look. That very feminine, telling look. *No. It couldn't be...*

Mitch crossed his arms over his chest. "Each time *what*?"

Maria sighed, her gaze going to the window. "I fell a little more in love with him."

Mitch's first reaction? *Holy shit.* Subsequent reactions were the same.

Immobile and speechless, he stared at Maria. She looked scared now as silence reigned in the room. There was a lot of eye contact between her, Brice, and Caroline, but eventually all eyes landed on him.

Maria was the woman Tommy had mentioned. Maria, Tommy's informant's *sister*.

Goddamn. What the hell had his friend been thinking? Breaking cover, sleeping with his informant's sister, getting himself killed—it was enough to make Mitch want to put his fist through the wall.

Maybe Maria was lying. JLo Junior had probably watched too many *Fast and Furious* movies. "So you and Tommy..." He had to think of some way to make sure she wasn't dicking them around. "You spent some time together, right? He told you about his childhood? His friends? His family?"

Maria met his gaze straight on. "He told me about you."

"Oh, yeah? What about me?"

"He said there was a fine line between being a criminal and a cop. That if it hadn't been for you, he would have ended up in juvie, maybe even prison."

Pressure rose in Mitch's throat, burned behind his eyes.

"He said you were his best friend. You and Kemp Rodgers. He *said*, 'those asshole training instructors at Quantico labeled us the Three Musketeers. Thought we'd hate the nickname, but we didn't. Any of us. Mitch twisted it around and nicknamed us the Holy Trinity, just to take a stab back at them.'"

Mitch held himself still. Maria was the real deal. She couldn't know all of that unless Tommy had told her.

He'd promised Caroline he would control his emotions, and no matter what, he was keeping a lid on the pressure cooker inside him.

Control came at a price. Caroline raised an eyebrow at him, and when he tried to speak, his voice was locked inside his chest.

Maria continued. "We had to be careful about our relationship. He never parked in my driveway and always came in the back door. Sometimes we met in places similar to this motel." She glanced around at the awful interior. "Made the most of our time together."

"Did he discuss the case?" Caroline asked. "The one involving Jesse?"

Maria fingered the strap of her purse. Her voice dropped a notch, sounding resigned. "He preferred not to, but I could tell toward the end—before he was killed—that things were eating at him. Things he wanted to talk about but couldn't. I was afraid for him, and for Jesse too, but he told me Jesse and I would be all right, no matter what happened. He'd make sure of it."

Caroline coaxed her on. "Do you know what made him think you and Jesse were in danger?"

The woman's ponytail swung as she shook her head. "He never gave me specifics, just that he was poking around and upsetting members on the taskforce. And their bosses. He told me..."

When she hesitated, Caroline leaned forward and rubbed Maria's arm. "It's okay. You're not in any trouble, and nothing you say will shock us, believe me. The more we know, the better off we are. You may hold the key to clearing Tommy's name and bringing the men responsible for his death to justice."

Good thing Caroline was there. If Mitch had said the same thing, it wouldn't have come out as caring or patient. Maria's shoulders fell as if she were done holding the weight of the world on them. She reached inside her purse, grabbed something, and withdrew her hand in a balled fist.

Her dark eyes rose to meet Mitch's. "Tommy told me to give you something if anything happened to him. I was devastated when I lost him. Scared and worried, too. Not for me, but for Jesse. I hid it for a few weeks, then I tried to find you and couldn't. I didn't know what to do."

Finally, his voice returned. "What did he give you?"

She glanced at Caroline who nodded. Slowly, Maria opened her fist.

In her palm lay a keychain. A round, gold keychain with a fleur-de-lis etched in the top. A symbol used by France and other countries, armies, and religions. It was also a symbol between Tommy, Kemp, and Mitch referencing the Musketeers.

A keychain? Tommy wanted him to have a goddamn *keychain*?

Caroline held out her hand. "Can I see that?"

Maria handed it to her. Caroline flipped it back and forth, eyeballing it. She ran her fingers over the symbol, around the outsides, then got up and walked to the lamp and held it under the light. There, she took a closer look. "Aha." She pushed the raised band at the bottom of the symbol.

Caroline held it up for Mitch and Brice to see.

Bingo. A silver USB drive had popped out.

Adrenaline pumped through Mitch's veins. He reached out and took it.

This was it. Tommy had left him a message, or files, or something that would explain this case and maybe why he'd been shot.

"I couldn't find you," Maria said to Mitch, "so I tracked down Kemp Rodgers. I didn't know if I could trust him with that." She pointed at the USB dangling from Mitch's fingers. "But since Kemp was part of your group, I copied a few files from it to a separate drive that I gave him. He was nice and thanked me for coming forward. Said he'd call me as soon as he had a chance to look at the files. Then I came home and waited for him to contact me. I found out the next day that he was dead too. That's when I got really scared. The news said he was murdered and that you were a person of interest. When you showed up at my door, I didn't know what to do."

A fresh rush of adrenaline tightened the muscles at the base of Mitch's neck. "When did you meet with Kemp?"

She clasped her hands in her lap and bent her head. "The night he was killed."

Caroline sat forward, squeezing Maria's hand. "Did you see who did it?"

"No!" Her head snapped up. "I didn't see anyone. He didn't know I was coming—I wanted to surprise him, see how he reacted when I told him I knew Tommy. Tommy had given me his contact information, but every time I called his office I got the run around. So I used money from extra shifts I'd worked last month to buy a plane ticket. I went to his office and the receptionist told me he'd left for the evening. Tommy had told me what a health nut Kemp was, that he drove an ugly green

Volkswagen hybrid, and that he did a daily run at Rock Creek Park. I didn't know Washington D.C. at all, but the car I'd rented had GPS. It took me nearly an hour to scan all the parking lots, but I found his car. I was nervous, but I waited. He came out and I approached him. He probably thought I was a stalker or a serial killer, but we talked. I told him I needed to know he was trustworthy and I gave him the USB I'd copied two of the files onto. I told him if he wanted the rest, he needed to help me. Get my brother immunity or whatever." She worried her bottom lip. "You don't think he was killed over those files, do you?"

Damn right, he was killed over these files. Or at least what someone believed was in them.

"You're lucky the killer didn't off you too. He probably heard you tell Rodgers that all the files weren't on that USB." Mitch closed the keychain and stuck it in his pocket, heading for the door. "Brice, stay here with Maria. Caroline and I are heading back to the RV. We'll have a look at these files and be in touch."

Brice looked less than pleased that he was babysitting again. "Why don't we look at it here on my laptop?"

Because I need to look at them alone. "As soon I know what's on it, man, I *will* call you."

He went out the door before Brice could argue further, Caroline on his heels.

"One more thing I think you should know," Maria called.

Mitch turned back and focused on Maria still planted in the chair. "Tommy said he never told you, and he always wished he had, but you were like a brother to him. The only person he ever considered family."

Mitch was quiet.

That alone obviously concerned Caroline because she kept looking over at him. Analyzing him like he'd turn psycho at any second. All he wanted was a few minutes to get his head together. To compartmentalize the emotional crap sawing him in half.

Twenty minutes into the ride to the RV, Caroline finally spoke. "What do you think is on that USB?"

Mitch, for once, was driving. He needed something to occupy his mind and Caroline was too doped up to complain. "Tommy knew he was in some deep shit, otherwise he wouldn't have secret files that he entrusted to his girlfriend. Whatever information is in those files, it's worth killing over."

"You don't really think Kemp was killed because Maria gave him a couple of those files, do you?"

He glanced at her across the seat. She was still pale and her eyes tired. So tired, in fact, she looked like she could barely keep them open. "You think it's coincidence? Come on, Caroline."

"Remember what I said about going off half-cocked and letting your emotions get the better of you?"

"This isn't about emotion, this is about information...information someone didn't want leaked. Tommy was about to blow the lid on something, I'd bet my ass on it, and it got him killed. Maybe whoever wanted those files was just going to mug him and he fought back. I don't know, but Maria met with Kemp, gave him a couple of the files, and he's dead now too."

"Why didn't they kill her? Whoever they are."

She was definitely tired and not tracking straight. "Because they need *all* the files."

"And she still had them."

"Exactly. Except, they didn't know where the others were, so they probably followed her back home."

"And broke into her house," she said, staring into the blackness outside. "But they didn't find the key ring."

He made a turn, heading north toward the lake. "They—

whoever they are—may have thought she gave the files to you. That's why you were attacked."

"They've been following her, and now us, the whole time? What if they go after her at the motel?"

"Brice will keep her safe. If they're smart, they'll be following us and leaving Maria alone."

Her fuzzy gaze swung back around to him and she gave him a loopy smile. The drugs were working her over and if he didn't get her to the RV soon, she'd crash right inside this filthy truck. "I love you."

"That's the drugs talking."

She scooted across the bench seat and tucked herself next to him. Her arm went around his and she rested her head on his shoulder. "You may be a little tarnished around the edges, but you still rock that shining armor."

He patted her knee. A stoned Caroline. What a gift. She was cozied up next to him, all warm and sleepy, and it reminded him how sexy she was after an orgasm. How much he loved this Caroline.

"Someone might be following us," her voice trailed off as she yawned—"the goons maybe."

"We're clear. I've got my eye on the rearview."

Except for Donaldson. His old boss had been following them since the hospital. Why, Mitch wasn't sure, but he'd had no trouble losing him a few miles back.

Caroline rubbed her cheek on his shoulder. "Good. I need sleep. Drugs are making me loopy."

By the time they reached the lake, she was fast asleep. Mitch did a heat run, taking a bunch of back roads until he was one hundred and ten percent sure they didn't have a tail. Then he parked the truck behind some trees and carried Caroline to the camper.

Inside, he laid her down, took off her shoes, and covered her up. He booted up her laptop and rubbed his finger over the fleur-de-lis while he waited for the start screen.

One for all and all for one.

The computer was ready. Mitch plugged in the USB and cruised the files. The first one he opened was labeled "Mitch."

One was a memo from Atkinson to various agents reminding them of the importance of discretion regarding Operation Bulletproof. They weren't under any circumstances to discuss their activities. Period. The next file was a summary of purchases made by a guy whose name Mitch didn't recognize. All fourteen weapons were semi-automatic rifles. Had to be a straw purchase, otherwise, what the hell did this guy want with fourteen semi-automatic weapons?

Mitch closed the file, went back to the directory and scanned the list again. Three documents marked with consecutive months were titled *Meeting Notes.* Click. Encrypted. Interesting. He sat back, thought about possible passwords. If Tommy intended him to have these files, the password would be something they'd both know.

Musketeers, he typed.

No dice. He drummed his thumb against the computer, running ideas through his mind. Names. They'd often joked about who would be which Musketeer. By Tommy's way of thinking, Mitch was Athos, the protector. And since Tommy left this drive for Mitch...

Athos.

Had to be. Tap, tap, tap.

The file popped open to what looked like Tommy's slanted handwriting. Scanned document. At the top of the page was the date and "TF meeting."

Taskforce meeting. Had to be. Tommy had noted something about guns being found at a murder scene just across the border. Jesse's name was written beside the note. What did that mean? Had Jesse purchased one of the weapons?

Mitch closed the file, clicked the next one. This one contained photos of dozens of semi-automatics and handguns confiscated from a warehouse. Beside the photo, Tommy wrote "straw."

Jesus.

Sickness rolling in his stomach, Mitch closed the file. Next file was an email from Tommy to ATF ASAC Atkinson warning him of the number of weapons agents were letting walk as part of Operation Bulletproof.

Covering his ass. Good old Tommy.

The next document was the response from Atkinson blowing smoke up Tommy's ass about his dedication to the job being honorable. He was also told to stand down. The plan was the plan and ATF had it under control.

Whatever that meant.

At some point, it started to rain. Mitch made coffee and stepped outside for air, the small awning keeping him dry. He stared at the lake, part of his mind filled with the information in Tommy's files, the other half wondering about the encrypted ones. Caroline had woken up and he heard her moving around, but gave her what little privacy he could in their cramped quarters. After a couple of minutes, he went back inside. She'd taken off her pants and was dressed solely in her shirt. Her bra had disappeared, too, and never had he enjoyed that white button-down as much as right now.

"I crashed. Sorry. I don't suppose you waited for me to look at those files, did you?"

He handed her his coffee. "You needed the sleep. How's the head?"

She brushed her fingers over the bandage. "Sore, but I'm tough. Takes more than that to put me out of commission."

He hadn't slept, but he didn't need to. He was wired. "Good, because we have a lot of work to do."

She eyed him. "What's on that USB?"

He'd had time to think everything out, but there was something he needed to do before he showed her the files. "Nothing that can't wait for a few more minutes."

Before she could protest, he lowered his head and kissed her.

19

The world needed a Mitch Monroe support group. A program. Somewhere women like Caroline could go to save themselves because she wasn't just about to fall off the wagon. She was about to dive head first. Twelve stories. Onto cement.

And nothing good could ever come of that.

Mitch was a wild card. She knew it and yet...

This is bad.

But the triple orgasm from last time? That was good. Very good. A solid twenty-five on a scale of one to ten.

With Mitch, it was all about the closeness, that skin-to-skin, soul-to-soul connection—the heat—she hadn't experienced with anyone else. Mitch was it. Then. Now.

Always.

Setting his hands on her cheeks, he backed away from the kiss, ran his thumb gently over her jaw and—wow—when he touched her, the stress of the job—life—melted away.

She hooked her fingers into the loops on his jeans and pulled his hips forward. "Let's finish what we started last night."

He nodded. One solid jerk of his head, but the gesture, one she'd seen from him thousands of times and was always so self-assured, so *determined*, suddenly felt...off. Hesitant. "Mitch?"

"It can't be like last time."

Um, why? "My three orgasms from last time beg to differ."

What she considered a fun, snappy comeback earned her an eye roll. He dropped his hands from her face and stepped back. "You think it's funny. This is what I'm talking about. It can't be another night-that-never-was."

Another...what? She stood for a second, stymied. Clearly her lame joke had unleashed something. For years now, sarcasm and innuendo had been their standard way of communicating. The status quo. What she knew and had adjusted to.

Now he wanted to change it? She held her hands up. "Okay, relax a second. I didn't mean to be flip."

He poked a finger at her. "If we do this, you'd better be in it for the long haul. My two oldest friends are dead, Caroline. I'm —" he dug his fingers into his scalp and squeezed his eyes shut. "Shit."

"You're what, Mitch?"

Please let him tell me what I need to hear. Whatever that might be.

He lowered his hands, opened his eyes and stared at her with an intensity—*sorrow*—she'd never seen before. The cocky smart-ass was gone, his normally amused eyes doused like a dying fire.

She held her hands out, fingers spread wide, ready to grab hold of anything he'd give because, dammit, she needed to hear whatever it was. "Please talk to me."

"Broken. I'm *broken* and—hello—the fact that I'm even admitting that is a fucking nightmare. You know me, you know how hard that is for me."

"Mitch—"

"I can't wake up tomorrow wondering if you'll regret it. Last time, I thought I had it made. We had a great night. Superior night."

"I loved that night."

He let out a sarcastic laugh. "You loved it until you didn't. That wasn't a one-night stand for me. That was my future. Finally something good to grab on to. I was all set. And if the Bureau didn't like the fraternization, no problem. Plenty of government agencies to work for. I would have walked away from the Bureau for you. So, yeah, for me, that night wasn't just a lay." He stopped, shook his head and let out a huff. "At least until you made it one."

"Oh, come on!"

That was so unfair. He was the one always making jokes, being slightly crude, laughing everything off and now he blamed her?

"Admit it, Caroline. Call it what it was. I was some dick who happened to get you through a tough night. Back then, I could handle it. Now? I'll lose my fucking mind. One more loss and I'm cooked."

Mitch Monroe unleashed. Who knew? With every layer she peeled back, she found more. And worse, she'd misjudged him. Horribly. "I didn't know. Back then. I didn't know you felt this way. I'm sorry."

"Well, now you know. The new Mitch Monroe. The one who talks about his feelings. Here I am and I can't do a replay of the night-that-never-was. If you want to start again, yeah, I'm all for it, but you'd damned well better be in it for the long haul. I'm a federal fugitive and you'd be laying your future on the line. If we do this and you walk away from me again, after losing Tommy and Kemp, I swear to God, Caroline, I will never recover. I need you, but I won't risk that. I'll leave right now. It would be the hardest damned thing I've ever done—and that's saying something—but I've been on the run long enough. I want my life back. When this is done, whatever happens, I'm done running."

"I love you," she said.

The words tumbled out, in a rush, without thought or a willingness to stop them.

He shook his head. "You said that before."

She reached for him, but he stepped back, putting distance between them. "Yes. And it's not the drugs. On the-night-that-never-was, you terrified me. It was so good that it was scary good. And I'm talking about the sex. Sex that good doesn't happen unless there's trust and affection. There's a purity to it. You know what I'm talking about. I know you do."

"That's what I'm saying. We're good together. On all levels. But being with me will wreck your career."

"Only if this goes bad."

"Which it probably will."

Finally she grabbed hold of him, gripped his forearms. "Then screw it. Let it go bad. We'll figure this out. Together. I have no idea what'll happen, but I'm here. Right now. I'm here. I'd have never done this a year ago. Never. But I know what I want now and somehow, my job doesn't matter." She yanked him forward. "So quit talking and screw me blind."

She kissed him, hard, the way she remembered it from last time and he finally gave in and smacked his hands over her ass, dragging her closer—skin-to-skin close, letting her feel the press of his erection against her.

I love him. For so long, she'd fought it. Knowing it and acknowledging it were different. Opposites that couldn't quite come together. Now...now the ends came together.

She wrapped her arms around his neck, slowed the pace of the kiss. Not this time. This time they'd go slow. She'd waited too long for him, for the *experience* of him.

Pulling back, she nipped at his bottom lip. "I want slow."

"We still have a lot to do and not much time."

"We can't do anything with those files until morning. Until we find out what happens in that meeting with Donaldson and the others."

"So, we've got the rest of the night and I'm used to no sleep."

"Good. Because after we're done in here, I've got my eye on that lake. I want what I didn't get last night."

Mitch laughed. "Oh, you'll get it, Caroline. You'll get it."

She loves me.

How was that possible? After everything he'd put her through, after the way he'd treated her. Bottom line, how could anyone love him in his current state?

Caroline's legs went around Mitch's hips, her arms wound around his neck. He carried her to the bunk bed, kissing her along the way. They didn't quite fit, but it didn't matter. Like two lusty teenagers in the backseat of a car, they contorted their bodies to accommodate each other without missing a beat. Setting her butt on the cheap mattress, he kept kissing her and went to work on getting his clothes off. Caroline helped, her fingers undoing his belt as he shucked off his T-shirt.

She loves me.

She said she wanted slow, and he did too. He wanted to draw out their time together and revel in the feel of her, the taste. But like always, the moment they were skin-to-skin, that searing sexual chemistry between them became nitrous oxide. *One damn fine explosion coming up.*

His belt was loose, his zipper down, and Caroline's hand went for the gold, slipping inside his briefs and taking hold. But she didn't yank or squeeze. She tickled him, the mere touch of her fingernails against his erection nearly sending him over the edge.

He plucked a condom from a pocket before his jeans hit the floor. Yes, he'd bought a couple of condoms from the dispenser in the mall restroom, and thank the good Lord in Heaven he had. She took the one in his hand and tore open the package. In seconds, he was sheathed. Caroline removed her conservative button-down, letting the edges slide over her shoulders and down her arms. She spread her legs and leaned back to grab the opposite edge of the bed.

Wanton. That was the look she sent him, her dancing eyes as tantalizing as her tickling, teasing fingers.

With their next kiss, Mitch entered her. Not fast and hard, but slow...inch by hard inch.

Caroline scooted forward, heels digging into his ass cheeks trying to speed things up. *Slow, huh?* He grinned against her lips.

"What?" she said, bucking against him.

He held perfectly still, refusing to give in to her body's demands. "I want to make this last, remember?"

"I know, but...but..." She was moving again and closing her eyes. "Oh, God, you feel so good."

"Caroline?"

"*What?*"

"Open your eyes and look at me."

Her lashes flew open, the dark orbs of her eyes animalistic. "I know what I said, but I changed my mind. I need it fast and hard and...well, fast."

She grabbed his ass cheeks, goading him to move. He took her by the wrists and wrangled her upper body so it was pinned down on the bed.

"Hey," she complained, her dark hair fanning out against the white of her shirt lying under her.

"Let go, Caroline. Relax. Let me do the work."

Miss Control Freak resisted for a moment, then arched her back, shifting her pelvis to take him deeper. "Mitch, *please.*"

Begging? Or bitching? At least she wasn't fighting. He caught both of her wrists with one hand and pinned them above her head. With his free hand, he massaged one breast and then the other. At the same time, he set up a slow, leisurely rhythm.

"Damn you," she whispered, but her eyes stayed locked on his the way he wanted.

"You've already damned me to hell and back, Caroline. Why don't you give up that precious control and just enjoy the ride?"

She rolled her hips, taking him deeper. His body defied his mind, wanting her. All of her. Against his will, his rhythm picked up. He gritted his teeth, hanging on for control. Damn woman. He was breathing hard and he hadn't even gotten a good start on her.

Releasing her wrists, he grabbed her hips instead and held them still, lowering his mouth to one of her nipples. She squirmed but moaned as his tongue flicked over the sensitive bud. Drawing it into his mouth, he sucked it between his teeth, gently. Her hips surged.

Tightening his hold, he gave proper attention to her other breast for a long minute. She cussed him again, but laughed, too, and finally, he felt her let go. *Really* let go.

Her legs spread wider, giving him fuller, deeper access. Her hands swept into his hair, pulling his face to hers so she could kiss his lips.

She loves me.

Mitch plunged deep, taking all she offered. She met him stroke for stroke, until a few seconds later, her orgasm broke over her and she yelled his name into the night.

Hearing his name on her lips, he followed her over the brink.

· · ·

Forget the support group. Caroline didn't need it. Nope. Experiencing the glory of a New Mexico sunrise over the lake with Mitch after a healthy orgasm was definitely the way to go.

Caroline tilted her head back as streaks of purple and orange splayed across a sky dotted with clouds, each one stacked against the other in an endless layer. No artist could create such magnificence. Impossible.

From behind her, Mitch snaked his arm under hers and held out his hand. "You didn't drop that soap, did you?"

"Nope."

She smacked it into his hand. Day three of their trip and the heat wouldn't let up. They'd stepped into the lake at 6:30 and the temperature had already hit eighty degrees. And without the use of a washer, Caroline was now out of what Mitch called her Bureau-wear. Today would be a jeans and tank top day. Unless they found a Laundromat.

"Don't hog that soap," she said. "I've got about ten layers of grime."

"Oh, that's romantic."

Caroline snorted. "Do you want a smelly girl?"

The look he gave her—mischievous and playful—should have been her first warning. He snatched his arm out again, grabbed her around the waist and tossed her sideways. She hit the water in a splash and came up sputtering.

"Really?" She wiped water from her face. "You want to play?"

"I do," he said.

Then she was on him, trying—and failing—to push him under.

"You'll never win, Caroline. I'm taller. I can stand here."

"Damn you, Mitch Monroe."

She shoved away from him, gave a little splash, and continued to soap up, a relentless happiness buzzing inside. *This is no time to be happy.* "I like starting the day like this.

When this is over, we should become adventure travelers. See the world. Hop from country to country."

He handed her back the soap. "And live on what?"

"Look at you suddenly all Mr. Technicality. I'm the one usually being the spoilsport."

He grinned. "You must be rubbing off on me."

What a tragedy that would be. She soaped up her legs, scrubbing as hard as she could. What she needed was a loofah. "Donaldson's meeting is at eight. We've got some time to kill. Let's look through the rest of that thumb drive. How much was on there?"

"I went through a few files, but there are a bunch more. We need a printer. Something tells me they're all part of a timeline we need to build."

"God, I love when you talk like that."

"I know you do. It's all part of my grand plan to brainwash you into being my love slave."

Little did he know the brainwashing might already be complete. She glanced back at the morning sky, the sun glinting off the still water. If she could stay here for another hour, life would be perfect. Her, Mitch, the quiet—Mitch quiet?

She laughed at that. Maybe quiet was overrated.

"What's funny?" he asked.

"Nothing. Let's get to work."

Minutes later, she slipped into jeans and her red tank top and stuck her still-wet hair into a ponytail. Mitch stood by the table, his gaze on her, creating heat that made the temperature outside look like an arctic freeze.

"Damn, you look good," he said.

She glanced down. "You might need glasses."

"I've never seen you like this." He motioned his hands up and down. "Jeans."

"Oh, stop it. You've never seen me in jeans? That's ridiculous."

"No, Caroline. I haven't. You're always in Bureau-wear."

She stopped, thought about that a second. As much as she hated to admit it, he could be right. In their time together, she'd been so uptight about being seen as a professional—one of the guys—she'd never considered wearing anything but work clothes around Mitch. Particularly around Mitch. With him, her goal had always been to keep her clothes on. Her business suits insured they kept things on a professional level.

At least until they hadn't.

Sigh.

She walked to him, tugged on his T-shirt, and kissed him quickly. "Well then, I suppose you've broken me. Now, let's get to work, Studly."

He winked. "There's only one chair. We'll have to share."

"Fine with me, we shared a hell of a lot more than that last night."

Mitch laughed as he sat, pulling Caroline onto his lap, the movement so casual like a couple who'd been practicing for years. She smiled at him, enjoying the moment of lightness before they dove into the hell that had been Tommy Nusco's life. Or at least what was left of it.

Mitch was already clicking files though, focused on the screen. "I left off here."

A scanned email popped on the screen and Caroline sat forward. "Okay, we've got an ATF document. Looks like an internal memo."

Mitch leaned in and the two of them silently read. Department of Justice. Strategy. Straw purchases of assault weapons. Allowed.

Whoa.

"Holy shit," Mitch said.

Holy shit was right. Caroline went back to the top of the document and read it again. Her shoulders and chest locked and stinging prickles shot up her neck. *Bastards.* According to the memo, the Department of Justice was on board with the taskforce strategy. Which meant George Atkinson, the New Mexico U.S. Attorney and an arm of the Attorney General and the Justice Department, knew about the taskforce's activities.

"They knew," Mitch said. "The sons of bitches knew and they let it happen."

Something nagged at her, poked at her about some report she'd read—was it a report? Her mind went back a few months. Was it only a few? Maybe more. *They let it happen.*

"Oh, Mitch."

"What?"

Can't be. She swatted Mitch's hand off the mouse and started clicking. *When was it?* Spring. Maybe late winter.

"What?"

"I'm looking for something."

Scanning her directory, she sorted the files by date and started clicking, opening multiple files at once. If she saw it, she'd know it. She closed the top file then the next. Nope. Next one. There. The email from Donaldson. His weekly round-up. Third paragraph.

She pointed to the screen. "There it is. Son of a gun."

Mitch read the document and grunted. "So, during a briefing, the president said his administration has been directed to take aggressive steps to stop the flow of illegal assault weapons."

"Yes. That was in April. When did Tommy become part of the taskforce?"

Mitch shrugged. "Maybe June? I remember it was warm. We went fishing one day and he told me he'd be going to New Mexico. He couldn't give me details."

"Talk about a timeline. Unless we are way off base, which we could be, the president knew about this taskforce in April. Whether it was his idea or someone else's, my guess is he knew something was in the works."

"Jesus," Mitch said. "This could go all the way to the top."

Caroline angled sideways and lunged off of Mitch's lap for her burn phone sitting on the strip of counter next to the tiny sink.

"Who're you calling?"

"Donaldson. I want some answers."

"He won't tell you anything."

"He will if I threaten to go to the Judiciary Committee."

"Whoa. Let's think about this a minute."

"Oh, now, this is a first. *You're* telling *me* to take a breath? No, Mitch. Judiciary is the way to go. If New Mexico's U.S. Attorney knew about this operation, it stands to reason his ultimate boss, the *Attorney General* of the *United States,* did too."

"And since the Attorney General is responsible for all things Justice Department, including ATF's fuck-ups, well, our options are limited on who we can go to for help. And where's the deputy AG in all this? He's the filter for his boss. He has to know."

"Even if the AG and DAG *didn't* know, the minute an agent wound up dead from a gun used in a federal investigation, they'd be brought up to speed. In Tommy's case, this makes sense. The AG and DAG are told Tommy died from a gun traced back to this straw buying operation and suddenly we have a sealed case file."

Mitch propped his elbows on his knees and dropped his head in his hands. "This is fucked up."

"Mitch, we have to move on this."

Finally, he sat up, shoulders slumped. Where was the Mitch Monroe Warrior King she knew? *Buried under a mountain of grief, that's where.* She squatted in front of him and rubbed her hands over the sides of his thighs. "It's okay. We can do this. I know what I'm doing."

"You're wrecking your career. You know they'll all say you blew it for me. A woman destroying her career because she couldn't keep her legs closed. It's the one thing you never wanted. And now you're going to walk straight into it. Caroline, slow down and think about this. What about your father? His company has government contracts. You don't think the government will retaliate by cancelling those contracts?"

Her father. She hadn't considered that. For once, she'd let her emotions rule and had ignored the obvious. *Mitch Monroe strikes again.*

But really, she couldn't blame him this time. This time, the responsibility sat with her. Outside of Mitch initially asking for her help, he'd done nothing but remind her of the risks.

Risks she'd willingly accepted.

She lowered her head to his knee, rolled it side to side and breathed in. The clean, fresh scent of his jeans made her think of the lake right outside this broken-down camper and the quiet pleasure she'd experienced that morning.

I want that life.

Risks be damned—her father would want her to do the right thing.

She brought her head up and studied Mitch's face. His hair was loose around his face, his jaw sporting a couple days' worth of stubble, and his eyes...tired, disheartened, worried. Did he really want her to back away from this? Or was he saying that to relieve his own guilt?

Either way, his bland expression—the relaxed mouth, the slightly raised eyebrows, the steady gaze—gave away nothing. Nope, this was all up to her.

"I'll call my father and give him the short version. I guarantee he'll tell me to go for it. A good man is dead and he won't stand for that."

Mitch ran his hand over the top of her head, then tugged her ponytail. "Just be sure. I don't want this to be my fault. That's all. I couldn't stand that. This has to be your decision."

"It won't be your fault." She stood, but bent over to drop a kiss on him. "I promise. This time, it's all me."

. . .

Caroline—God bless her secret rebellious, scheming heart— had lost her fucking mind.

Mitch sat back in the cheap chair and stared up at the ceiling while Caroline was outside talking to dear ol' dad. If this went bad for her, the guilt would kill him. All this time, he'd been obsessed with what could have been with Caroline and now here they were again, taking a shot. The way his luck was running, that shot would wind up severing his balls.

To that, he laughed. "Damn, Monroe, you're a magnet for bum luck."

But hey, there was no time for this boo-fucking-hooing. He jumped out of the chair, gave his ass-dragging body a good stretch, and listened for the sound of Caroline's voice through the camper's vinyl walls.

Silence.

Maybe she was done with her Dad. He swung the door open, ducked out and scanned the area. She stood by the lake, arms at her sides, staring out at the water. The morning sun skittered across the surface leaving glistening peaks where fish —or whatever else—disturbed the surface.

He made sure to give the door a good slam and she angled back.

"You finished?" he asked.

She gave the lake one last look then marched back to him. "I am. Talked to my Dad. I told him I was working a sensitive case and couldn't share details. He wasn't happy that I lied, but he understands. He also told me to do what I needed to do. He'll support me."

"Does he get what we're up against here?" Caroline rolled her eyes and he held up his hands. "Hey, I'm just making sure you've outlined it for him. That's all."

"I did. He's aware we're about to piss off the federal government."

"Now I know where you get it."

She smiled. "What are you talking about?"

"No gray areas with you. It's right or it's wrong and you have no problem acting on it if it's wrong. I guess you get it from him."

"Pretty much. I also left Donaldson a message. If he doesn't give me answers I go to Judiciary. It would help if we knew someone connected to either the committee chair or ranking member. I think the chair is Senator Colson."

A bird whipped by and cruised above the lake's surface. Right then, standing on the shoreline taking in nature, Mitch decided in his next life he wanted to be a bird and fly around all day. Helluva life.

"Mitch?"

Laughing at himself, he shook off contemplations of reincarnated birds. *Senator Colson.* "The one from Pennsylvania?"

"No. Arkansas."

Mitch thought about it. "Grey knows someone on Oversight. It came up after The Lion case. I'll call him."

"All we need is a contact. It doesn't have to be the chair or ranking member. That would help though."

Mitch pulled his phone from his back pocket, ran his thumb over the screen. This was it. If he made this call and Grey knew someone, there'd be no turning back. He glanced at Caroline.

She stepped closer, set her hand on his chest, her palm flat against him and the realization that everything had changed hit him. Before last night, she'd never have touched him like this. For that alone, he should be thankful.

"It's okay," she said. "All for one, remember?"

Tommy's face, laughing and happy, flashed through his

mind. Kemp's followed, his last jabs at Mitch that night at Rock Creek making him smile through the fist squeezing his heart.

One for all. He scrolled his contacts and hit Grey's name. Voicemail. So, okay, that would buy them some time to see if Caroline heard from Donaldson.

Once again, they were rolling, he just wasn't sure where they were heading.

20

At 10:30 Caroline's burn phone rang. She checked the ID. Donaldson's number. She glanced at Mitch, once again behind the wheel of the truck as they headed to the motel to relieve Brice. The poor guy had been awake all night, and with Maria safely at work in a hospital with massive security, he'd gone back and crashed in her room.

At least he'd get a real shower. Caroline might have to make use of that bathroom herself because, despite rinsing her hair in the lake, it wasn't clean.

"It's Donaldson," she said tapping the button. "Foster."

"Foster, if you were a man I'd say you stuck your dick in the wrong hole."

That set her back some. Donaldson was an idiot, but he'd never—ever—used that kind of language with her. Later, she'd thank Mitch for insisting on driving—and forcing her to relinquish control—because after hearing Donaldson's crude statement, she'd have run them off the road. "Sir?"

"My meeting is over. The Deputy Attorney General joined us via video. I was not aware he'd be attending."

Caroline snapped her head sideways and Mitch gave her his *what the hell* face. "The deputy AG?"

"Shit," Mitch muttered.

"Foster, you might as well put me on speakerphone. If Monroe will hear this, I want him getting it straight from me. No miscommunication."

Caroline put the call on speaker and held the phone between her and Mitch. "Yes, sir. We're both here."

"You are in the shit now. The deputy AG ripped us all new ones for allowing this operation to get so far out of control."

Mitch made a left into a supermarket parking lot and parked in the nearest spot. "I need to concentrate."

Caroline nodded and went back to Donaldson. "So, the DAG and the AG knew?"

"I don't know how much they knew, but on some level, they did. Now they're scrambling."

Mitch rubbed his eyes. "Well, yeah. They don't want this shit-storm connected to the White House."

"What are they going to do?" Caroline asked.

"They're going to start by issuing a warrant for the arrest of Jesse Lando. They need to do something to save face."

Caroline gasped.

Mitch banged his open palm on the ancient steering wheel and the thump vibrated inside the truck cab. "Knew it."

"But, sir," Caroline said, "Jesse was Tommy's informant. He was cooperating."

"Well, that cooperation might have just bought him a life sentence."

Oh, the damned politics of it all. Caroline squeezed her eyes closed. The big-shots, as Mitch suspected, were about to tidy this mess up. "Sir, that's not right."

"I know, Foster. I know."

"We need to do something."

"Hold up here," Mitch said. "Where is Tommy in all of this?"

Donaldson went silent.

"You son of a bitch."

Caroline stared at Mitch, once again gawking. He'd definitely lost his damned mind. "What?"

Without looking at her, he pointed. "Go ahead, you motherfucker, tell her."

"Mitch!"

"No, Caroline. They're going to do *exactly* what we thought. They're going to fuck Tommy over to save their own asses. *Goddammit*, I hate politicians."

Well, she wasn't willing to let that happen. Not when any agent, like herself, could have been in Tommy's position. "Thank you for this information, sir. I'll be sure to keep you out of this."

"Look, Foster, I'm a lot of things, but I protect my agents."

"I know that, sir. We may disagree on certain things, but I know you go to bat for good agents."

"Damn straight. This is bullshit. But I don't know how much I can do."

Could they trust him? She didn't know. Honestly didn't. But simply having this phone call could get him fired and he, being the SAC of the D.C. field office, was acutely aware of that. And he still chose to have this conversation. Which meant she might be able to nudge a bit more from him.

"There's one thing." Mitch shot her a look and she made a slashing motion to shut him up. "We could use a list of all the agents involved in this taskforce. The agent we've been in contact with...well, I don't need to get into it. We need to find another agent."

Silence streamed through the phone line, but Caroline waited. Mitch shifted in his seat and if she knew him at all, she suspected he was about to say something. She held her finger to her lips. What Mitch had failed to learn about Donaldson was, that in the war of silence, he always flinched.

Always.

"I'll get you the list."

Always. Caroline punched a fist in the air. "Thank you, sir. *Thank* you."

"Watch your ass, Foster. One of my agents may have been involved, but this has always been an ATF operation. I'm a minor player. If you go down, there's not much I can do."

"Understood. Thank you."

Donaldson disconnected and Mitch shoved the truck into gear. "I hate that guy. He's such a pansy."

"But he's our pansy. And he's the only one we've got right now."

With Maria at work, Grey checking on his contacts at Judiciary, and Brice taking a combat nap to recharge, Mitch and Caroline killed another hour at a diner for lunch. That gave Brice a solid four-hour nap. Way more than Mitch got. Then again, he'd had his battery charged in a different way. A way he very much liked and hoped to do again soon.

He glanced at Caroline and blew her a kiss.

She rolled her eyes. "I don't even want to know what you're thinking."

"I'll tell you later. In very explicit terms."

"Terrific. Can't wait."

Mitch parked the truck in the nothing-special motel parking lot outside the nothing-special room twelve. Pretty much, this place looked like every other circa 1970 roadside motel. Cheap, clean—somewhat—and easily accessible. He glanced around, making sure they were alone and damned sure weren't going to sit in this truck like deer about to get picked off.

The cops hadn't nabbed Caroline's attackers and Mitch was too paranoid to believe it was a random mugging.

"Let's get inside," he said. "We'll wake up Sleeping Beauty and fill him in. We've got a few hours before Maria is off-shift. Between now and then, we'll piece together what the hell was going on with Tommy. Maybe figure out who jumped you."

"It has to be whoever Jesse is working for."

"Why?"

"What do you mean, why? They have the most to lose. They've been buying assault weapons by the truckload under this operation. If we expose it and shut it down, no more guns."

Mitch knocked on her head. "Think harder, babe. If we've got a cover-up happening, maybe local ATF wants to shut us up."

She scoffed. "You think our own government attacked me?"

"I think anything is possible and you need to keep an open mind. You're fucking brutal when you get too dialed-in."

Before she could yell at him, he hopped out of the truck and waved her along. Caroline hauled her laptop with her and followed Mitch to the door. "You didn't have to be so rude."

"Seriously, you're going to deny you get hyper-focused?"

"Well, no, but '*brutal*' is a bit harsh."

Mitch laughed and banged on the door.

"Don't be a jerk about waking him up."

"I won't."

He banged on the door again then gave it a kick. Why not?

"Did I not just say don't be a jerk?"

"Trust me, that wasn't being a jerk. That was waking him up gently. He told me he sleeps like the dead."

A minute later, the door swung open and Brice stood there, his hair all kinds of crazy-assed, his shirt a wrinkled mess, and his basketball shorts not looking too good either.

"Wake up, sunshine."

Brice ran his hands over his face as Mitch and Caroline marched into the room. "Time?"

"One-thirty," Mitch said. "I gave you just under four hours."

"Yeah. I'm set."

"Good, cause that's all we can spare." Mitch propped against the short dresser while Brice locked and bolted the door behind them. "We found some funky shit on that flash drive. It's time the three of us started piecing this thing together and Maria can fill in the blanks."

Brice yawned. "What about Donaldson?"

Caroline set her laptop on the desk against the far wall. Good spot. Away from the windows. "I spoke to him earlier," she said. "The Deputy AG called him and the ATF higher-ups into the meeting and lambasted all of them for letting this case get out of control."

That got Brice's attention because he did a double-take. "He told you that?"

"He did. Underneath all that schmuckiness, he wants to do right by a good agent. He said he'd get us the list of agents on the taskforce. Hopefully that'll come soon. Then we go down the list and find someone who will talk to us."

"Caroline wants to take this to Judiciary," Mitch added.

Brice jerked his head back. "Judiciary? Seriously?"

She shrugged. "Where else can we go? We know from Donaldson that the Deputy Attorney General is now aware of this operation. Who knows when he became aware of it, but he's in spin mode now. If the DAG knows, you think his boss doesn't?"

"Well, shit," Brice said.

Mitch crossed his arms simply to have something to do with them. "Yeah. I tend to agree that if the DAG knows, this thing probably goes all the way to the top, which would be why, according to what Kemp told me, the White House rumors about invoking Executive Privilege might be true. Again, how long they've known is in question, but it's been at least since they traced that weapon to their straw buying operation. Short of it is, I don't trust any of these fuckers."

Brice sat back against the headboard and crossed his legs at the ankles. "If we get that list from Donaldson, I can start working that. I might know some of the people on the list."

Mitch nodded. "I have Grey checking his contacts in Judiciary. Maybe we'll get lucky."

Caroline finished booting up her laptop and spun the desk chair toward them. "Based on what we found on that flash drive, we can assume Tommy was getting information from Jesse, a known straw buyer, in the hope of busting whoever Jesse was buying the weapons for."

Brice nodded. "And we know he was buying massive quantities because Marty from the gun shop told us."

"Right," Mitch said. "So Tommy is basically sitting in his car, watching these straw buyers buy these guns and he's told to stand down. To not arrest them because the bigshots want whoever Jesse is buying weapons for."

"And then Maria busts in on a meeting."

Fucking Tommy. Should have known better than to get emotionally involved with his informant's sister. Rookie mistake. Mitch gritted his teeth. *Too late now.* "Considering what we found on that flash drive, I think Tommy panicked. He's got this informant and he's involved with the guy's sister. If the informant goes down, the sister will be devastated. Tommy, from what Maria says, was in love with her. He's in deep trying to figure out a way to keep Jesse's status from being blown— these gunrunning cartels would have strung him from a tree. On top of that, he's got Maria to worry about. In short, he's fucked five ways to Sunday."

Stupid bastard.

Caroline spun back to her laptop. "Maybe that's when he started complaining about the operation."

She clicked the mouse a couple of times and Mitch walked over, eyeing the two files she'd pulled up and aligned side-by-side on the screen.

"Look at the dates," she said. "The memo to his ASAC was sent on August 12. The response came on August 13." She closed both documents and opened a few more. "Knew it."

"What?"

She tapped the screen. "These are his handwritten notes regarding his activities. Look at the dates. He started documenting everything on August 14."

Brice hopped off the bed and joined them at the computer. "He started documenting everything six weeks before he was killed."

"That can't be a coincidence," Caroline added.

"Jesse could have panicked."

"Ya *think*?" Mitch cracked. "Maria has never said Jesse knew about her relationship with Tommy."

Caroline tapped her index finger against her lips, closed one eye then the other as she thought about it and Mitch nearly laughed. Typical Caroline.

A solid minute later, she gave up on thinking and shook her head. "No. She's never said. Jesse could have found out from someone else."

It all made perfect sense to him. "Exactly. If Tommy was stuck, Jesse was just as stuck. He's the informant and now his sister is involved with an FBI agent. Maybe Jesse gets spooked and realizes if his status is leaked to whoever he's buying guns for, he's dead, and his sister's just as dead."

Brice sighed. "Crap. The easiest way to rectify that situation is for Jesse to do an end run and leak Tommy's name to whoever he's buying for."

Mitch reached up, pretended to ring a bell. "Ding. Ding. He plays innocent and tells his contact that he's got some heat from this guy connected to the FBI and ATF."

"And they take him out," Caroline said.

"And they take him out. Taking him out protects Jesse *and* Maria. Sure, she's brokenhearted, but Jesse can live with that. Better brokenhearted than dead. That still doesn't tell us who worked you over in the parking lot."

She waved that away. "We have to find Jesse."

They'd definitely do that, but Mitch wasn't giving up on Caroline's attackers. He wanted those fuckers in his crosshairs. "As soon as we pick up Maria, we get her back here and ask her what Jesse knew. If she thinks he sold Tommy out, she might flip on him."

"My God," Caroline said. "What was Tommy thinking?"

"*He* wasn't," Mitch said. "His dick was."

Worse than I thought.

If that was even possible.

Caroline ran the heel of her hand over her forehead. They should get out of New Mexico. Now that she'd been attacked, both the FBI and ATF knew she—and probably Mitch—were here. And here, they were vulnerable. Limited funds, limited contacts, limited places to hide. If they went back to D.C. they'd be more nimble and definitely more productive.

She checked her watch. One hour until Maria was off work. "I think we need to go home."

Mitch spun on her, his mouth hanging open. "Go *home*?"

"Yes. Before you start yelling, think about it. We have no resources here. If we go back to D.C., Grey and his techie guy can help us. We even, so it seems, have Donaldson. If we can make contact with a member of Judiciary, we'll have that too. All we have to do is convince Maria to go with us. We'll get her to tell her story to Judiciary and we're off. All around, I think we're safer in D.C."

From his spot on the bed, Brice made humming noises. "She might be right."

"I'm not debating that," Mitch said. "But I'm sure as hell not going anywhere without Maria. The minute we're gone, she'll disappear. And maybe not by choice. Get my drift?"

Caroline stood, paced a few steps while wagging her finger. "We'll take care of her. She won't be happy about going back to D.C., but she loved Tommy. As much as she loves her brother, Tommy is dead and she wants justice for him. If she didn't, she wouldn't have tracked Kemp down to give him that thumb drive and make sure he was trustworthy." She stopped pacing, propped her hands on her hips. "I hate to do it, but we need to scare the hell out of her, make her think going back with us is the only thing that'll fix this mess."

Mitch eyed her and her mind zipped back to their Bureau days. How many times had she seen that look? He'd channel all his frenetic energy into one task and the intensity of it, the sheer force of him propelled the case forward.

Ignoring Brice, she jumped out of her chair, walked to Mitch and squeezed his cheeks with both hands. "I love when you have that look."

"What look?"

"The I'm-about-to-kick-ass look."

For a few seconds, the room went quiet—even the ancient air conditioner ceased—and Caroline stood there, cradling Mitch's face in her hands, her heart slamming so hard it hurt, knowing she'd never love anyone as much as she loved long-shot Mitch Monroe.

He'd probably wreck her life. No. She wouldn't allow that. Him wrecking her life meant allowing him to do so. And she wouldn't.

Not this time.

If this didn't work out, she'd survive. She'd done it before, she'd do it again.

She simply didn't want to just survive. "We have to make this work," she said.

He brought his hands up, wrapped them around her wrists and squeezed. Somehow, standing there, gazes locked, he understood she wasn't talking about the case.

"I know. It won't fall apart this time. I promise you."

"Hey, now." Brice smacked his hands together and leapt off the bed. "This is all super-romantic, but I'm gonna grab Maria. Give you two a few minutes to—" he motioned with his hands, "—do whatever it is you do when you're alone. Jesus, my mind just fried. It's like a Monroe-Foster porno in my head. And that's some ugly shit."

Oh, now that was funny. Caroline, needing to torture poor Brice for another few seconds, made panting noises. "Oh, Monroe!" she gasped.

At that, Brice laughed. "You are sick. But I like it. I'm gonna grab our witness and then we'll talk her into a road trip. My blog is gonna go viral. I can feel it."

He left the room and Mitch turned back to her. "Are we driving back to D.C.?"

"Not if my father will let us borrow his jet again. With any luck, we can be on a plane back to D.C. by tonight."

21

*C*aroline wanted to go home.

Whether Mitch agreed completely with her logic he wasn't sure and really didn't give a shit. But he was close enough to agreeing that he'd take a flyer. If Caroline wanted to go home, he'd get her there.

From his spot on the edge of the bed, he glanced over to where she was just about done sweet-talking her father into ponying up the plane. If he did nothing else right in his goat-fuck of a life, he'd make it work with Caroline.

Whatever it took.

He checked the digital clock on the bedside table. Brice had been gone thirty minutes. Another twenty and he should be back.

Then Mitch would go to work.

Caroline set her phone on the desk and gave it a spin so Mitch wandered over. "We all set?"

She nodded. "The plane is in D.C. He said he'd find their pilot and send him. If all goes well, we'll be out of here tonight."

Suddenly, the idea of leaving New Mexico had merit. Maybe Caroline's theory about being on home turf had triggered something in him. "That works. We need to get Maria on board, no pun intended."

"They'll be back soon. Let's talk about how we're doing this. Before she knew you were Tommy's friend, she was intimidated by you. Let's capitalize on that. I'll be the understanding female. I hate pulling this nonsense, but she's loyal to her brother and she needs to be convinced that Jesse could be involved with Tommy's murder."

Involved? The way it looked, Jesse was their killer. That sounded too tidy though. And if so, why hadn't Jesse been arrested when that ballistics report came back? Although, the government could be looking to wrap this up as fast and as quietly as possible and sacrifice Jesse along with Tommy. The big shots probably figured whoever Jesse was working for killed Tommy, but they'd let Jesse take the heat because his puzzle piece fit.

Mitch nodded. "I'll take care of it. She may not like me when it's over, but she'll be on that plane."

"I could use about a gallon of scotch right now," Caroline cracked.

He rubbed her shoulders, digging his thumbs into the knots, and dropped a kiss on her head. "It's like the old days. The two of us making a plan, working a case together. I miss those days."

"Maybe if we figure this out, those days can exist again."

She didn't really believe that. "Uh, Caroline, I'm never going back to the Bureau. You know that, right?"

"Why not? Once your name is cleared, you could reapply."

"Trust me, I know. Not only would they never hire me, I don't want it. I don't miss the politics and the bullshit. If I did anything, I'd work with Grey on his Justice Team. He's got enough work there for ten people. And, even better, he's the one dealing with the political garbage."

She rolled her head as he continued his battle with her

shoulders. "But you'll come out of hiding, right? When this is over?"

Yeah, that he'd do. Once they cleared Tommy's name, he still had to prove he hadn't killed Kemp, but now, with Maria giving Kemp those files, he couldn't help but think the two murders were linked. Once he uncovered who'd set Tommy up, he'd go to work on the Kemp connection. Then he'd make a deal with Donaldson. He'd turn himself in if Donaldson made sure Caroline's career stayed on track. He couldn't tell her about that, though.

"I'm tired of running. When we get back to D.C., I'm officially back on the grid."

At the door, the lock tumbled and Mitch stood. "Who is it?"

"It's me," Brice hollered.

Mitch glanced down at Caroline, ran his fingers under her chin. "You ready for this?"

"I guess I have to be. Let's roll."

Maria looked tired. Brice was tight-lipped. And Mitch figured it would be a helluva ride.

"Bolt that door," he reminded Brice. The former ATF agent looked annoyed, but did as instructed.

When Maria moved to the chair by the window, Mitch held up his hand. Time to start taking extra precautions. Just in case. "Not by the window. Over here, by the bathroom."

Even with the drapes closed, a shooter could find its target. If she wasn't sitting in front of the window maybe they had a chance of her not taking a round. Maybe.

Brice, ever the gentleman, moved the side chair to the cramped area between the closet and the bathroom door. Mitch sat on the end of the bed with Caroline across from him, the two of them pinning Maria with her back to the wall. Exactly as he'd planned.

Human beings were animals underneath the clothes and

attitude. One glance to Mitch, then one to Caroline, and Maria's face morphed from tired nurse into cornered prey.

"You've gotta be tired," Mitch said, "so we'll make this quick."

"I'm fine."

"Hungry?"

"Not yet."

"Good."

She fidgeted. "Brice said you had questions."

Mitch jerked his head. "We went through the flash drive. Not all of it, but we got a good idea of what was going on. Tommy complained about the operation to his superiors. His complaints escalated and he threatened to go outside of New Mexico with major damning information. Were you aware of that?"

"Somewhat. He was extremely frustrated. And worried."

"We could tell from his notes," Caroline said.

Maria worked her purse strap between her fingers. "I didn't want Jesse involved anymore. It was too risky."

Mitch held out his hand. "How much did Jesse know about you and Tommy?"

"About our relationship? Nothing. We never told him. I wasn't comfortable with it, but Tommy thought it was best. Jesse figured out I was seeing someone because he would tease me about my secret guy. I wanted to tell him."

"But you didn't?" Caroline asked.

"No."

Time to amp this up. Mitch rolled his eyes, made a show of not taking her seriously. "Jesse isn't stupid. I think he knew."

As Mitch had hoped, Maria responded with a skin-melting glare. "I'm good at keeping secrets. He didn't know."

Now he'd get answers. "Maybe he came by and saw Tommy's car in your driveway and figured it out."

"Tommy never parked in the drive or anywhere near the

house for just that reason. He parked around the corner a block down in the parking lot."

Around the corner. Tommy had been killed on the next block over. Mitch's shoulder blades twitched, that feeling that he'd struck gold. *Holy shit.* "Was Tommy leaving your place when he got shot?"

Maria paused and her dark eyes filled with tears. She blinked a couple of times and swiped under her eyes. "Tommy had talked Jesse into turning over a bunch of guns to him. I guess from what Jesse told me later, Tommy stuck them in his car that night to take to a meeting with some bigwig as proof about what was happening with the taskforce. Jesse gave him the guns and took off to meet up with some of his friends."

"How did he explain the guns going missing to whoever he was buying them for?"

"He never told Balboa he bought them. Tommy reimbursed Jesse for the cost of the guns and Jesse bought more guns for Balboa. He never knew Tommy took the first set of guns."

The stash of guns found in Tommy's car had to be worth fifteen grand. Tommy must have taken the money from his own account. Had to. Considering other ways he'd have gotten that money didn't help Mitch's argument that Tommy was clean. "What happened the night Tommy died?"

"I got home late and he was waiting for me. He stayed for a couple of hours, then said he had to go to a meeting. That's when he gave me the flash drive and said if anything happened to him, I should give it to you or Kemp. He gave me Kemp's contact info and a phone number for you, but that number didn't work."

No doubt because it was one of his burn phones. He never kept one longer than a week or two.

Her fingers tightened on the purse strap and tears leaked from her eyes. Her voice was barely a whisper, but she met Mitch's gaze straight on. "I heard the shots from my house."

Mitch's heart triple-timed it. *Dear God.*

Caroline, the one equipped with the sensitivity gene, leaned over and touched Maria's hand. "What did you do when you heard the shots?"

"At first, nothing. I thought it was just fireworks or something." Her lips screwed up and she sobbed slightly. "Then it hit me. My next thought was *Jesse.* I ran out the door to figure out where the shots came from. I didn't see anything so I ran to the end of the block. It was dark and I couldn't see anything from the corner. All the parking lot lights were broken years ago. I was in a panic and walked toward the lot. My eyes adjusted and I saw Tommy's car. I knew, I just *knew.*"

Mitch's blood pressure soared. "Did you call 911?"

"I started running toward the car, saw Tommy lying on the ground, but before I got to him, a man stopped me and told me to stay back. I told him I was a nurse, but he said Tommy was already..." full-on sobs shook her body "...that Tommy was dead."

Caroline gave Mitch a look. "Ethan?"

Mitch nodded. "Did you see anyone leaving the crime scene?"

She shook her head. "The man asked the same thing but, no, I never saw anyone or any vehicle leaving the parking lot. I didn't want to leave Tommy, but I had to find Jesse. I ran home and bolted the door shut. Jesse wouldn't respond to my calls and I haven't seen him since. The next day, I knew I had to do something with that flash drive. I couldn't locate you, so I copied a few of the files and found Kemp. I wasn't sure if I could trust him, so I gave him a separate USB drive in the park that night."

"We need to talk to Jesse," Mitch said. "Right now he's looking like our suspect."

Maria's shoulders flew back. "Jesse? No. He wouldn't."

"How do you know? Maybe he found out about you and

Tommy. Maybe *Balboa* found out about you and Tommy. Can't have the straw buyer's sister involved with a federal agent. That gets things all kinds of muddy."

She shook her head, glanced at Caroline—bingo—aiming for support. "He wouldn't."

On cue, Caroline squeezed her hand. "How do we find him?"

Her shoulders were bowed, her eyes now pinned on a threadbare spot in the carpeting. "I don't know. I've called every friend and acquaintance he had—at least all those I knew of—and none of them have seen him. I'm afraid he's...dead."

"He may well be, and we believe you're in danger, Maria." Mitch didn't really feel like playing hardball with her, but they were all in too deep to turn back now. "We're heading to Washington in a few hours. You need to come with us. We need your testimony along with Tommy's files to provide the Justice Department with solid proof to investigate. We don't know for sure who was behind the operation to let the guns walk and we don't know how high this cover-up goes, but if we're going to clear Tommy's name and find his and Kemp's killers, we need your help."

Her head came up, ponytail swinging as she shook it. "I can't. I can't leave here. I have a job, and what if Jesse comes home? I need to be here for him."

"Your brother was involved with a gun-running organization, and you got involved with a Bureau agent working undercover investigating that same organization. Your boyfriend was gunned down two blocks from your house, and another man was killed over a flash drive. Not only is the killer still running around, he must have guessed you didn't give all the information to Kemp, so now he's after you *and* us. The attack on Caroline was not some random mugging. You really think you're safe here, Maria? Especially after we leave?"

Her eyes went to Caroline, back to Mitch. "Can't you just tell the Justice people what I said?"

"No," Mitch said. "You need to give your statement in person. Plus, after we leave, who's gonna protect you?"

She looked at the carpet again. "I can't. I just can't."

"Well, I guess you didn't really care about Tommy like you claim."

Her face was fierce when she met his eyes. "I *loved* him."

"Then do the right goddamned thing. You have a chance to clear Tommy's name and you won't. What's your angle, Maria? Is this some kind of sick game? You know what I think?" He felt sorry for her, being tangled up in this mess, but his blood was boiling, and Bad Cop went on the attack. "I think maybe Jesse killed Tommy and this whole big story of yours is just that. A story to protect your lousy, no-good brother."

"Mitch," Caroline said in that tone that warned him he was about to go too far.

Too bad.

Maria sucked in a sharp breath. "You don't know anything about me or my brother."

"I know he's a criminal and all this talk about being in love with Tommy is a joke. You led him on and made him think you were in love with him while you and Jesse planned his murder, didn't you?"

"Mitch!" Caroline hollered because—yeah—apparently he'd gone too far.

Maria reached out to slap him, but he caught her wrist. She swore at him in Spanish and tried to jerk away. "How dare you."

He released her wrist. "Prove it. Prove to me that you and Jesse didn't screw Tommy. Come to D.C. with us and give your testimony."

Caroline inserted herself between them, shoved Mitch back a step and turned to Maria. "Don't do it for us. Do it for Tommy.

If you help us with this, I'll do what I can to clear Jesse's name and bring him home."

Again, Maria's gaze ping-ponged between Mitch and Caroline. Mitch saw it the moment the fight went out of her. Her eyes softened and fresh tears filled the corners. "I loved him. You may not ever believe that, but we had plans. Good plans. Ones that would take us out of here. I wanted a life with him."

Caroline inched closer and set her hands on Maria's arms, not gripping, but a light touch that allowed her to connect on a personal level. She'd always been good that way, worming her way in on an emotional level while Mitch was pond scum.

"Then help us, Maria. You may not have that life with him, but you can save his reputation, let everyone know what a good man he was."

Maria took a second, breathed in and out, chin against her chest, fingers mashed together. When she looked up, her hard gaze went straight to Mitch. "Fine. But I need to go back to my place and grab a few things. And what about my cat?"

"Who took care of the cat before?"

"My friend Lisa. I suppose I could leave her there again."

Caroline rose, grabbed a pad of paper and a pen off the desk and handed them to her. "Give me a list of what you need from the house and Mitch and I will go."

Caroline followed Maria's instructions and located her migraine medicine in the bathroom. Brice and Maria were parked two blocks down behind an abandoned gas station and Mitch was on lookout duty while Caroline threw clothes and toiletries into a go-bag for Maria.

Home. Back to D.C. And none too soon. Caroline's life and career would never be the same, but she could feel this fiasco about to explode. She'd deal with the fallout, put it behind her, and move on.

Hopefully, with Mitch by her side.

Muffled footsteps on the stairs made her pause her hunt for Maria's makeup bag. Mitch appeared, but didn't stop, passing the bathroom and heading for the second bedroom.

Caroline poked her head into the hall. "What are you doing?"

"Leaving Jesse a note." Mitch flipped a piece of paper onto the bed.

A note. With Mitch doing the composing, this should be interesting. She left the bathroom and peeked into the bedroom to see what the note said.

I have your sister. Under the statement was Mitch's phone number.

Caroline quirked an eyebrow at him. "You really think he'll come back?"

"He's already been back." Mitch pointed at a half empty pack of cigarettes on the nightstand. "That wasn't here last time."

"What a louse," Caroline said. "He's hanging his sister out to dry. He doesn't even care that her life's in danger."

Mitch glanced out the bedroom window. "If I find out Jesse had any involvement in Tommy's murder, I will hunt the prick down and put a bullet in him myself."

"I'll help you."

He met her eyes and that whoosh between them, that ingrained energy, surged. *We're sick. Getting turned on talking about killing a criminal together.*

Two minutes later, Caroline climbed into the backseat of Maria's car and handed the woman a bag of her stuff. The truck was running on fumes, so they were leaving it behind. Mitch sat up front with Brice for the ride to the airport.

Maria was quiet as they drove. Mitch was too. Caroline touched her cheekbone. The wound was healing, but she had a nasty bruise. *Wait 'til Dad sees that.* Maybe she could avoid him after they got home, at least for a few days.

Quick flicks traveled up her neck, the warning she'd experienced several times in her life, but had learned to appreciate as her body's instinctual distress call. She angled her head sideways, not much, just enough to catch sight of a black SUV pulling in behind them from the corner of her eye. Her nerves, already taut, tensed a little more. Was she paranoid? She had good reason to be. "Brice?"

"Yep," he said from the front seat. "Already saw them."

"Them, who?" Mitch checked the side mirror. "Black SUV?"

Brice took a left turn without preamble, throwing Caroline off balance and causing the seat belt to dig into her neck. She grabbed the door handle with one hand and reached for Maria with the other. "Get down. Now."

Mitch peeked between the seats, gaze focused on the back window. "Still with us," he said to Brice. His attention shifted to Caroline. "You get down, t—"

The back window exploded, sending shards of glass, compliments of a bullet, raining down on Caroline's head.

Maria screamed. *Help her.* Caroline shoved her to the floor as Brice accelerated and took a hard right. The squeal of tires and the acrid smell of burning rubber, rushed through the car, the momentum of the turn vaulting Caroline sideways over the seat. The damned seat belt ripped into her skin again. *I'm done.* "Mitch?" she yelled.

"I'm all right." His face filled the gap between the seats again, this time lower. "You okay?"

"Someone just shot at me. I'm pissed."

He grinned, of all things. Grinned! "Give me your gun."

The car flew around a curve. Maria sobbed, her overnight bag gripped tightly in her hands as she lay curled on the floorboard. Caroline grabbed her sidearm, staying low over Maria, while checking the magazine. "If anyone's returning fire, it's me."

"I have a better angle."

"Who is it?" Maria cried. "Who's shooting at us?"

I wish I knew. Caroline released her seatbelt and crouched onto the floor, positioning her back against Mitch's seat so she could raise up and fire through the open window. "How close are they?" she said to Brice.

"Three car lengths. I can lose them on the next turn," he replied.

Maybe she wouldn't have to shoot.

Pop-pop-pop. Another round of bullets hit the car and Maria howled, all her stress balling into a high-pitched wail that pummeled Caroline's system. *Ignore her.* Focus.

Mitch spoke close to her ear. "I have a better vantage point. Give me the damn gun."

"The hell you do." Caroline ran through the logistics of the scene in her head. *Pedestrians. Cars on either side. Possible collateral damage everywhere.* "Now shut up and tell me when I have a clear shot."

Brice weaved the car all over the road, continuing to throw her off balance, but she braced her back more firmly against the seat.

"Straighten it out, Brice," Mitch said. "Now, Caroline!"

Caroline popped up, gun at the ready. The instant she cleared the edge of the back window, she held the oxygen in her lungs, aimed and fired.

Bam-bam-bam. The gun recoiled in her hand, spent rounds flying and adding to the mess of broken glass surrounding Maria. Caroline dropped again, taking cover should another round come at them. Seconds later screeching tires—the sound abrasive and ear puncturing—followed by crunching metal refocused her.

"Nailed 'em," Mitch shouted.

Wanting to see her handiwork, Caroline inched up again. Sure enough, she'd busted a couple of holes in the SUV's windshield. She'd also hit a tire, or maybe the driver. The vehicle swerved, lost control, and hit a telephone pole.

"Go back," Mitch barked. "Let's see who's in there."

"No," Caroline and Brice fired back in unison.

"It's our one chance to find out who's after the flash drive!"

Caroline watched the mangled SUV grow smaller as they sped away, but no one bailed out. "Cops will show up any minute and we can't risk being there when they do."

Maria lifted her head, her brown eyes red from crying, a silent plea shining in them.

"I'm sorry," Caroline told her, keeping an eye on the road behind them. "We'll keep you safe, Maria. This will be over soon."

She hoped she could keep that promise.

22

*M*itch's gut sank as he looked out the window of Caroline's father's private jet to the runway below. Red and blue lights flashed in whirling circles, cutting through the shadowy night. "We've got trouble," he said.

Caroline leaned over him and took in the sea of lights. "Dammit."

Brice unbuckled his seatbelt and shot across the aisle, letting out a string of curses.

Maria paled. "What is it?"

"Cops," Mitch answered. His fugitive status was done, and now the three people with him were about to pay the price. "They want me. You guys stay out of it and let me handle this. I'll exonerate you the best I can."

The plane's wheels touched down, bouncing all of them and sending Brice falling back to his seat. He sank down and put a hand over his eyes, looking strung out and exhausted. Mitch was right there with him.

Caroline grabbed his arm and squeezed. "We're in this together, remember?"

He couldn't look at her. Not after all of this. He'd wrecked her career and probably her life. *No time for this shit.* Instead, he pinned Maria with a death glare. "You've got the number I gave you, right?"

She nodded. "Justice Greystone. I memorized it."

"And you've got the copy of the files?"

Caroline, the always Type-A personality, had made a backup of Tommy's flash drive and a backup of the backup just in case. Her thoroughness might drive him crazy, but at times it came in handy.

Maria patted the waistband of her slacks where Caroline had sewn in the flash drive. "I won't give it to anyone but Mr. Greystone. Unless they arrest me too."

Which was a strong possibility, but his gut told him Maria would walk. "Just tell the cops I coerced you. That you didn't want anything to do with me but I forced you to help out. You haven't broken any laws. They can't hold you."

Caroline poked a finger at him. "Stop taking all the blame."

"Someone has to get that flash drive to Grey. He'll take it to his contact at Justice."

As always, Grey had come through. He'd set up a private meeting for the four of them with Connor Lane, the head of the Office of Special Counsel, an independent federal agency inside the Justice Department. The OSC protected the rights of federal employees and whistleblowers. They'd give Lane the evidence and see what he advised them to do.

"We are so screwed," Brice said from behind the hand covering his face.

"I'll call Lane," Caroline said.

Mitch studied the flashing lights, his stomach sour from the misery of having always known at some point, somewhere, the choice to stop running would be taken from him. "Not if you're in jail."

"I get one phone call. Guess how I'm going to use it?"

He glanced at her face and saw her grinning. Damn they

were a twisted combination. "You are some woman, you know that?"

"You better believe it."

The plane rolled to a stop and the pilot came over the intercom. "Sorry, Ms. Foster. I was under oath from your father not to tell you about this."

Caroline issued a flabbergasted sigh. "My *father* did this?"

Brice rose and helped Maria up. He motioned for Mitch and Caroline to go first. "Might as well pay the devil his due."

They drew on their jackets and gathered briefcases, laptops, and overnight bags while vehicles pulled into position around the plane. A cop with a bullhorn told them to come out with their hands up.

Mitch went first, tossing his bag down the stairs in front of him and raising his hands. "Nobody get twitchy," he called to the cops. "I give up."

A plainclothes officer approached, cuffed him, and led him to an unmarked car. While he was being patted down and read his rights, Brice received the same routine, only his charges were related to releasing a sealed document.

Caroline and Maria stood back while three men approached.

Donaldson, in his usual ugly brown suit, sent a smug smirk in Mitch's direction. Mitch flipped him off even though his hands were cuffed behind his back. The officer opened the unmarked car's rear door. "Get in."

Mitch ignored him, watching the man leading the pack of Donaldson and the third man. He wore a gray suit with a tan trench coat and looked vaguely familiar. The third man lingered behind, his face drawn into serious lines with a set of peepers that matched Caroline's.

"Dad!" Caroline left Maria's side and strode toward her father. "What have you done?"

Donaldson intercepted her. "He cut a deal to save your ass, Foster. Show some gratitude."

"Get. In," the plain clothed officer said to Mitch, shoving him into the backseat.

The man in the trench coat didn't stop for the Foster family drama, but called to the cop. "Hold up. I want to see him."

He came to stand in front of Mitch, his gaze sizing up Mitch's long hair, and reading his Roswell alien T-shirt that said *Property of Area 51. Do Not Confront.* "Mitch Monroe. We finally meet. Agent Donaldson has told me about you." The man smiled a thin, knowing smile, and pinned his brows together. "But to tell you the truth, I'm a bit disappointed. I thought you'd be..."

"Shorter?" Mitch smarted off.

"More *clever*," the man countered. "I was enjoying the chase, but now..." He tsked. "You've dropped right into my hands."

The guy wasn't FBI—he didn't carry himself like an agent. His blond, Robert Redford hair and good looks gave him a definite Hollywood vibe. Mitch scanned his memory. He was sure he'd seen this dickwad on TV, but he couldn't come up with an ID. "Who the fuck are you?"

The man smiled for real now, slow and antagonizing, and Mitch wanted to pop him. His voice dropped a few octaves. "I'm your worst nightmare, Monroe. Your very worst nightmare."

Mitch shrugged, going for unconcern as all his instincts screamed *danger*. "Lame line, but let's see what you've got. Meantime, the rest of the kids here are innocent. This was all my doing."

"I bet it was." The man chuckled as if this was the most fun of his life and glanced over his shoulder at Maria while speaking to the officer. "Bring her too."

"Bring her where?" Caroline demanded. "On what grounds?"

The man held out a hand. "I don't believe we've met, Agent Foster. I'm Sean W. Straling, Deputy Attorney General for the United States of America. I strongly urge you to keep your comments, ideas, and opinions to yourself, or I'll be forced to renege on that little deal I made with your father."

She started to say something, but Mitch coughed loudly, drawing her gaze. "Agent Foster knows how to follow orders. She won't give you any problems."

For once, Caroline shut her trap. Mitch loaded her up with eye contact and she nodded. If even *one* of them stayed out of jail and got the information to Grey, they had a chance.

Donaldson eyed the DAG. "Where *are* you taking them?"

"Don't worry, Harold." Straling patted Donaldson on the back as he walked past him. "I'll take care of this minor mess and have charges brought up first thing in the morning, once I interrogate your ex-agent. Go on home."

The officer shoved Mitch into the backseat. Brice was already in the back of a different cruiser, and Maria was being cuffed as Mitch's official escort pulled away. He chanced a glance at Caroline and saw her lift her chin. "Whatever it takes!" she yelled loud enough for him to hear.

"Whatever it takes," he mouthed back to her. He wasn't going to let her down.

As Caroline watched the police cars drive away with Mitch, Brice, and Maria, her heart didn't just sink, it drilled right through the tarmac. The DAG said something to Donaldson, then walked back to the hanger. Caroline turned on her father. "Dad, why did you do this?"

Her father looked grim. "You transported a known fugitive wanted for murder on my plane. You didn't tell me about *that*." He brushed a finger across her bruise. "What happened to you?"

"I apologize for keeping the truth about Mitch from you, but he's innocent, and..." Donaldson caught her eye and motioned her to follow him.

She left her father sputtering and calling after her and jogged over to her boss. "I need to know where he's taking Mitch and Maria."

"Maria? That's the woman?"

Caroline nodded and retrieved the tiny USB she had hidden in her waistband to show it to him. "She was Tommy's...she's the, uh, sister of Tommy's informant and she can confirm sensitive information Tommy stored on this flash drive about the operation. There are men after her. She's in danger."

Donaldson spread his feet and crossed his arms over his chest. "Well, she'll be safe in jail while waiting for her bail hearing."

"Bail for what? Straling doesn't have any reason to arrest her."

"She was conspiring with a fugitive, Foster. I'm sure *if* he wants, the DAG can come up with a dozen other charges."

"Where are they taking them?"

"I don't know."

They locked eyes for a second. Caroline refused to give in. Not a chance.

Donaldson finally sighed in that way that told Caroline he knew just how stubborn she could be. "I'll look into it and find out where they're being held." He reached into his pocket and brought out a folded piece of paper. "In the meantime, I have that list of Thai restaurants you asked about."

Thai restaurants? She accepted the paper, saw a list of names. "Thank you." *I think.*

"Some of them are pretty noisy, if you know what I mean, or at least they used to be. But if you need a solid source of *indigestion*, you'll find one on that list. A few of the restaurants might have closed down or moved to another town, so it might take some digging to find them."

Good thing he didn't work for the CIA...coded messages were not his strong suit. Didn't matter. She clutched the paper tightly in her hand. The list, as her boss had promised, contained names of taskforce members who'd made noise about the operation or Tommy's death and been transferred, or otherwise shut down, to keep them quiet. "I'll get on this right away."

"Be in my office first thing in the morning. We have things to discuss before you resume your job."

She still had a job? "I'll be there, sir."

She gave her father a quick hug and a peck on the cheek with a promise to explain everything in a day or so. First, she had to make phone calls. Not only to the guys on the list, but to a few lawyers. Mitch, Maria, and Brice were going to need them.

Her car was at the airport where she'd left it. After retrieving her bags, she headed for the abandoned army base. On the way, she called Grey. "Mitch has been arrested," she told him. "So have Brice and the woman we told you about. We brought her with us to talk to Connor Lane and give her testimony, but now the DAG has her."

"Damn it." Grey was quiet for a long moment. "But they let you go?"

"My father cut a deal. The Deputy Attorney General showed up at the airport with Agent Donaldson and my father. He arrested Mitch, Brice, and Maria, but he never said what the charges were against Maria. Donaldson believes he'll use conspiring with a fugitive as the main one. I'm worried about her. And worse, with all of them being arrested, I think whoever is behind the cover-up searched her house, beat me up, and shot at us trying to stop this investigation. What if they kill her?"

Grey swore under his breath. "Where did they take her and Mitch? D.C. Metro?"

"I don't know. The DAG wouldn't say. Donaldson is looking into it." She took a turn off the interstate. "I'm heading to your office. I need a secure line to make a few calls."

"Teeg and I will meet you there."

Mitch saw little of the five-story building as he was hustled inside and down a long, dark corridor. Most of the lights were burned out, and the few actually working projected weird shadows on the graffiti-filled walls.

The cop cars had split off earlier, the one with Brice heading for downtown. His and Maria's unmarked cars heading for this abandoned building on the far edge of the city. At one time, it might have been a housing development of some kind. Definitely not a police station or FBI headquarters.

Trouble. Big, bad trouble, is what this was. The kind that smelled as ripe as the hallway he walked down.

Nerves banged around under his skin. He logged the layout, the entrances and exits he could see. Two officers escorted him, one in front and one behind. A third man waited for them at the end of the hall. Burly and in plain clothes, he looked like a bouncer at a club. Mitch suspected he was about to be released into the hands of an interrogator.

Maria was nowhere in sight. Had they taken her in through a different door? Her life could very well be in danger but how could he get to her when he was cuffed and surrounded by meatheads? With guns.

No words were exchanged as his two guards handed him over to the interrogator. The man's bald head and dark, beady eyes reminded Mitch of a trainer he'd had at Quantico. Cobra, they'd called him. The hardass trainer's ears had stuck out from his head like a Cobra hood, earning him the nickname.

After a grunt from the interrogator, the officers left. Mitch and the man locked stares.

This wasn't an arrest. This was a kidnapping.

What was this guy going to do to him? Silence him like someone silenced Tommy and Kemp?

Bring it on, motherfucker. "Where's the picnic?" Mitch asked. *Get to Maria. You have to protect her. But where was she?*

And what about Caroline? Would the killer go after her?

The man opened the door behind him and stepped aside. A single light bulb hung from a long electrical wire in the ceiling. Old wooden steps led down into a murky basement with a beat up table and a metal chair. Dark stains littered the floor. Dried blood?

"Move," Cobra growled, shoving Mitch forward.

"Wait!" Someone snapped their fingers. "I want to talk to him first."

Mitch turned and saw Straling motioning Cobra to escort him into a room off the hallway. Perfect. Maybe Mitch could get some answers about Maria's location before the meathead went to work on him.

The DAG's bouncer pushed and prodded Mitch back down the hall to the open door. Inside, it looked like an apartment in serious need of a decorator's touch.

Mitch was led into what was once the kitchen, and if he had his directions correct, it faced east. Most of the cabinets and appliances had been torn out, leaving gaping holes in the walls. The yellowed ceiling boasted a Rorschach of water stains and a chair was toppled on its side. Cobra righted it, shoving Mitch into the ripped seat.

The flexi cuffs on his wrists dug into his skin. *Use the pain.* Whatever was about to go down would be rough. He sensed it as his body stiffened and adrenaline flowed. He needed to stay alert and find or make an opportunity to get away.

Sean W. Straling planted his feet in front of Mitch, while his goon stayed to the left. "I hate that messy basement," Straling said. "So dank and dark. Better for us to discuss your future—however short it might be—up here."

"What did you do with the woman?" Mitch asked.

The DAG seemed cheered by the question. "Worried about her, are you? Good. Hand over the flash drive and she'll stay in one piece."

"What flash drive?"

Straling's cheer faded. He gave a nod to the goon and the man punched Mitch in the jaw.

The hit sent Mitch to the floor, pain exploding in his face and traveling to his eyes. Shaking it off, he staggered to his feet. "Afraid to mess up your suit, Straling?"

Another nod from the DAG and the goon shoved Mitch back into the chair. "Let's not play games. You have information I need. Do I have to search you myself?"

"Touch me and you'll have a problem."

"Is that so?" Straling jerked his head at Cobra. "Search him."

Mitch kicked the meathead in the shin, but the man's fist connected with his temple at the same time, sending Mitch to the floor again. White flashes blinded him and he squeezed his eyes closed for a second. *Breathe.* The goon flipped him on his back and searched his pockets.

"You're going to regret that," Mitch mumbled, his temple throbbing like a bass drum inside his head.

"Shut the fuck up." Cobra kicked Mitch in the hip. "He's clean," he said to Straling.

"Where are his bags?" Straling asked, frowning down at Mitch.

Cobra shrugged. "Your guys only brought him. I didn't see no bags."

Mitch opened and closed his mouth a couple of times to work the pain out of his jaw. His temple pounded and Straling's dress shoes faded in and out of his vision.

Straling snapped his fingers again. "The girl probably has it. Keep an eye on him. I'll be back."

Mitch blinked to clear his vision and called after him, "Did you kill Tommy Nusco?"

Straling stopped. "Me? Kill an FBI agent? Why would I do that? Donaldson said you loved a good conspiracy theory and I can see that now."

His brain might have been slightly scrambled from the hits, but pieces of the puzzle rearranged themselves and dropped into place. "Why did you want all those guns to walk?"

The shoes disappeared from view and Mitch stayed down, hoping Cobra would think he was harmless. He closed his eyes and listened to the DAG's retreating footsteps, the sound of a door opening and closing. Faintly, he heard the man making noise in the hall, then the sound of his shoes climbing stairs.

Maria's upstairs. At least he had a general idea of where to find her when the time came.

But she had one of the flash drives. She was no agent, no undercover operative. If Straling threatened her—*when* he threatened her—she'd hand it over without a fight.

He actually hoped she did. Straling was a priss and wouldn't dirty his hands, but he'd have Cobra work her over if it came to that.

...wouldn't dirty his hands. Another puzzle piece spun and dropped into place. The DAG wouldn't pull the trigger. He'd have someone else do it.

Someone who was still in New Mexico hunting for Jesse.

And getting his windshield fixed.

But why? What was Straling after? What was every politician in D.C. after? *Power.*

Mitch sat up. "Get him back down here," he told Straling's goon. "I'm ready to talk."

· · ·

Caroline paced the concrete floor in Grey's war room. That's what she'd decided to call the army base's main space. This time, he'd left up his bulletin board and the notes from various cases he was working. Since she'd put her career on the line for Mitch, Grey must have deemed her trustworthy.

Teeg, the computer expert, was at his desk, and Grey was somewhere in the building on a private phone conversation. Teeg stared at multiple screens and said nothing as she paced and waited for Donaldson to call.

Nine out of ten former taskforce members on the list he'd given her had shut her down before she'd asked the first question. Still, she'd warned them she was taking a boatload of evidence about the gun walking operation and Tommy's murder to Justice first thing in the morning.

Since the sun was already rising, first thing in the morning quickly approached.

Mitch, I hope you and Maria are okay.

Brice had been taken to Metro P.D., but no one could locate Mitch or Maria. Why separate them? Brice could have just as easily had the information as Mitch or Maria.

But Brice was never directly connected to Tommy. Caroline paced faster.

The one taskforce guy who'd spoken to her, Zachariah Nunnely, had put her on hold while he retrieved his notes on the operation. He'd eventually come through and the two of them reviewed the case in detail. Like Tommy, Zach had been suspicious of the straw buying operation. After Tommy's death, he'd gone to his supervisor, and for his trouble, he was now in Fargo, North Dakota twiddling his thumbs and chasing down cigarette traffickers.

But Caroline had hope. Zach had agreed to come to Washington and meet with Connor Lane. He was taking the first flight out and would be in town by early afternoon.

I just hope it's not too late.

Distrust and doubt itched under her skin. They knew the cover-up went high up on the chain of command, but how far? Who could they trust? The Deputy Attorney General had hustled off Mitch and Maria, and no one could find them. It didn't bode well.

Grey came walking in, his face a thundercloud.

"Anything?" Caroline asked.

He shook his head. "There's no reason for the DAG to meet your plane and take Mitch to an undisclosed location. None. If he was bringing him up on charges, Mitch would have been processed like any other detainee."

"He said he wanted to interrogate him."

"Same result...Mitch would be taken downtown and interrogated, but neither he nor Maria are there. I've called everyone I know and there's nothing on them. Even if the Deputy Attorney General is keeping things hushed up, one of my sources would know if Mitch was in the system. No one has seen him or heard anything about his arrest."

Caroline flapped her arms. "What the hell is going on?"

"I wish I knew."

"Incoming call," Teeg announced from his computer.

A second later, Caroline's phone rang. She glanced at Grey. "How does he do that?"

"You don't want to know."

"He better not have bugged my phone." She glanced at the screen. "It's Donaldson."

"Maybe he had better luck finding them than I did."

Caroline punched the talk button. "Foster."

"Don't ask any questions, just listen," Donaldson said, his voice low. "What I'm about to tell you goes no farther and you didn't hear it from me."

Caroline signaled Grey to stay quiet and put her boss on speakerphone. "Yes, sir. Whatever you tell me is completely confidential."

He grunted as if he'd looked through her phone and knew she was lying. "During his last State of the Union address, the President leaned heavily on instituting stronger gun control measures, especially in the southern states after the Milan incident in Mexico."

Yolanda Milan, a Mexican diplomat's daughter, had been killed outside her home by a weapon that had entered Mexico illegally from Texas. Mexican officials had put a lot of heat on the U.S. over her death and asked for an in-depth investigation into the illegal flow of weapons into Mexico.

"This," Donaldson continued, "kicked off the taskforce operation and gave the president more ammunition to enact stricter gun control legislation. The Republicans went ballistic."

Caroline frowned at Grey as Donaldson paused and let out a slow breath. It took all of her willpower not to fire off the questions swimming through her brain. "Okay. You're saying the Justice Department, as the parent department to ATF, was directed to get the guns off the street and came up with this operation?"

Donaldson responded with silence.

"So someone inside the Department of Justice approved letting guns walk? But isn't that ass backwards if they were tasked with getting guns *off* the streets?" She'd opened the dam and the questions kept coming. "Did the DoJ want the president's agenda to fail?"

"No, but the Republicans and the NRA put up such a wall against gun control measures, the president couldn't get over."

Her stomach knotted. "Is it possible this thing could go as high as the president?"

Silence again. Terrific. Her nerves stretched a little tighter. "Where did Straling take Mitch and Maria?"

"I can't confirm, but there's an abandoned building off I-395.

It's been used by the CIA, FBI, and a host of others for training and various purposes."

"A safe house?"

"Not exactly. There are some things you're better off not knowing, Foster."

"Give me the address. I'll meet you there."

"No chance. I can't get involved any deeper in this, and you need to be careful. I've saved your career at the moment, but if you go rushing in there, throwing around accusations, you could end up in jail with Mitch."

She was sick and tired of him holding her career hostage. "Good men have died over this. Mitch's life could be in jeopardy. You really think I care about my job right now?"

A heavy sigh came from Donaldson's end. He rattled off the address. "Don't say I didn't warn you...but look, if you get there and you see anything illegal going on, call me. Got it?"

"I've got it."

She disconnected and exchanged a look with Grey.

"You want me to drive?" he said.

For once, with the level of anger shredding her, she knew it would be better to let someone else take the wheel. "I'll meet you around back. I need to grab a few things from my car."

One of which is my rifle.

23

From the front seat of Grey's car, Caroline stared up at the T-shaped five-story apartment building where an unaccounted for number of goons held Mitch hostage. From their vantage point half a block down she couldn't see much, but that would change soon.

"What do we know about this building?"

Grey's face was hidden behind a long-range Burris scope. "It went into foreclosure ten years ago and the DoJ scooped it up. They use it for training exercises. And apparently, for other reasons too."

Caroline lifted her binoculars, brought the building into focus, and scanned the top floor. Ten windows on the one side. "He's in there somewhere, but we don't know where."

"We're assuming he's in there."

"Well, the goon at the front entrance might be an indicator."

Grey shrugged. "Maybe he's not our goon."

"So, you think we have random people standing outside the building Donaldson told us would be a good place to hide Mitch and Maria?"

"I don't think anything. I'm just not ready to say Monroe is in there. Not when we don't know."

Caroline lifted the binoculars again and scanned the block. Across the street from the building in question sat a vacant manufacturing plant—*one, two, three*—seven stories high and facing the hostage taker's location. A row of windows stretched across the top floor. Caroline swung the binoculars back to her target area. *Could work.*

"If I can get up to the roof of the adjacent building, I can use my scope and check each room on the front side of the building."

"That could take a while."

"Well, Greystone, unless you're busting out a drone that can help us find them, I'm going with it."

"Mitch told you about the drone? He never could keep his mouth shut."

Huh? Caroline knew her mouth dropped open, but *holy cow.* "You have a *drone*? Seriously?"

He shrugged. "Teeg likes his toys." He lowered his scope. "Screw this. You get your gear and set up on the roof. While you're doing that, I'm gonna deal with the ox by the south entrance. Once I'm in, I'll locate Monroe and call you."

He handed her the car keys, opened the door and made a move to get out, but Caroline grabbed hold. "Hang on, cowboy. You don't think that guy will shoot you on sight?"

"Not if I badge him. I'll walk up, flash my badge, and tell him I work for Donaldson. I know enough to be dangerous and he won't risk pissing me off. Now, get your gear and make your way behind those trees to that building. Keep your phone handy."

"Grey!"

Ignoring her, he kept walking. If she got out of this car and chased him, she'd most likely be seen by the goon half a block down.

Resigned to this insane plan—no wonder Mitch and Grey got along—she slouched down in her seat to give Grey a head start. Then she'd worm her way out of the car, grab her rifle case from the back seat and head to the roof of the abandoned building to hopefully save Mitch's ass.

Grey strode toward the King Kong wannabe standing in front of the south entrance to the apartment building. He wore a navy suit—solid, no pinstripes—and a white dress shirt that stretched across his massive chest. If given the opportunity, this guy could probably crush him.

If given the opportunity.

Already Kong had taken three steps left, completely blocking the steel double doors. Shoulders back, feet wide in that state of readiness men assume when they anticipate a threat.

Smart man.

Grey held up his hands as he approached. "Justice Greystone. FBI."

"Stop right there. Let me see your creds."

Reaching into his inside jacket pocket, Grey grabbed his badge and snapped it open, holding it until Kong gave him permission to approach.

Instead, Kong came to him and the power shift was on. First rule in the world of alphas. Never relinquish power. By coming to Grey, Kong had most definitely relinquished his power.

Arms at his sides, Kong studied the badge a second, intermittently flicking his gaze to Grey then back to the badge.

"Mitch Monroe is my former partner. Special Agent in Charge Donaldson sent me to talk to him. He thinks the pain in the ass will listen to me." Grey patted the breast pocket of his jacket. "I have a note for the DAG from Donaldson. He tried to reach him by phone, but no go."

Kong narrowed his dead blue eyes. Eyes like that, this guy had nothing in his soul. Stone-cold killer. Slowly, he set his hand on his hip. Right by his sidearm.

Yeah, I see the weapon, pal. It won't help you.

"Let me see the note."

"Sure." Grey reached into his pocket, grabbed his wallet where he had a folded slip of paper. The paper contained Sydney's ongoing Christmas list he'd insisted she give him so he didn't screw up. Kong didn't know that though, and Grey needed him distracted for a few seconds. And crotchless panties being the number one thing on the list—thanks to Syd's twisted humor—would definitely distract this guy.

After handing the folded note over, Grey shoved his wallet back into his pockets to free his hands. Kong focused on unfolding the note and Grey curled his right hand into a fist, shifting slightly and giving himself an unimpeded opening. *Another two seconds.*

Kong's bottom lip curled out. "What the?"

The second Kong lifted his head, Grey swung—*whap*—one shot to the throat. Momentum brought Kong's chin up and—*whap*—Grey cracked him again across the jaw. The big man's head snapped back, then forward again, his gaze straight on with Grey's but his eyes, those cold, dead eyes had gone spacey. They rolled back and—nighty-night—Kong went lights-out.

Excellent. Syd's note was still in his hand. *Ooh, can't lose that.* Grey snatched it up and shoved it into his jacket pocket. He'd put it back in his wallet later. Right now, he had to find his friend.

Drawing his weapon, he helped himself to Kong's two-way radio, clipped it to his belt and swung the steel door open, clearing the entryway. Empty. Perfect.

Staying close to the wall, he crept the empty hallway, taking note of the rat droppings along the way. The paint on the cement walls had long since started peeling and the floors didn't look much better. Grey stepped lightly, avoiding the heels of his dress shoes clicking.

Being a believer in his own instincts, the ones screaming he should take the stairwell coming up on his left, he did just that. At the second floor, he opened the door and listened. Nothing.

Maybe he'd go all the way up and work his way down.

The minute he hit the fifth floor landing, he heard it. He stopped, stared at the ceiling, listening, observing, taking it all in. Voices. In the hallway. Something about another go. He stuck his ear to the door. Definitely voices. Coming closer.

Shit.

Grey jumped to the opposite wall, weapon at the ready, waiting for the door to open. The voices faded as the men strode by heading to the north end of the hallway. He couldn't risk opening the door to check.

Caroline. He'd told her to keep her phone on. By now, she should have been in the building with her scope set up.

He shot her a text. FIFTH FLOOR. VOICES. I THINK FROM NORTH SIDE. CHECK ALL WINDOWS.

Inside of five minutes, Caroline had shattered the window on the back door to the manufacturing plant and let herself in. If this were the movies, she'd have picked the lock—which she could have done—but since the broken-down building appeared to have been without life for at least a decade, she saved herself time and aggravation and busted the window.

With her rifle and carry bag slung across her shoulders, she made her way through the empty building, kicking her way through random garbage and machine parts that littered the filthy floor. A rat skittered away and Caroline's heart slammed. *Hate those damned things.*

In the far corner, she located a set of stairs and made her way up to the fifth floor where she stood on a catwalk lining the interior of the plant. Above her was the open area she'd spied from the street. She needed to get up there, but the steps ended at the fifth level. Had to be another way up. She glanced around and inhaled the suffocating dust of the deteriorating building.

Should have brought a water bottle. Above her, the ceiling sat low and she scoured the area for another set of steps that would lead her upstairs. Nothing. She headed across the catwalk to the far end where she found an ancient elevator with a gate closure. Deathtrap. Right next to it—*bingo*—were the stairs.

If they could be called that. In essence what she had equaled a rusty thrill ride that would send her plummeting five stories to the cement floor where she'd meet her death.

Plan B.

Back to the elevator. She analyzed the open space above where emergency climbing rungs had been bolted to the side wall. Whether those rungs were intact or not, she couldn't know, but on closer inspection, they looked solid. She slid her rifle and carry bag crossways across her body, curled her fingers into the elevator gate and gave it a test shake. The cables seemed intact and the elevator barely moved. She'd have to risk it.

At least she'd worn flat shoes. But wow—she'd prefer to be in her cargo pants instead of slacks and a lightweight shirt. Whatever. Digging one foot into the gate, she boosted herself up and—upsy-daisy—climbed over the top of the car. The elevator swayed and she grabbed the cable to steady herself. Her stomach flipped. Long way down.

Only way to go was up. Breathing heavy from her climb, she swiped her arm across her forehead to dry the dripping sweat then reached for the climbing rung. *Whoa, baby.* The elevator car swayed again then stopped. Stretched across the top of the car and the side wall, she gave the rung a yank. Solid.

"Here we go."

Hanging on to the elevator cable, she moved one foot to the lower climbing rung. When it held, she said a lightning quick "Glory be" and swung fully onto the rungs.

The Glory be paid off because the rungs held. *Thank you.*

She quickly made her way up the rungs, checking the security of each before she put her weight on it. Near the top, one bolt broke away. Just *pop!* That sucker flew.

Fire ripped across her shoulders as half her body hung in the air. *Move.* Still gripping the lower rung, she let go of the bad one.

She'd have to jump to reach the next lever, and if she missed, well, it had been a great thirty-three years. *Dammit.* Only a few feet from the top and she'd hit a snag. She dropped her head, closed her eyes and breathed in. Slowly, she exhaled and envisioned the leap. Envisioned grabbing on to that rung. Envisioned flinging herself over the top. Envisioned Mitch and his life that needed saving.

She threw her shoulders back, willed away the frying sensation and focused.

"I'm hanging in the middle of a fucking elevator shaft. Mitch will love it."

Her front pants pocket buzzed. Terrific. Text coming in. Grey had said to leave her phone on. Well, he'd have to wait a second. *Can't talk now, hon.* She stared up at the rung, took a deep breath, counted three and leaped. Her body was airborne for half a second, but it could have been an hour and then —*foom*—she grabbed hold of the rung, tightening her fingers around it. The soles of her flat shoes slid down the concrete wall—*oh, no*—and she scrambled for a better grip.

Fierce stabs of panic plunged into her. *No, no, no.*

With her other hand, she clutched the rung and hung there,

her feet loose as her arms and shoulders absorbed the agony of holding her body weight. Sweat slid down the center of her back and her arms quivered under the pressure. *Hang on.* A vision of her dead body sprawled across the floor filled her mind. Not today. *No dying today.*

"You got this, Caroline."

And then her foot hit a chip in the wall. Just a small indentation but it was enough for her to prop her toe into it and get traction. *Go.* She heaved herself over the top, her breaths coming fast and hard and painful as her cheek lay against the disgusting floor, but—hey, it beat falling five stories to her death.

Dirt she could deal with.

Death, not so much.

Damn you, Mitch Monroe.

Breathing hard, she jumped to her feet, retrieved her phone and checked the text that had come in. Grey. Windows. North side. Got it. Thirty seconds and she'd be in place.

Running to the window, she set her bag on the floor, lifted her rifle, snapped the bipod legs open and placed them on an open sill. *Lookie here.* The target building faced due west where the sun would be directly in her face. How she loved a challenge. She dropped to her knee and adjusted her scope to 10 power for a wide view. Starting at the far end of the building she scanned the first window, then the second. Nothing. Third window. Pay dirt.

She switched the scope to 50 power bringing her target window into narrow focus. A sheer curtain with a six-inch space in the middle hung in the window. Behind it, a man in a black suit paced back and forth, his movements quick and jerking. Stressed. For a split second, he turned toward her. The DAG. That son of a bitch.

To his left, another target stood, arms crossed, feet spread as if waiting to be summoned to action. He stared down at a man in a chair and—*oh, God*—her skin caught fire again. Sitting in that chair, his head drooped forward, the side of his face battered and bloody, was Mitch. This man that drove her crazy, that she'd threatened to shoot countless times, that she *loved*, had been beaten like a rabid animal.

Can't allow that.

"Sons of bitches. You're going down."

Caroline closed her eyes, let the fury wash through her, and reminded herself she was an FBI agent trained to handle these types of situations with swift efficiency. She could not, would not get emotional.

At least not yet.

When Mitch was free, she'd get emotional.

Donaldson had told her to call if she saw anything illegal. Did she have time for that? Would he consider this illegal? One would hope, but she didn't know anymore. Forget Donaldson. She opened her eyes again. "Okay, boys, let's see what we've got."

In the window, her target continued his pacing, staring down at an unmoving Mitch. *He's pissed.*

Well, so am I.

But if she had to take a shot, it would be a cold bore one. Through a veiled curtain.

This shot was all about precision with a custom fit weapon. Caroline knew her rifle—the length of the barrel, the curve of the butt against her shoulder, the crisp two pound pull of the trigger—like she knew her own body. She breathed in. Precision and breathing she could control. Bad cartridges, *fliers*, she couldn't, but her accuracy percentage clocked in at .5 MOA. No doubt—she could make the shot.

Not. A. Problem.

Her phone rang. She backed away from the scope. Grey. She punched the screen for the speakerphone and set the phone by her feet. "I'm in place. Can you hear anything?"

"No."

She went back to her scope. Across the street, her target stomped around, back and forth, back and forth, his movements jerky. On her rifle, she grabbed the bolt, chambered a round, and locked it down.

"You ready?" Grey asked.

"I'm ready."

"Wake up, asshole."

Mitch opened his eyes, or at least the one that wasn't swollen from being punched. The deep voice belonged to another of Straling's goons, this one a long-haired hippy type with a tattoo on the side of his neck. During the night, he and Cobra had dragged Mitch up to the fifth floor and taken turns beating the shit out of him, mostly for fun, it seemed.

His hands were tied to the chair, forcing him to face front. The morning sun cast faint light from the window onto the cracked kitchen flooring where Mitch's blood had pooled and dried in spots. His head pounded, his ribs ached with every breath, and he needed to take a piss. "Where's Straling?"

"Right here." The man stepped in front of him in a fresh suit and tie, smelling of soap and shampoo. "Ready to confess your crimes?"

The bastard had gone home and showered. Probably even slept for a while. Could be good or bad. Either he'd left Maria alone or he'd gotten what he wanted from her even before Hippie Douche Bag had given Mitch a black eye.

Man, he needed a drink. Or a toothbrush. His mouth was dry and his sore jaw had trouble forming words. His time in between beatings had given him opportunities to think about the DAG's involvement, but he was still missing the man's motivations. Politics, no doubt, but maybe in the end, it didn't matter. Right now, he had to convince the DAG that Maria was an innocent party. "You don't need to hurt the girl. She was sleeping with Tommy but she doesn't know anything."

Straling shook a finger at Mitch as he paced around him in a circle. "She actually knows quite a lot. More than is good for her health, I'm afraid."

"She's too scared to talk, and I'll give you all of Tommy's files if you let her go."

"Files?" Straling seemed to consider the offer. "Oh, you mean these?"

He fished two flash drives from his jacket pocket—the red one Maria had been carrying and Mitch's blue one. He waved them in front of Mitch's good eye. "Looks like your bargaining chip is off the table. I have everything I need to wrap up this little operation and make sure the United States of America continues the good fight."

Goddamn. He had the files. Now what? "You don't have Jesse Lando. Is he your inside man? The one who set up Tommy?"

"Oh, please. Lando couldn't think his way out of a paper sack. He's a varmint like those nasty little scorpions they have down there near the border. He had a simple job. One simple fucking job, and that was to buy guns and deliver them to Balboa. That's it. But your friend, Agent Nusco, had to get involved and poke his dick where it didn't belong." Straling tsked, continuing to pace.

"Who shot Tommy? You don't have the balls."

The DAG gave Mitch a questioning look. "Goading, Mitch? After all of this, you're still itching for a fight?"

When Mitch didn't answer, Straling smiled. "Doesn't matter. You'll be dead soon anyway. How does it feel to know you can't hurt me?"

Oh, I'll hurt you, fucker.

"Lando got cold feet, decided to back out. Do you know how long it took me to set up that operation? Two years. I had that pussy Will Atkinson in place, doing whatever I wanted in order

263

to keep his big brother as the attorney general in New Mexico. He harassed the gun shop owners, kept me informed about all the whining the taskforce members were doing. Right from the start, I knew Nusco would be a pain in the ass. Two years of planning and organizing and making promises. Promises I still have to keep. Our nation's safety depends on it. My *job* depends on it."

"You're insane. Letting guns walk doesn't make our nation safer."

"The border states, with all the smuggling and rampant crime...need stricter gun control laws. The president has been trying to enact such laws, but Congress keeps burying the bills with bureaucratic bullshit. I knew I could move the immovable force."

Either Mitch was lightheaded from lack of sleep and water, or Cobra and Hippy had rattled his brain. This guy sounded like he'd just escaped from the loony bin. "What the fuck are you talking about?"

"Newton's first law of motion...in order for the motion of an object to change, a force must act upon it. In this case, the object that needs to change is Congress, and I'm the force acting upon it by proving we have an illegal firearms problem."

He couldn't be serious. "So you flooded the market with guns? You wanted to increase violence in New Mexico in order to pass a fucking gun control law?"

"Brilliant, no?"

No. Far from it. Lunatic. "How many innocent people died or were injured because of your cockamamie plan?"

"Now see, I thought you had vision. The AG is bailing after this term. Who do you think is in line for that job? You of all people should understand that sacrifices have to be made for the greater good."

Sacrifice. Mitch knew too much about sacrificing himself and his friends for the fucking greater good. His voice came out low and ragged. "Who killed Tommy? If it wasn't Lando, then who?"

Straling spoke to Cobra and Hippy. "Get the girl."

The DAG turned back to Mitch. "That's where it got interesting. Tommy sent me an email—*me*—asking me to look into the operation. Then he wouldn't stop. That prick rattled every cage available. He had to go. Atkinson wasn't too happy about it, but what choice did he have? He'd already strong-armed the gun shop owners. And his brother was on the hook with us. Hell, he's the top federal law enforcement officer for New Mexico and he was letting guns walk. Sacrificing the reputation and life of one agent was nothing to those boys."

The son of a bitch set Tommy up and made it look like he went rogue and was selling ATF confiscated guns.

The DAG's smile widened. He enjoyed gloating over his success. "Atkinson wasn't as bright as I'd hoped. He left the gun on Tommy's body to make it look like the exchange had gone wrong and the gunrunner had offed your friend." He touched his temple. "I knew when the ballistics came back on the gun, it could be traced to Lando, so I took a precaution and ordered the file sealed."

Mitch's guts cramped. "How many other people has Atkinson killed for you?"

"Only Agent Nusco."

At the look of hatred Mitch gave him, Straling shrugged. "Nusco was going to blow the whole thing. I couldn't let that happen. Too many people were counting on me."

"Like the president?"

"The election is only weeks away. We're going to win it."

Mitch rolled his head, trying to shake the fog loose. "So President Perkins agreed to your plan because it would help him get reelected."

Straling moved to the far side of what would have been the living room. A filthy, sheer curtain hung on the window, and a moment later Cobra and Hippy dragged Maria into the kitchen from what must have been the bedroom.

Dirty and bruised, she staggered in, her bottom lip bleeding and swelled. Her eyes were ringed with red from crying. "I'm sorry," she murmured, looking at Mitch. "I'm so sorry."

The DAG walked to her and snapped his fingers at Cobra. "Hand me your gun."

Maria jerked back, her gaze whipping to Straling's face. Hippy held her in place as Cobra handed over his weapon.

"Wait," Mitch said, struggling against his ties. "The only way to get Jesse to come in is if she's still alive."

Straling gave Mitch a *boy, are you stupid* look. "That may be true, but like I said, Jesse isn't that bright. He won't talk, but his sister here? She will. She's already told you and Agent Foster what she knows."

"You can't kill all of us," Mitch said.

The DAG smiled. "Agent Foster will keep her mouth shut or her dear father will pay the price. You're wanted for murder, so you'll be going to prison for a very long time. And if you open your mouth and say one word about this?" He raised the gun and put it to Maria's temple. "This is what I'll do to your girlfriend."

Mitch yelled Maria's name, but all he heard was the gun going off.

"Gunshot! Go!"

Grey's voice thundered through the phone and adrenalin poured into Caroline's brain. She blinked twice, focused on the shot.

Take the shot.

Not ready. Not ready. Caroline drew a breath, letting half of it out and holding the rest as her target turned to a side profile and swung his gun to Mitch. Screaming in her head, relentless and demanding, pounded at her to take the shot because Mitch was about to die and she was in a full blown panic. Her heart slammed—*take the shot*—stealing her breath, trapping all that good, healthy oxygen inside her. *Take the shot.* She blinked. *Not ready.* But Mitch couldn't die. Not in front of her. Not when she could have stopped it.

But what if she missed?

No missing. When's the last time she'd missed?

She centered her target's temple in her crosshairs—*not ready, stay still.* But that gun was pointed straight at Mitch. She squeezed the trigger and...*boom!*

Across the street, the window shattered and her target leaped toward the door,

Shit.

Missed. *Go.* She racked the bolt back, ejected the spent case, shoved it forward and chambered another round. The second target drew a weapon, pointed it at Mitch.

Quick bursts of air shot from her lungs and she concentrated on controlling her breathing. In, out, in, out, in, out. The chaos in her mind tunneled into sharp focus. The window, the distance.

Go.

One. More. Try. She found the spot on her target's head where, when hit, his reflexes wouldn't cause his body to flinch and fire the weapon in his grasp.

She squeezed the trigger.

Boom.

The shot connected and the target dropped. "Target two down! First one on the move. Go!"

"On it," Grey said, his voice calm and controlled.

Caroline sat back, propped herself against the low wall and blocked out the screaming while her tightly wound energy unraveled and spewed inside her. *Breathe.*

From somewhere, a siren sounded. Unrelated maybe. She

didn't know. Didn't care. In a minute she'd make her way to the street.

In a minute.

Right now, all she knew was she'd just made the shot of her life.

24

Mitch wasn't sure exactly what had happened. Maria was down, the goon's body on top of her, and Straling had jumped clear. Someone had fired a shot through the window and glass lay on the floor at Mitch's feet... and if he took a guess, he'd bet Caroline had something to do with the bullet in Cobra's brain.

His heart jack-hammered and he tried to stand. His legs were tied to the chair, his hands cuffed behind him, and his balance was totally off. He nearly toppled left, then right and realized he couldn't feel his feet. His circulation had been cut off for too long and everything below his waist was numb.

Just inside the threshold leading to the hall, Straling, coward that he was, squirmed along on his belly. Another few feet and he'd be out of sight from the window and would bolt.

Numbness in his feet or not, Mitch had to tackle him before he got clear of the doorway.

In the distance, he heard a siren. Reinforcements. Good. Toppling into the counter, he bounced off, and propelled himself into the hallway. He went down hard on his knees, the chair seat cutting sharply into the back of his legs. A grunt left his cracked lips and his center of gravity shifted. Sweat poured down his face as pain knifed at him, plunging deeper and deeper. Three feet away, Straling continued to squirm.

Mitch held his breath, readied his body for the second attack and hurled forward. He ended up on the DAG's back, the chair with his ass tied to it rising into the air. His forehead smacked into the back of the DAG's head and his already busted nose sent a fresh, sharp stab of pain into his frontal lobe.

"Well, that's an interesting interrogation pose," a voice said as a pair of black leather dress shoes came into Mitch's view.

He knew that voice. In fact, it might be the best voice he'd heard in the past few hours. "Grey? What the hell are you doing here?"

"Saving your ass." Grey's hands wrapped around Mitch and lifted him back into a sitting position. Mitch's cracked ribs screamed in pain. "Again."

Grey shoved his hoof into the DAG's back and put his Glock to the back of the man's skull. "Move again and I put a bullet in you."

The DAG stayed put as Grey cuffed him. Grey started on Mitch's ties, but Mitch shook him off. "Check Maria. She's under Cobra."

Grey didn't question the goon's nickname. The wrist restraints came free and Grey made quick work of the ankle restraints as well. "Here. Keep an eye on this asshole while I check her."

Mitch flexed his fingers twice and took over Grey's sidearm.

Blood and brain matter were splattered on the wall, a chunk of Cobra's bald head gone. Grey quickly shifted the big man off the smaller body underneath and bent down.

Hard to tell where Cobra's blood stopped and Maria's blood began. Grey searched for a pulse on Maria's neck, and after a second, his head snapped up. "She's alive. Barely, but still hanging on."

"Call 9-1-1."

"Already did." Grey gently repositioned Maria, then stripped his dress shirt off and used it to staunch Maria's bleeding. "Caroline's across the street. She took out your friend here. You two need to bug out and see Connor Lane at Justice. Immediately. I've already alerted him that we have a new witness and we're expediting the meeting. He's waiting for your call and will meet you at his office. Leave dumbass here and I'll have the PD hold him until I hear from you."

Mitch had known Grey for a handful years. Years that had tested both of them to the extreme. They knew each other's demons, understood what made the other tick. Grey pursued justice above everything else. It's what drove him to be the man he was.

It took a lot to push Justice Greystone over the edge, but Mitch could see the truth in his friend's eyes. If he turned Grey loose on Straling, the DAG wouldn't live to see that day's sunset.

Caroline and a few others might find it hard to believe, but vigilante justice had never appealed to Mitch. From the time he was a kid, he'd always wanted to work for the FBI. To bring criminals to justice but assure they were tried and sentenced fairly. Yes, he had a problem with authority, and yes, he liked to do things his own way, but when it came to the United States Constitution and the justice system, he still believed that everyone had rights and even the criminals deserved a trial by their peers.

Mitch rubbed his wrists, avoiding the open wounds the plastic cuffs had caused. He tested out his legs. Wobbly, and his feet were asleep, but now that he could stand up straight, his circulation would solve those issues.

"No. I'm not letting the son of a bitch out of my sight. He's coming with me. Caroline and I will take care of him." Mitch forced Straling to rise and shoved him toward the stairs. "You make sure our star witness here lives."

Caroline tore through the back door of the manufacturing plant, gun case slung across her body. Grey had called and said Mitch, along with the handcuffed DAG, would meet her at the car. For extra caution, she weaved through the clump of trees running the length of the block. No sense being seen now. Although, with the bloodbath they'd just created, she wasn't sure being noticed mattered.

All she could hope was that they were right about this cover-up. At the very least, she'd acted accordingly. She'd witnessed a woman getting shot and Mitch was next. Caroline had to act. Had to.

Still, with the DAG involved, this would be a media feast. They'd pick the meat right off her bones. At the very least, her job was gone.

She could always go back to teaching.

Her ankle caught on a branch and twisted, sending spikes of pain through her foot and up her calf. Damn. She winced, but kept moving.

Get to Mitch.

That's all she needed to do. Just get to Mitch.

At the car, she popped the trunk and stowed her gun case.

"Caroline!"

Mitch. And, God, the sound of his voice felt like a warm sun after a hard winter. She slammed the trunk and there he was, walking toward her, his steps faltering on every other one, favoring his one side, but shoving Straling along with him.

Even twenty feet away she saw the blood. Dried and fresh streaming down his cheeks. Reddish-brown streaks covered the front of his T-shirt as if he'd used it to wipe his face clean.

And his nose was bent sideways.

Jesus, God, what they did to him. Bile backed up in her throat and she squeezed her eyes shut. Getting emotional was the dead last thing she should do. But she loved this man, and seeing him in this condition and not getting emotional would make her the coldest bitch living.

She opened her eyes and ran to him, meeting him near the front bumper of Grey's car. Up close, the wounds were worse. Open cuts on his left eye and lips and a gash down his right cheek. She lifted her hands to cradle his cheeks, but he blocked her.

"I'm a mess."

"I'm so sorry. I can't believe they did this to you."

"We have to go. Grey said Connor Lane is waiting on us. Straling here is coming."

He wanted to meet with the head of the Office of Special Counsel at the Justice Department looking like this? "Mitch, you need a hospital. And Straling is *coming*?"

"I'll live. It's a busted nose and maybe a couple of ribs. We can deal with it later. Just get our prisoner into the car because until we figure this out, he's not leaving my sight. Check the child safety locks so he can't get out. I lifted a couple of pairs of the flexi-cuffs off one of the goons. See what we can cuff him to in the back seat. No chances."

It took all of three minutes for her to engage the safety locks and truss Straling up like the pig he was. Mitch stood guard making sure Straling didn't try anything, but really, in his condition, she wasn't sure how much he'd actually be able to do.

"We're already behind," he said. "Can you drive?"

Oddly, that made her laugh. She always wanted to drive. "Of course."

She walked Mitch around to the passenger side. Getting inside the car turned out to be an effort and he hissed out a breath the minute his butt hit the seat. "Goddammit, I'm busted up."

"Please let me take you to a hospital."

"No. Let the fuckers see me. Our hero here can't spin this one. Where are we on our ATF witness?"

"Zachariah Nunnely. His flight landed twenty minutes ago. He said he'd grab a cab and head to his hotel." She handed Mitch her phone. "Call him—I added him to my contacts. Tell him we're moving the Lane meeting up. He has to get there ASAP."

Slamming the door, she ran to the driver's side and fired up the Charger. In *three* days they'd blown the lid off of a cover-up involving ATF, FBI and the U.S. Attorney's office. And they still didn't know exactly what they were dealing with.

She hit the gas and glanced at Mitch who left a voicemail for Zachariah. "We're in this now, Monroe. No turning back."

"You idiots," Straling screamed. "I'll have you in a cell by nightfall."

Mitch flipped him off. "Yeah, well, you should have made sure I was dead before you turned tail."

"What happened?"

"That fucker. He set the whole thing up. He created the taskforce so he could flood the border states with guns. All under the guise of catching gun runners. It was all bullshit."

"Liar!"

Mitch waved a hand. "Blah, blah."

"I don't understand."

"With so many guns hitting the streets, gun violence skyrocketed. And what do politicians do when gun violence skyrockets?"

"They bitch about gun laws."

"Exactly. The president couldn't push his gun legislation through congress. Straling wanted to change that. He also wanted the top job at Justice, didn't you, Straling? Figured if he could create a situation where the level of gun violence forced congress to act on the president's proposed legislation, it would score points and he'd slide right into the AG spot next term. Except Tommy started yapping."

Caroline stopped at a light and banged her forehead against the steering wheel. "Who thinks of this crap? All the lives lost to political ambition."

"Pfft, it's collateral damage to this asshole. He ran the whole thing, Caroline. He wouldn't admit to having Tommy killed, but he came damned close. He was taking out whoever got in his way."

"What about Jesse?"

"No idea. He's gotta be on the run."

The light turned green and Caroline hooked a right, merging into snarled D.C. traffic. "So, we think Straling had Tommy killed because he was talking too much?"

From the backseat, Straling snorted. "You'll never prove it."

"Yes," Mitch said. "We will."

Caroline tapped her nails against the steering wheel. "Stands to reason that he was behind Kemp then too. Maybe Kemp was asking questions and Straling figured out you all were friends?"

Mitch shrugged. "I guess we're about to find out. Aren't we, Straling?"

Connor Lane met them at a secure back entrance to the Department of Justice headquarters because dragging a handcuffed Deputy Attorney General through the lobby wouldn't bode well. Lane smuggled them up a service elevator to his office.

"What in God's name happened to you?" Short and balding, the Special Counsel stared at Mitch through Coke-bottle lenses and spoke with a slight southern drawl.

Every inch of Mitch's body hurt and the vision in his one good eye was hazy. He blinked and refocused on the man, and then on the chair Lane motioned him into.

Caroline, helping Mitch into the chair, answered. "He was beat nearly to death by some men working for Sean Straling."

"Lane," Straling said, "get these handcuffs off of me or I'll put your ass in a sling. Don't be a fool. This man is a federal fugitive."

Lane sat in his plush, leather chair, the back rising high in the air and making him look like a munchkin in the Wizard of Oz. "Sir, I will need you to be silent until I hear the full story. If you cannot do that, I will have you removed to another room. Under guard."

Caroline had brought her laptop and held it up in one hand and her flash drive with its copies of Tommy's files in the other. "May I show you our research?"

Lane motioned her forward and Caroline went to work with her laptop and lists, talking nonstop for several minutes as she laid everything out in chronological order. Listening to her no-nonsense voice soothed Mitch's nerves. This was her thing—creating a timeline, providing the facts, listing motivations and the results of those motivations in a calm, convincing manner that forced even a shocked Special Counsel to listen intently.

"These are serious accusations, Agent Foster," Lane said, reading something on Caroline's laptop screen. "Mr. Greystone said you had witnesses. Where are they?"

Mitch pulled out his cell phone and opened a message from Grey with a picture attached. He handed it to Lane. "Maria Lando is on her way to the emergency room, sir. This is what Straling did to her. At the very least, you can arrest him for assault on me and attempted murder on her."

It was a graphic photo and Lane flinched. He did a visual of Mitch's injuries again and let out a hefty sigh. "Will she testify?"

"If she lives," Caroline said.

"That's bull, Lane," the DAG yelled, jumping up from his seat. "Uncuff me. Now!"

Lane stared at him over his glasses. "Sir, do not make me call a guard. You will sit down. *Now.*"

For a little guy, Lane had a spine. Caroline slid her sidearm from the holster and leveled it at Straling.

"Sit," she said. "I'm sure you recall what a good shot I am."

Straling stared at the weapon then brought his hateful eyes back to Caroline. Mitch grunted. This idiot didn't realize he'd lose. Right now, nobody in this office gave a crap about his title.

Eventually, he sat.

Mitch took back his phone and eased himself into the chair once more. "The gun Straling used on her is at the scene under the watch of Justice Greystone. You should get a warrant to search Straling's car, house, office...everything. Who knows what he's hiding?"

Lane's desk phone buzzed. He punched the speaker button. "What is it, Miss Kote?"

"Sir, you might want to turn on CNN."

The three of them exchanged a look and Lane grabbed a remote from the desktop, hit a button, and a television Mitch hadn't noticed on the far wall came to life. It was already on the news channel and President Perkins' face filled the screen. He stood at the podium in the White House briefing room, a crowd of reporters in their usual seats in front of him. At the bottom of the screen, the ticker read, "President Perkins denies knowledge of ATF-FBI taskforce cover-up..."

Mitch let out a barking laugh. "Straling, you are fucked. He's already throwing you under the bus. This is getting good now, kids."

Straling's body went rigid, his whole demeanor stiffening as rage contorted his face.

Oh, yeah. Definitely getting good. Maybe Mitch could help this along. "What do you think Straling? How long is it going to take for your boss to make you the administration's sacrificial lamb? With a dead agent, you'll be lucky if you get out of prison by your 80th birthday."

Straling drew air through his nose and held it.

"Yep, suck up all that oxygen, pal. The air in here sure beats prison air."

"That son of a bitch," Straling said, his voice low and gravelly and filled with hate.

Mitch moved in for the kill. "What did the president know?"

Straling glared at him. "The big guys want plausible deniability, so he didn't know the operational details, but he knew ATF was working on a new operation to curb gun violence. I waited. I planned this whole damned thing down to the letter and waited for his bill to pass. Then I'd tell him. Then Nusco's death was all over the news and that stupid reporter asked about the FBI agent that was gunned down in New Mexico and what that meant for the president's gun control agenda. Perkins called the AG and suddenly *I'm* in the hot seat. After what I did for him? This is what I get?"

"They screwed you," Mitch said.

Straling raised his cuffed hands to wipe his brow. "Of course. But I was ahead of everyone. All I had to do was tell the president Nusco had been working the taskforce and went rogue. Atkinson backed me up. He'd already confiscated all of Tommy's files. Case closed. Until I found out Nusco had made a backup of his files."

Good work, Tommy. But the other Musketeer needed justice too. "What about Kemp? Was he one of your messes?"

The DAG made an exaggerated frowny face. "Kemp Rodgers was an unfortunate bystander. He should have never gotten involved, but just like Tommy Nusco, I guess he couldn't resist a pretty face when Jesse Lando's sister showed up with her sob story."

The office door swung open and three men filed in, Lane's

assistant on their heels telling them they had to wait. Ethan, from the New Mexico office, and another man Mitch didn't recognize.

"What the hell is this?" the DAG wanted to know.

Ethan shook Mitch's hand. "Interesting company. You look like hell."

"Beats being dead."

As Ethan shook Caroline's hand, the second man stepped forward and introduced himself to Mitch. "Nunnely. Zach. We spoke on the phone earlier."

"Thanks for coming."

"Anything for Tommy. He was a good friend of yours, huh?"

"The best."

"Lane," Straling hollered, "are we done here? I have work to do."

Lane ignored him and spoke to Ethan and Nunnely. "You're here to testify about the gun walking?"

Nunnely shrugged off a backpack, unzipped it, and produced a laptop and files. "Here you go, sir." He handed the files over and set the computer on the man's desk next to Caroline's. "You'll find a detailed journal of Operation Bulletproof on my laptop, and copies of all the reports, testimonials, and other facts I could gather before I was told to keep my mouth shut and got shipped off to North Dakota."

"By whom?" Lane demanded.

"The ATF Director."

"Of New Mexico?"

Nunnely shook his head. "Of the entire agency."

Lane frowned and Ethan motioned for the third man to come forward. "This is our ace in the hole, Mr. Lane."

The man had hung back and been staring at the floor, but when his eyes came up, Mitch's pulse skipped. They were an exact match to Maria's.

Caroline drew in a sharp breath. "Jesse Lando?"

He gave her a reluctant nod and dug a note out of his pocket. The one Mitch had left on his bed. "Yes, ma'am." He held out the note. "I'm here for my sister."

Connor Lane sat forward and started sorting through Nunnely's files. "Have a seat, gentlemen. I'll need statements from all of you. And we'll get Special Agent Donaldson on the line."

"Donaldson?" Caroline asked.

"Yes. He needs to arrest the Deputy Attorney General."

Caroline smiled at Ethan and returned to her seat next to Mitch. She took his hand and squeezed. "We did it."

His heart constricted and his throat tightened. God, he loved this woman. He entwined his fingers with hers. "You did it, Caroline. You saved my life."

She laid her head on his shoulder and softly pinched his arm. "Don't make me regret it."

Mitch's entire skull ached from his hairline to his jaw, a dull throbbing synched with his pulse. Every breath he took, every move he made sent sharp stabs of pain through his chest, like nails being hammered into the birdcage protecting his heart.

But when Caroline looked at him with that gleam in her eye —the one that said he'd done the impossible and uncovered the truth behind his best friends' deaths, all the pain was worth it.

Three hours later, the ER was a riot of sounds and white coats swishing in and out of privacy curtains. How much privacy did they actually provide? Not much from what Mitch had seen sitting on a gurney and waiting for the results of his tests.

"Let's get out of here," he said to Caroline, sliding off the edge of the bed. "I'm tired of waiting."

She grabbed his arm and squeezed. "Not until we get the all clear."

"I'm all bandaged and sewn up. If I had a concussion, it would be evident by now."

"Not necessarily." She stared into his one good eye as if she had her own internal CT scanner or something. "Occasionally, brain injuries don't show up for days."

"All I need is a mega dose of pain meds and a few hours of sleep."

"The doctor may want to keep you for observation for twenty-four hours."

His swollen eye was a nuisance, making it difficult to give her the full Mitch Monroe charming look, complete with a wink. He went for it anyway, grinning and winking and hoping it worked. "Twenty-four hours with you in bed would do me more good."

"You have three cracked ribs. Acrobatics in bed are not advised."

He laced his hand through hers and kissed the end of her fingers. "I'm sure you could work around my injuries."

A flush rose on her cheeks and she laughed, shaking her head at him. "You are incorrigible."

"But you love me anyway."

She laid a soft kiss on his bad eye. "Yes, I do."

Her cell phone beeped and she checked it. "It's a text from Grey. Maria's awake. The surgeons removed bullet fragments from around her left ear and the ear canal, and a large fragment lodged at the base of her skull, but the bullet missed all of the major brain regions and didn't hit her spinal cord. She'll probably be deaf in that ear but her prognosis is good. She'll need physical therapy, but hopefully won't have any paralysis or memory loss. Jesse's with her now."

"I'm glad the kid showed up. For Maria's sake as well as ours."

Caroline pocketed the phone. "I told her I'd keep her safe and I didn't."

The same guilt gnawing at Caroline ate at him too. He'd screwed up a lot of things in his life, but allowing Maria to be shot would always haunt him. It would haunt Caroline too. "We'll do everything we can to help her recover, Caroline. It's the best we can do now. Allowing the shoulda-woulda-coulda demon to set up residence in your head makes you crazy. Take it from me. It's no way to live."

"I know." Her eyes were wistful. "I just wish I'd done things differently."

"Me, too." Enough of this hospital bullshit. "Tell Grey we're heading out. Ethan can stay and keep an eye on Jesse to make sure the kid doesn't take off before Connor Lane can get him in front of the attorney general or whoever needs to hear his testimony."

Caroline didn't try to stop him this time, but the curtain flew back and Donaldson blocked Mitch's exit. "Where do you think you're going?" he said.

As far away from you as I can get.

But that was the old Mitch and the old way of thinking. "I was about to come and see you. I'm turning myself in."

"Huhn." Donaldson reached into his coat pocket and drew out two sets of papers. He handed one set to Caroline. "This is for you."

Mitch saw the agent in her come to life, the past few hours of stress and anxiety rolling off of her like rainwater off a duck. "What is it?" she asked, her fingers nimbly opening the folded papers to read them.

Donaldson lowered his voice. "The warrant we'll be using to search the Deputy Attorney General's house and vehicles. I figured you'd like to go with me and my team."

Her eyes lit up. "You bet I would." Then she glanced at Mitch and her face fell. "But I can't leave him."

Oh, bullshit. "You don't need to babysit me, Caroline," Mitch said. "Grey can drive me to the Bureau and I'll wait there like a good boy for *Special Agent* Donaldson to return."

He emphasized Special Agent a little too hard, making it sound sarcastic—force of habit. Still, when Donaldson's watery eyes met his in challenge, Mitch didn't look away.

Donaldson held out the second set of papers in his hand. "Shut up before you make me change my mind and tear these up, you SOB."

Mitch hesitated. There was something in the way Donaldson held the folded papers out to him that made his hackles rise. Was this a warrant for his arrest? "I told you I'm turning myself in." He glanced at Caroline, and she smiled a sad, but proud smile at him. "I'm done running. I'll take whatever consequences are coming my way."

His old boss rolled his eyes. "Will you take the goddamned papers?"

For a half a second, Mitch's pulse skipped a weird tempo. If it was an arrest warrant, Donaldson would be handcuffing him and leading him away, not holding the damn thing out to him like an olive branch.

Against his better judgment, he accepted the papers, unfolded them and started reading.

The moment his good eye skimmed across the words, "...*all charges dismissed*..." his knees went weak. He glanced up. "I don't understand."

"What's there to understand?" Donaldson turned and motioned for Caroline to follow him. "I'm not going so far as to offer you your old job back, but I'm dropping the charges against you."

He turned and looked at Mitch over his shoulder. "And I don't ever want to see you in my office for any reason. Clear?"

Mitch stood completely stunned, watching as Donaldson walked past the nurse's station and nearly ran over an orderly. Caroline was on her phone texting. Her phone beeped and she raised her head. "Grey's on his way down. He'll drive you." She rushed back and kissed Mitch on the lips. "Isn't this righteous? We're taking down the Deputy Attorney General! We're getting justice for Tommy."

Justice for Tommy. All he'd wanted. Well, that and Caroline. His face hurt when he smiled, but he smiled anyway. He was a free man. Straling was going to face the music. Caroline loved him.

"Righteous," he echoed.

Across from the nurse's station, a TV in the waiting area showed a replay of the president on a news channel denying any knowledge of Operation Bulletproof.

Caroline followed Mitch's gaze. She made a derisive noise in the back of her throat. "He didn't waste any time distancing himself from all of this."

"Don't worry." Grey was suddenly beside them, looking sharp as ever in a fresh suit. "He's not above the law. One of these days, he'll get what's coming to him."

Caroline eyed Grey suspiciously. "In what manner?"

Grey patted Mitch on the back and smiled at Caroline "Let's just say, karma's a bitch."

As Grey led the way out of the emergency room doors, Mitch followed, ignoring Caroline's questioning looks. He paused for a moment in the sun, taking a deep breath, even though it caused him pain. *I'm free.*

Caroline blew Mitch a kiss before jogging off after Donaldson. "I'll call you later."

Grey's Challenger pulled up alongside the curb. Mitch eased himself into the passenger seat.

"Quite a girl you've got there, Roe."

"She's the best," he said. "I don't deserve her."

"No, you don't, but then, you always were a lucky bastard."

"Lucky?" He snorted at the irony. "I lost my career, the girl, and my friends. I was on the run for months and accused of murder, and you think I'm lucky?"

Grey shrugged. "You have me."

Even though it cost him, Mitch reached over and punched Grey's arm. Not hard, just a friendly guy punch. Sort of like a hug, but not. "Damn right I do."

Grey grinned and Mitch grinned back. "Shall we?"

Mitch held up his get-out-of-jail-free papers. "I'm a free man. How about we get a beer?"

Grey put the car in gear. "A beer? Hell, after all of this, I'm buying you a whole damn pitcher."

Lucky. Mitch stared out the window as Grey pulled away, tasting the warm, familiar bite of homesickness inside him.

But now, he welcomed it. This was his new life. With Caroline. With Grey. With a world of possibilities stretching out in front of him.

"I *am* lucky," he muttered, and held out a fist to Grey. "All for one, and one for all?"

Grey looked a little confused, but fist-bumped him anyway. "You're coming to work for me officially now, right?"

"Only if you're paying me. This volunteering shit is over. And none of that stupid election fraud case."

"Even if the fraud goes as high as the president?"

Mitch hiked a thumb back toward the hospital. "Is that what you were talking about back there?"

"Karma's a bitch, or in this case, the Justice Team is."

Mitch laughed. The president might be able to distance himself from the blowback over Operation Bulletproof and his Deputy Attorney General, but in the end, he would get what was coming to him. "I'm in."

"The Justice Team rides again," Grey said.

"Really? A western theme?"

"You just quoted The Three Musketeers."

"You're right. The Three Musketeers are so yesterday." And

the past needed to stay in the past. "How about The Avengers? Brice would like that."

"Brice? Is he joining our team too?"

Mitch thought about it. "Might not be a bad idea. We have to break him out of jail first."

Grey sighed. "Of course we do."

25

Two days later, Caroline sat on a counter stool in Grey's kitchen staring at the stainless steel double oven while this puzzle of a man—who knew he had such fancy taste in appliances—poured her a club soda. He wore track pants, a plain grey T-shirt and his hair was damp from an obviously recent shower.

Having never seen him in casual clothes, Caroline wondered if he wore his suits like she wore hers. The armor that kept them focused on the work and only the work. Protection from emotional entanglements.

She glanced down at her jeans. No armor tonight. For once, it might be a good thing. "Sorry to interrupt your evening."

He slid the club soda in front of her and propped his hands on the granite countertop. "You didn't interrupt. What's up? Everything okay? Monroe driving you batshit?"

She laughed at that. On any given day it could be true. Just not today. "As crazy as it is to believe, no."

Then again she hadn't spoken to him today. As of last night, he planned on apartment hunting all day. Mitch Monroe, back on the grid. Maybe now they'd actually manage a normal relationship. Not that either one of them knew what the heck normal would be.

A drip of moisture rolled down the side of her glass and she ran her finger over it. Stalling. Really? When had she become such a wussy-girl? She slugged half the club soda.

"You sure you don't need a scotch?" Grey cracked.

Not a bad idea. "I have a favor to ask."

"Sure. Let's hear it."

As if changing the course of her life were that simple. Sharp tingles zipped down her arms and she threaded her hands together. "Well, uh, okay, but feel free to say you can't do it. It's fine."

"Caroline?"

"Yes?"

"You're pissing me off. Spit it out."

The tension wracking her body vanished. Just poof. Gone. She snorted. No wonder he and Mitch got along. "I feel better now. Thank you."

"Whatever it is, let's talk about it. If I can't do it, I'll say it."

She believed him. One thing about Mitch, his ability to read people was spot-on. If he trusted Grey, it meant something. That's all she needed. "I talked to Donaldson this morning."

Grey tapped his fingers on the counter. "My favorite person."

"I know. Which is why I'm here. He said I'm not fired."

Grey boosted himself to a sitting position on the opposite counter, settling in for a chat. "That's good, right?"

A few days ago—heck, yesterday—she'd have thought so. Now? After all they'd discovered, she wasn't sure. All she knew was she wanted to do good, to serve the people of her country and, as cliché as it was, put the bad guys in jail.

Somehow, the circumstances surrounding Tommy's death didn't give her hope that her role with the FBI would achieve those goals.

She shook her head. "I should have been thrilled and I wasn't. It's been a long few days. I've learned more than I wanted to and the lessons weren't necessarily good."

"I get it," Grey said. "I was there myself not too long ago."

"I know. That's why I'm here." A thunk sounded from the fridge. Ice cubes dropping into the tray. Something she'd heard thousands of times in her apartment, surrounded by the quiet of her No-Mitch life.

She slugged another gulp of her club soda and set down the glass. "I'd like a job. On your team. As crazy as the New Mexico trip was, I came alive while we were there. I liked playing outside the lines. Mitch is a rebel. Always will be. He's used to being a pain in the ass. I'm always the obedient one. At least until New Mexico. We may have broken the rules, but it was for the greater good. That's what I want. And I think your team does that."

"What team?"

Okay, so he was going to play hardball. Make her work for it, even though he knew she was aware of his current assignment for the Bureau. "The Justice Team. I know what you do and why. I know you and your team are ghosts and that's the way you want it because that's how you get things done. But you stand for something that's very real. Justice. I want real."

Grey scratched the back of his head and stared out at the darkening sky beyond the wall of windows and glass doors lining the kitchen. "It *is* what we do. I'd love to have someone like you on my team."

"But?"

He shrugged. "You need to be comfortable doing the work and getting none of the credit. Being a ghost isn't easy or fun. It's messy and dangerous."

That she knew. She'd heard the rumors about the team, but no proof could be found. Anywhere. They kept big secrets, worked under the radar, and covered their tracks. "I'd be okay with that."

"What about S.W.A.T.?"

For a second, she held her breath. *You didn't consider that.* If she went to work for Grey, she'd have to give up S.W.A.T. All her training and hard work—not to mention the respect—would be sacrificed.

"Caroline, you'd have to walk away. Think of this as WITSEC. No one can know. You can't talk about it to anyone outside of team members."

The FBI had their own version of the Federal Witness Protection Program, and suddenly she wanted to give up everything for it. "I know and I'm ready for that. After I got done with Donaldson, I stopped at my desk for a few minutes. Nothing about it felt right anymore. Knowing what I know now, about Tommy and the politics and how he died, I'm questioning everything. And I can't work like that. I need to trust the people around me."

"What'd you tell Donaldson?"

"I thanked him and went back to my desk. What could I say? Go screw yourself? I couldn't do that after he'd helped us find Zachariah."

Grey rolled his eyes. "Don't kid yourself, he was saving his own ass. He knew you and Mitch were on to something. As Tommy's boss, he had to approve the taskforce assignment. And that's a potential landmine for him. But bottom line, my feelings about him don't matter. In fact, I wouldn't mind putting the screws to him by stealing one of his best agents. Don't take this the wrong way, but a woman with your looks and skills? I can use that. In a lot of ways."

Yes. Caroline bobbed her head like a five-year-old waiting for her ice cream. "I'd like that. As corny as it sounds, it would give me something to believe in."

"It's not corny. *That*, I actually understand."

"So, what do you think? Can you make room for me on your team?"

He hopped off the counter, wandered over to her and stuck out his hand. "Welcome to the Justice Team."

She shook his hand, staring at him the whole time, because it couldn't be that easy. Could it? "That's it? You don't have to clear me with your boss?"

"I have a couple of calls to make, but no, I don't have to ask. If this is what you want, my boss won't give me a hard time about it."

A beep sounded, then the front door slammed. "Honey!" A woman's voice. "I'm home!"

Immediately, Grey's face lit up, all serious G-man reserve vanishing behind a grin. "Kitchen!" Ten seconds later a tall brunette, completely stunning in heels, a tight pencil skirt, and a clingy sweater strutted in. This had to be Sydney, Grey's girlfriend.

Her laser sharp eyes landed on Caroline. "Hello." She set the grocery bags she carried on the counter and turned to Grey. "Why is there an attractive female in your kitchen?"

He laughed and dropped a quick kiss on her lips. "This is Caroline."

"*The* Caroline?"

What did that mean?

"I only know one Caroline, so it must be."

Sydney reached across the counter and shook Caroline's hand. "Mitch talks about you. A lot."

The sting of jealousy, that ugly blast of heat suddenly prowling inside her, hit Caroline full force, reminding her of all the nights she sat on her sofa, alone and heartbroken, texting Mitch, checking on him, wanting to know if he was safe and where he was.

And never receiving an answer.

Sydney was the lucky one. Caroline straightened her shoulders. *This is silly*. Childish even. Mitch was allowed to have friends. Only problem was, Caroline wanted to be the one talking to Mitch.

Sydney went back to unloading groceries. "You're staying for dinner, yes?"

A banging noise on the glass behind Caroline drew everyone's attention. She swiveled her chair and found Mitch and one of his cocky grins standing on the other side of the glass door leading to Grey's deck.

"Come on!" Grey hollered. "Seriously!"

"He does it to annoy you," Sydney said, eyeballing the steaks she'd set on the counter.

Grey stalked to the door, threw it open and sent it careening off the door stop. "Quit fucking breaching my security."

Mitch shrugged. "Not my fault you can't figure out how I do it."

These two. Such infants.

Sydney rolled her eyes. "I go through this every time. Grey is easy bait."

Then those dark eyes drifted to her and the heat from her little jealous snit converted to a whole different kind of warmth.

"Look who's here." Mitch marched over and kissed her. Long and slow. Right in the middle of Grey's kitchen. With an audience.

She loved it.

Yes, things had definitely changed.

Backing away from the kiss, he nipped at her bottom lip. "Hey, Caroline."

How she loved when he said that. "Hey, Mitch."

"You okay?"

She met his gaze and his mundane question took on its true meaning. What he really wanted to know was if she was okay after eliminating her target. They'd yet to discuss it, and if she had her way, they wouldn't. He of all people knew the emotional fallout she suffered after an incident. This time though, pulling the trigger meant saving Mitch's life.

End of it. "I'm great."

"What're you doing here?"

Unsure of how much to say, Caroline made eye contact with Grey.

"I just gave her a job," he said. "On our team. You two will be working together. Any issues with that?"

"No shit?"

"No shit."

"Um," Sydney said, "who is staying for dinner?"

"Both of them." Grey jerked his head sideways. "I need to talk to you a second."

"Oh, Fed Boy, I love when you want to be alone with me."

Mitch gagged. "Beat it already."

Once Sydney and Grey were gone, Caroline spun to Mitch and set her hands on either side of his face. The ugly cut above his eye had started to heal, or maybe she'd simply gotten used to the ugly black stitches and the bruising across his jaw and cheek. "Mitch, you look like a tractor plowed you."

"I feel like a tractor plowed me." He wedged himself next to the empty stool beside Caroline. "You're leaving Donaldson? Grey told you about his rules, right? Top secret and all that crap."

"He did. I'm ready."

He tugged on her ponytail. "Ha. You liked going rogue. I knew it."

"I did, actually. It was for the right reasons. That's what I like about Grey's team." She gripped his T-shirt and squeezed. "And I'd get to see you every day."

Slowly, he inched forward, his gaze on her, all that amused mischief softening. "I love you, Caroline."

Years she'd waited for him. Maybe she hadn't pathetically pined for him, but down deep, after comparing every man in her life to him, she'd hoped he'd come back. "I love you, Mitch."

Voices drifted from the hallway. Grey and Sydney coming back. Sydney entered the room first, clipping her long hair back. "One of you boys go light that grill. I bought Grey's favorite rib eyes. I'd planned on freezing the extra ones, but we'll just cook them all."

Mitch backed away—darn that—and leaned on the counter, resting on his elbows. "So, Syd. Are you officially moved in here yet?"

"Yes," Grey said.

"No," Sydney said.

Okay then. Communication barrier?

Grey grabbed a lighter from a drawer and waved it. "Your stuff is all here. Just say you've moved in and be done with it."

"Not all my stuff. I still have my furniture at my place."

"Which is stupid. You're paying rent on a place you're not living in."

Oh, Caroline saw where this was going. Leave it to Mitch. He never did anything without a reason. The reason might be half-assed, but he had a reason.

Sydney—Syd—cocked her head, gave him a syrupy smile. "There's a little thing called a lease. And mine is not up for two months."

"Excellent." Mitch smacked his hands together. "Have I got a deal for you."

"Oh, Christ," Grey said.

Caroline snorted. She'd missed this. The male banter, the frenzy Mitch always managed to create.

But Syd, being the smart woman she was, leaned in a little, slowly nodding. "What kind of deal?"

"I've been apartment hunting all day."

Yep. Always a reason. And, oh, how Caroline's heart opened up at the idea of Mitch having a home again.

"Everything in my price range is too small—whatever salary your boyfriend is going to pay me won't be nearly enough to afford anything decent in D.C.—or it's in a crappy part of town. Plus, I have no furniture. Since you're shacked up with Greystone here, I figure I can slide into your place and take over your lease."

"Huh," Syd said. "That's not a bad idea."

Lighter in hand, Grey walked to the door Mitch had come through. "It's a great idea. I think you should take that deal."

Syd held up a finger and followed Grey out the door. "Give me one second to talk to him."

Caroline gripped Mitch's hand. "A lease. You're sure you want to do that?"

"I need a place to live, Caroline."

"I know, but..."

"But nothing. I told you in New Mexico. I'm done running. I want my life back. I've been cleared of all charges, and I want my new life to include you. If you'll have me. And if you will, it means I need a home where you can come and visit." He snuggled into her neck and licked behind her ear. "A home where I can do naughty things to you. I'm officially back on the grid. Hopefully, with you. Whaddya say?"

What did she say? Please. He'd probably give her a hundred —a thousand—different reasons to want to kill him every day, but life with Mitch would never be boring. She loved him. Good or bad, all those months without him made her realize that wherever he was, a piece of her went with him.

Mitch tugged on her pony tail. "We're good then? No more Bureau-wear?"

Ah, no more Bureau-wear. "One condition."

"Uh-oh."

"Since you're back to living like a civilized person, I want you to cut your hair."

"That's your stipulation? A hair cut?"

MISTY EVANS & ADRIENNE GIORDANO

She returned the ponytail tug. "The long hair is fun, but it's not you."

He pushed off the counter and walked to the other side, rifling through drawers as he moved down the length of the island. "There they are."

"What?"

Something silver flashed and he tucked his hand at his side until he came around the island and held the item out. She glanced down. Scissors. Oh. My.

He nudged them closer. "Take 'em, Caroline."

"You want me to cut your hair? I don't know how."

"You don't have to. Just cut the ponytail and I'll stop somewhere and get it cleaned up when we leave here."

"Mitch, I can't."

Having heard enough, he grabbed her wrist, turned her hand palm out and slapped the scissors into her hand. "Yeah, you can. I want you to."

"You're sure?"

He took the stool next to hers and spun around to give her access. "Yep."

After this, he'd never let her wear a suit again. And suddenly, the idea of that made her more than a little giddy. She leaned in and brushed her lips against his ear. "Mitch Monroe, wait until you see the wicked boots I bought last month."

Keep the adventure going!

Thank you for reading *Cheating Justice*. If you'd like more of the Justice Team Series, check out *Exposing Justice*.

As a Public Information officer for the US Supreme Court, Hope Denby knows how to spin a story. A journalist at heart, she loves being in the middle of a juicy scoop and has her sights set on future Press Secretary for the White House. When

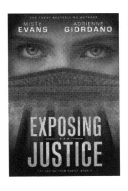

the Supreme Court Chief Justice is accidentally killed in a road rage accident, and a high-profile conspiracy blogger claims it was premeditated murder, Hope has to shut down the paranoid blogger—which should be a slam dunk until she discovers he's not as crazy as she thought and she has more in common with the secretive, hard-hitting investigator then she'd like to admit.

Cyber resistance against government corruption isn't just a theory for Brice Brennan on his blog, The First Amendment Patriot. As a former ATF agent who blew the whistle on his superiors, he's no stranger to government cover-ups and scandals. An anonymous tip on the Chief Justice's death sends him searching for answers. What he finds is a sexy, young idealist about to blow his private, behind-the-scenes world to pieces.

Brice and Hope couldn't be more opposite, but exposing justice makes them partners—and puts them on the track of a ruthless killer. As their investigation takes them into the dark underbelly of Washington politics and murder-for-hire, it also takes them into the bedroom where passion erupts and emotional walls crumble. But when the killer makes an attempt on Hope's life, will Brice be able to keep her safe? Or will blowing the whistle on corruption and greed mean losing the one person he's allowed himself to love?

READY FOR YOUR NEXT JT
ADVENTURE?

o undercover with Brice and Hope in *Exposing Justice*

Chapter 1

Brice Brennan sat alone at his computer watching a blinking cursor. He needed a story. A kick-ass story that no one else had.

And time was running out.

It was only three o'clock in the afternoon, yet he sat in the dark, courtesy of his blackout curtains. Today's blog had to be up by nine. Fifty-five thousand and sixty-three fans, and six new advertisers, were waiting for it. After he'd exposed the United States' deputy attorney general and the ATF's collaboration on a gunwalking scandal recently, his readership had exploded.

His readers wanted scandal. Real journalism, not sugar-coated updates running ad nauseam or ratings-whoring gossip passed off as investigative reporting.

Tick-tock.

Brice tapped his thumb against his desktop. Three big news stories had flooded the blogosphere today. Each held potential for him, but none yet had generated any calls from his covert, and oftentimes dissident, sources.

Knowledge was power. Once he hit on a story, he became engrossed in it. He wouldn't let it go until he exposed the truth.

As if summoned by his sheer desperation, his phone rang—the private tip line running through his computer. Brice's pulse jumped. This could be it. The tip he was waiting for.

"'The duty of a true patriot is to protect his country from its government.' This is Hawkeye. Go."

The Thomas Paine quote was his motto and what he founded the blog on. He recorded all his tip calls through the computer, which meant all of them ran through the speakers since he never used headphones. When you were always alone, what did you need headphones for?

"Hawkeye, this is Lodestone."

Lodestone was a government employee who seemed to enjoy being Brice's informant. He'd never said as much, but Brice knew the type. Knew the man had connections Brice could only dream of, and best of all, Lodestone never asked for money. "Go ahead, Lodestone. I'm listening."

"I have information about the death of Chief Justice Raymond Turner."

A spurt of adrenaline shot through Brice's limbs. "The road rage accident?"

"It's no coincidence that he got held up on that bridge." A pause—Lodestone deciding how much he could share? "A sensitive case was on the docket for Turner to decide whether the Supreme Court would hear it or not. Look into it. You never know what you might find."

The line went dead.

Brice disconnected and stared blankly at the screen. If Turner's death wasn't an accident...

The screensaver had appeared on his computer. The Patriot Blog's logo of an eagle. He tapped a key to wake the computer up, ready to start digging, when three loud knocks on his door interrupted him.

The first three were followed by a single knock.

Brice hung his head.

The coded knocks meant only one thing.

The Justice Team had arrived.

Maybe if he didn't respond, they'd go away.

"Open up, Brennan," Justice "Grey" Greystone called from the other side.

Brice swore under his breath. If he played possum, pretended he wasn't even there, Grey would...

"Or I'll have Mitch pick the locks. Either way, we're coming in."

How long was this going to go on?

Jumping up from his office chair, he hustled to the door, unlocked the three deadbolts and doorknob, and cracked the door open two inches.

"I'm not interested, Grey," he told the leader of the Justice Team standing on his front porch looking like the Federal agent he used to be. Dark clothes, fake smile. Batman in his Bruce Wayne persona. "We've already had this discussion. Six times by my count."

The weak smile on Grey's lips struggled to stay in place. The man never smiled unless his fiancé was in spitting distance. He was trying to appear friendly and inviting. Mostly, he looked constipated.

"There are perks." Grey glanced at Mitch, aka, Robin, and nodded.

When all else fails, go to your wingman.

"Like what?" Brice asked, chewing on the side of his thumbnail. "Being shot at? Having to send your girlfriend undercover as a stripper? Oh, yeah, that sounds better than medical insurance and vacation days." He switched his gaze to Robin. "Oh, and how about being framed for your best friend's murder? It's hard to top that as a perk."

Grey's hard eyes turned to pure steel. Although the Justice Team's past operations had all ended successfully, each one had put the members in extreme situations where things could have gone south in a hurry. Brice had been in on one of them in New Mexico with Mitch and his girlfriend, Caroline. Brice was lucky he was still breathing. They were all lucky they weren't in jail.

Mitch grinned and shoved his way inside. His coat was unzipped and it fell open to reveal a T-shirt that read, *I put the Hot in psychotic*. He took up residence in Brice's leather recliner with a big plop and Grey followed. "Jesus it's dark in here. Are you a vampire or something, Brice?" He didn't wait for an answer. "As far as perks, you get to look at my handsome face every day, Brice buddy. Best. Perk. Ever."

Psychotic did not begin to describe Mitch Monroe. Brice left the door ajar and went back to his chair. He didn't like people in his space. Especially not Batman and Robin. "I'm sure Caroline enjoys that, but it takes more than a pretty face to make me want to give up my blog."

"You don't have to give up your blog, right, Grey?" Mitch nodded without waiting for his boss to agree. "Investigating conspiracies is exactly what we want you to continue doing."

Cyber resistance against government corruption wasn't just a theory for Brice. *The First Amendment Patriot* blog was his life. While he valued his privacy and didn't like to call attention to himself, he had a strong internal sense of right and wrong and had no trouble blowing the whistle on corrupt politicians and government agencies. Others appreciated what he did. Donations to the blog paid his bills and he cared little about material wealth or possessions. As long as he kept his lifestyle lean, he'd be fine.

Tick-tock.

Grey didn't look all that happy about Brice keeping his blog. "We have nine open cases right now that involve crooked politicians, lobbyists, and potential cover-ups. Your skills and contacts would help tremendously."

Flattery. Grey was pulling out all the stops this round.

Brice's ego did indeed like it, too. He was damn good at running his blog, and he'd once enjoyed being part of a task-force. Lived for his job as an undercover ATF agent. The commendations in his folder had proven his worth, and the team of men he'd worked with had always had his back. Failure had never entered his mind.

Until his boss—his former partner—and the ATF sent him down in flames. The men he'd been closer to than his three brothers turned on each other.

Those days were over. Lesson learned. *Never trust anyone.*

Facts were more trustworthy than people. Detachment and autonomy were important to doing a good job. Exposing government coverups and bringing dirty cops, politicians, and even heads of the most powerful agencies in the world to heel from the safety of his computer was what he excelled at now.

"I'm no longer a team player." Truer words had never been spoken. Swinging his chair around to emphasize his point, he turned his back on the two men he had let into his personal circle and now regretted. The safety of his computer beckoned. "I just got a lead on a breaking story, and I'm not coming to work for the Justice Team. Show yourselves out, ladies."

Behind him, the leather chair squeaked as Mitch stood. An uncomfortable silence followed, complete with strained murmuring—Batman and Robin trying to figure out their next move.

Let 'em talk.

"What story?" Grey asked.

"Chief Justice Turner. The road rage accident that killed him may not have been an accident at all."

"Murder?" Mitch slapped him on the back. "Make you a deal, Brice, ol' buddy. You join the Justice Team, and I'll help you investigate your lead on Turner."

He was grinning like his offer was an obvious slam-dunk. Brice stood, grabbed Mitch's arm and hustled him to the door. "I don't need your help, Mitch, *ol' buddy*, and I can investigate Turner's death on my own."

Mostly true. *If* there was anything worth investigating.

Grey stood at the computer, looking at the screen, one hand cupping his chin. "What makes you think Turner's death was murder?"

"I got a tip from a very reliable source." Brice didn't need to prove anything to these men, and yet, the investigator in him liked the credibility. "Claims Turner had a sensitive case on his docket that he was deciding on whether the court would hear it or not. Maybe nothing, but he told me to look into it."

"Sounds far fetched to me. The Chief Justice probably had a long list of possible cases for the Court to hear."

Mitch jerked his arm out of Brice's hand. "Yeah, and every one of the plaintiffs believes their case is sensitive. It's going to take a lot of work to dig into each and every one of them."

A smile—the genuine thing—crept over Grey's face. "How about *I* make you a deal, Brice? We help you get Turner's list and do the digging. Save you a lot of time. If, of course, you help us out with a few of our cases."

He itched to jump on this right away, but he didn't need help. What he needed was for these two to leave him alone. "I'll think about it and let you know my decision in the morning."

Grey seemed unfazed by his delay. "Fair enough."

After Batman and Robin left, Brice dropped back into this chair. A few clicks of his keyboard and he had the phone number for the Public Information Office of the Supreme Court.

He'd do his own investigation, like always. If that lead nowhere, he'd consider Grey's deal.

As the phone rang on the other end, he smiled to himself. Nothing like a good conspiracy to get the adrenaline flowing.

"Denby! Get in here!"

Ooh! Hope Denby shot up, sending her rickety government-issued chair sailing against the back of her cubicle. She peeped over the wall in front of her at her cubemate, Rob. "Ohmygod, she's insane today."

Rob didn't bother looking up from whatever he was reading on his computer. "Seriously fucking deranged. You'd better get in there."

Because experience dictated she had thirty-point-two seconds to appear in front of her boss or she'd be bellowed at once again.

"Coming!"

Hope scooped up her legal pad and a pen and hustled to the boss's office just twenty-five feet away. Working at the Public Information Office of the U.S. Supreme Court meant each day brought something new. It could be working with reporters wanting to cover a case, preparing transcripts, or press releases, all of it fascinating and tedious and ripe with possibilities.

Today was no different. Eight hours earlier, the Chief Justice of the U.S. Supreme Court had been accidently gunned down on the Gaynor Bridge while trying to resolve a road rage dispute.

And now, it was all over the news and her boss, Amy Ripling, the Public Information Officer, had been in full-blown crisis mode all day.

"Denby!" Amy screamed again.

Hope kicked off her sky-high heels, left them sitting in the corridor—no time to stop—and picked up her pace. She swung around the doorway, grabbing the frame to slow her down. "I'm here. Sorry."

Amy sat at her desk, random files and papers and notes strewn across the top. Two ringing cell phones sat on top of the mess joined by the incessant beeping of the desk phone. Amy picked up the handset, tapped the hold button and handed Hope a note. "Call this guy. He's bugging the shit out of me and I'm trying to deal with the networks."

She glanced down at the name. The First Amendment Patriot. Interesting. But, woohoo! Finally, her boss ponied up an assignment on a major case, albeit a tragic one. "Yes, ma'am. Who is he?"

"He's a blogger."

A *blogger.*

The Journalism major in her wailed.

"Damned, bloggers. I am *on* it, Amy."

"I knew you'd love it. You're an animal, Denby."

"Thank you. I think."

Amy waved it away. "Yada, yada. He wants a statement, but be careful. He's one of the those conspiracy theory nutcases. Tell him something that won't hurt us. Until we have more on what happened on that bridge, we're going with what we know."

"Sure. But—"

Amy glanced at the still beeping phone, *beep-beep-beep,* then came back to Hope, her taut skin barely restraining her impatience. "What, Denby? *What?*"

Ignoring Amy's tone, she stood a little straighter. "Yes, ma'am. What is it exactly that we know?"

All day long, Hope, like everyone else in the office, had been monitoring the news channels to see who was saying what. For their part, the Public Information Office had released very few details. Mainly because they'd been given very few details.

The police and the FBI were handling the press on this nightmare.

"What *we* know," Amy said, "is that the Chief Justice and his security detail, consisting of one Supreme Court police officer, were en route to work today and got stuck in a traffic jam on the bridge. The FBI is looking into that. Apparently, there's some confusion as to why that lane was closed. They're talking to DDOT. Anyway, two cars ahead of the Chief Justice some whacko jumped out of a cab and started arguing with the driver of the car next to them. The argument became heated and the judge's officer got out to diffuse the situation. Justice Turner— God rest his soul—defied his security officer's order to stay in the car and got out to see if he could help. While the officer tried to convince the judge to get his ass back in the car, the guy who jumped out of the cab fired a gun; the shot missed and accidentally hit the judge. The shooter ran. That's what we know. But you're not telling our blogger friend that. For him, you're keeping it simple. Road rage, two men arguing, gunshot. D.C. Metro and the SC police are handling it from here."

"Got it. No problem."

"Good. I'm heading into a meeting with the Justices. I'm guessing it'll be a while. Make sure everyone knows they should only disturb me if the building is on fire. Or someone else is dead."

Ew. "I'll handle it."

She spun toward the door.

"Denby?"

"Yes?"

"Where the hell are your shoes?"

Hope pointed over her left shoulder. "In the hallway. They were slowing me down. I didn't want to irritate you."

"Ah. That's what I like about you. You're good on the fly.

Now get rid of this goddamned blogger. Bloggers we don't need."

"Yes, ma'am."

She hit the hallway, found her shoes in the exact spot she left them as people stepped over them in a rush to get to wherever they were heading. How insane were the people she worked with that no one questioned a pair of shoes, wickedly pretty shoes, sitting in the middle of the floor?

Craziness.

She slipped her shoes back on and swung into her cubicle. Of all the assignments she could have gotten, a blogger wasn't on her wish list. Bloggers were trouble. They had the freedom to write whatever they wanted. To be careless. To say "oops" when they screwed up. Fact check, people! Second sources, people!

Well, she wouldn't have it.

No pain-in-the-rear blogger would spread unvetted information about a murdered Supreme Court Justice. Not on her watch. She studied journalism for four years and was halfway to earning a Masters and these hacks thought they knew how to report the news?

Forget it. Everything with them was fair game. Off the record didn't exist. At least not in Hope's mind.

She ditched her notepad just as Rob's head appeared over the top of the wall.

"Whatcha got?"

"Blogger." She glanced at the note. "*The First Amendment Patriot.*"

"Shit."

Hope rocked her chair back. "He's that crackpot, isn't he? The one involved with the case against the deputy AG. He's the king of conspiracy theorists."

"That's him. People love him. We're talking cult following." Rob scrunched his face and made a tight fist, squeezing until his veins and knuckles popped. "Balls of steel, this guy. He outs the ATF like they're a bunch of toddlers. I want to be him when I grow up."

Okay. So maybe that fearless thing was impressive, but she didn't trust him or any other blogger. She'd deal with it lickety-split before he sent something viral.

Stabbing the buttons on her desk phone, she dialed the number on the note Amy had given her. "Rob," she said, "do me a favor. Make sure everyone knows Amy is in a meeting with the Justices. She said, and this is a direct quote, not to disturb her unless the building is on fire or someone else is dead."

"Ew," Rob said, echoing Hope's earlier thought. "How incredibly tacky."

Tacky. That was one word for it.

On the other end of the line, the ringing stopped and Hope dropped into her chair, receiving the usual squeak.

"'The duty of a true patriot is to protect his country from its government.' This is Hawkeye. Go."

Hawkeye! Dear God.

"Hello, Mr. Hawkeye." *Mr.* Hawkeye? Whatever. "This is Hope Denby from the Supreme Court Public Information Office."

"Finally," he said. "I've been calling you people for hours."

Hope rolled her eyes. A Supreme Court Justice—the *Chief* Justice—was dead and the blogger had issues because they hadn't returned his call earlier? "Well, guy, kinda busy here. What can I do for you?"

"I received a tip regarding Turner."

That earned him a second award-winning eye roll he couldn't see. "I'm sorry, we're not commenting on it at this time. We've released information and it can be found on our website."

Gotta go. Buh-bye. She shook her mouse to bring her computer out of sleep mode and scanned the latest emails.

"Yeah," he said. "I got that. Didn't help. My source said it's no coincidence that Turner got stuck on that bridge."

Hope stopped scanning. Did he say...? She abandoned the mouse and picked up her pen because crackpot or not, this blogger had just referenced the lane closing the FBI was looking into. "Wait. What?"

"That got your attention. The Chief was about to deliver a ruling on whether or not a landmark case got a hearing."

It sure did get her attention. Particularly when he was insinuating the Chief Justice had been assassinated due to a ruling. "Mr. Hawkeye—"

"Just Hawkeye. No mister."

"Fine. *Hawkeye.* I have no comment on that. It was an unfortunate and tragic road rage incident and the police are doing everything they can to apprehend the shooter. Whatever the judge's ruling would have been, we'll never know. Obviously, you cannot quote me on that."

And now she should shut up. She'd already gone off script and with her luck this Hawkeye character would bury her with it.

"Quote you on what? You didn't give me anything."

"Check the website. We've released everything we have."

"Ms. Denby, you do realize I'm going to run with what I have if you don't give me something."

"Mr.—"

"No mister."

"Hawkeye." *Whatever.* "Who is your source of this information?"

She didn't expect he'd tell her. Any reputable journalist wouldn't. Maybe she was testing him. Maybe not. Either way, trying to identify his source wouldn't hurt.

His chuckle was low and deep. "Ms. Denby, did someone hit you in the head with a two-by-four? I'm not telling you my source."

For a split second, she smiled. That two-by-four line was a good one. She'd maybe use it herself some time. Bonus, he'd passed one test. That got him a rung up on the credibility ladder. The chuckle gave her a couple of goose bumps. Not more than two or three, but still. His voice had a definitely goose-bump-inducing quality.

"One moment please."

She punched the hold button and hopped up to peer over the cubicle wall.

Without a glance up from whatever he was working on, Rob pursed his lips and slowly moved his head back and forth. "You gotta get rid of this guy. He's totally playing you."

Voices from her right closed in and she waited for two of her co-workers to pass. "I know," she said, keeping her voice low. "But he got a tip that Turner might have been assassinated because he was about to rule on a hearing for an important case."

"Shit."

"Amen to that. Still want me to get rid of him?"

"Even more so, but—" Rob flopped his lip out as he considered her question, "what are we categorizing as landmark? This is the Supreme Court. Could be anything."

"Dang it."

"What?"

"I don't know."

Rob laughed. "Okay."

She sat back down, took a deep breath. She could do this. No blogger would bring her down, even one with a sexy voice and dangerous sounding chuckle. She'd get rid of him and quietly poke around about cases the Chief Justice might have been about to grant hearings on. Easy-peasy. If nothing else, she'd blow this crazy conspiracy theory—and Mr. Hawkeye— out of the universe. Just blow them both to bits.

Easy.

Peasy.

Still standing, she punched the button again. "Let me call you back."

"I'm so looking forward to it." The sarcasm in his voice hinted that that was a lie. "When?"

"I guess that depends on when I have information, doesn't it?"

"Uh, no."

"No?"

"I'll give you until 8:00 PM. After that, I piece together what I have and run with the story."

Great. Threats. "But you don't have a story. That's why you called me."

Another chuckle, and yep, a couple more goose bumps rose on her skin. This time in the area right under her ear as if his lips had just made a trail there. And hello? They had a situation here and she was fantasizing about a *blogger*?

"I have enough to write a post planting the idea that the Chief Justice was murdered over more than road rage."

Dammit. Eight o'clock. She tapped the mouse again and bent over to check the clock on her computer. Four hours to figure out what case may or may not have gotten a Supreme Court Justice murdered.

"Eight p.m., Ms. Denby. Please don't let me down. I'm out."

She straightened, throwing her shoulders back. "Wait."

The line went dead. Well, the line went dead after the extremely loud click. He hung up on her. *Balls!* She dropped into her chair and sent the usual annoying squeak echoing through the cubicle. Stupid chair. Feet planted on the faux wood mat that allowed her to roll her chair within the cube, she shoved off. Momentum carried her into the corridor where she could see Rob.

"Comin' in hot." Cliff Cody walked by, swerving to avoid a collision.

"Sorry, Cliff."

From inside his cube, Rob spun to face her. "Don't even tell me you're gonna get into this. Company line, Hope. That's it. Until Crazy Pants Amy gives us something else to distribute, it's company line."

Forget that. Sort of. She couldn't get too aggressive on this thing or her butt would wind up with a major spanking and the potential loss of her career. But something told her this Hawkeye wasn't going away. And given his success on the case against the deputy AG a few months back, he had—God save her—credibility on his side. Oh, she could see it now, the *blogger* writing a column about how the now deceased Chief Justice planned on denying a hearing on some big case the same day he was gunned down.

The Internet would explode.

People would tweet and retweet and post and share and within an hour the Public Information Office would be doing major spin control.

She glanced down the hall to Amy's office where just minutes before her boss had told her she wasn't to be disturbed.

Hawkeye had only given her four hours.

She went back to Rob. "I have until eight o'clock or he's running with what he has. So, I can sit around wasting time until Amy is available, then ask permission to pursue this."

Again Rob slowly moved his head left and right in his signature move. "Hope—"

"—or I can start gathering info, just background stuff, and be ready when Amy comes out of her meeting." Hopefully before eight o'clock. With a dead Chief Justice, what were the chances of that? "Rob, you yourself said the guy has a cult-like following. I need to debunk this."

He laughed. One of those sarcastic you-have-lost-your-mind laughs. "Good luck to you then because I'm not touching it. No way, sister." He pulled himself back to his desk. "All I know is I want your desk when you get your ass fired. You've got an end unit."

"Oh, ha-ha."

"Seriously, what are you gonna do?"

She rose from her chair, entered Rob's cube and leaned close enough so she wouldn't be overheard. "Relax. I'll just chat with one of Turner's clerks."

"Which one?"

"Bigley. He has the loosest lips."

This she knew from rumors and her general snooping and digging around about the court staffers. A little research for her files for emergencies—like now—never hurt.

"Oh. My. *God!*" Rob said, his voice sotto voce but total drama queen. "There is no way a clerk will comment."

"I guess we'll see about that, won't we?"

Grab your copy of *Exposing Justice.*

WANT MORE OF SEXY THRILLERS?

The Justice Team Series

Stealing Justice

Cheating Justice

Holiday Justice

Exposing Justice

Undercover Justice

Protecting Justice

Missing Justice

Defending Justice

SCHOCK SISTERS MYSTERY SERIES

1st Shock

2nd Strike

3rd Tango

MORE BY ADRIENNE GIORDANO

DEEP COVER SERIES

Crossing Lines

PRIVATE PROTECTORS SERIES

Risking Trust

Man Law

Negotiating Point

A Just Deception

Relentless Pursuit

Opposing Forces

THE LUCIE RIZZO MYSTERY SERIES

Dog Collar Crime

Knocked Off

Limbo (novella)

Boosted

Whacked

Cooked

Incognito

The Lucie Rizzo Mystery Series Box Set 1

The Lucie Rizzo Mystery Series Box Set 2

The Lucie Rizzo Mystery Series Box Set 3

THE ROSE TRUDEAU MYSTERY SERIES

Into The Fire

HARLEQUIN INTRIGUES

The Prosecutor

The Defender

The Marshal

The Detective

The Rebel

JUSTIFIABLE CAUSE SERIES

The Chase

The Evasion

The Capture

CASINO FORTUNA SERIES

Deadly Odds

JUSTICE SERIES w/MISTY EVANS

Stealing Justice

Cheating Justice

Holiday Justice

Exposing Justice

Undercover Justice

Protecting Justice

Missing Justice

Defending Justice

SCHOCK SISTERS MYSTERY SERIES w/MISTY EVANS

1st Shock

2nd Strike

3rd Tango

STEELE RIDGE SERIES w/KELSEY BROWNING
& TRACEY DEVLYN

Steele Ridge: The Beginning

Going Hard (Kelsey Browning)

Living Fast (Adrienne Giordano)

Loving Deep (Tracey Devlyn)

Breaking Free (Adrienne Giordano)

Roaming Wild (Tracey Devlyn)

Stripping Bare (Kelsey Browning)

Enduring Love (Browning, Devlyn, Giordano)

Vowing Love (Adrienne Giordano)

STEELE RIDGE SERIES: The Kingstons w/KELSEY BROWNING
& TRACEY DEVLYN

Craving HEAT (Adrienne Giordano)

Tasting FIRE (Kelsey Browning)

Searing NEED (Tracey Devlyn)

Striking EDGE (Kelsey Browning)

Burning ACHE (Adrienne Giordano)

MORE BY MISTY EVANS

SEALs of Shadow Force Series

Fatal Truth

Fatal Honor

Fatal Courage

Fatal Love

Fatal Vision

Fatal Thrill

Risk

SEALS of Shadow Force Series: Spy Division

Man Hunt

Man Killer

Man Down

The SCVC Taskforce Series

Deadly Pursuit

Deadly Deception

Deadly Force

Deadly Intent

Deadly Affair, A SCVC Taskforce novella

Deadly Attraction

Deadly Secrets

Deadly Holiday, A SCVC Taskforce novella

Deadly Target

Deadly Rescue

Deadly Bounty

Deadly Betrayal

Deadly Threat

The Super Agent Series

Operation Sheba

Operation Paris

Operation Proof of Life

Operation Lost Princess

Operation Ambush

Operation Christmas Contraband

Operation Sleeping With the Enemy

The Justice Team Series (with Adrienne Giordano)

Stealing Justice

Cheating Justice

Holiday Justice

Exposing Justice

Undercover Justice

Protecting Justice

Missing Justice

Defending Justice

SCHOCK SISTERS MYSTERY SERIES w/Adrienne Giordano

1st Shock

2nd Strike

3rd Tango

The Secret Ingredient Culinary Mystery Series

The Secret Ingredient, A Culinary Romantic Mystery with Bonus Recipes

The Secret Life of Cranberry Sauce, A Secret Ingredient Holiday Novella

ACKNOWLEDGMENTS

As with any big project, there are people to thank for offering their time and knowledge (and patience!). Thanks to John Leach for never changing your email address and allowing Adrienne to bombard you with so many questions.

To Jeff Rinek, thank you, thank you, thank you for sharing your expertise. Your insight regarding federal law enforcement was invaluable. Milton Grasle, thank you for always being willing to brainstorm action scenes. Working with you is an unbelievable amount of fun and we look forward to the next one.

Amy Remus, you are a treasure and always keep us organized. Thank you for your ongoing support.

And, finally, thank you to our readers for taking another journey with us in the Justice Team Series.

Cheating Justice

Copyright © 2014 Misty Evans and Adrienne Giordano

Excerpt *Holiday Justice* © 2014 Misty Evans and Adrienne Giordano

ISBN-13: 978-0-9888939-8-6

Cover Art by Fanderclai Design.

Formatting by Author E.M.S.

Editing by Valerie Hayward and Judy Beatty

ABOUT ADRIENNE

 **Adrienne Giordano is a *USA Today* best-selling author** of over forty romantic suspense and mystery novels. She is a Jersey girl at heart, but now lives in the Midwest with her ultimate supporter of a husband, sports-obsessed son and Elliot, a snuggle-happy rescue. Having grown up near the ocean, Adrienne enjoys paddleboarding, a nice float in a kayak and lounging on the beach with a good book.

For more information on Adrienne's books, please visit www.AdrienneGiordano.com. Adrienne can also be found on Facebook at http://www.facebook.com/AdrienneGiordanoAuthor, Twitter at http://twitter.com/AdriennGiordano and Goodreads at http://www.goodreads.com/AdrienneGiordano.

Don't miss a new release! Sign up for Adrienne's new release newsletter!

ABOUT MISTY

USA TODAY Bestselling Author Misty Evans has published over seventy-five novels and writes romantic suspense, urban fantasy, and paranormal romance. Under her pen name, Nyx Halliwell, she also writes cozy mysteries.

When not reading or writing, she embraces her inner gypsy and loves music, movies, and hanging out with her husband, twin sons, and three spoiled puppies. She's a crafter at heart and has far too many projects to finish.

Don't want to miss a single adventure? Visit www. mistyevansbooks.com to find out ALL the news!

Check out her humorous pen name Nyx Halliwell for magical mysteries https://www.nyxhalliwell.com .

Made in the USA
Middletown, DE
12 January 2024

47740207R00188